Praise for *Rise and Shine*

"Stands on its own as a writerly achievement, [Quindlen's] best so far . . . Sentence by sentence Ms. Quindlen is the soul of brevity."
—*The New York Times*

"[A] classic story . . . Anna Quindlen has developed an enormously likable writing voice." —*The Washington Post Book World*

"The dialogue sparkles, the insights are right on . . . and the characters are appealing. . . . [It] has humor, heartbreak and drama. . . . [A] pleasure read."
—*The Charlotte Observer*

"Engrossing . . . [with] pungent observations about both life in class-stratified New York City and about family dynamics. The situation is ripe with comic potential. . . . The prose is top-notch." —*Publishers Weekly*

"New friends await readers in Anna Quindlen's latest work of fiction, characters you will delight in getting to know and miss once you've finished the book. . . . [*Rise and Shine* is] well worth reading." —*St. Louis Post-Dispatch*

"Quindlen pens a lavishly perceptive homage to the city she loves, while her transcendentally agile and empathic observations of the human condition underlie the Fitzmaurice sisters' discovery of the transience of fame and the permanence of family." —*Booklist*

"The chief pleasures of this very readable novel are Quindlen's observations of and specific detail about life and social mores in New York City."
—*Rocky Mountain News*

"A thoroughly engaging story peppered with memorable characters, who are humorously and touchingly drawn. Highly recommended."
—*Library Journal*

"Insightful . . . It trains a sharp eye on the things that keep us apart . . . as well as what draws us together: our common humanity and our desire for decency." —*The Kansas City Star*

RISE AND SHINE

A NOVEL

ANNA QUINDLEN

RANDOM HOUSE TRADE PAPERBACKS

NEW YORK

2007 Random House Trade Paperback Edition

Copyright © 2006 by Anna Quindlen
Reading group guide copyright © 2007 by Random House, Inc.

Published in the United States by Random House Trade Paperbacks,
an imprint of The Random House Publishing Group,
a division of Random House, Inc., New York.

RANDOM HOUSE TRADE PAPERBACKS and colophon are trademarks
of Random House, Inc.
READER'S CIRCLE and colophon are trademarks
of Random House, Inc.

Originally published in hardcover in the United States by Random House,
an imprint of The Random House Publishing Group,
a division of Random House, Inc., in 2006.

Grateful acknowledgment is made to Harvard University Press
for permission to reprint an excerpt from "Fame is a bee"
from *The Poems of Emily Dickinson*, Ralph W. Franklin, ed.,
F1788, Cambridge, Mass.: The Belknap Press of Harvard University Press,
copyright © 1998 by the President and Fellows of Harvard College.
Copyright © 1951, 1955, 1979, 1983 by the president and fellows
of Harvard College. Reprinted by permission of the publishers
and the trustees of Amherst College.

ISBN 978-0-8129-7781-3

LIBRARY OF CONGRESS CATALOGING-IN-PUBLICATION DATA

Quindlen, Anna.
Rise and shine: a novel / Anna Quindlen.
p.   cm.
ISBN 978-0-8129-7781-3
1. Sisters—Fiction.   2. Women journalists—Fiction.
3. Women social workers—Fiction.   4. New York (N.Y.)—Fiction.
I. Title.
PS3567.U336R57   2006
813'.54—dc22   2006045207

Printed in the United States of America
www.thereaderscircle.com

2 4 6 8 9 7 5 3 1

Book design by Jo Anne Metsch

For Maria Krovatin, the star.

Fearless, powerful, utterly amazing.

I want to be you when I grow up.

Fame is a bee.

It has a song—

It has a sting—

Ah, too, it has a wing.

—*Emily Dickinson*

RISE AND SHINE

FROM TIME TO time some stranger will ask me how I can bear to live in New York City. Sometimes it happens when I am on vacation, passing the time in a buffet line filled with the sunburned and the semi-drunk. Sometimes it comes up at a professional conference, drinking coffee in the corner of a hotel meeting room with a clutch of social workers, most of them wearing the dirndl skirts and dangling earrings of the socially conscious woman of a certain age. My aunt's friends will ask, although they live only a half hour north, up the Saw Mill Parkway, but in a state of bucolic isolation that might as well be Maine.

Even in New York itself I will sometimes hear the question, from the old men on the Coney Island boardwalk who knew Irving Lefkowitz when he was a bar mitzvah boy and who, from their benches on the Brooklyn beach, envision the long and slender island of Manhattan as an urban *Titanic*, sinking beneath the weight of criminals, homosexuals, and atheists, sailing toward certain disaster.

"And you live there why, sweetheart?" one of them once asked me with an openmouthed squint, his neck thrust forward from the V of a ratty cardigan so that he looked like a Galápagos tortoise with a wool-Dacron argyle shell.

Sometimes, if I'm tired, I just shrug and say I like it here. Sometimes, if I'm in a foul mood or have had a bit too much to drink, which often amounts to the same thing, I will say I live in New York because it is the center of the universe.

Most of the time I say my sister lives here and I want to be near her, and her husband, who is like a brother to me, and her son, whom I covertly think of as at least partly my own. The old men like that answer. They make a humming sound of approbation and nod their mottled hairless heads. A good girl. A family person. They peer up at Irving. The next question will be about marriage. We flee to Nathan's for a hot dog.

I do like it here. It is the center of the universe.

And I do want to be near my sister, as I always have been. We have our rituals. Every Saturday morning, unless she is covering the Olympics, the Oscars, a disaster, or an inauguration, my sister and I go running together in the park and have breakfast either at her apartment or at the Greek diner down the street from mine. She will tell you she is forced to set a slower pace because I don't exercise enough. She sees this as evidence of my essential sloth. I see it as emblematic of our relationship. Our aunt Maureen says that I was a baby so plump and phlegmatic that the only reason I learned to walk was so I could follow my older sister. Some of my earliest memories are of wandering down a street of old Dutch Colonials and long-leafed pines, the backs of a covey of eight-year-old girls half a block in front of me, the demand from the one at their center carrying on the breeze: "Bridget! Go home! Go home now! You can't come!"

I'm always a little breathless when I run with Meghan on Saturday mornings. But I'm accustomed to it now. "Listen and learn," she has said to me since we were in high school, and I always have.

"How weird is it that we were at the same dinner party last night?" she said one overcast March morning as we began to trot down the park drive in tandem, and I tried not to hear that long-ago plaint in her comment: *Go home, Bridget! You can't come.* It had indeed been strange to enter a vast living room, beige velvet and Impressionist paintings, and see her at one end nursing a glass of sparkling water. Our hostess had attempted to introduce us, since no one ever suspected Meghan and I were related. Then she had disappeared to hand off the bunch of anemones bound with ribbons I had given her at the door.

"God, flowers, Bridge?" my sister said, running around a stroller-size class of new mothers trying to trim their baby bodies. "I couldn't believe you brought flowers to a dinner party. That's the worst. With everything else you have to do when people are showing up, you have to stop to find a vase and fill a vase and cut the stems and then find a place for them and if they're blue, Jesus, I never know where to put them in our apartment, and then—"

"How is it possible that you can make bringing someone flowers sound like the Stations of the Cross?"

"Sometimes I just leave them on the kitchen counter and toss them with the leftovers." I knew this was not exactly true; Meghan had long had staff to toss the leftovers, and the people from Feeding Our People, the big society starvation charity, sent over a van to pick up the excess food from her larger dinner parties. "Just bring wine. Even if they don't want to use it they can put it away for cocktail parties. Or wait and send an orchid plant the next day. I don't know why, but every damn living room on the East Side has to have an orchid plant. I think they're creepy, like big white bugs. They don't look like flowers at all."

"I thought you loved them. You always have one on that chest under the windows."

"What can I tell you? I'm a slave to fashion."

We always see the same people when we run: the soap opera actor with the carefully tinted hair and heavily muscled legs, the small woman with the spiky gray hair who had the ropy muscles and sharp bones of a marathoner, the Chinese couple who wore identical fashionable warm-up suits and ran with a pair of borzois. One of our regular anorexics streaked past us, collarbone draped in the shroud of an extra-large Harvard sweatshirt. "You know that woman who does the financial news? Grace Shelton?" Meghan said.

"The one with that great haircut?"

"I don't understand why everyone says that. That haircut is not that great."

"Okay, fine. What's the point?"

"Someone told me that she doesn't eat anything except apples and Triscuits."

"That can't be true."

"Probably not, but you never know."

A runner in front of us turned and began to run backward. Meghan dipped her head so that the bill of her cap covered her face.

"I want to go back to the dinner gift issue," I said. "How much does an orchid plant cost?"

"A hundred and fifty dollars. You have to send the ones with two stems."

"Jesus Christ. That's a lot of money for a stranger who invites you to dinner."

"Accepted and acknowledged," Meghan said. Like the aunt who raised us, Meghan has a variety of expressions that she uses constantly and whose meaning is somewhat obscure on their face. This one has endured for decades. I think it was even beneath her yearbook picture. Once she told me it meant "I know but I don't care."

On the sidewalk, glittery with mica in the late winter sunlight, a solitary glove lay, palm up, as though pleading for spare change. Meghan barely broke stride as she lifted it and blew through the doors of her building. "Good morning, Ms. Fitzmaurice," the doorman said. The modern honorific was articulated plainly, a sound like a buzzing bee. The building staff know our Meghan.

"Can you see if someone dropped this?" she said, handing over the glove. "It's a shame this late in the season for somebody to find out they're one short."

"Of course," he replied.

"I'm such a good citizen," she muttered as we got into the elevator and Meghan took off the baseball cap that shaded her face so conveniently.

"Oh, get over yourself," I said.

"I am so over myself."

"As if."

We are creatures of habit, Meghan and I. At the diner we have western omelets and rye toast; at her house we have oatmeal and orange juice. This works fine because we live in the city of habit. New York is so often publicly associated with creativity and innovation that outsiders actually come to believe it. The truth is that behavior here is as codified as the Latin Mass. The dinner party the night before had been no exception. The dining room walls glazed red, the tone-on-tone tablecloths, the low centerpiece of roses and some strange carnivorous-looking tulips. The single man on one side of me. "I hear you're a social worker," he said as we both lifted our napkins and placed them on our laps, as so many had said before him.

That was best case, of course. At the home of one donor to the women's shelter where I work, two men who were equity traders spent an entire dinner talking to each other about the market within spitting distance—literally—of my face, bent so close above my dinner that I couldn't reach my bread plate. At the duplex apartment of a woman who worked with my brother-in-law at Sensenbrenner Lamott, I'd turned to the man on my left and asked, "How do you know Amelia?" and watched his face crumble and tears run into his beard. Everyone at the table ignored the display as he talked of his wife, who had been our hostess's college roommate and who had left him for a well-connected lesbian who lived in London. With very little help from me he worked his way through their college years, marriage, apartment renovation, career changes, and the dinner party (of course) where he himself had been the lesbian's dinner partner, the hostess having mistaken her for a more conventional single woman. He had invited the woman to their home for brunch because the two shared an interest in Fiesta ware, an interest his wife had never, in his words, "given a tinker's damn about." ("Oh, God, he's gay himself," Meghan had said at our next breakfast. "What kind of straight man even knows what Fiesta ware is?") In the face of his grief and rage, the table had fallen silent except for the torrent of words from one stay-at-home mother, who was doing a monologue about her child's learning disabilities.

It wasn't always that bad, of course. I once dated a professor at NYU for almost a year after I met him at a dinner party given by a woman who'd graduated from Smith and whom I met at an alumnae phonathon. I developed a firm friendship with a lighting tech who works on Broadway shows, an Irish expat named Jack who was seated next to me at a neighbor's annual Fourth of July potluck.

That was a good dinner, excellent company, excellent food. There were figs with goat cheese stuffed inside, and pumpkin bisque, and rack of lamb with broccoli rabe. The men all run together in my head, all the lawyers/filmmakers/academics/brokers/editors with whom I've been paired. But I almost always remember the food, even the bad food. There was a lot of that in the early days, before all around me grew rich while I moved from a studio to a bigger studio to a small one-bedroom to a one-bedroom with a window in the kitchen, that window that will be presented by brokers to apartment supplicants as though it were a fresco by Michelangelo. As, by Manhattan standards, it is.

For some of us the kitchen with the window means we have finally arrived at some precarious level of prosperity. For others it was a momentary triumph, a way station between the first book proposal and the third bestseller, the summer associate's job and the partnership, the husband who teaches comparative lit at Columbia and the one who runs the big brokerage house. One moment a kitchen with a blessed window, the next a kitchen with two imported dishwashers, two glass-fronted fridges, terra-cotta floors, stainless countertops, an extra-deep sink, a tap over the restaurant range for the pasta pots, designed in consultation with the caterers because they use it more than the homeowners. The kitchen is always hidden in the back of the apartment, away from the pricey views of Central Park and the master bedroom with the cherry chest at the foot of the bed that holds the television, which rises up out of the chest at the touch of a bedside button. It's funny how everyone feels they need to hide the TVs and the food, since both are the things they talk about most often. Meghan's kitchen has a flat-screen television, although Meghan hates to watch TV when she is not working.

"Where's Evan?" I mumbled with my mouth full.

"Evan? Evan who? Oh, you mean my husband? That is his name, isn't it? Evan."

"I'm sorry I asked," I said.

"Evan is at the office. The office here, not the office in London or the one in Tokyo, although God knows he's spent enough time in both in the last six months. When he's in New York, he usually comes home when I'm already asleep. I turn over and look and say to myself, Yep, that's him. Every dinner party now, he says, I'm exhausted, can you go without me? And people accuse me of being a workaholic. Which reminds me: Where the hell do the guys keep the Tupperware?"

Only the team of Robert and John, who made the meals, served the meals, and cleaned up after the meals, had a clue where anything was stored in Meghan and Evan's kitchen. Except for Leo, my nephew, he of the take-out Chinese and late-night ramen noodles, of the endless bowls of Count Chocula and the ice cream eaten straight from the container. He'd shown me where the Tupperware was one night when we'd eaten enough rice pudding to kill us both.

"In the square cabinet over the wine fridge," I said.

Another reason not to bring flowers: the lady of the house doesn't know where the vases are kept. If she had to find the vacuum cleaner or the Windex, the world would stop on its axis.

"Why do you need Tupperware?" I asked.

"We're doing a Tupperware party on the air on Monday morning, and apparently I'm going to have to do something called burping the Tupperware. We talked ad nauseam about whether it would be better if it was clear that I didn't know what the hell burping the Tupperware meant or if I burped it convincingly. With authority, I think they said. I opted for authority."

"Of course you did. On the other hand, it's hard to figure how anyone can look authoritative with Tupperware. I mean—Tupperware. Who cares?"

My sister gave me a long level look, her lip slightly raised on one side. "Maybe you're preaching to the converted here?"

"Hey, who am I to talk? I spent yesterday trying to break up a bootleg sneaker ring that apparently is being fronted by two of the women living in our shelter. The precinct was nice about it, but they said either we could shut down the Nike Air operation or they could shut us down."

"Don't tell me about things like that when I'm practicing Tupperware burping for a national audience. Yesterday I interviewed a guy who wrote a book about how hard it is to meet women, and after that the first woman pastry chef at a four-star restaurant. Then you come over here and talk about people who get burned out of their houses and kids in foster care. You just make me feel like my life is absurd."

"That's so condescending. What, suffering is always real and success is always a fake?"

"No, women who sell bootleg Nikes to try to feed their kids are real and a woman who talks about Tupperware on TV is fake."

"How do you know they're feeding their kids? Maybe they have a crack habit."

"Okay, now you're just looking for a fight. Hand me that big yellow bowl."

All the Tupperware was stacked neatly. My sister is the messiest person on earth, except in her mind, which is as orderly as the inside of a nuclear reactor control room. Meghan's life is so full that she has had to jettison the peripherals. Kenya, you can shout at her, and she can tell you who runs the country, who is trying to oust him, what the most profitable industry is, and how much foreign aid the United States shells out. "Isn't it weird," Leo once said, "that my mom knows all this stuff you didn't even know you needed to know?"

But she can never find her BlackBerry, and I now write her cell phone numbers in my book in pencil because she loses the phones so often. Her schedule is kept and enforced by a brace of young assistants. Her jewelry is mainly kept in a dressing room chest, to be coordinated to her clothes by trained professionals, adept in the art of deciding which neckline cries out for hoops, which for pearl buttons or gold studs.

"Voilà," I said. "Like this." I popped on a lid, lifted a corner, and let out a *pfft* of air, then closed it all the way. Lift, *pfft*, lift, *pfft*. "How did you ever avoid learning to burp Tupperware?" I asked. "Aunt Maureen had as many pieces of Tupperware as she had photo albums. I think she taught me to burp Tupperware when I was a toddler."

"We still lived at home when you were a toddler." By *home* Meghan means the big gray house with the white shutters, the house where we lived until our parents died. We moved to the smaller Cape with Aunt Maureen and Uncle Jack when we were six and ten. Meghan lifted the lid off a large bowl, then put it back and let the air out. "It would have looked like I was a moron if I'd messed this up," she said, but she practiced three or four times more. The last time she burped the Tupperware and looked straight ahead, her head tilted slightly to one side. My sister is the host of *Rise and Shine*, America's number one morning show. She is the most famous woman on television, which means that she is probably the most famous woman in America. The camera doesn't want to see the top of Meghan's head, although the colorist makes sure her roots are never darker than the rest. It wants to see her face.

She thumped the top of the Tupperware and tried to lob it back up into the cabinet. I took it from her and put it on the shelf. It's funny that I'm so much taller than Meghan, that she wears a size 6 shoe on her stubby-toed feet while I have vast gunboat 10s that look designed to bestride entire continents. Meghan is far larger in all the ways that matter. That's why from now on I will bring wine to parties instead of flowers.

"Red," she'd said flatly. "For some reason white is totally over." And like the rest of the country, when she talked, I listened.

"Don't wear black tonight," she said as I left her apartment. "It really washes you out."

"Thanks for doing this, by the way," I said. "It's really important. They'll raise a lot of money. Some of which they've promised will actually get to us. We're figuring on a new furnace because of you, and maybe another aide for the kids."

"It's just strange that it's a Saturday night. No one gives a charity dinner on a Saturday night."

I shook my head. "Do you know why it's on a Saturday night? Because they were told that because of your schedule you could only do it on a Saturday night."

"Hmm. I probably should have known that, shouldn't I?"

"I'm wearing black," I said as the elevator doors closed.

EVERYONE WAS WEARING black, except for a few adventurous souls who had decided to hell with convention and were wearing black and white, and the older women, who still dwelled in the land of lavender and teal. The reception area outside the Grand Ballroom of the Waldorf was choked with guests for the annual dinner of a group called Manhattan Mothers Guild. Manhattan Mothers is made up of socialites who raise money for poor women and children by hosting lunches, dinners, even breakfasts. The event programs are rather unvarying. There is a video that is usually long on shots of cute black kids with enormous dark eyes. There is a testimonial, from either a former foster kid who has gone on to Harvard Law School or a woman who was beaten bloody by her boyfriend and now counsels others in the same spot. And there is an honoree, chosen because of fame, fortune, and the ability to fill a couple of $100,000 tables. There is fierce competition for honorees; the CEOs of various corporations every week turn down three or four invitations to be cited for their commitment to a better life for all New Yorkers (or for all New York children, or schools, or landmarks, or parks).

In the world of fund-raising events, honoring Meghan Fitzmaurice, who has anchored *Rise and Shine* for the past ten years, is the ultimate double threat, publicity and philanthropy both. Coverage in the newspapers, perhaps the local affiliate of the network, a brace of tables, a crowd drawn by the opportunity to hear and see her. She does not disappoint. Unlike some other honorees, Meghan always shows up sober. She always looks good. She always speaks well. She is always cordial to those who approach her table, even the young television reporters who say they have been watching her since they were in elementary school, which makes her feel a hundred years old.

We were raised with good manners, first by the housekeeper, then by our aunt. We let them down only when we are alone.

I rarely go to events like this. Meghan doesn't ask me. She doesn't even ask Evan, her husband, unless the event is particularly high profile or she suspects that there will be lots of other investment bankers and that he can therefore turn it into a business opportunity. Once, years ago, Evan, Alex Menninger, and Tom Bradley got pleasantly drunk at a dinner party and created what they called the Denis Thatcher Society, an organization of men married to powerful public women. Any time the Denis Thatcher Society is mentioned, all the men roar with laughter and all the women get very still, their faces flat.

Occasionally Meghan brings Leo to one of these events as her date. In this way her son has met the president of Ireland, two presidents of the United States, a couple of Supreme Court justices, and that guitar player who organizes all the big relief rock concerts and is now a lord. "Today it's boring," Meghan said once when Leo groused in the car on the way to the hotel. "Tomorrow it's history. Think of the stories you'll have to tell your kids."

"I'm not having kids," Leo always says.

"You'll change your mind," Meghan always says.

I arrived too early and circulated busily with a glass of wine in my hand, looking as though I was looking for someone when I was merely trying not to look like someone who knew no one. The wife of one of Evan's partners was doing the same, and she seemed overjoyed to see me although we'd met in a perfunctory way only once before. She talked for ten minutes about their newborn twins, a conversation that seemed to take place underwater in slow motion. Baby nurse, teak crib, glub, glub. She drifted off and was replaced by Meghan's associate producer, the one she had been threatening to fire during our Saturday morning Central Park runs for at least three months. I could tell he hadn't gotten my name because twice he referred to my sister as "the queen of all media."

"You," came a throaty voice from behind me, and I turned to Ann Jensen, who was the chair of the event. "You. You. You."

"Yes," I said.

"You are my hero. Or heroine. Do you mind which? Because whichever it is, you are it. All day I have been saying, Bridget Fitzmaurice is my hero. Or heroine."

"It was nothing. Really. I was happy to do it."

"Nothing? Four hundred and thirty additional guests is nothing? Last year we made a million dollars at this dinner. This year it will be one point six million. That . . . is . . . not . . . nothing."

Manhattan Mothers had given the women's shelter program where I work a good-size grant the year before. In exchange I had delivered Meghan for this year's dinner. I was a hero. Or a heroine.

"And let me tell you something about your sister," Ann Jensen said, leaning in more closely so that I could look directly into her eyes, which had the preternatural stare of someone who has had lower and upper lifts. People always feel the need to tell me something about my sister, as though we don't know each other well. "Oh, I could tell you a few things, honey," I was tempted to reply, but instead I looked rapt. I tried not to look down. Ann Jensen had on a strapless gown, and she had the kind of cleavage about which Irving likes to say, "You could park a bicycle in there."

She held on to my hands insistently. "No demands," Ann continued. "Do you know how rare that is? No demands. We had someone several years ago—I can't even tell you. A certain size car, a helicopter from the country house. And then they wouldn't even come for dinner. In at nine-oh-five for the award, out by nine-thirty. Your sister is not only coming for the meal, she is coming for cocktails."

"And staying for dessert and dancing," I said.

"What did I say? No demands." It's an odd thing about irony in New York; either you find yourself in situations where it is the only language spoken or those in which it falls on utterly deaf ears. Ann probably spoke French for shopping in Paris and pidgin Spanish to give instructions to the housekeeper. She did not speak ironic. "My hero," she said as she was led away by a woman with a clipboard and I began my aimless circulating again.

My sister came in at seven. Usually I can tell because the cameras start to go off with a sound like a swarm of insects. It was easier this time because she was wearing a white dress. Meghan never wears underwear under her evening wear. I suppose Evan and I are the only ones who know that. Or maybe everyone knows it. The dress she was wearing that night followed the lines of her body perfectly. It looked like a very simple white halter dress until you realized that it was covered with tiny round shiny things. "Those things," she'd said that morning at breakfast. "You know. They're not sequins. Damn. You know."

"I have no clue." I still had no clue, but they looked wonderful. The dress looked like water, which seemed apt. Meghan has the body of a swimmer, long strong muscles, broad shoulders, slim hips. Every day after the show she takes off the makeup, calls me, has a cup of coffee, goes to the gym, and swims for thirty minutes. She says it's the only time she can really be alone.

"She's much better looking in person," someone behind me said.

"She has to have had work done," said another.

She hasn't.

Evan was next to her, his hand at the small of her back. Evan and Meghan met when they were children, he eight, she six. We lived in the nicest section of Montrose then, and so did he. They were at a birthday party together. Legend has it that he said she had spots on her face. "I have freckles," she said with the dignity she had even as a kid. "They look like spots," he replied. She pushed him in the pool. I have heard the story so many times that I can see it all in my mind's eye. Evan is wearing a polo shirt that's buttoned too high on his thin stalk of a neck. Meghan's knees are knobs, her legs skinny, her hem drooping because our mother was so careless with our clothes, insisting they be so expensive that they needed dry cleaning or ironing, then ignoring whether they were cleaned or ironed. He is speaking out of self-protection because she is so sure of herself; she responds out of outrage at being made to look foolish. Of course I have no way of recalling any of this; I was two years old at the time and was probably at home in a playpen watching the housekeeper wash dishes, which apparently was one of the ways I

whiled away my toddler days. I've been told too many times to count that
Meghan called Evan "Stupid Head" as he flailed in the deep end, and
that he was led away, dripping and dazzled.

I'm sure Evan had never encountered anyone like Meghan before.
Evan's parents are the quietest people on earth. When she's feeling
froggy, his mother will say, "Oh, you," to her husband, and he'll squeeze
her forearm. That's the equivalent of all hell breaking loose in the Grater
household. I sat with Evan's mother at their wedding lunch, and I remember how her eyes filled and shone as she watched the two of them
move around the dance floor. Evan had taken ballroom dancing lessons
as a surprise for Meghan, and he was guiding her firmly through the
turns and twirls. "He's beside himself," his mother had said.

It's a variation of that dance when Evan steers Meghan through
crowds like the one at the Waldorf dinner. She never really has to move
at all, never has to thread her way like I do through the waiters' trays and
the glasses held high and the eyes wandering away to someone more interesting or important. Like a spot in the cosmos, she becomes that area
around which all matter begins to circle. The chair of the event. The
vice chair. The woman whose son was in Leo's class at the Biltmore
School before Leo went away to boarding school (the kid who beat Leo
bloody in fifth grade). The woman who is married to one of Evan's partners (and who once tried to seduce Evan in a powder room during a
party). The president of the network.

Somehow my boss, Alison Baker, the executive director of Women
On Women, has wound up at Meghan's side. She leans in to whisper in
my sister's ear, and the gracious, slightly frozen smile that Meghan has
been wearing and that fits as perfectly as the dress widens into something
authentic and wicked, and over the camera click-click I hear the gut-
tural and very loud sound that is Meghan's real laugh. Once a men's
magazine said it was the sexiest thing about her.

The Grand Ballroom of the Waldorf looks like the throne room of
some small second-rate monarchy, Liechtenstein, maybe, or Monaco.
The hotel knows its market, and the lighting is soft and pink and designed to shave ten years off your age. It takes forever to make your way
through the tables, which are arranged even more tightly than the guests

arranged themselves during the cocktail hour. Ann Jensen was right; the evening's take would be enormous. I looked inside my little calligraphed seating card, but I knew my table number. I was at table 1. Meghan is always at table 1.

"Thank God it's you, Bridge," Evan said as he slipped into his seat next to mine, Meghan trailing behind with the network president. "I thought I was going to have to talk to one of those women all night. You know what I mean."

"Where were you this morning? We had breakfast at your house."

"Working."

"Have you talked to Leo?"

"I keep missing the chance because of the time difference between here and Spain. I get ready to call and then I realize it's the middle of the night. Knowing Leo, he's probably out and about in the middle of the night, even in Spain, but I don't want to take the chance I'll wake the guy up. Meghan talked to him after you left, I think. I think that's what she said."

"I'm so, so honored," said Ann Jensen as she came up behind him, and I grabbed his left hand and squeezed as he grimaced down at the gold-rimmed dinner plate and then pivoted deftly, breaking into his company grin. "I'm such a fan of your wife's," she added. Now there's the kind of thing a guy loves to hear.

Meghan was across the table from me, an explosive spray of flowers between us, so that I could see only the top of her head. She never changes her hair for these events, or for the camera. It waves around her face. In her last contract, the network offered her her own makeup person, but Meghan said it wasn't necessary. The women in the makeup room don't forget that. When the circles under her eyes are darkest, they are there during commercial breaks with concealer and powder. One of them comes to the apartment and does her hair and makeup for evenings like this one. Her copper-colored hair shines in the light from the ballroom chandeliers. Her freckles shine through her makeup by design. She is forty-seven and looks thirty.

It would have been rude for me to monopolize Evan, but luckily on my other side was a pleasant older man with a handsome head of silver hair, a ruddy complexion, and blue eyes that smiled when he did, which is quite rare in New York. Meghan has frequently remarked that this is how our father would have looked had he had an opportunity to age gracefully, which is apparently how he did most things. At least according to Meghan. When she speaks of our parents, it is in breezy set pieces, as though they are people about whom she once did a story. Their death together in a car on a Connecticut curve merely seems like the obligatory coda. If the intention was to make me scarcely believe in them, it has worked. "No one knew him well beyond the obvious," our aunt Maureen had once said tartly of our father. "Nice looks, nice voice, nice manners." This stranger at my elbow seems much more real to me than the idea of John J. Fitzmaurice, a man whose reality was apparently so tenuous that he managed to join the Yale Club although, as we discovered some years later, he had never actually gone to Yale.

My dinner partner had just returned from climbing Machu Picchu and was discursive without being a bore about it. He spoke about the sense of peace he felt after the difficult climb. "Almost makes you believe in God," he said.

I told him about a pilot program we were doing at Women On Women, to have the women who were living in our shelters act as aides in our preschool so that they could use what they learned to raise their own kids. Talking to people at dinners like this is a win-win proposition for someone in my line of work. A year ago I piqued the interest of an older man at a dinner party in some weird old loft building on a dirty block by the Hudson River; inside was ten thousand square feet of apartment, much of it made over into a facsimile of an English manor house, with a dining room large enough to seat forty-three. The man, whose name was Edward Prevaricator—and who spent five minutes convincing me it truly was his name, eventually showing me his platinum Amex as proof—was one of those rare New York men who ask after your work and then listen when you respond. He was the only dinner partner I'd ever had with an encyclopedic knowledge of early childhood education, and he told me a charming story about reading *The Cat in the Hat* to a grandchild who would move her lips because she'd memorized the book. He'd also had the most memorable blue eyes I'd ever seen, like those eucalyptus mints that taste like Vicks VapoRub and remind me of the illnesses of my childhood. When I mentioned his eyes, Edward Prevaricator had replied, "They are my one grace note." It was as though he was a character from a Victorian novel brought to life, one of the good ones, the ones who liberate an orphan secretly and watch him prosper from afar. In some sense he was exactly that, for the following week he sent WOW a check for $100,000, the largest unsolicited gift we had ever received.

"You smoke the pole?" asked Tequila, our receptionist, when the check arrived in the morning mail. Tequila thinks everything is about sex or money, and often about the two together.

"He didn't even make a pass. I didn't even know he was rich," I said. "I swear."

Alison looked hard at the check. "Can this really be this guy's actual name?"

"Let's wait and see if the check clears."

"Do you know a man named Edward Prevaricator?" I asked the man now sitting at my left, who was trying not to stare at my sister across the flowers.

"Here tonight, I think," the man replied. "He's a very philanthropic character. From Kansas City, I think, or Chicago. One of those midwest places. Very successful business." He had lapsed into Manhattan shorthand. It's as though the city is too busy for verbs or transitions.

At the other side of the table, I heard Meghan thanking one of the event chairs for holding the dinner on a Saturday night so that she could attend. She does a lot of work at events like this. She has always felt the need to do more than a single thing at once: the mail while on the phone, the newspapers on the treadmill. No matter how tedious the company, she interviews her dinner partners, and frequently finishes coffee with at least one idea for a story, on monetary policy or public health or Asian-American relations. This is disappointing only for the wives of the men who are seated next to her, who ask what they talked about, what she told them, what she was like. "She seemed interested in my work," the husbands say, and the wives sigh or snort, depending on their dispositions and how long they've been married.

As the waitstaff was clearing the entrée course, I ducked to the back of the ballroom to the Women On Women table. All around the vast rococo space you could hear the hum of dinner conversation interspersed with the sharp impatient accented exclamations of the Waldorf waiters: Excuse me! Excuse me please! Meghan once did a story on why the Waldorf had no women waiters. Now there were a few women waiters among the men, wearing the same tuxedos, fetching the same vegetable plates for the vegetarians and the decaf for the older guests.

At good-conscience dinners, representatives from the various charities are seated at the tables so far back in the ballroom that the people with money would go nuts about the placement if they were at those tables themselves. It's insulting largesse, but largesse nonetheless. The people seated at these tables are the only ones who praise the ballroom food. WOW had two tables, and because of Meghan we would get a nice chunk of the evening's proceeds. We run a shelter for homeless women, a job training program for the women in the shelter, and an early childhood program for their kids, along with a little covert drug rehab that we prefer not to discuss with donors. Half of our staff was at table 82, so far in the back that six more feet and they would have been sitting in the foyer. Tequila was wrapping dinner rolls in her napkin and putting them into a shopping bag beneath the table.

"You brought a shopping bag to the Waldorf?" I said.

"Oh, Miss Smarty, that shopping bag is full of good stuff! You got lipstick, nail polish, a copy of *Cosmo* magazine, a nice T-shirt, maybe a little small for me but nice, some kind of candy bar—"

"Protein bar," said one of the other women.

"Whatever. I still didn't get to the bottom."

"You're supposed to take your goody bag on the way out," I said.

"Look at all these people! You think they have enough bags for all these people? No way! And with my luck I get outta here, someone goes, Oh, no, sorry, Tequila, we got no candy bars for you—"

"Protein bars," the woman repeated.

"You look at the color of the lipstick?" I asked. "Because usually the cosmetic companies give them whatever they can't sell, and you wind up with some coral stuff, the kind of stuff grandmothers wear."

"It's actually a nice subtle pink, Bridget," Alison said. "She showed me."

"I got it on," said Tequila.

"You're right, it's a nice color. What did you say to my sister coming in, Al? It was the most fun she's had all night."

"I told her that joke about the nun and the rooster."

Tequila laughed. She has a kind of he-he creaky door laugh. "That's a filthy joke," she said.

I felt a hand on my shoulder, and by the wide-eyed, slightly open-mouthed look of every woman at the table, I knew who it was. "There's nothing I like better than a filthy joke," said Meghan, wrapping her arm around my waist.

"It's the birthday girl," Alison said.

"The bride," Tequila said.

"I guess this is sort of bridal, isn't it?" Meghan looked down at herself. "That's probably what it was meant to be, the perfect dress for a third wedding." Meghan's hand rested on my hip; Alison had one of my hands in hers. A finger poked insistently into my hip. I hadn't been felt up so much since eighth grade.

The finger belonged to a small girl in a flowered dress holding an autograph book. She looked up as I turned and shook her head. Not you. At least she was direct. I elbowed Meghan. She bent from the waist so she and the little girl were face-to-face. "What's your name?" she said, and she signed accordingly: "To Kirby. You rock! XOXO Meghan Fitzmaurice." It was Meghan's newest autograph salutation. "Please, Mom, stop, you're killing me," Leo had said, but it was short and snappy and made Meghan seem hip. It had at least a year before the statute would run and she would move on to something else.

There was a ruckus at the door directly behind us, a cavalcade of men in black suits with lapel pins. Behind them came a balding man with a bad comb-over and a tux with too-wide lapels. He was carrying a plaque in one hand and fussing with the hair with the other. His face when he saw Meghan was like an acting improv exercise: displeasure, fear, followed by feigned joy and then long-rehearsed warmth.

"Meghan! My favorite morning host! And the country's, too!"

"Hello, Mr. Mayor. How was the ribbon cutting at the Armory?"

"God, she's good," I murmured to myself. I shouldn't drink at these events. Meghan never does.

"You know my schedule better than I do. Probably the president's better than the Secret Service."

"The president is at Camp David this weekend, actually, with the British prime minister."

"What did I say? Did I call it, ladies? This lady knows everything about everything."

"Picture!" said the official photographer, and Meghan and I pulled Tequila into a shot with the mayor, who was hustled afterward to the front of the room by his security detail. If Tequila finally killed her youngest child's father, a course of action all of us at WOW would support, that photograph would wind up on the front of the tabloids.

"He's got to do something about that hair right now!" Tequila said.

"He's ridiculous," Meghan said. "I did an interview with him during the campaign that left him looking like a fool in six minutes, and he doesn't even have the balls to hold a grudge. I'd respect him a whole lot more if he'd just cut me dead when he sees me. Instead it's all, Oh, Meghan, great to see you."

"Smarmy," said Tequila.

"Unctuous," Meghan agreed.

"Get the dictionary," said Alison. "Here come the vocabulary words."

"She means the man is one kiss-ass mayor," said Tequila.

"Exactly," said Meghan.

"You going to keep the lipstick from your goody bag?"

"I don't know," said Meghan. "Is it one of those really bad colors? It's not easy for redheads, finding good lipstick colors."

"You never even take the goody bag," I said.

"I might if the lipstick was a good color."

Tequila narrowed her eyes and pursed her lips. "I'm wearing it right now," she said, "and I'm thinking it's too pink for a redheaded girl like yourself."

The waitstaff eddied around us, crying, "Excuse me! Excuse me!" like some breed of urban bird. The dessert was something pink in a chocolate cup with raspberries and the obligatory sprig of mint. The chocolate cup was the official emblem of charity dinners.

"Meghan, thank you so much for getting me those tickets last month," Alison said, lifting her spoon.

"Oh, no problem. I was happy to do it. Oh, God, I almost forgot, I have to go to the ladies' room, that's why I came back here in the first place. And to see you girls, of course. Bridget, come with me. I'm on in about ten minutes and I don't want to be at the podium thinking I have to pee."

"What'd I get her tickets for?" she muttered as we picked our way through the ballroom foyer.

"No idea."

"Oh. Okay, great."

Ladies' rooms are a nightmare for us. This one was not so bad. Only one woman reared back from the sink and cried, "It's you!" Sometimes they say "It's you" and sometimes they say "You're Meghan Fitzmaurice." Either way they seem to feel that Meghan needs to be told who she is. Mostly they seem stunned by the three-dimensionality of her: in the park, in the restaurant, in the toilet stall.

"If I didn't wash my hands, it would wind up in the columns," she said.

"You went back to see some of the clients," Ann Jensen cooed when we returned, threading our way around table after table. It was like doing the wave: table 43 stares, then table 28, then 11, then the single digits.

"I know them," Meghan said. "They're friends of mine."

"So gracious. So gracious."

And she was. The mayor declared it Manhattan Mothers Day, the executive director of Manhattan Mothers introduced the film clip, Ann Jensen announced that the dinner take was close to two million dollars, and then she presented Manhattan Mother of the Year to Meghan. It was a crystal obelisk from Tiffany. Someday an archaeologist is going to be investigating ancient cultures and find blue box after blue box filled with crystal objects in Bubble Wrap with the name Meghan Fitzmaurice engraved at their bases. And he will wonder what in the world they were for. As did we.

"It's past my bedtime," she said as she stepped to the podium, cradling the obelisk. And everyone laughed. Everyone knew that while the rest of Manhattan is watching the late news, Meghan is in bed, that in the empty hour just before dawn, when the streets are almost clean of cars and only the windows of insomniacs burn silver in the darkness, Meghan is in a black car on the way to the studio.

"I wish my son, Leo, was here tonight, but he is spending three weeks in Spain, perfecting his skills in a language I don't even understand. He is making himself more cosmopolitan, more educated, more a citizen of the world than his parents are." She looked down at Evan and smiled slightly, to include him, but he was looking at his hands in his lap, threading his fingers together tightly. I smiled back at her.

"That's what every Manhattan mother wants for her children. Mothers rich and poor, black and white, Christian and Muslim, uptown in Harlem and downtown in Tribeca. We want our children to do better than we have done. We know that our families are the most important things we have or do."

And she was off. I don't remember all of the rest. I've heard a fair number of Meghan's speeches, and I still can't quite understand how it is that she can make a small bit of alliteration, the repetition of a phrase, a pause and a tightening of the lips and a raised voice evoke the same sort of emotion that music does. It amazes me.

"What we all want for our kids," she said at the end, "is for them to rise and shine." Oh, such a smoothy, I wanted to say cynically, to close with the name of her own show. But it was perfect. She stepped back, and they all stood up. Evan had tears in his eyes.

I wouldn't want anyone to think, in retrospect, that it was a night of great moment or triumph, although in the coming weeks a photograph of Meghan on that night, in that slender glittering fall of fabric, holding the plinth of crystal to her heart, would appear in the papers over and over again. In many ways it was a typical night of a sort that happened perhaps eight or ten times a year. Afterward I stood to one side as people asked her to sign their programs. It never varies, what they say: I never miss the show. You're prettier in person. You gave an amazing speech. For Linda. For Jennifer. For Bob. For Steve. I stood to the side and held the blue box. In the car on the way home, Meghan handed me the obelisk, and I rewrapped it. It didn't feel like the end of anything.

"That wasn't a really terrible one, was it?" Meghan asked Evan, her head thrown back against the seat.

"It was fine," he said.

"You were great," I said.

"You're quiet," she said to Evan, who was looking out the window at the shadowed walks of Central Park.

"I'm just tired," he said without turning his head. I could see his face reflected in the glass. He looked exhausted, maybe even ill.

"Ev?" I said.

"Bridge?" he replied. We've known each other a long time, Evan and I. Meghan tucked her hand through the crook of his arm. His bony fingers began to play a tattoo on the leg of his tuxedo pants. But still he kept his head turned away.

"We'll be in the Caribbean in a week," Meghan said. "A week of no calls and no meetings and no snow. A week of reading and tennis and snorkeling."

"Sounds good to me," I said.

"I wish Leo could come. He gets back from Barcelona and goes right up to Amherst to work on some big English paper. His life is as crazy as ours."

"His life is great," I said, still looking at the back of Evan's head. His hair had gotten thin on top. I hadn't really noticed it before.

I tripped over the curb on the way to my apartment building, fumbled for my key in my clutch bag. "Bridge," Meghan called, leaning forward. "Bridget!"

"What?"

"Paillettes."

"What?"

"The things on the dress. That's what they're called. Not sequins. Paillettes."

"How did you finally remember?" I asked.

She shook her head. Meghan describes her hair color as auburn. She hates it when anyone says it's red. Her hair is red. So is mine. "I had someone at the office look it up. P-A-I-L-L-E-T-T-E-S." And as if they heard their names called, the sparkling circles undulated as she leaned forward, Northern lights in the backseat of a Town Car.

"Accepted and acknowledged," I called as I unlocked the door.

"It was like the end of an era," I said several days later to Irving as footage of Meghan in the dress ran over and over on the news.

"Get a grip, kid," he replied. "We're not talking World War Two here."

BAD NEWS COMES to you in strange ways in New York. Before a friend can tell you about the lump she found, you've run into a friend of a friend at the pharmacy, and you already know about the suspicious mammogram and the exploratory surgery. Before someone has gotten to your name in the Rolodex to tell you he's leaving the rat race to spend more time with the kids, you've overheard gleeful associates talking at the next table about how he was canned, his office cleaned out in less than an hour. You see the hook and ladder and learn of the fire, the yellow tape and know about the murder.

I got my bad news at the home of the nicest rich people in New York, Kate and Sam Borows. They had written a city restaurant guide that made them wealthy, and in the process they had become the best sorts of philanthropists, with not a hint of "get out the ball gown" self-congratulation. When I'd first met them through my sister, they'd lived in the same building they live in now, in a spacious apartment that had become an enormous one as they'd annexed a studio and two one-bedrooms on either side and a three-bedroom apartment above. When I'd gone to work for WOW, Kate had done some variation on the wish-there-was-something-I-could-do lament, and I'd told her she could come up to the Bronx a couple days a week and teach nutrition and cooking. It had been five years, and she'd placed at least fifty women in good jobs in restaurants and caterers, and she never mentioned it in interviews unless we wanted her to thump for WOW for our own purposes.

"Bridget," she said when I walked in on Monday evening and struggled out of my coat for the catering guy–cum-actor. "I didn't think you'd come."

"I told you last Saturday night that I was coming," I said as I handed her a bottle of red wine, which she handed off along with my coat.

"Oh, my God," she said, hugging me, and then the elevator was back, emptying directly into her foyer as the elevators of the wealthy do, so that no one will be subjected to the shared space of the hallway, the smells of strange cooking, the sight of strangers with their keys in the locks. Six other guests tumbled from the mahogany-paneled car, laughing and handing over coats and proffering wine. I found myself stuck in the foyer with a real estate agent who was making the sale of a duplex on Park Avenue sound like curing cancer. I'd gotten into trouble the year before with a woman like this, who had asked about my work and crooned, "I wish there was something I could do personally." "Write a check," I'd replied. In my defense, it had been a long hot day in an office that had bad air-conditioning, and one of the women in my work-study program had been shot by her ex-boyfriend. I still caught hell from my sister, who had heard through the Manhattan tom-toms that I had offended the sister-in-law of the managing partner of one of the city's largest law firms. New York is the biggest little small town in America. That's why it's so dangerous. Believe me: having your purse snatched is nothing compared with being mugged by Manhattan manners over rare tuna on toast rounds.

I moved into the living room, toward a waiter with wineglasses on a silver tray. "Wow—you're here," said Sam Borows, with the signature kiss on both cheeks that I guess you learn at John Dewey High School in Brooklyn.

"Why is everyone so shocked that I showed up at a dinner I was invited to?" I asked, and suddenly there was the answer in front of me, a spindly man with too-long hair who was grinning at Sam like a madman and performing a good-gossip monologue, the linchpin of any successful cocktail hour in New York.

"One of the great days of television," he said without preamble. "We'll be talking about this one for years to come. On the way up one of the guys was saying the network is spinning it like crazy. The question is whether there's any spin that can make this go away." A woman had appeared at his elbow. "It was like watching a car wreck," she said. "I mean,

I was on the treadmill and my mouth fell open. I don't think I've ever seen anything like it, and I was watching *Live and in Color* when what's-his-name started to slur his words talking to Yasir Arafat."

"What's-his-name was formerly Burt Chester," said the man, "and he currently runs a bookstore in Montpelier, Vermont. And insists in every interview that he's happier now. Right. Sure. Happier. My ass."

"Shrimp?" said a waiter, and as we all fell silent and poked the tooth-picks into fancy little lemon halves while we chewed, I could hear conversations all around us that were clearly on the same subject: Did you see it? How bad was it? What's the spin? This sort of knowledge deficit was the inevitable effect of working triage in the Bronx while most of Manhattan was going to the same restaurants, forwarding confidential e-mails, talking on the phone. I'd walked into one dinner without knowing that the president had been impeached, and another without knowing the mayor had called a press conference to introduce his fiancée, which came as quite a surprise to his wife. My usual day at the office was too full of lost public assistance checks, arson fires, black eyes, trips to family court, foster care placements, and calls from the cops to keep up with breaking news. Catching up on the conversation was a constant part of dinner party attendance for me. Except that Sam Borows had never kept his arm around my waist before, although by the end of any number of evenings men I'd known far less well had done so.

"You going to the Cape soon?" he asked the man and woman, who had the indefinable body English that told you immediately they were husband and wife of long standing.

"Oh, come on, you're going to try and change the subject here? I know you're her friends, Sam, but this is the only game in town." The man looked out over the jagged vista of the Manhattan skyline, black, gray, silver, and the occasional faint flickering blue light that marked a large-screen television in a skyscraper living room. "Look at that. The greatest city on earth, and I bet there's only one conversation topic going on anywhere in it."

"Not just in New York," said his wife.

"Sure, L.A. and Chicago and South Dakota. All anyone cares about at this moment—"

"Jack—"

"—is why Meghan Fitzmaurice self-destructed on the air in front of about twenty million people this morning."

Sam's arm tightened, and Jack raised his glass. "Rise and shine," he said, and his wife laughed and clinked his with hers. "And let's all hope there's another bookstore available in Montpelier."

"Tuna tartare?" said a waiter.

"I have to go to the bathroom," I said and I walked toward Kate, took her by the hand, and pulled her down the hall and into the pantry. As I left the living room, I heard the man standing with Sam ask loudly, "Who is that woman?" I didn't hear Sam's reply, but I didn't have to. He would have said the words I'd heard so many times that I might as well set them to music, needlepoint them on a pillow, have them engraved on a headstone. He'd have said, "That's Meghan Fitzmaurice's sister."

"What happened?" I asked Kate, backing her up against a wall of stainless steel bun warmers. "What does everyone but me know about Meghan?"

"Oh, Bridget," she breathed and placed her palm against my cheek.

Kate Borows is a good friend, to me and to Meghan. She ignored her guests to talk to me in the kitchen, and she told me that she would re-arrange her table settings so I wouldn't have to stay. "You don't look like you'd be able to stomach osso buco tonight," she said, and I shuddered. I wanted tea and ice cream, ice cream and tea and TV. "That jerk Ben Greenstreet," Kate said savagely as she called one of the cater waiters to get my coat. And I knew as she said it that out in the living room, and all over town, people were saying something else: That bitch Meghan Fitzmaurice.

Of course it was on morning television, the town square of public voyeurism, that the two of them had collided. Ben Greenstreet was the scandal du jour, one of the crunchy-granola child-men who had joined the billionaire ranks with the rise of the California computer culture. His favorite word was *dude*, his hair was never cut, and he was worth roughly five billion if you counted his stake in an arena football team he'd named the Live Wires. Every year at the stockholders' meeting he sang a Dylan song to the assembled, and he had once done the final leg of the Ironman triathlon naked, allegedly because of a chafing problem. He spent most of his time making money and what was left over telling people that he lived outside the system, dude, it was just his way. His last name was a gift to tabloid writers and late-night hosts alike.

Proving that marriage is the great enduring mystery of human relations, Greenstreet had been married since college to a woman named Dixie Cohen, one of those whip-smart women in a black pantsuit who sail up the corporate ladder as though filled with helium. Dixie was the CFO of the third biggest computer manufacturer in the world, and somewhere along the line she and Ben had suddenly realized that they had a nine-bedroom house, a five-bedroom apartment, a three-bedroom boat, and no one to put in the beds. They had forgotten to have children.

It was the kind of thing that happened a lot in their circle of friends. In my sister's circle, too. Meghan knew so many women who had gone right from fertility treatments to perimenopause that in an apartment in her building there was now a support group for mothers of adopted Chinese babies, including classes on the history of Confucian thought and the making of dim sum. I guess if you're a Chinese girl living in a triplex with a Rothko over the fireplace, it's important to be able to remember your roots.

The Greenstreet-Cohens had gone a different route, hiring a surrogate mother whose eggs were harvested and fertilized with Ben's sperm. Two successfully implanted, a boy and a girl, and all would have been well in the world in which the couple traveled in Pacific Heights, which is like the East Side of Manhattan only with chillier mornings and steeper streets, except that Ben, who is a vegan, insisted on visiting the surrogate with some regularity to keep tabs on her prenatal diet.

"Surprise, surprise," said Meghan, who had become prickly about marriage during the winter months, perhaps because Evan was spending so much time in Tokyo on a major consumer electronics deal. "They were both eating the same thing. Each other."

"Oh, yuck."

"I can't even take credit for that line. It's from one of the gay guys in my office. What's the deal? They get the fashion gene, the design gene, and the wit gene. What's left for us straight people?"

"Professional sports."

"They have all the figure skaters, too."

In one afternoon Ben Greenstreet left Dixie Cohen and she sued for divorce and custody of the twins, due to be born in six weeks. Ben countersued for desertion, saying that he and Dixie had not had sex for two years, and announced that he intended to marry as soon as possible "the mother of his children."

And on Monday morning it was the third lead story on all three morning shows, after the spike in the jobless rate and the death of the French president. *Morning in America* had the doctor who set up the surrogate arrangement. *The A.M. Show* had the surrogate mom's husband, a construction supervisor who was suing for custody of their own two kids, whom he brought on the air with him. And Meghan had Ben and the surrogate, whose name was Cindy, because for as long as most TV viewers could remember, Meghan always got the big guest. Before the Super Bowl she got the quarterbacks; if there was a war she got the president.

Dixie Cohen was the only one who had the intelligence or the dignity to stay off the air.

It was hard to tell from the clips I saw that night whether Meghan had been in a foul mood all morning or whether Ben Greenstreet set her off. A few days later, when I had more of an idea of what had really been going on, I asked Irving whether he'd seen the beginning of the show and whether she'd been sour from the top of the hour, when that unmistakable four-note opening played. "I'll give it to you like this, kid," he said. "You got the distinct impression that it was the French president's own fault he had the stroke." But it was when she had Ben and Cindy huddled together on the cornsilk-colored sofa on the living room set that Meghan really worked up a head of steam.

"Mr. Greenstreet, it's hard to even know where to begin," she said. "A man leaves his wife of eighteen years for the surrogate pregnant with their child—"

"My children," Greenstreet said. "There's two of them. And there's no DNA in there except for mine and hers. This is not a surrogate. This is the mother of my children." And he reached over and patted Cindy's belly.

"Let's leave the DNA for just a moment and backtrack. You and your wife, who is, according to *Pennywise* magazine, one of the fifty top female executives in America, contracted with Mrs. Benn to use her, in essence, to provide the baby you both badly wanted. Isn't that correct?" Meghan's consonants were as hard as pebbles in her mouth, and she had the flinty look in her brown eyes that I'd seen before. When I took a leave from college so I could work at Rock Hill stables. When I moved to Maine to throw pots full-time at a shop called Mud in Your Eye. You do not want Meghan ever to look at you that way.

She was wearing one of her signature black turtlenecks, and above it her pale freckled face seemed to float forward like a tribal mask. Even Ben Greenstreet, who was moving his hand in a circular motion over Cindy's enormous stomach, must have seen the hard glint in her eyes, because he began to babble.

"Look, love happens. It's just a plain and simple deal. Love happens. And I gotta say, the reason we're here is because both of us think maybe we've been playing God, paying for people to have babies. Maybe it's the natural order of the universe, that I would look at this woman whose body is sheltering my seed and that I would realize that we were meant to be together."

"So you see this as a commentary on the evils of surrogacy, and not as a case of a man leaving his wife for a woman fourteen years his junior who, by the way, was not in the least offended by being paid to have a baby when she deposited a check for twenty thousand dollars that your wife"—Meghan stopped and looked at the ever-present index cards in her lap, as though unable to be certain that what she had said was accurate, then nodded and did something unpleasant with her lips that suggested disapprobation—"wrote from her personal account?"

"She needed to write the check because she was the one who needed the help," said Cindy, who had an unfortunate singsong voice. You couldn't help but suspect that Ben would be suing her for custody of the kids in a year or two.

"Excuse me?" said Meghan. You don't ever want to hear Meghan say "excuse me?" either. She'd used it once on the vice president when he was insisting that eliminating the estate tax would enable the administration to increase Medicaid for poor seniors, and the president's poll numbers had gone down almost 10 percent in a week.

"Ben didn't need to pay anybody. He can have children. He has children. I'm living proof. She was the one with a problem. She had a problem where her tubes were scarred up."

"Endometriosis," Ben Greenstreet said helpfully, looking down at the belly he continued to massage and not up at Meghan. Who, I was in a unique position to know, had had two surgeries for endometriosis, one before she had Leo and one afterward, an unsuccessful attempt to provide Leo with a sibling.

"Mr. Greenstreet," she said softly, "would you characterize yourself as a moral man?"

"I have a strong sense of personal morality," Ben Greenstreet said. "It comes from the voice within. That's why I'm here. To say we've been on the wrong path where baby making is concerned." His hand stopped moving. His eyes narrowed.

"And what about a sense of personal privacy? In other words, is there anything you can say that would make the American people understand why you're sitting here telling them all this about your personal life?"

"Whoa, hey, you're the one who asked us to be here."

"She sent baby clothes," said Cindy. "Didn't she send baby clothes? Or was it the other one?"

"That's what we do in television nowadays, but there are times when it seems unseemly. This is one of those times. We'll be right back."

My sister has become famous in television because she has what is called "the common touch." It isn't, really. A common touch would be fulsome, approving, pitched to the lowest common denominator of America at the beginning of the twenty-first century. Meghan's uncommon touch is that she asks the questions and makes the comments that ordinary people would like to ask if the guest were sitting on their sofa, except that they wouldn't have the wherewithal to think of them, or at least not until hours later. The riposte you wish you had gotten off at the faithless friend? The disdainful comeback at the belittling boss? The throwaway line when you find your husband in bed with his trainer? Meghan is the person who has the broadcast equivalent at her fingertips always. Once the network did a focus group study of the morning show and found that the comment made most often about Meghan Fitzmaurice was "You gotta hand it to her." She has always been daring, ever since she jumped into the quarry in Montrose from the highest cliff on a dare from a group of high school boys. She was nine years old, and she went in cleanly feetfirst. They cheered; she climbed onto a rock by the water's edge and bowed. Next day my aunt Maureen discovered that she had broken a bone in her foot, the force of the water slamming her narrow instep. She wears orthotics when we run.

When we got older, I remember thinking that if she'd jumped from one of the lower spars, the crowd would have been just as impressed and her foot would have been saved. And that morning on the show she could have cut cleanly as well with that last comment. People would have said she was too harsh, but plenty of women (particularly the ones with endometriosis) would have put their heads together at dinner parties and said smugly that it was just what they would have done in her shoes.

She would have been fine if she'd left it at that. But somehow there was a beat of open air before the commercial, perhaps because Meghan had cut the interview short. And in television a beat is a lifetime, long enough to sink a politician or to kill a sound engineer who leaves it empty. There would be a lot of speculation about the technical reasons for what happened, whether someone with whom Meghan had been brusque had intentionally left the station on the air when she thought they had gone to commercial. I doubted that; the guys on the lower rungs loved her, the sound guys, the equipment guys, the gofers. She remembered their birthdays, sent home little keepsakes for their kids. Certainly it was hard to understand how someone with Meghan's experience had not noticed that she was still on the air, that her mike was still live. What is indisputable is that Meghan said, "We'll be right back." And then a moment later she snarled under her breath, "Fucking asshole." And then the network went directly to a commercial for Happy Heinies, the disposable diaper with aloe vera in the seat.

TOOK A cab home from the Borowses' building and spent a frustrating half hour trying to reach my sister. The cell phone number I had was out of service, the phone itself probably left in a restaurant and later canceled by one of the assistants, as so many had been before. The home number was useless. I never called my sister after 9:00 P.M., when she took an Ambien, turned on a white noise machine, switched off the phone, and went to sleep. There was nothing left to do but eat fudge ripple out of the pint container in a bathrobe that used to belong to Evan, plaid flannel with a faded Brooks Brothers label. The television was on, and the cat lay on the crest of the couch slightly above my left shoulder. Meghan says disapprovingly that I look like a caricature of a single New York woman when I do this. The ice cream carton, the cat, the tiny couch. This is one of my favorite ways to spend the evening, especially if my nephew, Leo, is with me, too, and I can put my feet up in his lap. A nineteen-year-old boy who doesn't mind giving a foot massage to his aunt is a thing of beauty, especially if he has wild red hair and a deadpan sense of humor.

I thanked God that Leo was somewhere in Spain, somewhere where I assumed all the television sets were tuned to soap operas and bullfights. The cat snagged the back of the bathrobe with her claws, and I backhanded her and went to the refrigerator for a wine chaser. It was nighttime, and I was watching my sister on TV, which was the network equivalent of sunset at noon.

We live in a time when the past can be present, and the moment eternal, on a continuous loop of film. The events of Monday morning had slipped by me, only to be resurrected and replayed over and over. Every channel was covering the story with that telltale combination of broadly acted disbelief and muted glee that marks discussions of fallen celebrities at the beginning of this century. I had missed the actual show, but like millions of others I hadn't needed to miss the critical moment, since it was played over and over on several cable channels: the right-wing channel (to illustrate the degradation of the mainstream media), the BBC (to illustrate the curious customs of Americans), and the comedy channel (because the truth was that it was funny). Some viewers must have been mystified, since when the clip was replayed, Meghan's words were blanked out to conform to the FCC regulations about obscenity that she had shattered in an instant that morning. Over and over the report was that she had said something unspeakable, and then all the viewers saw was a woman in a turtleneck fingering a stack of index cards as her lips moved.

Of course I can read Meghan's lips. Sometimes when I am at her dinner table and she is pretending to listen to the man on her left she is really listening to me, and if she feels I am about to go wrong, her lips will move. Republican. Divorced. Bankrupt. All the quicksands into which I might so easily step.

I reached for the phone, then replaced it in the cradle. It would be cruel to wake Meghan now, even if I could. She has to be up and in the shower at 4:45, in the car to the studio at 5:00, on the air two hours later, her skin glowing, her hair arranged so that it looks soft and pretty but never falls into her face. She is the only redhead on TV news, and is inevitably described by reporters as the best-known television redhead since Lucille Ball. In her early years in the business, when she was flying around the country as a general assignment reporter, she did her own makeup, and she laid the Pan-Cake on pretty thick, so that there was contrast between her dark eyes, her red hair, and her white skin. Then six months into her time doing the news on the morning show, one of her male cohosts made an offhand comment about Meghan's freckles being covered by the makeup people during a second-hour segment on the world freckle competition in Des Moines. ("You can't make this shit up," Meghan had said. "There's a kid at the table, Meg," my brother-in-law had replied, pointing his fork at Leo. "What?" said Leo, who frequently let his mind wander into a country different from the one his parents inhabited.)

Overnight an organization of proud redheads had formed, demanding that Meghan's makeup be lightened. I believe there was even a logo with the legend "Free the Fitzmaurice Freckles!" A celebrity news program—"an oxymoron," Meghan always says—interviewed a famous dermatologist, who had never met her or seen her in person but who said my sister didn't wear enough sunscreen and better take care of herself as she grew older because she had thin skin.

My sister had always hated her freckles; she found them infantilizing and had been thrilled when she realized that on-air she could trowel on the powder with no one the wiser. Now she wore a sheer foundation from which a sprinkling across her nose shone dimly, and at forty-seven she was happier to look like a distaff Tom Sawyer than she had been at twenty-four, when the phrase "taken seriously" came up in our conversations more than any other except, perhaps, "anchoring the evening news." I was Meghan's mind dump; she left everything with me, no matter how small, large, or forbidden.

My brother-in-law had his own phone line in his study with a light that flashed on and off in lieu of a ring tone so that the distant ringing would not wake his wife. He was the only person in America who had such a thing and was not hearing-impaired. I called his line six times in the next half hour, but there was no answer to the flashing light. Finally I left a message on Meghan's office phone, the private line only she answered.

"Why didn't you call me? I'm home now if you're up. If you get this in the morning, call me at home. It doesn't matter how early. Or call me as soon as you get off the air. I'll be at the office. Or call me on my cell. I need a full report. Don't panic." I stopped, breathed, and hung up after the last. For me to tell my older sister not to panic, my sister who had done a stand-up as the president was being loaded into the helicopter after the stabbing by that wacko at the Caribbean summit, who had once interviewed the Russian president while he had his hand on her ass, who had piggybacked me over to the community hospital when I was eight and she twelve and told the desk clerk flatly, "She needs stitches in her leg right now!"—if I was telling Meghan not to panic, I knew it meant we were in terrible trouble here.

When the phone rang, I jumped. "Hello, dear heart," said a voice with a bit of a rusty hinge in it.

"Oh, God, Aunt Maureen."

"Now, be still, Bridget. That's why I'm calling so late. I know you're sitting there worrying yourself to a sliver."

"Did you see the show?"

"I did. And then I had bridge club. Can you imagine? Lucy Selliger said she'd never heard a thing like that in all her life. And I said, Well, Lucy, I assume your husband never hit himself with the hammer when he was hanging a picture."

"Oh, God bless you, is there anything Meghan could do that you wouldn't stand up for?"

"Of course there is. There have been times when I've given your sister the lash of my tongue, but this won't be one of them."

"Of course not. That would be terrible for her. The worst."

"That's not the only reason. Elaine Lee said this morning, Well, I thought that man was an asshole, too."

"My God! Mrs. Lee said that! Isn't she a Mormon?"

"Her husband was a Mormon. She's Presbyterian. There was a big scandal about the marriage, apparently. But that's neither here nor there. I'm sure there were plenty of Mormons out there thinking that Meghan was speaking the truth."

"I missed the whole thing." The first Monday of the month was the only day I didn't watch *Rise and Shine* before work. I always had a staff meeting, and all the day's work backed up after it, all the weekend's crises knocking at the door. The ancient furnace breaks in our women's shelter on Mount Morris Avenue. One of the women in the transitional housing building down the street decides to try to scar up one of the others, maybe because she took her laundry out of the dryer in the basement or gave her boyfriend a blow job in the vacant lot. You never know what will set people off if they have no money, no home, and spend a lot of time watching television shows filled with people they'll never look like living in places they'll never be able to live. There had been the usual litany of need that morning, the usual litany of violence and poverty and want that would go on and on, more obscene than any words.

It's a different world up in the Bronx, where I work, the anti–East Side, rap and salsa from the doorways, squat buildings with metal grilles over the doors and windows, steep hills and layered graffiti and drive-by law enforcement of the "no one's dead, let's have coffee" variety. I know from experience that in a half hour on the train you can go from Lupe's Brides Delux, which rents elaborate lace dresses at an hourly rate for hurry-up marriages, to Bergdorf's, where the women stroll casually through the ground floor, putting out manicured fingers to touch a scarf, a bag, a sweater that may cost more than one of my women gets from welfare to support three kids for a month. I've watched those women sigh, frown, turn from one necklace to another, then with the dissatisfied not-quite-but-still look hand over a credit card for something they will scarcely use and barely remember enough to regret. If they went from their homes to Paris or Hong Kong, they would travel a shorter distance than if they were to take the Number 6 train to my part of the Bronx.

"I missed it," I repeated to my aunt. "I mean, I didn't really miss it. You can't miss it. They keep playing it over and over again. It's like she just snapped."

"I talked to her this afternoon, dear. She will be fine. She needs a bit of space. She's been in a brown study these last few months. I think it's sending Leo off to college and being in the same job for a long time. She's come up here after the show for lunch the last few weeks, and she hasn't said much, but I can tell."

"She's been coming up there?" My sister's schedule usually looked like the schematic for a nuclear power plant. Lunch with my aunt Maureen in Westchester seemed pretty far off the grid.

"The last month or so. She can't stay long, but I make her a grilled cheese sandwich."

"The patented Maureen Dougherty cure for anything that ails you. I still think I ought to make one anytime I get the flu."

"Everyone feels a little better after a grilled cheese sandwich. A real grilled cheese sandwich, none of that low-fat nonsense. Especially for your sister. She looks like a roof shingle in a high wind these days." Our aunt Maureen is the official queen of china closet aphorisms. I suspect she makes most of them up on the spot.

"She's in a high wind right now. She's going to blow right over."

"She will be fine."

"I can't get her on the phone. I can't get Evan, either. I'm going a little nuts here."

"Oh, I think she's under the porch, dear," Maureen said.

On Valentine's Day the year after we moved in with Aunt Maureen and Uncle Jack, our uncle had brought us home an Angora kitten. I'd like to say that I won the right to name her, but the fact is Meghan simply wasn't interested. I suppose it seemed too much like we were staying if she christened a cat. I named her Puff Ball. "That's the stupidest name I've ever heard," Meghan whispered that night as we lay in bed.

Despite her name, and her appearance, Puff turned out to be one of those cats who never met another animal that didn't look like dinner. With a grating, high-pitched yowl, she set slain moles, birds, mice, chipmunks, even frogs, on the kitchen floor. But sometimes she took on a possum, a raccoon, a neighbor's boxer, and the result was a deep puncture wound or a gash from ear to ear. We discovered what had happened only after the fact, too late for the vet, because when Puff was wounded, Puff went under the porch and nursed her injuries until the bleeding stopped and the healing began.

Whether it was when her best friend ran off with another group of girls in eighth grade, when she was unfairly denied the English prize at her high school graduation, when she was passed over for the weekend anchor spot, or when the doctors told her she would never carry another pregnancy to term, Meghan did precisely the same. She licked her wounds alone and in isolation, until only the sharpest eyes could see the scars. And then she went on as if nothing had happened. Once I had cried to my aunt, "Why can't she talk to me about it when she's really upset?"

"It's not in her nature," Maureen had replied.

Like Puff, who died quietly at age nineteen while lying on a pile of old sheets in the upstairs linen closet, Meghan always managed to recover. So maybe this, too, would pass. I should know better than to underestimate my sister. She'd taught me to ride a bike when she'd just learned herself, pulled me out of the Long Island Sound surf one afternoon when I was caught in a bad rip current, gotten both of us scholarships to Smith, had a baby when they told her she never would, pushed aside the occupant of the morning show spot without even seeming to do so, and kept the woman as a friend, or what passes as a friend in her circles in New York City, to boot. Maybe it would not matter that the viewers of *Rise and Shine* had heard the same two words that had killed off Tandy Bannister's radio show and landed him in Detroit doing syndicated car news, the same two words that had cost a gubernatorial candidate in Nebraska a sure primary victory.

At 7:00 the next morning I awoke, put on the TV, and it was as though nothing had happened. There was the intro music and there was the logo and there was the cheesy-looking semicircular desk. Except that instead of the usual opening—"Good morning. Rise and shine. I'm Meghan Fitzmaurice, and I'll be with you for the next two hours"—the program opened with Tom McGregor, a jovial guy who looked ten years older than my sister and who was actually ten years younger. Viewers loved Tom because he looked like an average guy who lived in the burbs, had three cute little kids, and played golf with his brother-in-law on Sundays; in fact, Tom lived in the burbs, had a fourth cute kid on the way, and played golf all weekend long. The makeup crew complained bitterly about trying to bring down his sunburn to manageable levels on summer Mondays. They'd wound up using the kind of foundation you use to cover serious scars and he still looked like an Irish guy in the third hour of the St. Patrick's Day parade. Meghan said he was smarter than he looked, certainly smarter than Bill Messereau, his opposite number, the single member of the team, who always wound up on those lists of the ten most eligible bachelors in New York.

"Good morning," Tom said with his serious look. "The Federal Communications Commission announced late yesterday that it would begin an investigation of the use of a profanity on this program during a broadcast interview. The FCC acted after several complaints from viewers, including the wife of the vice president. Network officials said they were confident that after looking into the incident, the chairman of the FCC would conclude that it had been an unfortunate production accident and that it was in no way deliberate."

It's funny how the way you deliver a line can make all the difference in the world. Tom was neither attractive nor authoritative, but he had sincerity that politicians must have wanted to tap and bottle. He was the Vermont maple tree of sincere, dripping with the sweet stuff, a little sappy but pure nonetheless. Having him do the story was the perfect solution. If network executives were intelligent, Tom would have finished there and the program would have gone on as if nothing had happened. But if more network executives were intelligent, television would be completely different than it is.

"Meghan?" said Tom.

My sister was wearing a pale pink blouse. It is the color they make her wear when they want her to look feminine, vulnerable, soft, sweet—in other words, when they want her to appear other than what she is. She wore that practiced look that people in her business have perfected, not quite a smile but friendly nonetheless.

"I want to take this opportunity to apologize to viewers who were offended by what I assumed were off-the-air remarks at the end of a particularly contentious interview. I lost my temper in front of a live camera and a live microphone. It's happened to others more distinguished than I am—presidents, prime ministers, and in one memorable case, the Prince of Wales." You could almost hear the chuckles. I could almost hear the computer keys. Meghan had written this herself. I knew the sound of her voice.

I knew the sound of the lawyers' voices as well. Occasionally I'd heard her mouth them when the network itself had been in the news, when they'd been sued by the family at the center of a made-for-television movie, when their weekend anchor had been arrested for drunk driving.

"It was not my intention nor the intention of the network to permit such language or to countenance its use," Meghan continued, and in case you weren't clear on the fact that she was reading a prepared statement, she was looking down at the papers on the desk, papers that even the most cursory TV-watching American knows are used just for show, so that anchorpeople have something to do with their hands. "The network is mounting a full investigation of the circumstances and will respond completely and appropriately to the FCC investigation."

Meghan looked up and smiled softly. This time the smile was in the mouth but not the eyes. Or perhaps I was the only one who noticed.

"At least that's what it says here," she added with the signature head tilt. "I'm Meghan Fitzmaurice. Rise and shine."

I'd heard her say it lots of different ways over the years, but I'd never imagined she could make it sound like that, make "Rise and shine" sound exactly like "And you can all go to hell."

"WOO-HEE," SAID TEQUILA when I walked into my office.

"I know."

"Things are happening fast," she said.

"I know."

"Her husband's here."

"What?"

I've known Evan Grater longer than I knew my own parents, or my aunt and uncle, or Irving Lefkowitz. The only person I've known longer than Evan is Meghan, but sometimes the two merge in my mind, and I really do believe I knew that tidy little boy who had to be pulled, gasping and affronted, from the Bensons' pool, humbled by his future wife.

But I don't think he'd ever been to my office. And why would he have? Evan has one of those Wall Street jobs that no one understands but that seem to consist of some mysterious ability to turn money into more money, a little like what Christ did with the loaves and fishes. He works near the Staten Island Ferry terminal in an office that seems to float over New York harbor; viewed from the right angle, the Statue of Liberty appears to be a paperweight on his Hepplewhite desk. From his office we watch the fireworks over the harbor on the Fourth of July. It's like being in the center of the starbursts. "Open these windows, Daddy!" Leo said once when he was small, and we all laughed, except Meghan, who shuddered slightly and buttoned her cardigan against the air-conditioning. Incredibly enough, my sister is afraid of heights.

My office is in the back bedroom of a narrow row house on Carolina Street just off Mount Morris Avenue. From my window, which is accented with a security grate locked into place with a padlock so junkies will be dissuaded from stealing my computer, I can see a backyard that we've asphalted over so we can keep our two vans there. We use the vans to take clients to and from the endless appointments that are the price of poverty in big cities. Welfare, immigration, the methadone clinic, the school. A couple of years ago, just after I arrived, Tequila had some buttons made up for one of our fund-raising events that said "Being Poor Isn't for Sissies." Actually, they'd originally said "Being Poor Ain't for Sissies," and we'd insisted on changing them, setting off a pitched battle about white grammar versus black street language or, in Tequila's words, "tight ass instead of talking true." We won because white folks rule the world and because Tequila's daughter, Princess Margaret, told her mother the original was trashy.

I've always got one of the buttons on my bulletin board, although people are always stealing it and I have to go back to Tequila for a replacement. It's next to my list of phone numbers: city agencies, hospital emergency rooms, shelters, the precinct. I've also got a pile of regulations held in place with one pushpin: eligibility for public housing, rules for visits by biological parents to children in foster care, all the things you're not supposed to do if you're on parole. In a corner there's a basket filled with ratty toys, since lots of the women I have to talk to come in dragging tired, sometimes hungry children. There are granola bars in a jar on my desk. I've got everything at my fingertips, which means that my office looks like one of those apartments occupied by an old person who won't throw anything out.

So I felt a combination of shock and shame, seeing Evan amid my junk when I got to the office. He was turning a page on the circular sent out by the precinct with the new rules for complainants in domestic violence cases, a fingertip away from making a move that would send all the papers on my desk crashing to the floor. "Ev, don't," I said as he put the one he'd been reading back.

For many years Evan was the closest thing I had to a dependable man in my life. If there was a mouse in my kitchen, I barricaded myself in the bedroom until Evan arrived with a trap and a rind of Jarlsberg. If I needed a mirror hung, I would ask for his help, although he was not much better with a hammer than I was. He bought me a locket when I graduated from high school and perfume on my birthdays and cashmere at Christmas. He is a good listener, a quality rare in the circles in which he travels. I know that he is shy, although most people do not; Meghan's aura of sociability has rubbed off on him. I suppose he was a hybrid, the brother-father I'd never had.

My sister and I are orphans. People like that. I know it sounds harsh, but I could see it even when I was young, the round-eyed looks, the lowered voices. Everyone around us went limp at the sound of the word. I see it at work now, too. It's so much easier for us to find a placement for three siblings if the parents are gone for good, dad shanked in Attica, mom frozen to death in an abandoned building after an alcoholic blackout. That's a real case; those kids are living in a split-level house on a half-acre lot in Jersey now, although the littlest one still hoards food under his bed from the years when he was starving. I helped place them myself. Their mom was one of our clients, and on a good day she was a pleasant churchgoing woman with scars all around her eyes. On her bad days she was, in the words of her middle kid, the devil.

Meghan and I weren't orphans the way those kids were orphans, but no matter what facts surround the word, it still has a certain punch to it, a Dickensian shorthand that means lost, sad, needy. There's one photo of us that I think of as the orphan photo. It was taken at Easter; our parents had died in December, on their way home from a holiday party in their black Lincoln. In the picture we're wearing the kinds of clothes working people think the upper-class wears on special occasions. And we're dressed identically, turned into twins by tragedy. Navy coats with small rounded collars and pearl buttons, white straw hats, white gloves, and patent leather shoes. Elastic under our chins to keep the hats on. There are two versions of the picture. In one we are both looking at the camera, Meghan, tiny and almost translucent, as though she's a vision halfway through a disappearing act, and me dopey, mouth a little open, square and short, going through a chubbette phase. The second picture was probably taken accidentally, my aunt's finger coming down on the button of her old Brownie a moment later. We are still in place, but Meghan is staring off to the side and I am hitching up the socks that have crept down into the heels of my shoes. My nephew, Leo, has these two pictures in one of those hinged stand-up frames on his bureau for reasons best known to him.

Meghan tends to conflate her childhood with my own. Four years is not much of a distance now that she is forty-seven and I am forty-three, but in childhood, four years is the difference between toddler and girl, middle school and high school, innocence and sex. Sometimes Meghan will say, "Do you remember when Mother wore that horrible lavender bouclé suit?" or "Do you remember when Father brought home the beagle puppy and then decided we weren't dog people?" But I don't. I have hazy memories of the big foyer and the little telephone alcove tucked behind a door beneath the stairs, of Mother's dressing room with enormous roses on the wallpaper and a chair with cracked green leather in Father's study. But sometimes I'm not sure if I'm remembering right or if those are scenes from some movie that imprinted itself inside me, a facsimile of our lost life. Sometimes Meghan will sniff the air like a pointer dog at a cocktail party or in a department store, and I know that she has scented someone wearing our mother's perfume. The smell means nothing to me, not that one or cherry pipe tobacco or wet oilcloth or any of the other vaguely Englishy things with which our parents apparently tried to disguise themselves.

Meghan had a big chunk of childhood in that world, in our old house, among those people. And then it was over as though an enormous blade had sliced through the front walk. On the other side were our aunt and uncle, who moved fifty miles southeast so the two of us could stay in the same town. They'd probably decided it would be best to uproot us as little as possible, but the smaller, shabbier place on the down side of Main Street and the palpable sympathy of virtually the entire town combined to suggest that this was a mistake. They should have taken us away instead of raising us in the long shadow of before. I didn't feel it much, but Meghan did. She spent eight years waiting to leave. After her first year at Smith, she never lived there again.

She didn't really know Evan until college, despite the oft-evoked dunking. He went to the local boys' school. It was the brother school of the one we attended, but there wasn't much mixing until the students were older, and by then he'd graduated and moved on to Amherst. It was an old story; he went to a college party, she went to a college party, they were both surprised to see each other out of context. She was shaken by Smith, by the glut of smart girls who, like her, dreamed of being successful writers. He was bored by Amherst, which had begun to feel like a slightly more grown-up version of high school. They went to see a French art film projected on a blank wall of the Smith museum, and both thought it was pretentious and silly. There are stupider reasons for marriage, I suppose. And perhaps part of Meghan's reason was that Evan was a last vestige of that past life, when we had parents, a sunporch, a patina of privilege.

I just loved the guy. The day they married was one of the happiest days of my life.

"Ev," I cried, "what are you doing here? How did you get here? Do you want coffee? We have really horrible coffee."

"There's a recommendation," Evan said.

"Sit. The leather chair is comfortable." It was. One of the board members had redecorated her den, and we'd gotten all the old furniture. Why should a woman who has just lost her apartment in a fire and lost her kids because she lost her apartment have to sit in a straight chair?

"I can't believe you found this place," I said.

"The driver couldn't believe this was where I wanted to go. He kept saying, 'Mr. Grater, you got the wrong address there.' "

"Black car?"

"What else?"

"Yeah. The driver's either from the neighborhood or grew up in the neighborhood, or one just like it. Bet he locked the car the minute you got out."

The black car could be the official icon of New York, or at least the New York Evan and Meghan call home. It's usually a Lincoln Town Car, apparently not unlike the car in which our parents died. New Yorkers with pretensions but middle-class means take one for airport trips or special occasions, an anniversary at the River Café or a black-tie event at the Waldorf. Up-and-comers get them to drive around with clients, or the company picks up the tab when they take one home late at night, when a prospectus or a brief has slopped over into the early morning hours. If you walk down Park Avenue in the Fifties at midnight, you'll see black cars bumper to bumper double-parked from the old Pan Am Building to Fifty-seventh Street, with the logos of some of the Fortune 500 richest companies on small signs in the windows.

Then there are people like Meghan and Evan, who have black cars all the time. The most enduring memories of their work life will be sitting in the back of a spotless Town Car, reading the *Times* and trying to drink coffee from a sip cup without getting stains on their suits when the driver hits a pothole. A car picks Evan up every morning, returns if lunch is in midtown, takes him to the restaurant or the hotel for dinner or (rarely) to the apartment for an evening in. Elsewhere in the country teenagers are taking photographs of the limo that picks them up for the prom, but in New York there are children who take one to school every morning. A lot of them. In fact, Meghan chose Leo's school in part because it had the fewest black cars double-parked in front on the morning they went for their family interview.

Before Leo went away to boarding school, a black car would take him to Randalls Island for soccer and softball games. From the Triborough Bridge during the early rush, you can see a strange sight in the spring and fall: fields full of the bright blues and greens and yellows of school sports uniforms, with a phalanx of black cars on the verge, the spectators in dark suits moving back and forth from field to car as they watch, cheer, cry encouragement, then hasten to the backseat when a cell phone chirps. Once I was at one of Leo's games and a dad emerged from the back of a black car with a big grin and high-fived Evan. "I just made seventeen million dollars between innings," he said.

"Way to go," Evan said.

There had been no black car outside when I came in, slogging up the hill from the 149th Street subway station in a bitter wind that carried bits of greasy paper and some strange carbonized city dust with it. I would have noticed. I would have assumed it was Meghan, straight from the studio. She and Evan had once gotten into each other's black cars by mistake when he had an early morning flight. They had talked about it at dinner parties for months after.

"Luis drove me," said Evan. "He's a good guy. He's the guy who drove us to and from the Waldorf the other night. He's just never driven me to the Bronx."

"Yeah, but he knew the neighborhood, right? I'll tell you where he is right now." I was moving toward the door, which required only half a step since my office is the size of what they call the maid's room in a big New York apartment, which is big enough for a twin bed, a cheesy dresser, and the maid. "He's around the corner getting a Cubano sandwich and a good cup of coffee, the kind you can stand your spoon up in. It's what I have for lunch at least once a week." I closed the door and sat in my desk chair. "And that's the end of the chitchat. What the hell is going on?"

"What?"

"You. Here."

"You know."

"I know the world of morning TV as we know it has blown sky-high, and that Meghan gave the most insincere apology I've seen since she told that guy who came to dinner at your house who kept calling her Maggie that she was sorry about the coffee spill. But I figured I'd talk to her about that, not you. No offense. If she ever calls me."

He searched my face, then slumped and looked at his hands. "So you haven't talked to her?"

"Not since Sunday. Saturday we ran. Saturday we all went to that deal at the Waldorf. Sunday she called me while she was prepping for Monday. Monday I had to go to court with one of our women who might lose her kids, so I missed the show. Monday night I find out all about it at a dinner at Kate and Sam's, walk in cold and discover that my very own sister is the toast of New York, emphasis on *toast*. I couldn't call her line because of the telephone switch-off at nine. I called your line and got no one. I called her office line and left a message. Several messages by now, I guess. And this morning I watched her give the finger to the network and the FCC. Tequila," I hollered—we didn't have an intercom because the place was so small we didn't need one—"did my sister call yet?"

"No, ma'am," called Tequila, who didn't like being hollered at.

"So I figure she's probably sitting and fuming, and when she cools down she will call and I will yell at her about not calling sooner. Sounds like a plan, right?"

Evan took a deep breath and did something unnecessary with the knot of his tie. "So you haven't talked to Meghan since Sunday afternoon."

"Honey, you're scaring me. What's the matter? What's really going on here? This isn't about some stupid television screwup." I touched his bent shoulder. "She's sick."

"No. God, no."

"You're sick?"

He shook his head. His lanky body was so accordioned in the chair that the point of his pink tie was touching the floor. He was going to be covered with dirt by the time he got back into that black car.

"Jesus, Leo?"

"He's fine. He's living for a few days on some family farm in the middle of the Spanish countryside. I talked to him briefly yesterday. I didn't want to stay on long. He sounded busy, but good, really good, you know how he is. Just . . . happy. When that kid's happy, he's really happy. I didn't tell him about the Greenstreet interview. I was thinking it might upset him, being so far away, and I didn't want to do that. And afterwards I thought he'd just laugh. He'd just say, 'That's my mom,' the way he always does."

"He's always had her number. Boy, I miss him. Did Meghan get a chance to talk to him?"

He looked up at me. "Meghan's not at the apartment. She's staying at Harriet's place. Harriet is in Africa, I think. There are photographers and TV camera guys all over both entrances of our building."

"Well, that's okay. Give me Harriet's number. I'll call her there."

"I don't have the number there. I'm not living there. I'm living at that new Four Seasons downtown."

I'm slow. I've always been slow. Meghan says that when our aunt told us our parents were dead, I went into the kitchen and rummaged through the cabinets and finally came out with a box of Cheerios. "Like, what do you mean, dead?" I said. "Like, dead dead?" Probably at the time they thought it was shock. But the truth is that I'm a little slow on the uptake.

"We decided on Sunday night to split," he said, mumbling so that his words were barely intelligible.

"You and Meghan?"

"Well, me, really. I did, Bridge. I'm so sorry. It's just— I don't know, there's really nothing there anymore. I mean, it's not like a marriage. It's not even like a friendship. I don't come home and say, Hey, honey, I'm working on this big deal and I have this kid working on it with me and he's good but he keeps making mistakes and, by the way, I ran into Ed Lawrence from college today, remember him, he works for the Justice Department now and he has a kid at Cornell. I don't sit in front of the TV and watch the news with my wife and say, Man, that scumbag, I hope they fry him, or get up in the morning and read the papers and say, Hey, Meg, look, they're closing down the overpass to the highway, that's going to kill us when we leave for Connecticut on Friday nights. Because we don't go to Connecticut anymore, we're way too busy, and when I'm having breakfast Meghan's already gone and all I see is the coffee mug to prove she's even been there and at night she's sleeping with that eye mask on and the only time I see her at dinner we're with some other couple at Le Bernardin or at a dinner party where she's at one table and I'm at another and sometimes I just look at her and I think, That's not my wife, that's not that woman I used to swing in the hammock with or read to while she drove the car. When's the last time she drove a car, Bridge? I look at her at some dinner party with people I don't like in an apartment that looks like every other apartment in New York, and I think, Damn, that's Meghan Fitzmaurice."

This was the longest comment on anything Evan had made since he gave the Class Day speech at Amherst. It was followed by silence, or what passes for silence in a neighborhood in which at least one car alarm is always going off.

"That's why she clobbered Ben Greenstreet Monday morning," I said softly.

"Yeah. I mean, I think she would have clobbered him anyhow. But that's why she clobbered him in the particular way she did."

Outside I could hear some woman yelling, the way women have yelled since time began, "You get your ass in here. Now! Don't make me come over there!" Oddly enough, it didn't really fill the silence.

"You've been married twenty-two years," I said.

He nodded again. "I want a normal life," he said.

"I am coming out there," yelled the voice from the back.

"Don't you dare say that to me," I said. And suddenly I understood what that poor schlub Greenstreet had faced. The anger started at my feet and moved up like a pitcher filling. Maybe this was what a hot flash would be like. I'd know soon enough.

"Don't you dare say that to me. Normal life? Jesus Christ, don't you dare. I love you, Ev, but she's my sister and you knew what she was and what she was like when you first met her. If you didn't want that, the time to back out was twenty-two years ago, not now. Not with a life and a history and a kid, for Christ's sake. What about Leo?" What about me, I almost said.

"Leo's at college. We see him five times a year. When he wasn't there it made it even worse. We had nothing to talk about."

"Oh, what is this, empty-nest syndrome? Am I going to read about this in the *Times* next week, the empty-nest syndrome for guys? All the more reason to stick around. This is chapter two. Or three. Or whatever."

"You have no idea what it's like."

"Oh, please." Then I stopped. I'm not that slow. "Oh, wait." The heat my anger was radiating had become so strong that I felt a trickle of sweat run down my side beneath my sweater. "Who is she, Ev?"

"Oh, don't start that. That's all Meghan could say. I just told you, it's the pace of it, like we're on some hamster wheel, like none of it's real. There's no there there, Bridge. We're never alone. We're never relaxed. Leo's gone. This is more of a conversation, this one I'm having with you, than I've had with Meghan in years. It's not even because of what Meghan does, although God knows that's hard to live with—Hey, Ev, saw the wife with the pope today. Hey, Ev, wanna grab some dinner, see Meghan's in Bangladesh—but half of those guys live this way, too. They don't even know their wives. They talk about the kids or they don't talk at all. I just don't want to do it anymore."

I leaned in close so our heads were almost touching. "Who is she?" I whispered. It was quiet out in the front room. Tequila was listening so hard it was practically aerobic.

"I feel like it's the invasion of the body snatchers, like one night while we were asleep these people took over our lives, this woman who never sleeps, who can't go to the corner without someone taking her picture, who hasn't been inside a grocery store in years. And then there's me, some sort of work automaton, who has the best skis and the best bike and the best tennis racket and gets to use each of them maybe once a year because I'm either at the office or I'm on a plane or I'm at some damn business dinner or I'm in the health club at the Four Seasons, and half the time I can't remember which Four Seasons I'm in, Prague looks the same as Dallas, as much as I see of either one. And like a year ago we were in a car on the way to some screening or something and I said, Let's just stop this. Let's just kick back and enjoy the rest of our lives. We've got the money. Let's take the time. You know what she said to me? She said, Buy yourself a red Porsche."

It sounded like Meghan.

"Who is she?" I said.

He shook his head. "I don't know why I thought you'd get it. I thought maybe you could convince her that this isn't about that."

"Ev," I said in a whisper. "It's always about that. When one of the women here comes in and says her man broke the TV and then left, he's gone to some other woman. When one of your partners leaves his wife, he's found another one just waiting to happen. When Ben Greenstreet split, it was for someone else. That's what guys do."

"And I always thought Meghan was the cynic and you were the idealist."

"You know and I know that Meghan is about as cynical as a baby. It's the conventional wisdom that says otherwise. And you're supposed to know a whole helluva lot more than conventional wisdom about Meghan."

"It's just too hard," he said.

"Try harder."

"I can't." He stood up. His pale pink shirt was dark from perspiration.

Betrayal is aerobic, too. "She's going to really need you, Bridget. I know you think it's the other way around. But you're the only person who keeps her sane. And normal. Or relatively normal."

"If it's someone we know, I will kill you, Evan. I swear to God I will kill you with a steak knife."

"I just came here to see if we can stay friends. That's why I came in person. We've been family for so long."

"You're the one who seems to have forgotten that."

"I just don't want you to hate me."

"I can't promise that, Evan. I can't. I can't even talk to you anymore. Just give me Harriet's number so I can call my sister and talk to her."

"I don't have it," he said. "I'll have my secretary try to find it and give it to you." And then he was gone. For a moment I wanted to follow and watch him get in the car. I felt as though I would never see him again. But of course I would: across the aisle at Leo's graduation from Amherst, in a crowded living room when we met the family of the girl Leo would someday marry. Somehow the thought was much worse than never seeing him again. It would have been better that he disappear than that he become a vaguely familiar face.

"Sometimes I can't believe she's interested in me," he'd told me once when we were having breakfast in the shabby apartment they rented one summer in Boston. It was the summer Meghan was an intern at the network affiliate there, the summer that would become the fat paragraph in every profile, and already she had started to shine like a copper ornament in the garden of everyday.

"I'm not sure it's going to work out," Meghan had said about Evan that same summer, and then, when she saw the look on my face, "Oh, God, Bridget, just stop. I can't stay with a guy because you want a big brother!"

Evan had three older sisters, and he never seemed to mind having acquired overnight a younger one. If Meghan was working for the summer as an intern in Boston and he was taking a course at Harvard, they enrolled me in an art history enrichment program and found a place with a sleep sofa in the living room. If the two of them were going on a ski trip with college friends, they insisted I skied as well as I walked. (That was true, I guess; for years I could barely get from the front door to the curb without falling down. When I was four my mother nicknamed me Clumsy, until my father apparently told her to stop because it was just country clubby enough to stick. Or at least that's what Meghan says.) When I graduated from college, Meghan was stuck on assignment at a coal mine collapse in Kentucky, but Evan sat with my aunt and uncle. He gave me a watch for a gift; he had picked it out himself. I've worn it ever since. I'm a creature of habit.

"Tequila," I called, "call Evan's office and ask his secretary for the number of a friend of Meghan's named Harriet. The last name is Kraft with a *K*, I think, but it might be with a *C*. Or maybe even two *f*'s—Kraff. And call Meghan's assistant at the office and get the number of her most recent cell phone. I just really need to track Meghan down."

"I bet everybody in the world is trying to find your sister, baby," she said, "but Tequila gonna make it happen." She came to the door. She was wearing stretch leggings so tight you could see her cellulite, and a sweater with a koala bear on the front, probably handed down from some charity grab bag. She'd spent most of the weekend having her hair braided. If she'd had wrinkles, she would have had a face-lift and a hairdo all in one, but Tequila was only thirty-five, although her oldest child was twenty.

"He taking a hike?" she said.

"Apparently."

"He got a girlfriend?"

"He says no."

Tequila let out a "huh" that sounded like the noise a weight lifter makes when he cleans and jerks two hundred pounds. "Men," she said. "Can't live with them. I'm gonna find your sister, baby, wherever she is."

She's under the porch, I thought.

"IT WILL ALL be over by tomorrow," I muttered to myself as I turned onto West Sixty-ninth Street, trying to convince myself. "It will all be over by tomorrow." A couple passed me, a forty-three-year-old woman talking to herself on the street, and didn't even look twice. When I first moved to the city, I figured that people who talked to themselves on the street were either actors going over their lines or crazy people. Now that there were these tiny cell phone headsets, every third person on Broadway was barking orders or chortling wildly. The whole town appeared to be peopled by unmedicated schizophrenics.

"It will all be over by tomorrow," I muttered as I turned the corner onto the block where I lived, passing the newsstand and the sweet-faced Indian man who smiled at me every evening. "Meg's Name Mud" one of the tabloid headlines read on the front page. Thank God they didn't know the real story: Meghan and Marriage, Over and Out. Tequila had finally somehow gotten Harriet's number, and I had gotten Harriet's machine. Harriet, according to her slightly breathy message, was in Kenya at a conference on malaria. "Meghan!" I yelled after the beep. "Meghan! Pick up right now!"

Meg Mum on Marriage, and everything else. It was Tuesday evening, less than two days since the Greenstreet interview, three since the dinner at the Waldorf, and yet I felt that a crack in the sidewalk had opened and swallowed my life as I knew it. I would not have been surprised to find my apartment building in flames, my furniture on the street, the subways stopped, the park gone. Instead I saw Irving Lefkowitz swinging down the street toward me, and the blanket of dread lifted. He had a spring in his step, a song in his heart, and a bottle of middling California chardonnay, proving that even the least kempt among us are not immune to the wine impulse.

"Talking to yourself," he said with a grin.

"What are you doing here?"

"I live here," he said. "You live here. I like it here. What the hell's the matter with you?"

"We can talk when we get inside," I hissed. My sister once told me that you never know where a reporter might be hiding.

The good thing is that my apartment is on the top floor of a five-story building, with a view of carefully landscaped town-house yards. The bad thing is that it's a walk-up. More than once Irving, who is twenty-four years older than I am, has predicted a coronary and an ambulance trip to Roosevelt Hospital on the third-floor landing. Then he gets inside, bends at the waist with his hands on his knees, breathes deeply a couple of times, and is all ready for a drink and a cigar.

"Look, you're overreacting to this," he said, putting the wine in the fridge and pulling out a beer. "Everybody's overreacting to this. It's got a day or two more in the news cycle, and then it's over. It'll follow your sister around for a year or two, and then before you know it people will be saying, Yeah, what'd she say?"

"Did you actually see the show?"

"Nah, you know I can't watch that crap. I slept on the office couch and took a shower in the commissioner's bathroom. Then I went out for a jumper on the Brooklyn Bridge, which turned out to be nothing."

"They needed you for a jumper on the bridge?" I took his beer and took a sip. The cat sat on the couch just behind Irving's left shoulder. They say cats can always sense those who hate them. Irving took the beer back, put his hand under the cat's behind, and flipped her onto the floor.

"Whatever," he said enigmatically.

Irving is the deputy commissioner for public information for the New York City Police Department. This is a position that is traditionally held by well-connected former reporters, what the rank-and-file in the department like to call "lame-ass hand jobs." But for some reason the mayor appointed a serious hard-guy cop as commissioner, and the commissioner appointed Irving, who is frequently called in the tabloids "a cop's cop." Much of this is because he looks, shirtless, as though he has a third nipple just below the one on the left. This is the scar of a bullet hole. Legend has it that, spewing blood and clearly on his way to a splendid police funeral, Irving nevertheless managed to kill the guy who shot him, who turned out to be a serial rapist who had used his gun in a fashion that was apparently impossible for him to use his penis. For this act of bravery, Irving won the department's highest honor and was christened by the *Post* "The True Blue Jew."

There are very few Jewish guys in the department. "Because," Meghan had once said tartly, during one of our many disagreements about Irving, "Jewish boys tend to go to college and then find remunerative work with regular working hours."

"Wait a minute," I'd replied. "Most of the guys you know work seven A.M. to nine P.M. when they're not on a plane to Bonn. Those are regular working hours?"

"None of them sleep on their office couches," Meghan said.

It was true that Irving led an irregular life. Often I kept track of him by watching the news and seeing him behind a bank of microphones, trying to wrap his mind around the word *perpetrator* when he would have preferred *scumbag*. If he'd been up all night, he looked it, with a dark jaw and a tie that appeared to have been recently balled up in someone's fist. He was good-looking, but in an old-fashioned way, with a thatch of gray hair and a big, square face full of nose and brows.

"I ordered a pizza," he called from the kitchen, where I heard him pop another beer. The cat strolled across the back of the couch and curled up on the spot where Irving had just been sitting. "I'd move if I were you," I said.

"Why'd you ask if I saw her this morning?" he said, executing a lacrosse sweep that landed the cat on the other side of the coffee table.

"You understand this stuff better than I do, but I'm pretty sure she made it worse. She was supposed to give this apology, but she did it as though she thought they were all morons. And I don't think I was the only one who knew that."

Irving clicked the TV remote and went to one of the cable stations. The retired anchor of a defunct morning show was talking. "Jeez, she's had a bad lift," Irving said, cranking up the volume with his thumb. "I'm not sure she can survive this in terms of her credibility with the American people," said the woman, her plumped lips pulled into a tight little O-ring. "It seems to me that the line between outspoken and inappropriate—"

"A line which she's always been in danger of crossing," said the host.

"Shut up," I said to the TV.

"Well, certainly there are those who think so. And there are many people who think it has now been crossed. She will probably have less supporters in-house and out."

"Fewer!" yelled Irving and I simultaneously. One of the things Irving and I have in common is a powerful affection for grammar.

"Sources at the network say they are putting Meghan Fitzmaurice on leave until the FCC takes a look at this," said the host. Then they ran again the clip of the end of the Greenstreet interview with the appropriate bleeps. *The New York Times*, in its inimitable fashion, had referred to Meghan's use of two barnyard epithets, which I thought sounded lively. Naturally the *Times* had not done a story on a network news personality swearing on air. That would have been beneath them. The paper did a story on whether standards had slipped in what they called "the everyday tenor of public conversation." Meghan was exhibit A, and the answer was yes.

The tabs just said she had a potty mouth and should be soundly spanked.

"What's Meghan say?" Irving asked.

"I haven't talked to her since Sunday. I can't reach her anywhere. I'm going out of my mind. I've left messages everywhere, and she won't call me back. She could be dead in a ditch for all I know."

"She's not dead in a ditch," said Irving. "I'd know if she was dead in a ditch."

"It gets worse," I said. "Much much worse. Evan came to my office this morning."

"Your office? Evan went to the Bronx?"

"He's left her. He says— Oh, God, I don't know what he said. They don't talk anymore. They have nothing in common."

"He's got a girlfriend. Bet on it."

"That's what I said!"

"Well, that explains everything. That's why she blew. She's got a mean temper. You know she's got a mean temper."

The bell rang. The pizza guy and Irving had a deal; Irving buzzed him in, then met him on the third-floor landing. Then Irving gave him twenty bucks for a ten-dollar pizza. It worked for them both, and Irving never worried about letting a strange man into the building since he tended to be wearing a shoulder holster when the pizza handoff was made.

"It's not really about the woman," Irving said around a mouthful of cheese. "It's just that, to have the balls to do it, he'd have to have another woman. Guys can't do the alone thing. Or straight guys can't."

"I asked him over and over who it was. If it's someone we know I'm going to kill him."

"Yeah, but who it is isn't important. It's someone ordinary, someone normal. She's someone not too famous. She's someone not too busy. That's the main thing. I'm surprised the poor bastard has hung in there that long."

"Hey! That's my sister you're talking about! And what I always thought was her supposedly happy marriage."

"Baby, I love you. But if people were always elbowing me aside to get to you, that could change pretty fast."

"It's Meghan's fault that her husband is bailing on a twenty-two-year marriage?"

"It's not anybody's fault. It is what it is. No guy wants to feel like he's a bag carrier for his wife."

"Which women have been doing for men for centuries."

"If we're going to have the interchangeable argument again, I'm going to come out where I always come out. It ain't so. The important thing is to figure out what kind of bounce this will take in terms of your sister's situation. If the brass knew she was under stress because of marital troubles, would they cut her a break?"

"It doesn't make any difference. She'd sooner cut her own throat than go public with something like this. Meghan Fitzmaurice, ditched? No way. That's why she's avoiding me. Actually, there's probably a lot of reasons why she's avoiding me. She knows how much I love Evan. Or how much I used to love Evan."

"Whoa," Irving said.

"And I talked to my aunt today and it seems like Meghan's been upset for a while, anyhow. Apparently she's been going up to Westchester and having grilled cheese sandwiches with Maureen once a week for the last couple of months."

"Is the grilled cheese sandwich symbolic?"

"Yes, wiseass," I said, hitting him in the shoulder. "It's what Maureen makes us when we're sick, or upset."

"So she saw this coming. The Evan thing. Not the work thing."

"How can that be? If she did, why wouldn't she tell me? We ran six miles Saturday morning!"

"Your sister doesn't do failure," Irving said. "Especially with you."

He narrowed his eyes. I've always suspected that it's the way he looked when he shot that guy, the last sight the guy ever saw: Irving Lefkowitz on his knees on a narrow street in Brooklyn outside an auto body store, bleeding into an oil slick, raising his weapon like a third eye.

"I gotta cogitate," he said. It's one of Irving's favorite expressions.

"This isn't your problem."

But he was making it his problem for my sake. He didn't like Meghan, and she didn't like him. Maybe that was inevitable, but it wasn't helped by their first meeting, which had been a disaster. Six months after I'd begun to go out with Irving, I brought him to a dinner party at Evan and Meghan's apartment. For so long she had been demanding that I find the right man, a man who was accomplished, secure, intelligent, mature. Irving was all of those things, as well as authorized to carry a gun at all times. And in New York City, where psychobabble, half-truths, obfuscation, and downright lies are the order of the day, he always, as he likes to say, calls a spade a spade. So does Meghan. That's precisely what she thought she was doing at that dinner when she called the senior senator from New York a moron. It was the sort of pronouncement she was used to having greeted with rapt attention.

"Nah, he's not," Irving said flatly, turning his fish fork over in his big fingers. "He's done a lot of dumb things and he's got a problem with how he handles himself in public, but he's actually a pretty smart guy."

Meghan assumed her attentive television face. A child could have seen that her neutral expression was insincere. "I appreciate that someone in your position would have to give him the benefit of the doubt," she said, "but I've interviewed him at least a dozen times on various topics, and I can tell you unequivocally that he's a moron." She began to turn to the man on her left.

"Nah, he's not," Irving said, a little louder this time. "We went to junior high together, so I've known the guy almost fifty years. Smart guy. Reads a lot, thinks a lot. Like I said, the problem is with how he handles himself, but even in junior high he was smart."

"Junior high?" Meghan asked, as though it was a technical term.

"Yeah, in Coney Island. I remember even at his bar mitzvah the old guys were talking about how he should go into politics. Funny, right?" Irving looked around the table. I remember that Evan gave him a grin. Meghan was flushed beneath her makeup. "The kid glad-handed everyone in the temple reception room. And he gave some great speech during the service, something about his Torah portion and Adlai Stevenson, maybe? The New Deal? Jeez, am I that old?"

Meghan replied sweetly, "I guess you must be."

"She's everything people told me she would be," Irving said afterward. And the more I pushed, the less he said. From time to time he had accompanied me to Meghan's house, but not very often. Four years in, and the two people I loved most were still in a battle for my soul, although Irving's chief weapon was passive resistance. Meghan preferred the barb, about his cheap cigars and rumpled clothes. Most of the time she simply ignored his existence, as though if we did not discuss him, he would cease to be. All the young lawyers and college professors and stock analysts and junior executives she'd fed and cosseted at dinner parties on my behalf, watching their eyes glow with the combination of merlot and proximity to power. And somehow I'd run through a personal trainer, an actor who worked as a bouncer at a club, the guy who made bread for a chain of caterers, only to end up at Irving, whose signature line, faced with a phalanx of microphones, was "Yo! Listen up!" He usually said this while pulling at his mustache, his mouth twisted to one side. When Irving thought deeply, he seemed to be acting out deep thinking in a game of charades. Ditto pissed off and reaching orgasm. It was one of the things I loved about him. There was no nuance. I have a red couch and a bed surrounded by mosquito netting and twinkle lights and a cat named Kitty Foyle. I hate subtlety. My least favorite color is beige.

"Are you married?" I'd asked when Irving first asked me to dinner.

"Not currently," he'd replied.

He'd been standing outside a burning building two doors up from our shelter screaming at the public affairs guy from the fire department over who was going to do a briefing. There was no doubt that a fire was involved, but it had apparently been preceded by the murders of a woman, her common-law husband, and three small kids. "Which is a goddamn police matter, unless you guys are suddenly investigating crimes, Jimmy!" Irving had yelled.

I insinuated myself between the two of them. "Can one of you gentlemen help me? I've got nine families standing out in the cold here in their pajamas and I'd like to send them back inside but I don't know if it's safe." Irving turned his face to mine with an exaggerated expression of rage. It was very convincing, and I took a step back. But behind me I could hear one of the little girls in our shelter, who had been burned out of her own house the year before when her father tried to set her mother on fire, wailing at the top of her lungs. I stood my ground.

"Lady, that's the fire department's call," he said and stalked off toward a knot of reporters.

Later, when two cops came up the steps of the shelter to find out whether any of the residents knew the victims and might know who had wanted them dead, Irving came with them to apologize. We made all the cops and firefighters coffee in the communal kitchen at the back of the shelter house, and Irving sent a car out for sweet rolls and more milk around dawn, when the burning house had gone from incandescent orange and blue to dead black, its paint blistered, its windows blown out. His third cell maxed out as the sun was coming up and I let him use our phone. Some of the kids were already downstairs foraging in their family cabinets for cereal, jazzed up on the combination of crisis and fear that had been their birthright.

"You want some instant oatmeal?" I asked him. His shirt collar had gone gray from the smoke, and his eyes were red. "Miss Bridget, is this your maaaaaan?" sang a boy named Taurus, and he did a little dance move.

"You leave that lady alone, Taurus," his mother called from the stairs.

We went outside and sat on the steps of the building, coughing a little in the smoke, our white breath mingling with the steam from the coffee cups. Irving ate three bowls of instant oatmeal and put a twenty in the locked donations box by the front door. The house had been a convent before we bought it, left over from a time when the Catholic schools in the Bronx had nuns to teach in them.

"You like Italian food?" he said.

"Who doesn't like Italian food?"

Irving had the best kind of black car, a police sedan driven by a rookie officer named Valerie Morales. He took me to a little red sauce place in Little Italy. After four glasses of wine, I said we probably needed a check. "I can tell you don't date cops," he said. There was no check. There was never any check.

He walked me to the door of my building. I'm tall, but Irving is taller, over six feet, and he looked down at me, his eyes glittering and his lower lip held firmly in his teeth. "The next time I take you out I'm gonna have you for dessert," he said firmly and walked away. But the next day a Circle Line boat crashed into a tennis pier in midtown, killing nine people, including a mixed doubles foursome from the East Side, and I didn't see Irving for more than a week except on television. Which seems to be a pattern in my life. Days go by and I don't see or hear from Irving. And then there he is at the door, pulling at his mustache, pulling off his tie.

"I don't get it," Meghan once said while we were running together on a Saturday morning.

"I don't think you want me to go into detail about this."

"Jesus, please don't."

"And aside from that, he loves me. He really loves me."

"Oh, for God's sake, Bridge, everyone loves you. You're the last lovable person on earth."

"Well, thanks. And yet somehow you make that sound like a bad thing. Besides, Irving's honest."

"Irving's crude. There's a crucial distinction between the two."

What Meghan doesn't understand is how much Irving and I have in common. Much of our work life consists of seeing, hearing, and resolving the kinds of situations that most people would turn away from in disgust. Neither of us is a stranger to the body bag or the room spattered with blood. Irving lives in the same New York that I do, the New York that Meghan and her friends will never know. They walk through the elegant foyers of their apartment buildings, through the limestone surrounds, into the car with its paper and skim latte waiting, then out and into other gleaming lobbies and up into their offices. This makes it possible for them to think that New York is a wonderful place and the mayor is doing a wonderful job.

There are three kinds of people who live in New York City. There are the ones who will leave as soon as they can, and the ones who will never leave. There are two groups of that second kind: the ones who are trapped by circumstances, and those who are trapped by love. I am of the second variety. So is Irving.

A disproportionate number of us live in Manhattan. Like a thief with his fist behind his back, the other four boroughs are clenched around a core of gold, and the gold is the island. Irving has an aunt in a nursing home in Elizabeth, a city whose name is a lot nicer than its reality, and when we drive back from visiting her, there is one steep curve on the highway that leads to a sharp rise, and when you are atop that rise, Manhattan suddenly spreads itself out. And I always think to myself: There it is. Irving shares the feeling, with more reason: He was born in Queens, lives in Brooklyn, spends most of his time on West Sixty-ninth Street. But like a convert, I am more overwhelmed and outspoken about my faith. I, too, think that New York is a wonderful place, but the mayor is an incompetent who cares only about the zip codes of Manhattan in which there are Prada boutiques and big-ticket donors to the Republican party.

"Meghan Fitzmaurice is one of the most illustrious residents of this great city," the mayor said that evening on the local news. "I'm confident she'll do the right thing."

"What the hell does that mean?" I asked, holding a pillow to my chest.

"It means nothing. He always gives saying nothing his best shot. He only gets in trouble when he says something that means something. Nothing works for him long term."

"He hates her. She says he hates her."

The next morning we both rolled over in bed when the alarm went off, and Irving clicked on the TV. Tom McGregor was wearing a tie with a small pattern that flickered on the screen like a disco ball. "Good morning," he said. "Meghan Fitzmaurice is off today."

"That is it!" I shrieked. "I need to talk to her now! And when I do, I am going to rip her limb from limb! How can she do this to me?"

"Calm down," Irving said, sliding out of bed. "I'm a cop. I'll find her. Let me make some calls."

But I'd underestimated the investigator I'd already assigned to the case. Tequila was on the phone when I got into the office. "Yeah, honey," she was braying, with a big, barking laugh. "I sure know that." Out back, to one side of our parking lot, two kids were blowing bubbles sitting on the stump of an ailanthus tree, the weed tree of the city so resilient that I once saw one growing out of a slag pit of chopped concrete at an abandoned urban renewal project. It was a sweet, old-fashioned scene, the puckered lips, the lifted chins as the kids followed the flight skyward. By the trajectory of their gaze, I could tell that the bubbles were flying into the fire escape on the back of our building, there to burst into little smears of soap. But it was a raw March day, with a steel gray cloud overhang, and the kids had no coats. "You two come inside and put on warmer clothes," I called out the window, a disembodied adult voice that froze them both.

Tequila let out a loud whoop. "Oh, girl, I know what you're talking about. Times I say to myself, Tequila, you're gonna get yourself in trouble. But the Lord sets a bar on my tongue." Tequila belonged to an evangelical church, but she was reasonably fluid in her piety. My feeling was that she liked the singing. She had a beautiful alto voice; to hear her sing "Natural Woman" full-throttle was an almost otherworldly experience.

There was a long whistle from outside my office. "Oooh, baby, you got the president on your tail, you better be careful. 'Cause if there's one thing we know around here, it's that the government, they don't care. They don't care about truth. They just do what they do. What. They. Do. That's all. They gonna twist up everything. That happened to me once with the police, they were trying to mess me up every which way—"

"Who are you talking to?" I asked, standing by her desk and digging in her candy jar for a Tootsie Pop.

"Hold on, honey." She put her big hand over the receiver. Tequila wore more rings than Liz Taylor, although it was hard to tell exactly what sort of metal they were made of, especially the older ones. "It's your sister. The president of the United States is after her. She better watch out."

"Meghan? You've been on the phone all this time with Meghan?"

"We been visiting."

"Put her through. Now."

A volcanic "huh," a muttered explanation, and then my interoffice line bleated feebly. We'd had our phones hot-wired by a former client who'd been recruited by the telephone company for a minority hiring program. "Good morning," Meghan said.

"Good morning? Good morning? I am not the television audience at home. This is your sister. Where in the hell have you been?"

"Put Tequila back on. She was much nicer."

"Meghan, I haven't talked to you since Sunday. I left messages everywhere. I've been beside myself. I almost had the police looking for you."

"I bet the police you know didn't want to find me."

"Oh, shut up. Why haven't you called?"

"Honey, in case you haven't noticed, I've been busy. Kissing the brass's ass. Making nice to the lawyers. Although I draw the line at Ben Greenstreet. If that little jerk thinks he's going to get a private apology out of me, much less a public one, he's stupider than I thought he was."

"I've been so worried about you. Are you all right?"

"Me? Of course."

"Don't 'of course' me."

"God, Bridge, you're starting to sound like Aunt Maureen."

"And don't try to change the subject. Why weren't you on the air this morning?"

"I was not on the air this morning because apparently there is some feeling at the highest level of the network that a cooling-off period is called for. For whom I am not sure. I certainly don't need a cooling-off period. I'm perfectly cool. But since I was leaving on vacation Saturday anyhow, it has been decided that I should begin my vacation a few days early. It would have been nice if anyone had informed me of this fact so that I wouldn't have gotten up at four in the morning and called the car service and found out from them that I wasn't on the schedule for a car this morning. But the network guys probably figured that if I could scream at some stranger named Ramon at daybreak it would cool me off a little bit so they'd get off easy. Which is not the way it eventually happened, but that was probably their thinking."

"Oh, God," I said.

"I can't even run," she said, and her voice seemed a little thin, as though that monologue had exhausted her. "Or swim. Yesterday was the first morning I've missed swimming in eleven years. When I covered the Sydney Olympics, I got off the plane and swam double laps to make up for the twenty-three hours in the air and the time difference."

"I'm sorry."

"Never mind. It's such a relief to talk to someone who doesn't go like this"—and turning her voice into something between a moan and a croon, she said—"Meghan, how aaaaaare you? Which of course really means, Jesus, girl, you are so screwed and I can't wait to report back at lunch about what a shadow of your former self you've become almost overnight. Which reminds me. Want to have lunch?"

"Where are you, anyway? I tried you at Harriet's and no one answered."

"How did you know I was at Harriet's?"

This is my particular area of expertise. I step in it. I am the person who once asked a woman who was not pregnant when she was due, who congratulated Meghan's producer on the great job she was doing at a party fifteen minutes after she'd been fired, who thought Meghan was joking when she said she was going to name the baby Leo.

"Bridge-et? Bridget Anne Fitzmaurice?"

"Evan."

"Evan called you?"

"Evan came up here to see me."

"Up to the Bronx. Evan?"

"Yesterday morning."

"Black car, I assume?"

"Duh."

"And he said . . . ?"

"He was upset." Oh, no. I let my head drop into my hands. I am the woman who asked the wife of the Nobel Prize winner in Literature whether she critiqued her husband's poetry three months after her husband had left her. For a twenty-two-year-old waiter at Repaste. A male waiter.

Perhaps I only imagined that the silence on the other end was vibrating. It might have been the connection. "Do you have a pen, Bridget? I'm at three thirty-two Central Park West, at the corner of Ninety-fourth Street. Apartment eight-N. I'll order out. Indian?"

"Sounds fine. Do you want me to bring anything?"

"Not a thing. Put Tequila back on, please."

From the other room I heard Tequila say, "Here, baby." Then there was a long silence. "I'll say a prayer for you," she finally added.

"What did she say?" I hollered out to reception.

Tequila came in unwrapping some Dubble Bubble, her eyes lifted heavenward. "She say if her husband come back here, I oughta cut his thing off."

"Oh, Jesus Christ."

"Taking the Lord's name never improved a damn thing."

"I have a date in housing court I've got to cancel."

"No you don't. That woman went to North Carolina. She called this morning, said to hell with this city and everybody in it. She say she going where it's nice and warm."

"I get that."

"Me, too," Tequila said.

ARRIET'S BUILDING WAS right around the corner from a building I'd lived in for two years when I was still working as a potter. In fact, there are few Manhattan neighborhoods in which, sooner or later, I do not walk past a vaguely familiar stoop and realize with a pleasant shock that I once had an apartment there. The tiny floor-through in the Federal house in the south Village with the fireplace in the living room out of which a terrified squirrel had erupted one day. The one-bedroom in Chelsea on that seminary block with all the trees that I'd had to vacate because a venture capitalist bought the house and wanted all six thousand square feet for his family of three. The place on Ninety-sixth Street where I'd lived while I was getting my master's in social work at Columbia and working nights at a restaurant on Columbus Avenue, making more in tips than I was now making as a social worker. Over the course of twenty years, it is possible to bounce through New York City like a stone skipping across the surface of the reservoir. You don't leave more than ripples. The first of every month the moving vans and U-Hauls double-park on the streets, and the new people come, identical to those who've just left.

"Hey," said Meghan when she opened the door. Without her makeup, in a T-shirt and sweatpants, my sister looks like a teenager. But she looked like a very tired teenager, and I didn't like the look in her eyes.

All the way up in the lurching elevator, with its smell of Windex and wax, I had wondered how to greet her. Perhaps this seems simple to you. Your sister has been publicly disgraced at work and, more important, has been ditched by her husband on virtually the same day. All evidence suggests that she has been unhappy, or at least unsteady, for some time.

So you wrap your arms around her, pat her back, murmur comfort. But all those actions assume that sympathy is welcome. Meghan did all those things for me upstairs after all the people had cleared out when the after-funeral lunch for our parents was done. Meghan did all those things for me when my apartment was robbed and when two of my clients were killed in a home invasion and when I was on a subway car that derailed. Meghan did all those things for me. It was not a reciprocal transaction.

I had done the same for her only twice. Once was in the hospital after her second pregnancy ended at eighteen weeks. The other, ironically, was the morning of her wedding, when I was fastening her veil. "What the hell am I doing?" she had wailed, turning in my arms. "I'm only twenty-five years old. I have no business getting married. Why did I let him talk me into this?" I'd patted her silk-satin back and offered to call a cab, and then she'd pulled away. "Oh, for Christ's sake, Bridget, be practical," she'd said. The moment gave new meaning to the direction to pull yourself together. The window of opportunity to see Meghan Fitz-maurice undone was, I had figured out, approximately five seconds. The next thing I'd known I was standing at one end of the college chapel and she was at the other, coming down the aisle looking utterly composed.

"Hey," I said back, reaching for her arm, still wondering what to do. She took it out of my hands. She moved forward and bumped me. Bumped me twice, and I bumped her back, and then we both made the face that went with the bump, a kind of rueful frown. The bump is how we show solidarity, camaraderie, one of us throwing shoulder and hip slightly into the other. It is a guy thing, I guess, the kind of thing men do to show physical affection when a hug is too much. I can't remember its genesis, but certainly Meghan must have invented it.

Harriet's kitchen, just large enough for a tiny table and two chairs at its end (but with a window, sure enough), smelled sharply of cumin. Meghan pulled containers from a shopping bag on the counter, and we put out all the food and filled our plates before we began to talk. I looked in the refrigerator. There was Tsingtao, Grolsch, Sapporo, Kirin, a United Nations of beer. I held up a bottle, and Meghan shook her head. She rarely drinks except when she has Mexican food, when she will hold up the beer between bites and grin. Dos Equis and enchiladas—perfect together. If only the manufacturers had known. Although she doesn't do commercials, either. A panty-hose company once offered her a million dollars to do one. Meghan always goes bare-legged.

"Tell me everything," she said.

"Wait, you're the one with the story. What's going on at work? Why are you at Harriet's? If you couldn't stay at home, why not the Carlyle?"

"Where the bellman would have sold the information to the tabloids, and a photographer would have managed to bring up my room service tray and take a shot of me in my robe? Get real, Bridge. Use your head. You're the one with the real story. Just talk. Start with the moment when Evan walked into your office, and talk straight through to the end. In detail, please."

"You know what he said. He said he already told you. I don't know, the two of you never see each other, you've grown apart, you're busy, he's busy. Isn't that what he said to you?"

"That's exactly what he said to me. And it's all bullshit. What planet is he beaming this in from, Planet Greenwich, Connecticut, where Mr. Man comes home every night on the six-thirty-two and someone is waiting in an apron to hear about his day? Is he going to be the only guy in New York who doesn't go out at night, whose wife doesn't travel, who has a schedule too busy for pillow talk? I didn't invent this. And I tried to cut it down years ago, when Leo was young, I'd say, Let's stay in tonight, I'd say, Let's not make plans. Half the time he would say we had to go to someone's house for dinner and they'd be upset if I didn't come along. It wasn't my fault that the Israeli prime minister had a heart attack and I had to fly to Jerusalem, or the president made a speech and I had to go to Washington. That's what I do. Did he think I liked being away from home in some lousy hotel room? Did he think I liked missing things at school or having to read over clips at night? That's what I do, and I'm not going to apologize for it just because he suddenly wants to go back to the fifties and play Ozzie and Harriet. I made certain choices over the years. He made certain choices over the years. His job was just as responsible for this as my job. And suddenly I get all the blame. And I'm not taking the blame. I've done the best I could under difficult circumstances. I went to the soccer games. I went to the school plays. I gave dinners for his partners. I acted like I was interested in their boring wives. It's not like he didn't know. This is me. This is the me I've become and it's too late for me to be any different now."

There are sights you see that shock you so much your mind refuses at first to process the information, like the old line about the unfaithful husband caught in the act by his wife who asks her, "Who you gonna believe, me or your lying eyes?" New Yorkers are pretty unshockable, but I'm sure there would be plenty who would have been stunned to see Meghan Fitzmaurice put down a piece of nan bread, bury her head in her greasy hands, and begin to sob. She cried with the gasping, repetitive sound of a child left at kindergarten on the first day of school, and just like that child's, her gasping gave way to a long, horrible wail. I went over and knelt at her feet and held her in my arms. I could feel each vertebra shivering under my fingers, and I tried to will warmth into her broad shoulders, the only broad part of her narrow, trembling body. After a minute she blew her nose into a paper napkin from the take-out place that said "Good karma" on it below the image of some goddess, the one with all the arms.

I'd often thought before that the distance from Saturday night to Monday morning is greater than thirty-six hours would suggest. From dinner date to desk, from house party to 9:00 A.M. class, from drunken sex with a stranger to numb on the subway. It's as though one has nothing to do with the other, as though the woman in the slip dress dancing in Chelsea with her hair unfurled behind her like a signal flag is a different person from the woman in the black pantsuit and dark glasses standing on the corner two blocks over flagging down a cab as the wan light of a city sun wavers over the line of buildings looming to the east.

"Bridge," she sobbed. "Bridge, I've been with him my whole life. My whole life."

"I know, sweetheart," I said.

The two of us had come a long way, from the shimmering paillettes of Saturday night to the profanities of Monday morning and the tears of this Wednesday lunch. And Meghan had come so far, from tucking her arm into Evan's in the car after that dinner to mopping her face with a paper napkin from the Indian restaurant. She blew her nose twice, hard, and then she lifted her chin, and it was as though she was suddenly another woman. I moved back onto my heels and then up into a chair.

"There's someone else," she said in a flat, dead voice, and it was as though she'd never, ever cried, not for a moment.

"I asked. He said no."

"What if I said I didn't care?"

"What do you mean?"

She sighed. There were lines in her face that you never saw when she was smiling, or when she was on television. Ten years of getting up when it was still dark, and she'd never looked as tired as this.

"Honey, half the women I know in this city have husbands who cheat on them. Half the women cheat on their husbands, too. The stories I've heard. In detail."

"Yech," I said.

"You have no idea. Did you know that Sam Borows once left Kate?"

"What? Why didn't you ever tell me?"

"Are you freaked out?"

"Totally."

"Then why would I have told you?" Meghan said wearily.

It was as though the door that had momentarily opened was slamming shut again, the door to the room in which I protected Meghan rather than the other way around. She stood up and began to clear the table, dumping everything into the take-out bag.

"Has anyone told Leo yet?" I asked.

Meghan shook her head. "That's the last thing I said to Evan. I said, If you're going to do this, then you're going to be the one to tell Leo." It was a terrible idea, a terrible idea that brooked no disagreement.

I could tell that Meghan regretted her tears. She put on the kettle for tea and sat back down at the kitchen window. "I like this place," she said. "It's a nice size. I suppose we'll have to sell the apartment, which doesn't really kill me. It was always too big. With Leo at college, it feels enormous. I like this place. Two bedrooms, one bath, a little den, a living room with a view of the park. Maybe I'll get a place like this."

I looked around. It was a lovely apartment, furnished by someone with a good eye and no money for a decorator. There were two striped couches facing each other across a glass coffee table, a leather chair, and some African tribal masks. Harriet was an executive at UNICEF. The last time I had seen her, two or three years ago, we had had an interesting discussion about female genital mutilation in Africa. Hers was the apartment of a woman of a certain age and a certain income and a certain situation. Meghan would never buy an apartment like this.

"What about work?"

Meghan waved her hand in the air through the halfhearted steam from the kettle. "Josh is nervous, but then Josh is always nervous. He's a producer, that's his job. The numbers are through the roof, which makes him less nervous. I'll go on vacation. The numbers will start to go down when the viewers realize it's only the two guys. Anyway, you know the news cycle. Someone will die, someone will get married, a train will derail, war will break out. I'm going to Jamaica, and I will return lightly tanned with copper streaks, and when I'm back on the air, everyone will write about how well I look. Did I tell you Ben Greenstreet's wife sent me flowers? A big bouquet of delphiniums and stock. My assistant said it looked like a lobby arrangement."

"And you can talk to Evan and work all this out."

Meghan poured the water in mugs and brought them back to the table. Then she narrowed her eyes and looked at me. "That's what I thought at first. Save the family and all that. But I've changed my mind. Leo is at college, and he's a strong person. He'll be able to handle this. And I can, too. If Evan doesn't know what a great life he has, that's his problem. And it is so going to be his problem, because in two or three years he's going to be talking up some big contact, and the guy is going to say, Didn't you used to be married to Meghan Fitzmaurice? And he'll know that he's a nobody, and that he made himself a nobody, and that he's going to be a nobody for all time." Meghan gulped at her tea and yelped, "shit!" and her upper lip began to bloom red. Underneath it all she has a redhead's vulnerable skin.

"I'm just going to go away for a while," she said. "I need a vacation. I'm entitled to a vacation. A vacation will do me good."

"What about Leo? I don't think it's such a great idea to have Evan tell Leo himself. Maybe you could both tell him when he gets back."

Meghan got a flinty look in her eyes as she looked at me over the rim of the mug. "Bridget, I know things seem a bit chaotic at the moment, but I'm still able to look out for the best interests of my son," she said.

"I'm just trying to be helpful."

"I know you are."

"I'm at a loss," I said to Irving that night when he crawled into bed at midnight smelling of cigars and Scotch.

"You taste like curry," he said. "You see your sister?"

I nodded. "It was like Sybil," I said. "She was about five different people in the space of three hours. I kept wondering which one will get possession of her body."

"It's got to be weirding her out. All these years she's got the world by the tail, everything just where she wants it, and in one fell swoop she loses her job and her husband."

"She didn't lose anything. She'll go back to work after she goes on vacation, and everything will be fine. And Evan needed her a whole lot more than she needed him."

"That the party line?"

"What?"

"Is that the party line? Because I'm not sure I believe a word you just said, and I'm pretty sure you don't believe it, either. You make it sound like this is a fender bender."

"It was an accident. She didn't know her mike was open."

"Yeah? There are no accidents, except maybe at stop signs. Maybe your sister was tired of being herself. Maybe Evan was tired of being her shadow. I know I get tired just being around them for five minutes."

"Where'd you get your psychiatry degree, Dr. Freud?"

Irving hooked an arm around my neck. "Both of us are more qualified to shrink people than the shrinks we know. We both spend way too much time figuring out why people do the crazy things they do. Except for you, when you deal with your sister."

"Now you're really making me angry."

"Okay, then, stop being the little sister. You're too big to be the little sister anymore. And a little sister is a drag. Like pulling a wagon, or something. Stop being a wagon."

"Since when are you an expert on family dynamics?"

"I'm going to sleep," he said, and then after a few minutes, "Nobody wants a wagon, kid." He snored softly right after that, the snore of the semihammered, and the sound of it put me to sleep.

T IS A testimonial to the topsy-turvy ethos of social welfare programs that I teach parenting classes. Actually, mothering classes
would be more accurate, since in the three years I've been doing it a father has never attended, and only a handful of the women there had
men in their lives on a regular basis. Tequila wasn't allowed to teach the
class because she didn't have a bachelor's degree, and Alison because
she didn't have some arcane state certification, and Jasmine, who runs
the shelter and has looked out for so many kids that the photo display in
her living room looks like the record of a smallish elementary school,
has a criminal record from a time in her teens when her boyfriend was
selling crack out of their apartment.

So I wound up teaching parenting skills one evening a week in the
community room at the Harriet Tubman projects, north of Yankee Sta-
dium, which happens to be where Tequila lives. Luckily, the community
room is on the ground floor or none of us would ever make it to the class,
since like most housing project elevators, the ones in Tubman break
with some regularity. Fat women are always making applications to the
housing authority to get moved to the second or third floor so they don't
have to lumber up the stairs a couple times a week when the elevator is
broken. Tequila scored a three-bedroom apartment there by saying she
didn't mind living on the top floor.

If the world made sense, Tequila would have been teaching the
course. She was one of our success stories. She had come to us ten years
before, a high school dropout with four kids, all of them in foster care.
She had called the police to make the father of her youngest one stop
beating her, and when they came, they took the man to Rikers, Tequila
to the station house to make a statement, and the kids to temporary fos-

ter care. *Temporary* in social welfare parlance means something different than it does in the actual world. Tequila showed up at our office six months after they took her kids. I wasn't there yet, but my predecessor said she was the angriest person she'd ever met.

The people at Women On Women told her to do all the things we always tell people to do. Find a decent apartment. Make sure there are enough beds and food in the fridge. Go to church and to AA or NA or whatever the hell your particular A happens to be. ("Someday I'm gonna set me up a Being Goddamn Poor Anonymous," Tequila said one day.) Enroll in a GED program and get a high school diploma. Tequila did every single one, and one at a time she got her kids back. One day when the unreliable receptionist called in sick with her regular Monday morning whiskey-sours-at-an-all-night-club flu, Tequila sat down at her desk and started answering the phones. That chesty "huh" was her signature sound. Every bureaucrat in the Bronx hated it, and her. "You know you got space for me," she would tell a drug treatment center, or "You hold up her food stamps, that baby's gonna starve and you gonna wind up on page five of the *Daily News*," she'd say to a petty bureaucrat with a paperwork deficiency. One of her sons was at the Police Academy, one was in community college, and the youngest one was on the honor roll at a charter school near the housing project where Tequila had scored a decent-size apartment on a high floor. Our biggest fear was that she was going to get shot by some drug dealer, since when she walked her kid home from the after-school program she was always calling them names. Not under her breath, either.

And then there was Princess Margaret, her only daughter. When Tequila had first gotten her out of foster care, she had despaired; the kid would leave for fourth grade in the morning and not come home until 7:00 P.M., her eyes red, her hair disheveled. She refused to talk about what she'd done or where she'd gone, and Tequila, using the skills she'd acquired in parenting classes, reluctantly decided not to beat it out of her. Then one Saturday when Tequila made the kids accompany her to the nail parlor, where she indulged in her only vice, the painting of flowers on her talonlike acrylic tips, they had run into the wife of the pastor at the Living Rock Church of the Merciful Jesus, which Tequila attended. "I have never seen a child read in my life the way that child reads," said the pastor's wife, who also worked part-time at the branch of the library on Mount Morris Avenue, on a block Tequila had told the children was dangerous. And that's how Tequila found out, first that Princess Margaret was a crazed reader, then that she was a genius. First, Tequila got her into a program for gifted kids in upper Manhattan, then a program that sent poor kids out of their neighborhoods and into the most exclusive private schools in Manhattan.

The idea of it gave me a feeling of falling off the high dive backward, but Tequila insisted that Princess Margaret was perfectly happy at the Carlisle Benedict School for Girls on East Eighty-eighth Street. This may have been because Princess Margaret was never forced to attend the social events that would have made the differences between her and her classmates so clear. Tequila almost never let her out of the house except for school. "The warden," Princess Margaret called her mother. "Ms. Fitzmaurice, tell her that a junior in high school needs some freedom. What's your nephew's curfew?"

"No nephew gonna get pregnant, mess up his life for once and for all."

"For the millionth time, I am not going to get pregnant. I just want to go out on Saturday night."

"You go out on Saturday night when you go to college," Tequila said. The college counselor had told Tequila that the Ivy League was Princess Margaret's best option. At the moment, Tequila was leaning toward Princeton.

From Tequila's apartment window, the Bronx looks every bit as magical at night as Manhattan does from atop Fifth Avenue. While most of the people I meet prefer to focus on the differences between where I work and where I live, I'm often struck by the essential similarities. Most days as I walk from the subway station to our buildings, I'm lulled by the ordinariness of life. Partly it's because it's morning, and most of the worst things take place under the soft, mottled cover of big city darkness, in the pockets of black between the streetlights and around the footings of the projects. Partly it's because the Bronx is just like anyplace else, only poorer. Sometimes I'm walking behind a gaggle of girls from Maria Goretti High School, their legs long and shimmery beneath the plaid uniform skirts that they have rolled up and will roll down when the school door is in sight. And I remember how we rolled our skirts at the Harper School, how Miss Means would stand in the doorway to shake our hands and say, one eyebrow cocked into an accent grave, "Have you forgotten something, Miss Fitzmaurice?" until I tugged my skirt down and moved on. And there are two little boys on our shelter's block who go to school together, their mother watching from the window with a baby in her arms, the two of them hand in hand. They are a little closer in age than Meghan and I were, but still the older boy, who can't be more than eight, has that proprietary sense and a rich quiver of demands: Come ooo-nnn. You're slooo-ooow. We're laaa-te. The old woman in the community garden rises stiffly and watches them as they go past. There's nothing for her to do in March except walk the perimeter of the lot and dream of May: tomatoes here, peppers next to them, marigolds to keep the bugs away. Bugs feast on vegetable gardens in the Bronx the way they do in Connecticut or Iowa or anywhere else, and boys walk to school, and girls show their legs. It's just ordinary life.

One day I abandoned my predictable adult conversation with Princess Margaret about her classes and her teachers and her friends to ask her if she didn't find it difficult to ricochet between a school at which most of the students considered it a tragedy if a cashmere sweater had a moth hole and a neighborhood in which a school shooting was a commonplace. ("You know why this is such a big story?" Tequila had said when the lead in every paper was two boys shooting up a school in Nebraska. "I give you three guesses. White, white, and white.") Princess Margaret has a fierce and dignified beauty that means boys of her own age will not see it until they mature, and an implacability that borders on torpor and that is surely a response to her mother's pogo stick of a personality. Flatly she replied, "It's pretty easy, Miss Fitzmaurice. You're just two different people. One there, the other here. And you have the whole ride on the train to turn from one into the other." I knew exactly what she meant, but I suspected even she didn't understand the full cost of life as a social Janus, one side facing the bright white limestone of Fifth Avenue, the other the grimy bulk of the Tubman projects, in which she lived but would never now be at home.

As housing projects go, Tubs, as the kids call it, is not in the first ranks of the truly terrible, mainly because there is a core group of pissed-off women who give hell to miscreants, at least the miscreants who are young and haven't yet taken to carrying weapons tucked into the back of their boxer shorts. The elevator that works smells like urine, which is the signature scent of housing project elevators everywhere, although in my years in social work I have never actually seen someone peeing there. Fortunately, the community room smells most of the time like frying chicken and cake because of the elderly woman who lives next door and who salves her loneliness by cooking as though her children are still at home, or at least likely to visit. I love the smells of grease and sugar; if I were to create a signature perfume, it would be called Donut Shop and would smell just like the community room but without the overlay of industrial cleanser. Unfortunately, the community room is also right next door to the laundry room, which means people are always coming in and asking us for quarters when we're talking.

"Can't you see we having a meeting here?" Charisse said, as she did every week to some teenage girl who would wander in with a crumpled bill in her hand, desperate to launder her low-rise jeans in advance of a big date.

Charisse had been coming to parenting class for two years, but it didn't seem to have stuck. Her fourteen-year-old had gotten his girlfriend pregnant, her twelve-year-old was in a youth facility because he'd been caught boosting computers from the charter school, and her eight-year-old had hyperactivity disorder so bad that a cocktail of meds that would have left most kids drooling in a corner barely made a dent. The fact that he adored his older brothers did not bode well for the future.

Yet still Charisse came on Thursday nights and discussed nutrition and boundaries, communication and directed play, just as she had the year before. She'd walked out with me one night on her way to the overpriced and filthy grocery store that served the Tubman projects and told me she was taking other courses, too. Yoga. Computers. Cooking. Somewhere along the line, someone had come up with the bright idea that the residents of the Tubman projects would be enriched by learning to do things that had meaning in the greater world but none whatsoever in their own, exercise classes in lieu of health insurance, job training in lieu of jobs, parenting classes to bring up kids who would soon be dead, pregnant, or in jail.

"Let's talk about corporal punishment," I began.

"It's not good," said one woman. "Not fair. Only the black men be getting it. None of the white ones, not even that one that killed all those people and put them under the floor. How is that fair? It's racial."

"You talking about capital punishment," said Charisse smoothly. "This is corporal punishment. Corporal punishment mean you be hitting the children to get them to behave." Charisse gave no hint that she'd made the same corporal/capital mistake the year before. (She was for capital punishment, racial or not. Eye for an eye, baby, it's in the Bible.) I'd considered changing the nomenclature, but I hadn't yet figured out how to begin: let's talk about whether we want to hit these kids or not.

"It depends," said Maria, the only Latina. "Like with Gabriella, I don't do nothing but look cross-eyed at her and she behaves. Cries, too, lots of times. But with Tomas, I started giving him a swat when he was real little because otherwise, he do exactly what he want to do."

"You got to hit the boys," said a woman who had four sons. "The boys don't mind otherwise."

"Spare the rod and spoil the child," said Charisse, who sang in the choir at the church located in a former synagogue on Mount Ararat Avenue. "You can't argue with the Book. The Book says it, it must be right."

"But does it work?" I asked. My handbook says that I'm supposed to use the Socratic method, to use "intellectual investigation to bring participants to a common understanding of the limitations of corporal punishment in molding behavior." It didn't say anything about the Book.

"With the boys it works. The girls don't need it," said Maria.

"By the time they need it they too old to do it," said another woman. "They give you this evil look. Hit you back, maybe."

"Girls are hard," said a woman who had three daughters and sent them back to live with her mother in South Carolina the moment they began to menstruate. Maybe they don't have sex down south.

"Boys hard, too," said the mother of sons.

"But are there better ways to make them mind than to hit them? And are you teaching them that violence is acceptable when you do?"

"See, you misunderstanding, Miz Fitz, because violence is one thing and giving them a tap, that's a whole 'nother thing," said Charisse. "We not talking about beating the children. Beating the children's not ever the thing. You be beating on them, you go to jail, they go to foster care, that's bad, nobody okay with beating. But swatting is different than beating. Swatting just the flat hand, just saying, listen up there, you in trouble now."

"When you have kids, you'll see," said Maria.

Most of the women in the class had no idea that I was the age at which women in the Tubman projects were usually grandmothers two or three times over, often grandmothers who were raising their grandkids while the generation sandwiched between worked two jobs, Ping-Ponged between rehab and addiction, or put in a deuce at Attica or Dannemora. All of them behaved as though everything else in life was the waiting room, and having kids meant actually getting in to see the doctor. And that despite the fact that some of them were attending parenting classes in the first place because a judge somewhere had decided they'd failed miserably at parenting, had given birth to babies who had cocaine in their blood or brought kids to the ER with cigarette burns or broken bones. Charisse was raising her sister's two girls, and while I was nattering on about healthy substitutes for soft drinks, she was worrying about whether her oldest son was having sex with his cousin. I'd met the girl, and I'd vote yes. It was also a cinch that Charisse would wind up raising her grandbaby, so maybe it made sense that she was back for a second helping of the class.

"Oh, that'll be a pretty baby," said one of the women, looking me up and down.

"Big baby. Look at how tall she is for a lady. That'll be a big nice-looking child."

"You got to see who the daddy is. Sometimes the babies take so much after the daddy, it's like the mama was just one of those things in the hospital to keep them warm—"

"Incubator," said Charisse.

"Could we get back to corporal punishment?"

"You got no children?" asked a pretty young woman there for the first time.

"No," I said. When I'd just begun at Women On Women, I would have said, "No, I'm not married." Now I knew that that would be a rebuke to virtually everyone in the class.

I don't even have a dog. I tell people I'm allergic so they won't think less of me. Instead I have a cat, the pet that ranks just above a throw pillow in terms of required responsibility. The closest I'd come to having a kid was Leo, who was my godson as well as my nephew. I'd held him at St. Stephen's Church, and when he cried as the priest poured water over his bald head, I had begun to sway from side to side in the gentle unconscious rhythm that later I'd learned to recognize in supermarket lines, waiting outside preschools. The unconscious slow dance of motherhood. I'd taken him to the carousel in Central Park, to eat ice cream at Serendipity, to solemnly observe the bears in the Bronx Zoo. Nannies would look from him to me and shake their heads. "You can tell who his mother is," they would say, and I halfheartedly corrected them in the beginning and then I just stopped. But I knew who I was. I was the maiden aunt, that staple of fiction and movies and real life, the one who is attentive and adoring and just a little odd, who takes the kid the places and has the conversations the parents can't or won't. On me Meghan's auburn hair is carroty, her muscled torso softened and elongated. She's the color picture; I'm the sepia version. Close enough. Leo called me Bridey because he hadn't been able to manage the back-to-back consonants of *Bridget* when he was small. He called me Bridey still.

"I like that kid," Irving had said once when Leo stopped over after school, before he went away to board at Crenshaw Academy. The two of them had watched a Yankees game on the couch together, talking in that impersonal, strangely intimate way that guys talk about sports. Leo had a mashed Fluffernutter sandwich in his backpack for which he'd traded someone at lunch—Meghan would have flipped at the thought; with all her running and swimming, she was very particular about what she referred to as the fuel that fed her family, even if she couldn't scramble an egg—and the two guys had split it companionably. "I never had one of these," Irving had said. "They are fantastic."

"God, you are so Jewish," I said.

"I don't think you should say that," Leo replied.

"Nah, it's okay, kid," Irving said. "Your family gets to make cracks like that. But if a stranger does it"—he smacked his fist into his palm—"to the moon, Alice."

"*The Honeymooners*," Leo said.

"I'm impressed. Went off the air long, long before you were born. Before your aunt was born."

"I watch a lot of old TV. Gilligan. *Hogan's Heroes. Beverly Hillbillies.*"

"Come and listen to a story about a man named Jed," Irving began to sing in his bass voice, and Leo joined in. Then they sang *The Flintstones* theme, and *Mister Ed.* I felt that sensation of physical well-being that bears a passing resemblance to lying on the beach at 3:00 P.M.

"I'm not a big fan of your sister's, but she must be a helluva mother," Irving said later.

Meghan is a very good mother. When Leo was a baby, she was living part-time in a garden apartment in D.C. while covering the Justice Department, and by the time he entered school she was doing weekend newsbreaks and a feature called "Real America," about the lives of ordinary people, that took her all over the country. But she would fly for hours to get back in time for a teacher conference, and he would fax his school papers to hotel rooms so she could read them over. And Evan was a wonderful father, good at roughhousing and reading bedtime stories. There was the nice Scottish nanny who stayed until Leo started school, and the great Filipino housekeeper who'd be around forever, whose name was Mercedes. And of course there was always me. We did look enough alike to be mother and son.

And then when Leo was seven, Meghan became the morning show newsperson. There were family dinners every night at six. Eighteen months in and she was given the big job, for what at the time seemed an

astronomical sum and now was slightly in excess of her clothing allowance. Her first day on the air I watched with Leo and Evan, the three
of us eating oatmeal. And when Meghan said, "This is Meghan Fitzmaurice. Rise and shine!" I burst into tears. It sounded just as it had
sounded when we were children, when the eight-year-old Meghan
would slide from her twin bed to wake her four-year-old sister with exactly that greeting. It sounded so promising, as if this would be the day:
the day to ride a bike without training wheels, to make it through the afternoon without a stained blouse and a scolding, to persuade the girl
next door to like me. To meet a man. To make a mint. To prosper. To
love. To live fearlessly.

But Leo had been truculent, and his freckled brow had dropped low
over his eyes, as though he was wearing a visor. "She said that on television," he muttered. "That's what she says to me, not what she says on
television." It was as though Meghan had blurred a line that Leo had expected she would maintain, a line between work and home. Evan and I
had looked quizzically at each other over his head. Finally Evan had
said, "I guess it will take some getting used to."

FOR MANY YEARS my date book had contained the overlay of someone else's family: M to Phila for convention, E in Tokyo all week, and everywhere L. L—soccer. L—exams. L—field trip. It was not that I made them all, but I was the backup parent. "This is Bridey," Leo said to his English teacher, his coach. The friends' mothers all knew me, the friends liked me. There was a common perception that I was less likely to narc them out, in their words, than a parent would be. This perception was wrong, but they'd tested it only once, when I was house-sitting for Meghan and Evan and found two guys in the steam shower with a beer bong. I turned the shower on and threw them both out onto the street dripping wet. Luckily, the other guys thought it was hilarious, and whenever they saw me they all started to chortle. "What is it with those guys and you?" Meghan said once, almost as though she was jealous.

"L to JFK," it said in my date book when I turned to the following week, and in this new atmosphere of domestic anarchy, I was stymied. Meghan had left for the Caribbean, Evan was somewhere in a hotel, and I was not prepared to be the one to tell their son that his father had moved out and his mother had become a national symbol for the degeneration of American society.

That last was not exactly accurate. First came the news stories, then the features, then the opinion columns, and not all the columns were bad. There were the pursed-lipped discussions of standards and the columns that called for Meghan to resign and those that said she should stay on but she made too much money and didn't pay attention to Kansas and Arkansas and what one pundit called "the great swelling midsection of the country."

But there had been plenty of columns that said that Meghan's temper was understandable, that you couldn't lionize people because they were hard-hitting and irreverent and then turn on them when they stepped over the line, that Ben Greenstreet would have tried the patience of St. Edward R. Murrow himself. "I stood up and cheered," wrote the only woman columnist at *The New York Times*. The flip side was the antifeminist who wrote always as though the fifties had been the most halcyon time in American life (although of course she would not have been able to write a column then) and who suggested that if Ben Greenstreet's wife had not been so busy with her own job, none of this would have happened. Meghan had read me that one over the phone. "So let me get this straight," she'd said at the end. "He's a jerk because she works?"

She had gotten claustrophobic in Harriet's apartment, much as she professed to love it, and gotten angry at her forced hiatus from the show, although she had been scheduled to take a week off anyway. "I'm leaving this afternoon," she said when she called the morning after our lunch, at least a half hour short of dawn.

"Oh, God," I said. "I wanted you to stay in touch, but not necessarily at five A.M."

"It's my body clock. Along with everything else, this show has totally screwed up my body clock." Then she gave me a list of clothes to get from the apartment for her trip. "Aren't you worried they'll take pictures of you at the airport?" I said. "I'm chartering," Meghan said. Ah, the chartered jet, the black car of the air.

I couldn't bear to watch the show with only the two men, both guys who seemed to think that banter was a small country in Africa. It would have reminded me of looking past the night table at Meghan's bed after she had left for college. Pillows stacked, comforter uncreased. A couple of times I'd jumped on it just so it looked as though someone had once slept there. I'd seen my sister almost every morning for the last ten years, mostly when both of us were in New York, but sometimes when I was in Washington and she was in London, I in Philadelphia and she in Baghdad. Most of the time I was drinking my coffee and she was drinking hers, although probably people think it is water in that big mug on the desk. And every morning she greeted me with the words she used to wake me in the morning when we were kids.

She somehow made it mournful in the first few days after the terrorist attacks of September 11, and then changed it to defiant after week two, so that one columnist said she had thrown down a gauntlet for those who thought the United States was out for the count. She embellished it from time to time, said "Rise and shine, Mr. President" the morning after the inauguration and "Rise and shine, Hoosiers" the morning after the NCAA finals. If the ratings are any indication, you probably saw her every morning, too.

"Who cares?" she had said the last time the numbers came out. "The morning shows are a joke. Thank God I got that 'no cooking segments' clause in my contract."

"You make ten million dollars a year," I'd said.

"You always bring that up. You and the tabs."

"It does mitigate."

"I know, but who really cares about the crap we do? Diet doctors, stonewalling administration officials, shrinks. Who watches that stuff?"

"I do."

"Yeah, but you only watch because you know what I'm really thinking. Now that would be great television, if it had subtitles and what was really going through my mind was at the bottom of the screen."

That would be an easy job for me. I've been a potter, a paralegal, a waitress, an art framer, and a social worker. I'm pretty sure that last one is the one that will stick, but if I ever decide the job of helping those who can't help themselves has lost its charm, I can always do *Rise and Shine* with subtitles.

Meghan to the bestselling mystery writer thumping his eleventh book: How would you compare this to your last?

Translated: Everything you write sounds exactly the same.

Meghan to the secretary of defense: I've been told you meet with the president every morning. How did that routine get started?

Translated: We all know the guy doesn't know anything about foreign policy and you make all the decisions.

Meghan to the actress thumping her new movie, in which she appears nude and during which she was sleeping with her costar, a married

Catholic with five children: Talk a little bit about the atmosphere on location.

Translated: Whore.

My sister has a filthy mouth in private, although she has a reputation as one of the most eloquent public speakers in America. The first word Leo said was *shit*, although he couldn't articulate the *sh* sound terribly well. Luckily, New York City playgrounds have heard many a toddler use the kind of language the FCC bans on television. Often in Spanish, too.

"It's how I let off steam," Meghan once said. "I know it sounds ridiculous, but to be charming for two hours a day in front of millions of people—it's a lot more exhausting than it looks. And before you start, I know how much money I make."

My sister liked the fact that I watched every morning. "What do you think?" she'll say when she calls at 11:30, after she's wiped off all the eyeliner and the lip gloss and done a postmortem with the production staff. "Was I too hard on the first lady?" I am the *Rise and Shine* target audience. "Oh, Jesus," a producer once said when he met me at a dinner at Meghan's apartment. "You're the sister? God, if I hear one more word about how the sister hated the supermodel segment, or the sister thought we should have Philip Roth on after Bellow died, or the sister hates the upholstery on the new chairs."

The sister ought to have looked at her calendar before Meghan left for Jamaica. When I saw the notation about Leo's return, I tried to call her on the new cell number her assistant had given Tequila. After ten rings, a mechanized message answered. I sighed and called Evan. A secretary made me spell my last name, which seemed harsh, and put me on hold for a very long time. I hoped she was a temp.

After a few minutes he came on. "What now?" he said in a thin, slightly shaky voice.

"Ev?"

"Oh, God, Bridget, it's you. This new woman said it was Miss Fitzmaurice and I thought it was Meghan."

"A week ago I watched you steer my sister around a black-tie event with your arm around her waist and now you're making her sound like Eva Braun."

"I'm sorry, but I can't reach her and when she reaches me she starts slicing me to ribbons. I appreciate that this came as a surprise to her, but for God's sake, Bridge, she's making it a million times worse than it needs to be. She knows it's not as if we had this idyllic marriage and, bam! I pulled the rug out from under."

"Actually, Ev, that's exactly what you did."

"That's what I did from where you're sitting. If you'd been with us day after day, year after year, you'd know I'm right."

"Evan, I practically live at your house half the time. I don't want this to turn into the fighting Fitzmaurices, but you did a pretty credible imitation of a happily married man."

"Exactly. An imitation."

"How's your new girlfriend?"

"What? What?"

"I know there's got to be someone."

"Do the two of you think with one mind? Speak with one mouth? Jesus. I have to go here."

"That's fine, I don't want to talk about this anyway. I just wanted to ask about Sunday."

"Sunday?"

"My day planner says Leo gets into Kennedy from Barcelona. Are you picking him up?"

"I thought Meghan took care of that. She always takes care of those things."

"Meghan has left for vacation. Remember? The two of you were going to go together to Jamaica on Monday morning for a week. She went early. I don't know what the plan was for Leo."

"She told me he wasn't even coming home. At least I think that's what she said. I think that's why we were going to Jamaica even though he was on the way back from Spain. I think she said he wasn't going to stop back home before he went up to school. I could be wrong, though. I'm so tired, what with the travel and the work and everything else. Maybe I got it wrong. Should I send a car?"

"A car? A car? Are you serious? Call me old-fashioned, but I don't think the proper response to welcoming back your son whose entire world has been blown up while he's been gone is to have the official greeter be some stranger in a black suit holding up a sign. Particularly when his mother may be on the covers of the magazines in the airport newsstand. Oh, and then there's your little piece of news. You want to have the driver break your news to him, too? I'll tell you what, Evan, you'd better get your ass out to Kennedy Airport on Sunday."

"I'm in Tokyo."

"What?"

"Didn't she tell you when she put you through? I'm in Tokyo for the next week on this deal. I went because I thought Meghan said Leo was going right from Spain back to school without stopping at home. I also thought Meghan wasn't going to Jamaica until Monday. I'm totally confused. Help me out here, Bridge."

Help me out here, Bridge. It should be programmed into their computers, left as part of the message on their machine. But it was always about Leo, and that had made all the difference.

"I'll pick him up. That's it. As for the timing, yours has really been off here. With everything that's going on, you could have backtracked on this separation stuff a bit and decided to let this whole thing ride for a couple of months, just to get over the publicity hump."

"You're going after the wrong person here. I suggested that to Meghan the last time we talked. So that the publicity could die down and we could find a good time to talk to Leo together."

"And?"

"Let's just say that Ben Greenstreet got off easy. Meghan was the one who said it was out of the question. Or words to that effect. Mostly obscenities."

"Okay, I'm just not going to discuss my sister with you at this point. Just tell me where I should take Leo after I pick him up."

"What do you mean? Take him home. He probably has to be back at school Monday, anyway. I think spring break is over. Take him to the apartment."

"There's no one there. I think Mercedes had the week off because you guys were going away. Is there even food in the fridge?"

"I can't tell you that. Meghan had the locks changed. She told the doorman someone had stolen our keys. I felt like a damn fool when I went to pick up my suits. I've been wearing the same two ties all week."

"Paul Stuart."

"No, they're both Zegna."

"Go to Paul Stuart. Buy new ties. Get over yourself. How the hell am I supposed to get in the apartment?"

"She said you had keys."

I looked into my purse. Meghan had sent me to her apartment to pick up the things for her trip as though she was afraid to go, afraid that the ghosts of a happy past would rise from the Oriental rugs and strangle her with memory. Or maybe it was the ghosts of the unhappy past. There were four photographers on Meghan watch outside, but apparently none of them knew about the side entrance. One of the doormen, Rafael, nodded at me solemnly. "Tell Ms. F hello for me," he said formally. The doormen liked Meghan because, unlike the jokey rich guys, she never pretended they were her friends. And unlike the jokey rich guys, she tipped big at Christmas.

I'd thought she was silly when she gave me the packing list—"white bikini, red bikini, black tank, navy tank, running shoes, running shorts, three prs. white pants, three white T-shirts, flip-flops, gold sandals, gold halter dress"—the packing list of a woman who planned to swim and eat expensive. But once inside the apartment, I was glad she'd asked me to do it instead of doing it herself. The air was so silent and still that it had mass. The weight of the past: The sleigh bed in which Leo had been conceived. The desk that had once been in Evan's father's den, with its green leather inlay. The detritus of various decorators: the chintz period, the Biedermeier period, the white period, the red period. Like most Manhattan apartments, it looked less like a life than a stage set for a production of a Noël Coward play. Meghan is not a slave to fashion, but various rooms had been made over at various times even though they'd looked perfectly fine. Leo had once told me that the words that struck fear into the hearts of private school boys in New York were "Why don't we look at wallpaper for your new room?" Trains. Soccer balls. Street scenes. Stripes. Plaids. Those poor boys had seen it all.

In my purse were two loose Tylenol, five credit card slips, a tube of Chap Stick without a lid, a very expensive wallet that Meghan had given me for my birthday, and Meghan's ring of keys. I wanted to think she'd given them to me because she'd remembered about Leo and knew he wouldn't be able to get in with his old set, or my old set. I couldn't bear to consider that she'd forgotten about her son, that she'd been so addled by adversity she'd overlooked the only person she'd ever loved in an unselfish and uncomplicated way. What a terrible feeling it would have been for my sweet boy, to come home and find the locks changed. And I say that as someone who sees kids every day who've been sleeping on the subway. Everything is relative, as Meghan liked to say sometimes when she'd throw her arm around me after a dinner party.

"Bridget?" Evan said. "Do you have the new keys to the apartment?"

"Yeah." I swallowed. "I do. You can't have one."

I N EVERY CITY in the world, the airport offers a disinclination to visit. It's not what they look like inside necessarily; in a couple of the southern cities they've got rocking chairs tucked into every alcove on the concourse, I guess so you can sit there and imagine you're on a front porch as the Airbuses lumber onto the runway. The problem is where the complex is located in the first place. No one wants to waste prime real estate on runways and hangars, so most airports are in the part of town that looks most like the place you'd least like to visit. In warm-weather countries, you're looking forward to a piña colada and water clear down to your toes, and you look out at disintegrating cinder-block buildings, ramshackle houses with no windows, and sometimes even the wreckage of a past plane. Irving and I went to Mexico together once, a big mistake since for Irving a real vacation is a shooting under the board-walk in Coney Island in July. He's the kind of guy who starts checking his messages the moment the landing gear hits the tarmac. In Mexico there was a half-finished hangar with no roof just off the left wing of the plane. Someone had scrawled a sentence on it in Spanish with black spray paint. Irving, who has learned Spanish by osmosis after years of being a cop, said the sentence was "You should die, you scum."

"We should feel right at home here," he said. And he did when he paid a courtesy call on the chief of police, who let him go along while they rousted a gang selling bootleg phone cards. I went snorkeling and took a Pilates class and threw out my back.

But as far as I can tell, there is on the face of the earth no airport to compare with John F. Kennedy Airport in New York. Every kid who passes through our shelters and transitional housing has at one time or another had to go on a field trip to Ellis Island, which has now been

retrofitted so that the early immigrant experience seems like a cross between a trip on a cruise ship and a celebration of diversity. ("Jesus, if it
had been like this, they wouldn't have sent my father home with the ty-
phoid," I heard an old man say once when I took the tour.) Our kids miss
the irony of all the "give me your tired, your poor" stuff they're fed by the
guides on these trips; they're kids, so they haven't entirely tumbled to the
fact that they are the tired and the poor of this generation. Maybe a generation from now someone will open a homeless shelter museum and it
will look like the floors were waxed and there were comfortable cots.

The modern incarnation of Ellis Island is instead JFK. First you fly
into Queens, over attached brick houses and small apartment buildings.
The water landing is over a stretch of ocean as gray as a battleship, the
sort of sea that looks utterly impenetrable, as though it would close over
anything that touched down there so convincingly that it would be as if
the thing never existed at all.

But it is the insides of the terminals that really say it all. Dun-colored,
dirty, with winding corridors that seem to go nowhere, then suddenly
give out onto vast open spaces of dark flooring and multilingual din.
Elsewhere in America, airports have begun to sprout day spas, Calder
mobiles, historical murals, indoor playgrounds, shoe stores, jewelry
stores, cosmetics stores, museum stores. Not JFK. Its arriving passengers
from other countries must wonder, just as those at Ellis Island once did,
what in the world they were thinking when they decided to come here.
Those returning to their own countries know the answer. Czech Air-
lines, Korean Air Lines, Varig, Aerocaribe: the lines snake between the
faded ropes, people traveling as companions to their packing boxes. New
microwaves, DVD players, flat-screen TVs, air conditioners, even Lava
lamps. They came, they drove through the single-family sprawl of
Queens to the Emerald City, they shopped at a favorable exchange rate,
and they went home.

"Tourists," we mutter when we're trying to hotfoot it through Columbus Circle and there is a family in shorts and "I (heart) NY" T-shirts
walking at a normal pace in front of us.

No one escapes the drab and hostile monotony of JFK. I know this
from experience. Meghan and I have gone on several trips together: the

spa, the think tank conference, the five days at the Ritz in Paris. We arrive at the airport in the way the rich and famous do. The black car pulls
up at a prearranged location. A woman from the airline is there in a
blazer and a colorful matching scarf. She holds a clipboard. She directs
someone who disappears with the luggage, which we will not see again
until it appears, a tiny islet of home, in the middle of the carpet in our
hotel suite. (Once, Meghan said, she never saw her luggage for an entire
trip. She was staying at a castle in Scotland, doing a story on the son of a
bus driver who had become the wealthiest man in England. The luggage had gone from the plane to the castle in a separate car, up a separate staircase, unpacked by the maids, and then stored in a separate
room. "Beam me up, Scotty!" Meghan had said of the experience. On
the air.) We are taken down a secret corridor into a special room and
from there down another corridor that suddenly opens onto the boarding area. We are boarded last, and when we sit down there is a sound like
bees swarming, which is the sound of everyone in First Class turning to
their seatmates to whisper, "Meghan Fitzmaurice." It's that *zzz* in the
middle that makes the noise.

There are two sorts of children of this sort of privilege: the little brats
who embrace it wholeheartedly, who order room service waiters around
and complain that the spa doesn't have good shorts for sale, and the
other kind. Leo is, of course, the other kind. He and I went together to
visit Stanford, a visit he had arranged for a weekend when Meghan was
speaking to a cybertech brain trust gathering in Seattle. I am never sure
how much of this is deliberate on Leo's part. I do know that Meghan is a
major distraction. Brides whose fiancés are up-and-coming network reporters or business associates of Evan's are always dazzled by the idea of
having her at their weddings. But the brides who are network reporters
themselves never are. They know that no matter what they are wearing,
who has done the flowers, how good the food, or how beautiful the
room, the guests will care only that Meghan Fitzmaurice is sitting at
table number 3. At Stanford, Leo would have had a different sort of tour
with his mother, the tour that included a meeting with the president of
the university, a walk through the campus with the valedictorian and the

head of PR, the avuncular calls afterward from alums who just happen to be studio heads or name partners in law firms.

With me he got the information session with a hundred people so nervous that the whole room turned clammy. With me he got the airport line and the security check and the inattentive flight attendant. Or as inattentive as the flight attendant ever is in First Class.

And with his friends he even got coach, and a lost duffel bag, and the security drone who pulled them out of line and patted them down. When he came down the long corridor with his headphones hanging around his neck, carrying only a single large bag and yelling, "Dude! Dude! Dude!" at another kid who was getting his yayas out by leaping into the air to skim the pocked ceiling tiles with his fingers, I felt a surge of happiness, and then of fear. I wondered if Meghan had felt it when we were children: No, Bridget, they're not coming back. No, we can't stay here. No, we can't have our own rooms. Meghan was a practiced bearer of bad news, especially now that she had been doing it for a living for so long. It didn't catch in her throat the way it did in mine. Meghan could tell you seven miners had been killed in a shaft collapse in Monongahela, Pennsylvania, without even stumbling over the name of the town.

Which comes first, I thought as I watched Leo hitch the ubiquitous backpack on his shoulder, his red head shining in the dull fluorescence that was part of the hideous Kennedy ambience. Which comes first, his mother's foul mouth on national television or his father's determination to leave? Which comes first, disgrace or divorce? The first he would laugh off. The second would break his heart.

"Bridey," he cried, "you irascible daughter of St. Patrick!"

"Leo FM Grater," I replied, "the pride of the Yankees." When he hugged me, I felt small. He is the only person who has ever made me feel that way. I don't know why I love that so.

"What are you doing here?" he asked, letting me go, looking around, searching the crowd. I felt a surge of rage at both Meghan and Evan. Then Leo grinned and pointed. To one side of the crowd was a limo driver in a dark suit holding a sign. WELCOME HOME, LEO! it said.

"That's not our driver," I said.

"No, that's the guy Mom sent. She called me in Spain and set it all up last week. I told her I couldn't stick around because of a big comp lit paper I've got to crash overnight. So she said she'd send a car to drive me right up to school. Beats the train." Leo chuckled drily. "Crossed signals?" he said. "Miscommunication? Duplication of effort? All of the above? Or are you just so happy to see me that you had to drive all the way out to Queens? We can get dinner, anyhow, and then I'll get the guy to drive me to school. But if I bomb on this paper, I'm blaming you, and you know your sister will be pissed. And when Mom is pissed, watch out."

The other boys eddied around us, some to cabs at the curb, others nodding to drivers and handing over bags, a few to their parents. "You want to offer anybody a ride?" I murmured against his boy-fragrant shoulder.

He pulled back and looked at me, his mouth up at one corner with what would be a smile if you were a person with a perpetual sense of irony. His nanny had always said Leo was an old soul. At the very least, he has eyes that will not lie no matter how much he bids them try. If Leo loves you, they are like lights behind copper-colored glass. If he disapproves they go flat as a mud puddle.

"I think just us, Bride." And I knew he knew about what had happened on the show.

"You guys all thought I was on a *farm* farm," he said when I'd sheepishly sent Meghan's car away and we'd climbed into the one Evan had insisted on sending for me. "But it was a farm like the Holdernesses' farm, or the Beltons'." Both were families who lived near Meghan and Evan's country place, and the closest they came to farming was that occasionally the wives would pick chives to throw into the eggs on Sunday morning, feeling extraordinarily domestic. I liked Vannie Holderness, who always acted as though Meghan was just another guest, but when she waxed poetic about how uppity and arriviste the Hamptons are, it was hard not to crack wise about her garden, which was planted with nothing but white flowers.

In the backseat, Leo cracked open a bottle of spring water. "These people had about three thousand acres and a whole stable full of horses.

Really, really nice, though. The mom was great. She just raises the horses, does stud stuff, shows them sometimes. He's in the government, but I think he must have done something else before. Or maybe she did. All I know is they have a Picasso over the fireplace." Leo looked out the window. "Like Mrs. Booth would say, a big Picasso. Not an etching."

Peter Booth is Leo's best friend. The fact that he is a great kid who wants to become a pediatric oncologist proves that it's nature, not nurture, that makes the man. His mother is one of the most loathsome climbers in all of New York, which is a little like saying someone is the chicest person in Paris. Hadley Booth was incapable of mentioning Leo without mentioning Meghan, which was why Leo and Peter spent most of their time at Leo's house.

"Anyhow, the señora is really smart and interesting, but just like you she's got her weird gossipy things she's interested in. And one of them is this magazine called *Olé!* which is filled with movie star stuff and the royal family and all that. And last week she's reading *Olé!* in the den, and she suddenly looks up as though she got bit by a bee. She goes into the kitchen and starts talking very quietly in French to Georges. The dad."

"French?"

"They speak German, too. English. Americans are so bad. They think one language is enough. It was kind of embarrassing to only speak two. I think I'm gonna take Chinese next semester. Anyway, their kid, who's another Georges, only they call him Googy, he's like, What's up? I said maybe one of their friends was in the magazine, but he said they don't have those kinds of friends. So we have a normal night, the parents go out but they're still acting wack, so we find the magazine in the trash and we're paging through it and there's a big story. Big story. Not as big as the one about the Spanish soap star and the soccer player, but still pretty big. You want to know how they say 'fucking asshole' in Spanish?"

"Watch your mouth."

"You're talking to the wrong person." It's true. Leo has been notoriously abstemious in the matter of profanity since he grew out of the purely imitative toddler phase. It is as though he feels one sewer mouth in the family is enough. "How's Mom, anyhow? Are the picture guys all over her?"

"She's away, hon. She left early for Grosvenor's Cove. Did she tell you about that?"

"Yeah yeah yeah, that's right. They're gone, huh? Yeah, she made this big thing about how they were supposed to leave just when I was coming back and how they would postpone so we could all be together, and I was, like, I'm not going to be there anyhow, save it until after this term's finally over and we can all hang out. How's Dad holding up? I bet he's digging this a little bit. He's been telling her for years that her mouth was going to get her in trouble."

"He's in Tokyo. He and I were both a little shaky on your travel plans. We should have known your mom had it all down."

"She went to Jamaica alone?"

I nodded. The car veered sharply around a cab on the highway with its hood thrown up and smoke rising from the engine, a man with a white turban kicking its side. A parabola of gray sleet spray rose and fell with a sound like gravel onto Leo's window.

"Weather sucks here," he said idly. "How's Irving?"

I leaned against him, and he put his arm around my shoulder. The rocking of the closed car made me feel sick to my stomach; that, and the dread. I had a little sign I put up during parenting classes: PARENTS ARE THE BEDROCK ON WHICH A CHILD BUILDS HIS HOUSE. I also had one that said "God couldn't be everywhere so he created mothers," and "Any man can be a father, but it takes someone special to be a Dad." They all felt like treacly clichés, and they were all true. The women in the class loved them.

I leaned harder into Leo. "Aren't you cold?" I said. He was still wearing just a T-shirt. Inside it said FIGHT THE POWER, but it was turned inside out so he could get a second day of wear out of it.

"Man, I missed New York," he said as the skyline rose on the other side of the tunnel.

"Yeah, but you've got a month more of clean air and green grass to look forward to."

"Way overrated," he said.

"Welcome home!" cried Rafael as he reached for the door of the car.

But Leo had it open before he did. "Mr. Sanchez," Leo said. My nephew is a prince. The doormen at expensive New York buildings are ritualistically stripped of their names the moment they put on the ridiculous faux-military coats that go with the job. Like the nannies and the housekeepers, they are reduced to first names, never mind honorifics. But Leo told me once he found that disrespectful.

The apartment occupies the entire eighth floor of the building, with the obligatory umbrella stand, hall mirror, and half-moon table ("The new money girls call it a demilune," Meghan said) to hold mail and keys and spare change just opposite the elevator. One of the doormen had thoughtfully provided a large basket to hold the mail, which looked as though it had piled up over the course of a year, not a week. Most of it was the usual: catalogs, magazines, engraved invitations to dinners and parties. Mailed, perhaps, before Ben Greenstreet and his surrogate had made the mistake of taking their love story to the unblinking eye of *Rise and Shine.*

"I thought Mom just left," Leo said, looking at the pile of mail, dumping his backpack on the black-and-white tiled floor, and peering at his own face in the mirror.

I opened the door. The place was even stuffier than it had been when I'd packed for my sister, and dust motes glistened in the half-light coming through the windows. I jumped at a faint staccato tapping sound and then realized it had started sleeting and the sharp little shards of ice were hitting the living room window.

Why is it that in horror stories they make a point of having pictures with eyes that follow you around the room? Don't they all do that? All the faces in all the silver frames filled with Meghan's utterly charmed life, Meghan and Evan in their wedding clothes, black and white; Meghan and Evan with Leo between them, left and right; Meghan and the princess of Wales, Meghan and the president, Meghan and the Dalai Lama. Meghan holding Leo. Meghan standing behind Leo. Leo standing behind Meghan. I looked out the window at the cars on Central Park West, the faint pinpoints of their headlights blurring in the sleet storm. A hansom-cab horse strained against his bit at the curb as motorists edged around him carelessly. Rafael the doorman stepped off the curb with a whistle in his mouth, and he must have blown it, because a cab veered toward the awning. But there was no sound through the triple-glazed panes except the sleet hitting the glass and falling.

I turned and Leo was gone. I walked down the long corridor to the bedrooms and found him standing by his desk, haphazardly handling things, picking up a book, putting down a pencil. The room of a boy who has left home is a sad and empty place. The pens in the mug are dried out, the clothes left in the drawers those that have been outgrown or never really suited in the first place, the photographs on the bulletin board dull and dusty and curled at the edges. I hoped Meghan stayed away from this corner of the apartment.

Framed on the bureau was a photograph of Meghan and Evan. They were cutting a cake, a five-tier monstrosity with overblown roses made of icing and a cheap plastic bride and groom on the top. In a cloak-and-dagger fashion that he'd obviously enjoyed, Leo had thrown his parents a surprise party two years ago, for their twentieth anniversary. While the customary caterers had produced the food, Leo had insisted we go to an ancient bakery on upper Amsterdam Avenue and get the most flamboyant and old-fashioned wedding cake imaginable, with icing that tasted like sugar and shortening. In the photograph, Meghan and Evan are grinning and holding an ivory-handled knife, her hand atop his. I no longer trusted their smiles. The invitation to the party had had a photo from their wedding, with the line "And they said it wouldn't last. . . ." above.

"So, okay," Leo said, not turning around. "My dad is in, what, Japan?"

"Tokyo," I said. "On business."

"On business. Right. And my mom is in Jamaica."

"On vacation."

"Right. Alone on vacation."

"At Grosvenor's Cove."

"Right." He turned and looked at me, his eyes narrowed. "What's going on, Bridey?"

"Things are weird around here, honey."

"Yeah. Yeah, I got that." Leo looked back down at his desk. Then he mumbled something. It almost sounded as though he was just clearing his throat.

"What?" I said.

He jammed his hands into his pants pockets without looking up and stared down at the snow globe on his desk, the one he used for a paperweight. Inside was the spiky skyline of New York. He didn't speak for a long time. I waited, and finally he said, a little louder, "Split?"

"It seems that way, sweetheart. I think you need to talk to your father about it. I feel like I'm as much in the dark as you are. I'm sorry. I don't get it, either."

"Oh, Bridey," he said softly. "You're too much. There's nothing to get. It just happens. People are married, then they're not married. You go away and come back and call a guy to hang out and, it's like, Oh, different apartment. My mom's apartment, my dad's apartment, my mom's new boyfriend's apartment. It happens all the time. All the time. Except . . . except I guess I just thought we were different." He kicked at the Oriental rug with his big shoes. "Stupid," he said. "Stupid."

One by one, tears began to fall on the toes of his walking shoes, staining them. Leo wears these white leather walking shoes, the kind designed for old men. He has about six pairs, and he somehow keeps them very clean. I wrapped my arms around him, and for a moment he shook all over and it was just like holding Meghan except that she is small and Leo is big, bigger than me now. But for both of them it was as though an earthquake was passing through their bodies, as though there had been a seismic shift in the plates of the sternum that protect the heart.

"Bridey, I can't stay here one more minute," he finally said.

"That's okay. Want to go out to eat somewhere?"

"Nah. Nah, let's go to your house. Is that all right? Maybe get some pizza."

"What about your paper?" I started to say, and then stopped.

By the time we got back downstairs, the sleet had turned to snow and it was beginning to stick to the tree branches angling across the stone wall from Central Park and to the back of that poor horse, whose driver was smoking a cigarette. But Rafael got us a cab.

"Thanks, Mr. Sanchez," Leo said as he got in.

"Vaya con Dios, Señor Leo," Rafael said, and when I looked up into the man's black eyes, they were so full of affection and sympathy that I shifted sideways in the backseat of the car so Leo would not see it. The door slammed, the windows clouded with condensation, and we drove off with a spray of salted slush.

HE MOST COMMON misconception about New York City is that you can lose yourself there. You can understand why people from Ames, Iowa, or Eugene, Oregon, might think this. There are apartment buildings that hold as many people vertically as many small towns do horizontally, and if you ride the elevators, you often get the sense not only that none of those people have ever spoken to one another but that none of them have ever made eye contact.

But New Yorkers know one another. Some of them know one another in the fashion of a man I once met at a cocktail party, whose sister was married to the younger brother of the first guy I dated when I moved to New York, which I suppose is the way people know one another in Savannah or San Francisco, too. But there is another way in which we know one another as well, as familiar strangers. I know the family who lives in the duplex apartment in the brownstone behind mine. The girl has a desk that looks out the window directly across from mine. She is a studious child who sits reading, taking notes, long after the light has turned from ash to slate gray. Her brother is older, and he pulls his blinds down often now, which probably means he is lying on his bed with the door locked and a skin magazine next to him. Unlike so many people in my neighborhood, the parents actually seem to use their kitchen for cooking on many nights, and sometimes when it is warm enough to have windows open but not warm enough to have the air-conditioning on, I can smell the sharp, savory aroma of a stew drifting from their windows.

It is like the smell of family life, a life I have known mainly second-hand. Our mother didn't cook, and the black woman who tended house, and us, made casseroles or desserts at her own home and then brought them to our kitchen to be reheated. Our mother and father ate at the club or at restaurants four or five evenings a week. "Now you girls eat something," our mother would say vaguely, waving a hand with a sapphire ring that looked like a cold blue eye. That's one of the few things I can remember her saying, that and "I couldn't be more exhausted," which she seemed to breathe into the phone no matter who was on the other end. (Later I realized that if that plaint was followed by an irate "You have no idea!" it probably meant she was talking to our aunt Maureen, who worked as a surgical nurse and so knew exactly what real exhaustion felt like.) More often than not, Meghan and I would make peanut butter sandwiches and put the food back in the fridge. "Oh, we went out to eat with our parents," Meghan said when Nelly asked. Even then she was inventing a facsimile for public consumption, so much better than the original. I learned early to keep quiet about the lies that made us sound like more than we really were.

I know at least a dozen people on my block by sight, and occasionally I will learn enough about them to give them names as well as faces. Not proper names, but classifications. There is the professor at Columbia— every block seems to have one of those—and the poetry editor. There is the mother of the three teenage girls and the mother of the badly behaved boys. There is the old man who is an improbable wizard on the computer and spends his days trading stocks online. And I am an amateur compared with Tequila. Sometimes we walk through the neighborhood around the office and she keeps up a commentary as though she is Thornton Wilder and this is a ghetto version of *Our Town:* this girl getting with a married man from work, that boy going to Bronx Community because he failed the firefighters' exam, this one pregnant, that one selling dope. "I hear stuff," she says to explain how she knows the backstory of every life that crosses her path on Mount Morris Avenue. That's why she's good at her job, too, because she hears stuff: a family who needs a housekeeper that might hire one of our women, an apartment opening up where one of our families might be able to live. If Tequila lived in Bees Knees, North Dakota, it would be impossible for her to know more about her neighbors than she does just by keeping her ears open while she pushes her cart at the C-Town or stands in line to register her son for the subsidized day camp at Fordham.

But more than that, it is impossible to get lost in New York because, by some defiance of the law of averages, you keep running into people you know on the street, on the subways, and in restaurants. Meghan has a name for this; she calls it the "boomerang effect," and she always says that it is those you least want to see whom you will run into unexpectedly. "For instance," she once said, "if I have a terrible assistant and I fire her, she will be in the ladies' at the University Club when I'm meeting someone for lunch, visiting someone in the same building when I'm going to dinner, or shopping at Saks when I'm on my way to buy a coat."

"You haven't been in Saks in years. They send clothes to the house for you."

"You get what I mean."

I got what she meant. When I was twenty-five and working as a potter, I began a relationship, if you can call a relationship something that consists of little more than sex and takeout—which is, by the way, the ruling principle of many New York relationships—with a guy named Ken who ran a shop called Potpourri. It was one of eleven unrelated shops in the Manhattan phone book by that name, which should have told me something about Ken's powers of imagination. He had a beard, which I found increasingly irritating, and a habit of striking yoga poses with no provocation, so that sometimes he would leap from bed and, rather than go to the bathroom, do the Crow or the Heron. A response seemed to be required, and my response, after four weeks, was to tell him that I wanted to move on.

"I think you'll regret this," he said. "I want to leave the door open."

In the weeks that followed, I saw Ken at Shanghai Palace in Chinatown, at a bank in Chelsea, on Eighth Avenue after the theater had let out one night, and at a party given by a friend I didn't even know knew him. In fact he didn't; Ken was there with his new girlfriend, a yoga instructor who, for some reason, called him Kenyon. The door was closed.

So I was not at all surprised when I took Aunt Maureen out to lunch for her birthday and we found ourselves in a restaurant in midtown a few tables away from Kate Borows. At some level, of course, it was inevitable; the restaurant was a brand-new Asian fusion place (which meant that everything on the menu, including the desserts, had either tamari sauce or ginger), and Kate, in pursuit of the *Borows Book on New York City Dining*, was frequently one of the earliest diners at any new place in town. When she waved at me from beneath what appeared to be a batik bridal canopy strung with Christmas lights, I scarcely blinked.

"There's someone I have to say hello to," I said to Maureen.

"Of course there is," she said with a smile. "You two girls know everyone. And I have to use the facilities. Take your time. I'm going to celebrate and order a drink with lunch."

"There are chocolate martinis on this menu," Kate said indignantly when I sat down next to her. "I don't even want to see the words *chocolate* and *martini* in the same sentence."

"You can't be eating alone," I said.

"I'm early. I'm so glad I ran into you. I was going to call you anyhow. I just wanted to let you know that I hear Meghan is fine. Sam was talking to Edward Prevaricator, who's on the museum board with him, and Edward saw her at Grosvenor's Cove. Playing golf, swimming. Apparently she killed him in a tennis match."

"That's my girl," I said.

"Anyhow, she wound up sitting with him and some other people at dinner one night and acted as though everything was fine, nothing had happened, vacation was great, life was great, blah blah blah. She talked about Leo, about you. I gather she talked about everything and everyone except Evan and Ben Greenstreet."

I sighed. "So you know. It's out, I guess. About Meghan and Evan, I mean."

"It's out, but she told me before she left. You know, the producers are morons, she can't find her gold flat sandals, oh, and that jerk she didn't really want to be married to in the first place doesn't want to be married to her."

"Business as usual," I said. "That's her area of expertise."

"I know. I remember when she had that last miscarriage. I was so shocked when she went to work the next day, but what was worse was that they had a segment on baby care with a couple of babies. She could have had one of the guys do it, or asked them to reschedule. Instead there she was comparing cloth and disposable diapers as though nothing had happened. She's one of my closest friends, and I still feel like there's a level I can't penetrate. I guess because you were kids together you get the full monty. Have you talked to Evan?"

"Yeah. We were kids together, too. I'm trying not to feel like he left *me*."

"He did leave you. That's what guys don't seem to get. They think they're leaving a woman, but they're really leaving a life. The jerk. There's someone else, isn't there?"

"He says not."

"Someday I'm going to meet a man who leaves his wife out of a deep sense of ennui and a feeling that there's something more out there for him. But I haven't yet. You know Carrie Dwyer." I nodded. She'd lived on the same hall as Meghan in college. "Her husband left her for their daughter's college roommate."

"Wow." Nearly everyone I meet expresses deep sympathy about the fact that I have never married. Sometimes I wonder why.

"I think Meghan will be fine," Kate added. "I think she just wants to pretend for a couple of days that nothing happened. She can pretend that she didn't blow up on the air, the network's not really giving her hell, and her husband had some business deal and couldn't get away or he'd be right there in Jamaica with her. It's a good time for her to be away for a week or two, anyway. This town is so savage. When Sam left, there were people who asked him to dinner and put him between two single women the following week."

"Sam left you?"

Kate leaned in and looked into my eyes. She has the sort of pale equine face that was fashionable during the Renaissance, and the ability to look right through you as though you were plate glass. "Don't pretend you didn't know. God, you and your sister are a matched set. Salt and pepper. Yin and yang. Mutt and Jeff. You can't lie worth a damn, and she's so opaque I can never tell what's really happening in her head. Anyhow, it was years ago, between the second and third baby. He lost his mind. I think he was just sleep-deprived. But there were a couple of women who turned him into an extra man the moment he started packing his shaving kit. I keep a mental list. You don't want to be on my mental list."

"I absolutely don't."

My aunt was threading her way between the tables toward us. She'd just had her hair done, and it glowed silver in the silly little white lights strung above the table. Kate rose to shake her hand, but Maureen kissed her on the cheek. "We've met before," she said, "at that nice party the network gave when Meghan had been doing the show for five years."

"I'm so sorry." Kate groaned. "My mind is a sieve."

"Don't worry, it will come back later on," Maureen said. "I remember everything now clear as a bell. I think it's because now that I'm retired I don't have all the clutter up there, whether this patient needed more morphine or that one should have had oxygen and so on. And all the household things are easier when you're shopping for one." She put her hand over mine. "I still can't find my keys half the time, but I can remember everything about this little girl. She was quite a cook, you know, on a little stool helping me make pastry. She stuck to me like glue whenever her sister was out of the house, and that's how we'd pass the time."

We went back to our table when Kate's lunch date arrived. It was not another woman, as I had assumed, but a man about my age with black hair and the kind of glasses that mean to call attention to themselves. Kate offered only my first name, bless her, so there would be no whispered questions about whether I was related to. Not for nothing has she known Meghan and me forever.

Kate introduced her luncheon companion as the architect who was putting an addition on the country house, but I did wonder. I wondered about everyone now. I'd even rifled through Irving's wallet one night while he slept. There were the business cards of several reporters, some lawyers, and a guy who apparently sold guns. There was a picture of his niece that was at least ten years out of date and a newspaper clipping about his nephew, whose Little League team won a county championship several years ago. And there was a small napkin with what looked like a soy sauce stain and the words "Where have you been all my life?" written on it. I'd written it drunkenly two or three years ago when I'd had to leave the apartment at three in the morning to deal with a water-main break at our shelter. Seeing it sandwiched next to a wad of twenty-dollar bills made me feel ashamed and triumphant.

Across the room I saw that the waitstaff had begun to drop tiny tasting dishes all over Kate's table like falling leaves, and I watched her wince slightly. They knew who she was, and the meal she was about to get would be appreciably better than that of the average diner. By association, we got the same treatment on the other side of the room. "Now, we didn't order this, did we?" Maureen kept saying, dipping in with her fork. "I'm not sure what it is, but it certainly tastes good. I like that woman. She and her husband do the food guide, don't they? She seems like a nice person."

"She's a good friend to Meghan. Sometimes I feel as though she knows her better than I do. I think I take Meghan too much at face value. Or too little. I was so angry at her when I went to get Leo at the airport, and then it turned out she'd made provisions for him herself very nicely, thank you very much, and I was only coming in as the second string. I guess I sell her short sometimes."

"Oh, I don't think that's the problem at all. I think sometimes the both of you just get a little stuck, if you know what I mean. Sisters tend to get stuck in their roles and they don't always know how to get out of them. The pretty one. The practical one. That's a hard row to hoe."

"So you think I let Meghan be the competent one? That's what Irving thinks, too."

My aunt shook her head slowly and took a sip of her wine. "That's a very simplistic way of looking at it, not like Irving at all. Meghan wants the world to be safe as houses. To do that she has to always be sure of herself."

"But she is always sure of herself! It's not a façade."

"Sometimes the façade becomes the building," Maureen said a little sadly. "I said something like that once to my sister. I needed her help making some decisions when our mother died. 'You're so good at those kinds of things,' she said. And I was. Sometimes we just wind up doing the things of which we're capable, whether we like them or not."

Ineffectual. That was the word Meghan used when she was trying to describe our mother, the pretty plump woman who'd made an entire world out of her mahogany bed, her lilac counterpane, her skirted bedside table, and her nearby bathroom. Perhaps it was all those consonants, but Meghan made the word *ineffectual* sound like a curse.

"I know it might be unfair to ask you of all people this, but was she really as bad as Meghan makes her sound?"

Maureen frowned at a scrap of scallop on her fork. "She didn't spend quite as much time in bed as your sister likes to suggest. I think a lot of that is Meghan's own metabolism talking. On the other hand, she was always a girl who liked her breakfast on a tray. She had certain privileges when she was younger. Our mother believed she had asthma, although I can't recall a doctor ever confirming the diagnosis. And she was the kind of person who didn't care to be seen unless she was wearing something nice and new."

"That sounds like half the women in New York."

"Oh, she would have been right at home here," Maureen said. "Not in the circles you girls travel in, but with some of those other women. You know what I mean."

"You two must have been an odd pair."

"My sister was not a strong person," Maureen said. "But that's no concern of yours. It's no great thing if a strong woman has two strong daughters. But if two strong women grow from weakness, that's a glorious thing. That means you made something out of yourself."

"Well, I had Meghan," I said.

"And Meghan had you."

"And we both had you."

Maureen waved her hand in the air. It had always suited her to suggest that she and her husband had done very little by uprooting themselves and taking in two young children, one standoffish and truculent, the other clingy and befuddled. She seemed to prefer the Greek myth approach, that both of us had sprung fully formed and functional into the world.

"My mind is a sieve, too," I said. "I hardly remember all that with the pastry making. Most of my childhood stories I know because Meghan told them to me. I can't remember much of the past, and now with everything that's going on, I'm beginning to think I really didn't know squat about what was happening in the present."

"Well, that's what the future's for, isn't it, dear heart?" My aunt patted my hand again. "And the future's always right around the corner. I don't know about you, but I intend to have dessert. How's Irving?"

"Same as always."

"That's good to hear." My aunt Maureen has always liked Irving. "That's probably because he's more her generation than yours," Meghan said once.

Here's the thing my sister doesn't understand about Irving Lefkowitz: he makes a girl feel like a million bucks. He is not a new man. He is a really really old man in the best possible way. Irving remembers a time when girls wore girdles and garter belts, when their dresses had belts and complicated buttons, when even those who were willing had learned a baroque fan dance of demurral and denial and so required six months of foreplay that crept ever southward. He remembers pregnancy scares and guilty tears and marriage plans based not on a proposal but on a lost hymen.

And then one morning he awoke, after wife number two had told him she preferred the weather in California, and found himself in a world in which the hymen was an anachronism, perhaps overtaken by evolution as the dentist said wisdom teeth would soon prove to be, a biological artifact. T-shirts slid easily up, sweatpants down. You could follow a girl into her apartment and before you'd had a chance to register the color of the couch and the posters on the wall she would have her clothes on the floor. Once he got over the shock, Irving wedded the hunger of a man long denied to the happiness of a man suddenly fulfilled. Instead of the casual clinical detachment of younger guys—"There. No, there. Is that good? What about this?"—he was a study in lust. Even after a year I would sometimes get into bed naked and see a look on Irving's face like the look Leo had had at his first birthday party, when he jammed a fistful of double chocolate cake into his mouth after a year of breast milk and pureed spinach. I still have the photograph somewhere. It might as well have a caption that reads "Amazement and Joy."

Irving threw back the covers and looked down. "Yum," he said.

Like that.

You have to love a man who acts as though you're ice cream and he's five, even if he is—as my sister has told me at least as often as she's told America about national defense, the nutritional pyramid, and the need to spay your pets—old enough to be my father.

Except that our father was apparently a fraud, as we discovered early on when the house was sold, the furniture sent to the consignment house, the will probated, the bills toted up.

Irving, by contrast, was completely authentic. His parents had been Communists, his grandparents itinerant illiterate Eastern European peddlers. He was a brilliant dyslexic who had flunked out of Brooklyn College, married a coffee shop waitress, left her for a bookstore owner who left him for California. He was carelessly flatulent and occasionally priapic, and in conversation he sometimes seemed to be a bigot, which proved to be completely inaccurate when you actually saw him with people who were black or gay or disabled. He didn't want to marry again, and he never wanted to have children, whom he said he found terrifying and boring in equal measure, except for Leo, whom he said didn't count as a child.

If I were ten years younger, I would have been concerned that I was sleeping with Irving and that my period was a week late. But a forty-three-year-old woman with a reasonably new diaphragm knows what that means, and I didn't want to tell him that I thought I was menopausal lest he leap into the air and yell "yippee." I was not one of those little girls who lovingly tended her dolls, but I had always imagined that some-day I would have children. Of course I had also imagined I would have a husband, a home I owned, and disposable income.

"Relax," he said, kneading my shoulders after he was done with my breasts.

"You smell," I replied. We certainly sounded like married people.

"Hah. You love it."

He was right. That busy man with the wine bottle under his arm, the one hurrying from his plastic surgery practice or the office with the panoramic view of the Chrysler Building: he never smelled of anything but shaving soap from Boyd's or the starch the Chinese laundry used on his cotton shirts, their thread count as high as that of his sheets. The men of my generation had become as careful of their skin and dress and hygiene and hair as young women, and it had emasculated them in my eyes. I vaguely recalled my father as a man who paid an inordinate amount of attention to his suits and his shoes and who smelled always of a combination of lemon, wintergreen, and Scotch. Meghan may have thought Irving was a daddy substitute, but when I sat at dinner parties and smelled those sharp, fresh scents mingled on some young investment banker, it occurred to me that he was exactly the opposite.

That was another thing Irving hated, dinner parties. Once a month he had dinner at a red sauce place downtown with a bunch of older cops who had come up in the department together, and once a month he had dinner with his aunt at the nursing home in Elizabeth, and several times a week he didn't have dinner at all because he was on the way to a triple homicide in Staten Island or just reaming some reporter out on the phone. He'd have his car screech to a halt in front of Gray's Papaya and he'd get three dogs and call it a day. Or he would come to my place and eat chicken with three nuts. Heh heh heh, as Irving liked to say. I went to dinner parties alone, although I frequently had to cancel because of a catastrophe. And not the catastrophe of having a sister on the cover of the *National Enquirer.*

On Tuesday, both Irving and I had been awakened from sleep—"Hotcha" is how the festivities had commenced that night—by the sounds of our cell phones. My first thought was that it was my sister, awake in the middle of the night, looking for someone to talk to. But then I heard Irving's phone ringing, too, and heard him groan, "A doubleheader." It happened only on occasion, signaling a disaster in the Bronx, like the one at which we'd met, bad enough to constitute an emergency for both the police and our shelter. The only upside is that with a doubleheader I can hitch a ride with Irving and don't have to persuade a Pakistani cabbie that it is possible to go to the Bronx in the middle of the night and survive to tell the tale at the hack garage next morning.

When I arrived, I was already exhausted. The small waiting room of our office was so choked with people that I could get the door open only wide enough to slither in. I stepped over two little girls in Pocahontas pajamas huddled together over a tattered copy of *Green Eggs and Ham.* Usually the clients don't wait patiently. They're complaining loudly about the chairs, which are hard molded plastic in the fashion of seating for the poor everywhere, hospitals, welfare offices, prison waiting rooms. Or their kids are taking the crayons we leave around and making a bee-line for the walls, figuring the walls are already so scuffed and marked that no one will complain.

But these people looked stunned and drugged, and no wonder. In the police car uptown, Irving had told me the story: Nine families in a small apartment building had felt a rumbling, heard a sound like gravel in a bag, and watched from their beds as the outside wall of their building fell to rubble into the maw of the vacant lot next door, which the city had been excavating because of complaints about an ancient leaking fuel oil tank.

I saw the pictures in the tabs the next day, and it looked like some ar-chitectural cross-section drawing. All the scanty and cheap possessions were laid bare for any passersby to see. The flimsy furniture rented from the thieves who made twenty-nine dollars a month sound like a steal until you realized you'd paid five hundred dollars over time for a set of bunk beds you didn't even own and you could have bought for a hun-dred dollars less. The vinyl floor on top of old linoleum on top of the wood that the original builders had installed. The kitchens that had been left untidy the night before, or maybe were never tidy. Slices of life, like having a camera crew come unexpectedly into your apartment on a day when you were promising yourself you'd get around to straightening up. There were nine families because three of them were already home-less and had moved in with relatives or friends. Or people who had once been friends, before being a friend meant sharing a bathroom, a refriger-ator, a closet that was already too small.

Tequila and Alison were both in the back room making lists. "We were already full before this," Alison said, shaking her head.

"We got to come up with something," Tequila said. "They go now, they go to emergency services, they're up all night in chairs, scrounging around all day looking for another place."

A sporting goods magnate from Long Island had once let us go through his damaged merchandise, and we had thirty sleeping bags. Ten were in use. Tequila called up the street to the manager of the shelter building and asked her to pull out the others. The living room in the transitional housing building had two couches and some floor space.

"Lopez?" I called out in the waiting room. "Delgado? Hurston?" The mothers had picked through our boxes in a back room and found sweat-shirts and even a few jackets for the kids, who were in their pajamas. I carried a little girl with bare feet on my hip up the street to the shelter building. It was late April, but the wind was blowing down the block, and she hunched her birdlike shoulders and buried her face in my neck. Her mother had a baby wrapped in a towel over her shoulder and a boy held by one hand. The boy was wearing the snow boots I stowed under my desk, shuffling along the pavement with the tops digging into his groin. Somewhere I had a list of places that gave us free shoes. I'd have to call as soon as one was open. Cheap sneakers in every size.

"Yo, Annette," I said when I got back to the office. The woman who rose to her feet had been in our shelter a year before with a baby and a toddler. Now she had a toddler and a kid.

"Annette, where you been?" I asked.

"All over, Miz Fitz," she said softly. "I went to my sister in Brooklyn, but she got evicted and went to Jersey. I got into a nice place by the nuns on Lefferts, but then my husband said come back and I came back up here and then he started again, you know." I did know. Annette had had three broken ribs the last time she'd been with us. "So then I go with my girlfriend and we sleeping with her kids in their room and whoosh—the whole thing just goes. And Delon was sleeping right up against the edge."

Delon looked at me. At least he had a coat on, and socks. I had a feel-ing he'd been sleeping in them. "Boom," he said. I figured he was about three.

"You know Mercedes from before?" Tequila said. "She moved up from the shelter to transition, she's got a nice room there. Maybe you can double with her and her kids."

"She's got nice kids," Annette said, pulling at her top lip. She had two deep scars on one cheek, and her nose leaned to one side. She was a pretty woman advertising to the world what she was willing to put up with.

"You got a girl in your office," Tequila said to me. "Had a baby in the crib by the one wall of the house. Baby in the crib went down with the wall."

I could hear her wailing before I even opened the office door, a heavyset black girl, maybe sixteen, maybe thirty. She'd already found my box of tissues and my box of butterscotches. The floor around her was almost decorative, a glittering plastic wrapper here, a white rosebud puff of tissue paper there, a paper circle of grief. She was either quite fat or heavily pregnant. I reached toward the candy jar and took a butterscotch drop myself.

"Take your time," I said as she blew her nose. I wonder why they don't teach that in social work school. It's the best all-purpose tragedy sentence I've found yet, because God help you if you should say "What's wrong?" or the even more egregious "Are you all right?" Irving said he'd once been at a scene at which a young officer, just a year on the street, had knelt down by a man whose left leg had been severed below the knee by a hit-and-run driver and said, "Are you all right?" Irving had been ready to give the kid a good clout on the back of the head, but even as he considered it the rookie had fainted, falling forward, knocking his head on a parked van. They'd had to call for a second ambulance.

"And today that cop is the commissioner," Irving always finished triumphantly, arms thrown wide. And everyone roared with laughter. Only a few people had ever tumbled to the fact that the story was true. Meghan had, of course, and when the commissioner was on the show to talk about recruiting more young people to the force, she had asked him about it.

"God damn her to hell," roared Irving, whose profanity was as old-fashioned as his lust.

"Take your time," I said to the young woman again, patting her on the shoulder.

"My baby," she finally wailed. "My baby gone."

"Take your time," I said again.

T IS AN occupational hazard in my line of work, that in facing great tragedy we quickly come to see the tragic as heroic. In this we are constantly abetted by the news media, who like nothing more than the story progression in which a bereaved mother transforms in the space of a week or so from an anonymous nobody to the central figure of a poverty pietà. Of course, they prefer it if later it turns out that she is neither. This is precisely what happened with our young mother, whose name was DeBra. According to Tequila, she had been a bad actor for a long time, and the days in which she was photographed, holding a pink Care Bear (snagged from our donations box) and wailing extravagantly over the white particleboard casket that the Romero funeral home donated to us whenever a child died just showed the corruption of human conduct and local television. "She crying over that child now, I hear she used to smack that child silly," Tequila said with her huffiest affect. "So why is she crying now?" Within a week we had to ask DeBra to leave because she was smoking crack and drinking Forties in the shelter. She complained to a local TV reporter, but the smell of Colt 45 had a chilling effect on her on-camera role of grieving mom.

"What's she doing drinking anyhow?" Tequila said. "She gonna lose this baby to Child Services, you wait and see."

"She's pregnant? I thought she was just fat. Sorry, heavyset."

"You can say fat to me, baby. I call a spade a spade, and you know it's true. I am big, black, and beautiful. She's fat and pregnant both. I'll be calling the caseworker on her in about three months because I won't have that poor baby on my conscience, I tell you true."

"Wow. I really thought she was all right. I felt so bad for her."

"She played you, honey," Tequila said. "We all got real good at figuring out what you white folks want and then playing the role. You should hear what all the girls who work as nannies say when they come home at night. Whoooooo. Curl your hair."

"Keep that to yourself."

"Always."

We were turning people away every day because of the building collapse, and I was working twelve-hour days, trying to find apartments, benefits, and school placements. I was calling all the mothers Mom. There just wasn't time to learn everyone's names. The kids were Honey, Sweetie, Handsome, Big Boy, and Pretty Girl. One-size-fits-all endearments are the last refuge of the overworked social welfare worker.

"Mom, should we keep her in the school she was in before or get her enrolled in the one closer by?" I said to one with a third-grader curled into her side sucking loudly on her thumb. The mother had unpacked her purse looking for some of her welfare paperwork, unloading so many meds that my desk looked like the will-call counter at the Walgreens store. She left the inhaler out just in case. In neighborhoods like ours, the inhaler is the icon. All the kids have asthma. Some doctor did a study that showed it's because of the cockroaches, but it could as easily be the crumbling plaster, the lead paint, the emissions from the Cross Bronx traffic, or the lousy nutrition.

"She wasn't going to school last week," the mother said. I looked down at the file. This one was named Jackie. "We were over by the park and she was going to school there, then they had a water-main break and we moved in with my sister and she went to school there, then I was trying to bring her back to the old place but they couldn't find the papers. She might need special ed. She's not reading so good."

No wonder. It turned out she'd been in six schools in three years. "Tequila," I yelled.

"You don't need to be shouting."

"Sorry. Is there any chance we can get this sweetie pie here into the charter school?"

Tequila made a clicking noise with her tongue, the one that means "You are always driving me crazy with your unreasonable demands." Then she made a huffing sound, which means "But I, Tequila Johnson, will somehow rise to the challenge." This is the Kabuki dance of our office. At the end I grin, tilt my head, and shrug. I am the straight man.

"You come up with me," Tequila said to Jackie, walking into my office. "Miss Fitzmaurice got a call anyhow. Some person named Joseph Murphy wants to talk with you, but he's such a big man he got some woman on the phone to say so. 'Is Ms. Fitzmaurice available to talk to Joseph Murphy?' 'I don't know,' I said. 'Is Mr. Murphy there, 'cause this don't sound like him.'"

"Wait," I said. I picked up the phone. A woman's voice asked if it was me, then said, "Please hold for Mr. Murphy." I handed Tequila the phone. "When he comes on, you say, 'Please hold for Ms. Fitzmaurice.'" Tequila loves putting people in their place. She sounded so snippy that her accent was almost English.

Joseph Murphy is the president of Meghan's network. Before that he was the president of a company that makes and sells cars, and before that the president of a company that makes and sells major appliances. At his first meeting with the staff, he had made the mistake of describing his strategy for the network as similar to his strategies for the other two. "Don't think of it as programming," he'd said. "Think of it as product."

Meghan had named him Joe-Joe the Dog-Faced Boy. The name stuck. Sometimes when he was leaving the newsroom, which he liked to visit to show that he knew, as he said, "where the heart of the network lies," people would bark. He thought it was a newsroom tradition, like insisting on going to the actual site of a big story when it would make just as much sense to him to take the feed from a local affiliate.

"Miss Fitzmaurice," he said. "I don't believe we've met. How are you?"

"Fine thanks, Mr. Murphy. Actually we did meet at the fifth anniversary party for *Rise and Shine*. I had a long talk with your wife." Apparently Joe and Rita were having a hard time cracking the code of New York City after the halcyon days of Detroit and Indianapolis. Media types thought they were too corporate, and corporate types were always enraged at the pieces the news side had done about their business practices. Rita was spectacularly indiscreet. She drank white wine like it was water and we were chatting in Death Valley at noon. I had liked her immediately. And she loved Meghan, could quote from her greatest hits on *Rise and Shine* the way I liked to think our parents would have done had our parents been in any way those kinds of parents. But that was before Meghan said "Fucking asshole" so that America could hear. I doubted that Rita was among those women who believed Meghan had done the right thing by calling Ben Greenstreet by his proper name. When Joe was named network chief, the first thing she'd asked him to do was arrange an audience with the pope.

There was silence on Joseph Murphy's end of the phone. I had breached the firewall of New York propriety: if someone believes you have never met, you must go with that belief if you are the less powerful of the two. How had I forgotten, given the number of anchormen, diplomats, writers, and hedge fund managers to whom I had been introduced three, four, five times?

"Mr. Murphy?"

"Call me Joe. And you are Bridget, is that right? I have a sister by that name." Along with Colleen, Maureen, and Mary Pat, I'd be betting. I heard adenoidal breathing on the line but thought it would be unwise to shout "Tequila!" Few Murphy clans think of Tequila as a name.

"The thing is, Bridget, I'm trying to reach your sister, and I'm having a dickens of a time. I've left a number of messages with her assistant and at her home, and I've even called her agent and her husband at his office. And I just can't seem to track her down."

"She's on vacation, Joe. She doesn't go often, but when she does she really likes to relax. Drop out of sight. Go off the reservation." I'd run out of clichés.

"Of course she does. So do I, although Mrs. Murphy complains that I'm still on the phone to the office too much. But I get out there and golf, play a little tennis. Your sister plays tennis, if I recall."

He recalled. She'd beaten the crap out of him at a mixed doubles match for charity. The poor guy had gotten so red in the sun at the tennis center that the EMTs in one corner of the court had been in a half crouch during most of the match. He recalled, and now he was going to rush the net, old Joe Bow-Wow Murphy.

"I'm sure she will be in touch as soon as she gets back, Joe."

"Well, there's the problem, Bridget. I need to be in touch with her now. Things are a little hot around here, and there are some issues that need to be ironed out with Meghan right now. And I know that she was at Grosvenor's Cove for the week. In fact, our old old friends the Braithwaites—do you know them, he's on the museum board?—they saw her there. Susan Braithwaite told Rita that Meghan was looking marvelous."

"Joe, I would bet you the concierge at Grosvenor's Cove would put you right through."

"Oh, he was happy to. He's a good man. Cecil, his name is, but the British way, you know. Ce-cil. Beautiful voice, too. The trouble is, she's checked out."

"Ah," I said. The breathing had stopped. Tequila was either thinking hard or calling Cecil on the other line.

"She stayed the week and then she left. And now it's been almost a month since we've heard from her. And someone said to me, Well, if there's anyone who knows how to track her down, it's her sister, they're as thick as thieves." It seemed an apt metaphor: the Fitzmaurice sisters, who had snatched quite a life out of not much of one. Or at least the elder had, and the younger had come along for the ride. "So here I am, calling you before I call the ambassador. Can you imagine being ambassador to Jamaica? Heck of a cushy job."

I was doing the mental scramble. "Gee, I assumed she'd left the number with the people at the Cove," I said. "I don't have it right here. Let me call you with it from home, Joe."

"I would appreciate that, Bridget. And when you talk to Meghan, tell her that she's in all our thoughts." And those of the FCC.

"Jesus Lord!" cried Tequila from the next room.

She and Alison both came into my office and closed the door. With three people in my office, it feels like the subway at rush hour. Tequila sat down and knocked a pile of files off my desk.

"She's gone," Tequila said.

"Don't be ridiculous," I said. "It's just that this Murphy guy can't find her. If you were his secretary, he'd be on the phone to her right now."

"Saying what?" said Alison.

"I went missing once," said Tequila.

"When?"

"Whenever. Sometimes you just don't want to mess with people. You don't want no questions, no ooooh-oooooh worrying-about-you nonsense, no looking at you like, Oh, no, Tequila, times are bad. You just want to keep yourself to yourself."

"One of the papers today said that Meghan is exploring other opportunities," Alison said.

For someone who has been indicted, it's a bad fact pattern. For a patient, it's a poor prognosis. But in TV, it's exploring other opportunities. That's the kiss of death. "It would be better if they said she was in rehab," I said, picking up the old, misshapen pot in which I kept my pencils. It was the first pot I'd ever fired. That's the kiss of death for a childless forty-three-year-old woman. The lumpy clay thing on her desk she'd made herself.

"One of the papers today said she was in rehab."

My phone rang. Tequila answered it with the haughty voice again, then put the call on hold. "You are a popular girl with the men today," she said. "It's Mr. Altercation."

"I don't know anyone named Altercation. In fact, I don't even believe there exists anyone named Altercation."

"That's not a real name, Tequila," said Alison.

Tequila presented her enormous rack for inspection, which is what she does when she is annoyed. Tequila has the breasts of a grandmother and the spindly legs of a grandfather. She heightens the effect by insisting on wearing leggings and the sorts of oversize shirts that were popular when she was a teenager, usually with some kind of spangles on the shirt. Today a sequined tiger lurched toward Alison and me as Tequila bristled, perhaps because in this case she was remembering how often it's been suggested that her name is not a real name, either.

"Altercation, Altercation. That man you know. That one who gave you all that money and you say no funny business but we think you lying. Him!"

"Prevaricator?"

"What I said!" said Tequila as the tiger lunged toward us.

"Miss Fitzmaurice," he said softly on the phone.

"Bridget, please, Mr. Prevaricator. How's your granddaughter?"

"My granddaughter?"

"The one who memorized *The Cat in the Hat.*"

He chuckled softly. "How good of you to remember," he said. "She's moved on to *Amelia Bedelia.*"

"I bet you enjoyed those," I said.

"As a matter of fact, I was discussing them with your sister not long ago. That's why I'm calling." As he spoke, I reached for a pad and pencil, knocking my Patrolmen's Benevolent Association paperweight and a jar of paper clips off my desk. I took notes, and Tequila and Alison stayed put. When I said, "How does she really seem to you?" both of them leaned forward a bit in the molded plastic chairs.

"Thank you," I said, and then, "I can't thank you enough," and then, "Thank you very much again."

"You were right," I said softly. "She just wants to disappear for a while. No cell reception. No phone. No address. But I do have a fax number." I pulled a sheet of paper off the pad and wrote in capital letters "WHEN ARE YOU COMING HOME?" Tequila took it from my hands, and a moment later I heard a birdlike beeping as the old fax machine handed down to us by a law firm began to send. Everything we had was hand-me-down, every chair, every computer, every desk. The beeping stopped. Somewhere in the kitchen of a small seaside house in a remote part of Jamaica lent to Meghan by Edward Prevaricator, who had run into her at Grosvenor's Cove and realized she needed a place to stay, there apparently was a fax machine and my words would spill out the other end.

"I'm tired," I said. "I'm going home."

"Your nephew called, too. He say nothing important, just to talk. And Commissioner Lefkowitz say he's out tonight at a meeting in Staten Island. He say that girl DeBra is at Rikers, got capped for drugs. She's crying, carrying on, say it's because her baby died."

"Jesus, I'm so tired." I could hear the rain hitting the metal hatch to the basement out in back of the house. The roof in the transitional building needed replacing, and I hadn't found a donor yet to underwrite it. I hoped it wasn't leaking. The rain started to come down hard. "You got an extra umbrella?" I asked Alison.

Next morning on my desk was a newspaper turned to a story on DeBra's arrest, a warrant for one of the moms in the shelter on an old drug charge, and a sheet of paper that said in capital letters "I'M NOT. DON'T WORRY." Somehow my pencil pot had gotten knocked down and broken into two big, ungainly pieces, so I stuffed the pencils in the drawer and threw the pot in the trash.

EGHAN ONCE TOOK me to lunch at a place in midtown that is famous because it is the place where people like Meghan have lunch. Actually, Meghan herself rarely has lunch out, preferring a salad at her desk or at home after she swims. But when she does eat, she eats at this restaurant, which has mediocre food and a media clientele. Part of its charm is that the staff now know anyone who is anyone in television or movies or print journalism. Many of those people have spent so much time with their noses pressed against the window of the true American aristocracy or the new American big-name money that to have a maître d' say, "Good afternoon, Miss Fitzmaurice," gives them a feeling of well-being no amount of overdone salmon can quench.

I don't quite get the point of the place, because it is impossible to talk about anything substantive there. The one time we went we couldn't trash the woman from another network who is always angling for Meghan's job because she was just a few tables over. We couldn't trash Meghan's producer, Josh, whom Meghan calls Josh 3.0—she likes to say that when the 4.0 upgrade comes out, it will have news judgment and a sense of humor already installed—because Josh's wife, an agent, was at the table on one side of us. And we couldn't even trash people who weren't there because sitting back-to-back with Meghan was one of the gossip columnists for one of the tabs, and he was listening to everything we said so carefully that next morning there was an item saying Meghan had criticized her Cobb salad. I had it, too, and I can tell you it was lame, not enough cheese or bacon and too much lettuce.

We had been reduced to talking the entire lunch about Leo's high school graduation, whether I should find a bigger apartment, and whether our aunt Maureen needed to be moved from her apartment to an assisted living complex. It was a real wow of a lunch, made worse by the sight of so many people who loathed one another kissing on both cheeks as though they had been born in France instead of the Chicago and Philadelphia suburbs. Most of these are not nice people, people who have risen triumphantly to the middle through the use of sharp elbows.

But there was one interesting moment, and that was when an entire table of guys—two television executives, one movie producer, and an agent—was disrupted by the sounds of their cell phones ringing simultaneously. They all took the calls, of course, rising from the table to move to more secluded corners of the dining room in case they were screwing any of their lunch companions in a business deal and were going to be told so by an assistant. General hilarity reigned when each returned, and before long the entire restaurant was in on the joke: three assistants had been calling to say that the fourth lunch companion would be late, while his assistant was calling to tell him she had told the others that he would be late.

"And he's not even late!" they all roared.

Then the restaurant manager came over to personally deliver the message they'd just received that Mr. Blah Blah was running a little late. And the place went wild. The fact that everyone thought this was the hilarious high point of the day goes a long way toward explaining how lame most movies and TV shows are, particularly the ones that are supposed to be funny.

And he's not even late! Cue the laugh track.

But the incident did illustrate how impossible it has become to tumble off the radar in our day and age. Yet that is what Meghan had managed to do, convincingly and utterly. Later she would show me a dusty stack of faxes from the network, pleading that she call and set up a lunch date with the president, asking that she meet and discuss her future, demanding that she respond immediately on when she would return, informing her that she was in breach of contract. But in a world in which everyone is instantaneously available, Meghan was almost completely out of reach. In a world that had become like that restaurant, friends and enemies and rivals and allies all with an ear cocked heavenward for the messages from cell phones and e-mails and lunch conversation, the only possible way to be silent was to disappear.

It reminded me of the first semester of Meghan's first year at Smith, when she had not come home until Christmas. I sent her long, discursive letters about the difficulties of algebra and the cat I'd acquired at the pound and the painting I was doing of the park across the street at sunset. I got a handful of postcards back, so perfunctory as to sound like fortune cookies: "Pet that kitty for me!" "Don't sweat the math!" "Freshman year is the hardest!" They sounded so unlike Meghan that I wondered if she had gotten them out of some big-sister primer. Only later did I discover that Meghan, miserable and feeling out of her league, had gone to ground and spent most of the semester in her room.

"There, and yet not there," one of her high school friends had said.

It was fine for my aunt to talk again and again about Meghan's determination to hide from adversity, to struggle alone, to go under the porch. But her disappearance was taking on a larger, more ominous tone, as though she was in a witness protection program for the walking wounded. Perhaps somewhere she was regaining her strength, but all I could think of was how shattered she seemed at a distance, how lost and weak.

The stories trailed off, the references to the FCC investigation became fewer after they'd levied a fine of $100,000 against the network, which was roughly commensurate to Meghan's travel and entertainment expenses in any given year. As for Meghan's whereabouts, the network couldn't let on that they didn't know and the other networks couldn't show they cared about a rival star. The straight papers don't cover that sort of thing unless they can do it as a business story—"Network in Ratings Slump as Morning Newscast Changes Personnel"—and the tabloids were preoccupied with a serial killer in Ohio, a sitcom star who had come out of the closet (unless you happened to be gay, in which case the announcement was about five years behind the times), and most troubling of all, a missing wife on the East Side. Long blond hair, two kids, what the tabs kept calling a $2 million co-op apartment, as though that would be anything larger than two bedrooms and a maid's room in this market.

The supermarket tabloids remained on Meghan watch, but after she left Grosvenor's Cove, they were reduced to reporting spurious sightings. Meghan on the yacht of a software mogul who was a rival of Ben Greenstreet's. Meghan in a Buddhist retreat center in Nepal. Meghan angling behind the scenes for the job as evening anchor, the job she had really always wanted, which was true. The always wanting, not the current angling.

One morning I got a phone call from Hadley Booth, the loathsome socialite. That's how Meghan always refers to her, as though it is her full name. She has had to be very careful over the years not to say this in front of Peter Booth, Leo's friend, Hadley's son.

"Bridget? Hadley," she said, as though we were the closest of friends. "I needed to check in. Leo seems so distraught. So. Distraught. Not at all the same boy. And we do think of him as our second son."

I shuddered, at the thought of anyone else thinking she was Leo's surrogate mother, and at the idea that that person might ever be Hadley Booth, who had once thrown a fit because she was shut out of a Chanel show after arriving late. But even from the collagened, lying lips of Hadley Booth, the notion that Leo might be suffering disturbed me more.

"I didn't know Leo and Peter saw each other when they were at college," I said.

"So close," she purred. "E-mail, phone, all those other techie things I don't begin to understand. Peter is a rock for Leo. I've told him that I've had so many friends come out the other side of all this. I've seen it over and over, and there is a light at the end of the tunnel."

"You've had lots of friends who misspoke over an open mike on national television?"

"That's the symptom, isn't it, Bridget, not the illness."

I refused to bite.

"I said to someone just the other day, I know Meghan Fitzmaurice, and Meghan Fitzmaurice will emerge from this crisis stronger than ever before."

"Tanner," I added.

"Excuse me?" Hadley Booth said, barely hiding her annoyance. She had taken time out of a very busy day of laser resurfacing, Pilates sessions, and shopping on Madison Avenue to get the scoop from the impoverished, obscure sister so she could spread it around town at dinner that night. And she was getting only sarcasm. It occurred to me that I sounded a bit like Meghan.

"She'll be tanner," I said. "She's at the beach. Hadley, I've got to run, I've got a crack addict and a cop waiting for me. It's always nice talking to you."

I was definitely channeling Meghan.

When I called Leo to report on the call, he just sighed into the phone. "Don't listen to Mrs. Booth, Bridey," he said wearily. "She's a complete bitch. And Peter never tells her anything. Besides, here's what I decided: It's kind of better this way. Dad doesn't really want to talk until he can do it with Mom, and Mom can't talk until she gets back. And if I don't have to talk about it, I have some time to get used to the idea, you know?"

"It's very sweet of you to make that sort of allowance for your mother," I said.

"I learned that one at the feet of the master," he said. I wasn't sure whether he meant me or Evan. That was a bad sign.

The network was letting the morning newsperson, a nice young woman who was always tripping over stray consonants as though they were heaves in the sidewalk of a sentence, sit in for Meghan, and even having her say "Rise and shine!" in a way that somehow suggested she spent a lot of time practicing in front of a mirror. I found this dispiriting. Leo might have felt as a boy that Meghan had cheapened a greeting that was theirs alone by turning it into common parlance, but to hear come out of the mouth of Susan Lomenta the words with which my sister had awakened me, first when our mother was taking her much-vaunted beauty sleep down the hall, then when our aunt was working the early shift at the hospital, was infinitely more jarring than Meghan's on-air imprecation against Ben Greenstreet had been.

"I don't believe you, Bridget," Evan said when I insisted I had no idea how to reach Meghan, which was almost true, as so many things are. I had not had a fax since that first declaration. But although I had given her assistant the fax number and insisted that she use it sparingly, I would be damned if I would have a stream of divorce documents scrolling their way out of thin air into the steamy, sweet-scented days in which I liked to imagine her, the blue sea spread before her like thin, shimmering cloth until it disappeared into the horizon somewhere short of Cuba.

Leo told me he planned to have dinner with his father every two weeks. Leo said the first two dinners were pleasant but, I divined, somewhat empty of content since he had declared a moratorium on any discussions of his mother, his mother's whereabouts, his mother's shortcomings, and his parents' marriage. I could imagine their time together, Leo sitting quietly at a Thai or Greek or Italian restaurant not far from Grand Central so he could take the train back, Evan returning to Amherst, where he was always preternaturally lively, as though to illustrate through simple bonhomie that he was somebody, he had been somebody. "He's gotten this bald spot on the back of his head," Leo said thoughtfully, reminding me that he was just as apt to make judgments and find the jugular as his mother, although with no ill will. When I asked what he and his father discussed, Leo said, "The Yankees."

"Go Yanks," Irving muttered when I recounted the conversation in the back of a cab.

"They suck!" the cabbie had said in heavily accented English.

"Mets fan?" Irving asked.

"Certainly. The Mets are the team of the workingman."

"You see?" Irving muttered. "This is why we should take my car everywhere." More loudly he said, "I'm a cop." The driver began to drive so slowly that Irving literally tore his own hair. "We're in a hurry!" The driver gunned the engine, and we jerked forward, nearly colliding with a man and his dog in the crosswalk. By the time we got downtown, I was carsick. Of course we were going to a clam house, which is one of Irving's three favorite kinds of restaurants. The man once sat across from me at a dinner and stared morosely at a bowl of cucumber gazpacho for nearly a half hour without speaking. He loves ketchup, nitrites, and crullers.

He loves me, too. He held my hair as the aroma of clam sauce and slightly ripe garbage overwhelmed me and I vomited in a gutter at the corner of Grand and Mercer streets. Then he gave up zuppa di pesce to walk me down to a little place that served pancakes and pie and other sweet, heavy foods that settle your stomach.

"You eat today?" I shook my head. "See, that's not good. You're under way too much stress, and you're not taking care of yourself. Take the day tomorrow. I'll take the day tomorrow."

"I can't take the day off," I said to Alison that night on the phone.

"Yeah, you can. You just think you're indispensable."

"Do not!" There's nothing like a little insight to bring out the youngest child in a youngest child.

So we took the day off and went to Coney Island. We even took the subway, which is a mode of transportation I love, particularly with Irving. What is it about him? Sometimes I look at him and imagine that he looks like a middle-level capo in the Gambino crime family, the prosperous head of a family company that sells cheap sportswear to Kmart, the principal of Sheepshead Bay High School, even a reporter at a tabloid. Maybe it's the eyes, which are deep brown but look black and are always a little narrowed. But if a guy is on the A train with Irving and he's carrying a knife, a gun, a box cutter, a can of spray paint, or is simply a little behind on visits to his parole officer, he knows Irving is a cop. There is a force field around him, and I am in it with him.

The old men watching the water rise and fall from their benches on the boardwalk gave him respectful nods. At the aquarium they let us in free to watch the beluga whales smile from the other side of the thick glass, showing off their pale bellies as they glided against the side of the tank. At Nathan's the counter guy handed over three chili dogs, two fries, and two root beers, and waved his hand when Irving gave him a twenty.

"You nuts?" the counterman said. "Paying?"

"You cops," I said as we ate.

"It's got nothing to do with the cops," Irving murmured, his cheek full of chili and bun. "When I was younger I used to take my nana here every Sunday. If we see an old lady, you watch. She'll act like I'm Jesus H. Christ on the cross."

"How come we don't see old ladies? All we see are old guys. And old ladies outnumber old guys by about ten to one. At the projects there are no old guys at all."

Irving did his close-one-eye-lift-the-lip-what-kind-of-moron-are-you? look. It's very effective. I saw him give it to the governor once at a press conference, and the governor deferred on the next three questions to the commissioner. "There are no guys in the projects over the age of twenty-five. Dead or incarcerated or got the hell out."

"It's not that bad."

"It's that bad. Here it's a different thing. Those guys on the benches are the last living husbands. Every day their wives throw them the hell out so they can wax the kitchen floor, then have lunch with their girl-friends. They got into a routine when they were younger: the husband goes to work, the wife cleans, watches the soaps, talks to the other girls. The husband retires, it's a nightmare. So they tell them—go out, exer-cise, get some fresh air, pick up some milk. You come out here in Feb-ruary, these poor sons of bitches are freezing in Russian hats and scarves and gloves, the whole nine yards. When my nana was here, there was one guy, been married fifty-seven years, he goes and leaves his wife for one of the widows in the building, lives three floors down. His son shows up, yelling, carrying on, says to his father in the lobby, What the hell are you doing, Pop? The guy says, She lets me stay inside during the day."

"You're making this all up."

"Swear to God."

Irving finished the last bit of my dog and crumpled up the trash. It was one of those deceptive spring days when the sun shines down so confi-dently that you begin to think of putting your winter coat away, one of those days that gets the weatherman an additional minute or two on the evening news, with film of kids playing ball in the park, a couple walk-ing amid the daffodils. Irving and I walked beneath the roller-coaster supports. The roller coaster at Coney Island looks like it's built of two-by-fours and spit. Irving swears by it. A homeless guy wearing a NEW YORK CITY MARATHON T-shirt with a mongrel dog lying alongside him held a sign: GULF WAR VET, AGENT ORANGE, NO BENEFITS, MY DOG IS HUNGRY, AIDS.

"Sign sucks," Irving said, dropping the twenty the Nathan's people had passed up into the guy's cup.

"I guess marriage is a mystery," I said, looking at two old men huddled together on one splintering bench as though for warmth in the thin May sunshine.

"A misery, more like it. Yo, Mr. Kanterman. Mr. Beck."

"Irving," one of the men called. "How's your nana?"

"She's dead," the other snarled at him, hitting him in the side with the back of his hand. "Four years ago. You sat shivah."

"It's okay, Mr. Kanterman. I forget everything, too."

"How's the wife?"

Again the hand, like a martial arts expert. "He's divorced! Idiot!" The man I assumed was Mr. Beck peered at me. His eyes were a blue so light that he would have looked blind had he not fixed them so accusingly on me. "Unless there's a new one."

"I'm just the girlfriend," I said. Mr. Beck looked disgusted at the notion that I actually talked, but Mr. Kanterman nodded and smiled and said, "That's good."

As we started down the boardwalk, Mr. Beck called, "Irving? Irving! You got your gun? You be careful. They're everywhere now."

"Your nana just died four years ago?" I said as Irving lit a cigar and puffed energetically into the wind off the ocean. On the horizon were two big tankers, bookends to the two big apartment towers where the old people lived. Maybe someday the buildings would be unmoored and sail away south, to Miami maybe. Maybe that was what all the residents were waiting for.

"She died in 1988. Mr. Beck thinks everything happened four years ago. He hits Kanterman so often I'm surprised the poor guy isn't black and blue all up and down his side."

"All that time and they all still remember you?"

"Nothing changes out here. The city, everything changes all the time. Here, it might as well be four years ago."

"That's what it was like on City Island. Remember when I told you I once lived on City Island?"

"Jeez, that place," Irving said, holding his cigar down at his side and throwing an arm around my shoulder. "That's an embalmed place, City Island."

"I loved it," I said, which like most simple declarative sentences was an oversimplification merged with a lie and overlaid by the mists of blessed memory. I had been invited to house-sit in City Island by my landlord, who had acquired a small home on the water there from an aunt who had recently died. He hadn't decided whether to keep the place or sell it, and he was convinced that, uninhabited, it would be vandalized or flooded or mysteriously decrease in value. The day I told him I was moving out at the end of the month, he'd asked me if I wanted to live rent-free for a while in this City Island house. It was the first time I'd ever heard of City Island, and because I was a New Yorker, it was the first time I'd ever heard the words *rent-free*.

"How do I get there?" I'd asked.

It's not easy to get to City Island. A train to the bus, the bus over the bridge. There's a reason for that. City Island is so different from the rest of the city that, on the few occasions during those three months that I left it, I would not have been surprised if it had disappeared into the mist, a mirage from a Broadway musical, a small New England fishing village within spitting distance of the blocky Soviet high-rises of the central Bronx. The house in which I lived was just as difficult to find, down a narrow, dead-end block tucked in behind the avenue overlooking the ocean. It had blue carpeting, a plaid couch in the kind of early American style the Puritans might have embraced had they shopped at discount stores, and a recliner chair in green Naugahyde equidistant between a small low-ceilinged kitchen and the television.

"Young girl like you, you won't last a week here," said the druggist at the corner who sold me Tylenol and maxipads.

It was the perfect place to live after a job dismissal and an abortion. I had a little money left over from my job at Stinson, Reilly and Jacoby. ("The name alone is a history of ethnic progress in New York," Meghan had said one night at dinner.) It was no wonder I'd been asked to leave, sandwiched as I was between two groups of enthusiasts, the older women, high school graduates whose vocation had been found in being handmaidens to a senior partner, and the young sharpies in black skirt suits, Ivy grads who were putting in the obligatory two years before going to Columbia law school and leaving SRJ in the dust of their seven-figure ambitions. A New York paralegal who thinks she shouldn't have to work weekends, or for that matter fewer than eighty hours a week, and who insists on wearing peasant skirts and clogs is a New York paralegal awaiting work as a waitress. I did that for part of the time I was living on the island, did the breakfast shift at the island diner from five until ten. But most of my time was spent lying on the couch covered by a brown-and-orange afghan with that unmistakable sweet, musty old-lady smell, watching TV and eating donuts. God, do I love donuts. I could eat donuts all day. And did. By the time the bleeding had stopped, I had gained ten pounds and become inextricably enmeshed in the story lines of *One Life to Live* and the rerun episodes of, ironically, *L.A. Law*. I was thirty-three years old, growing fat and stupid in Brigadoon, my only human contact a request for more butter on rye toast or more coffee as the sun rose half-heartedly in an always overcast February sky.

"God, this place is really a dump, isn't it?" said my landlord when he brought a friend in to give him an appraisal, and I nodded dumbly, although I had been thinking of asking him whether he would give me a two-year lease.

When Meghan arrived, I had just gotten home from my shift, taken off my uniform of white shirt and black pants and dropped them into the back of the closet, where they gave off their familiar smell of syrup and butter, and lain down on the couch in what my aunt Maureen would have called a housecoat. I'd even begun to wear clothes that had been left in the closet, smocklike shirts that snapped up the front, shapeless pants in slippery synthetics, robes with zippers and big patch pockets.

"Are there pancakes?" she said as she took off her black wool coat and tossed it over a chair. "Coffee?" I shook my head dumbly. She'd been misled by the aroma of the diner that clung to my hair and hands. I heard her rattling around in the kitchen, and finally she came out with a donut and a warm Coke. Meghan is adaptable, in part because of the time she has spent in war zones. She ate horse once, and dog, too, and maybe snake.

"You watch the show?" she said, looking at the game show on the small set.

"I work from five to ten. Waitressing."

She chewed thoughtfully. She still had a trace of TV makeup on her jawline.

"Mary Todd Lincoln," Meghan said. She was answering a question on the game show. "The theory of relativity," she said. "1914. The Boston Red Sox. David Copperfield. The Nineteenth Amendment." The windows were rattling in the frames, and outside I could see a small, half-dead apple tree in the yard of the next house bending at its gnarled waist. The weather is the constant background music of life on an island.

Meghan leaned over and turned off the set. "This place is like a little piece of Nantucket," she said, "before rich people ruined it."

"I love it," I said as unthinkingly as I said it years later to Irving. I suppose it was that that set her off.

"What's with you?" she said, pacing the carpet. "Look at yourself. You look like her. Don't you remember what it was like, her lying up in her bedroom all day, the smell of Chanel No. 5, God, it would kill you when you went in there, like dead flowers and Scotch all mixed together."

"I don't know what you're talking about."

"Oh, come off it, Bridget. Do you think if I spent all day, every day, in my bedroom reading trashy novels and having my meals on a tray and seeing Leo once a day to say, Oh, how was your day, darling? he wouldn't remember it?"

"I'm just saying, Meghan. I don't remember what you remember."

"You don't remember me getting your uniform skirts out of the closet in the morning? You don't remember me helping with your homework at night? You don't remember me showing you how to do division?"

"I guess."

"You guess? You guess?" She was yelling at me now, and for some reason I thought of how she had done a broadcast in the dark from someplace in Central America, whispering, "The rebels are firing all around us, yet for a moment it's so quiet you can hear your own breathing." Not a person in the world but me could deconstruct that sentence. If

Meghan could hear her own breathing, it meant she was breathing fast. And since Meghan has a resting heart rate of somewhere between coma and sleep because of all that swimming, if she were breathing fast, it meant she was afraid, which meant there was truly something to fear. She'd been pregnant with Leo when she went on that assignment. She said she didn't know until afterward, but I'd wondered.

When Meghan was yelling, it meant that something—or someone— was very, very bad. I hadn't told her about the abortion, but she had probably figured it out. She pulled the afghan off me and tossed it onto the floor. "Get up!" she cried. "Get up and take a shower and put on some decent clothes and get on with it. Get out of bed and get out of the house and do something with yourself."

"I'm not you, Meghan."

"No one wants you to be me," she said. "Least of all me. But Jesus, Bridge, isn't it time for you to be something? The pottery, the stupid jobs, the apartments. I've crossed you out and written you in in my date book what, nine times? Ten? Now this place? You might as well live in Asshole, Arkansas, as this place."

"So maybe that's where I'll go."

"No you won't. You'd miss Leo too much. He'd miss you. He keeps asking when you're coming to see him. He has Grandparents' Day on the twenty-seventh. Don't get me started on why a school in which most of the parents are in their fifties would have an event dedicated to grandparents, most of whom are dead or in a home or have Alzheimer's or are in Boca Grande."

"I always come to Grandparents' Day. Last year I even came to the mother-son softball game."

"Look, I was going to go to that, but I had to be in Washington for that Senate thing. You remember. That thing." But the truth was neither of us remembered which thing it was, only that it had seemed important at the time.

At the end of the month, I moved back to Manhattan. I started in the social work program in September with a loan from Aunt Maureen. At least I had refused to let Meghan and Evan pay for it, although they had

pushed hard to do so. For six years I had been living in the same apartment. For four years I had been seeing Irving. Once he had wanted to go
to a clam bar on City Island, but I had decided better not.

As he was beginning to breathe heavily that night, exhausted and content from a surfeit of sea air and processed meat, I said, "I'm going to
have to go get my sister and bring her home."

"See, when you do that I can't get back to sleep. I'm like on the edge
of sleep and then you interrupt it."

"Sorry."

"Besides, you keep thinking your sister is in exile. Maybe she's not.
Maybe she's just resting."

"Meghan doesn't rest."

"There's a first time for everything."

O N MY DESK the next morning were three enormous piles of paper, the price I'd paid for a day's vacation. Irving had left his three cell phones and his pager on top of the bureau, looking back at them only once as we walked out of the apartment. He let his deputy handle all crises for the day; according to one of the papers, the deputy had called the shooting of a civilian "an error," which is a term they teach you in public information school never to use. Both of us had gotten to the office early.

Atop one pile was a fax. In block letters it said, MOVE INTO MY PLACE WITH LEO. Somehow, somewhere, my sister had remembered that late May brought the end of the college year. I wrote NO on the back of a take-out menu for a deli and yelled, "Tequila!"

"Don't be calling me like I'm some slave," she mumbled. She was wearing a big T-shirt over capri leggings. The shirt said "PMS." It was the official shirt of Pelham Manor, the charter school that Tequila's youngest attended. Sometimes people just don't think things through.

Tequila held up the fax. "Don't you be snippy with that poor girl," she said.

"She's a forty-seven-year-old woman with a whole lot of responsibilities who has dropped off the face of the earth. She's lucky she's even getting an answer."

Besides, Meghan and I had a long, rich history of this form of communication. At various times during our childhoods, we had been temporarily estranged, an estrangement that had only become richer and more baroque when we moved from our parents' house to the smaller one our aunt and uncle had borrowed heavily to buy. There we needed to share a bedroom. There is no feeling quite like refusing to speak to a person only a nightstand apart. Meghan said years later that it was good preparation for marriage.

"Please return my mechanical pencil," a note on my pillow would read.

"Don't have it," I would reply, leaving a torn corner of loose-leaf paper on her desk.

"Liar."

"You lose everything."

"I saw it in your backpack."

"Stay out of my backpack."

It was always Meghan who would break the logjam, rolling over in bed and sighing, as though the last four days had never happened, "Why does Aunt Maureen think anyone wants to eat fish sticks?"

There was no need for me to move into Meghan's apartment, which had taken on a faint Miss Havisham air of both desertion and taxidermy, the elaborately maintained façade of something that had ceased to live. Leo had already moved into my apartment for the summer, which meant that my sofa now had that faint perpetual boy smell, not unlike the underground cheese room at L'Occidental.

One lucky aspect of being a grown child in Manhattan is that your parents and their friends will employ you in a variety of high-profile, albeit nonpaying, positions during the summer months of college. Leo had always had a certain contempt for the phenomenon, and as a result, while friends from the Biltmore and Crenshaw schools had lined up internships at *Time* magazine, U.S. Trust, the networks, the museums, and even Bergdorf Goodman, Leo had found himself at a loose end with the expectation that he would catch up on his sleep until well into the afternoon and early evening hours in my living room.

Fortunately, two happy accidents had dovetailed: the van driver who transported our clients around the onerous scavenger hunt required of the poor decided to move to Florida, and I discovered that Leo had a driver's license. To those who live in other parts of the country that might seem unremarkable, but in New York City, where teenagers think of transportation as the subway, and Leo's peers considered it driving when a man in a black suit with a black car took them from one location to another, the discovery that Leo not only knew how to drive but was legally able to do so came as a great shock.

"That program I did in South Carolina last summer, where we built the houses? We all had to be able to drive," he said, eating Corn Pops out of the box by pouring them down his throat. Something about the sight of his Adam's apple always made me feel tremulous. My sister had somehow given birth to a man.

"Get dressed," I said. "You're hired."

We took the subway together in the morning, walking past the Cuban sandwich place and the bridal shop and up the hill to the WOW offices. Leo had a schedule for the day that took him from the shelter to the hospital's satellite clinic to the welfare office and the housing projects. The first thing our departing driver, LeMar, taught him to do was lock the doors from the inside.

"You carry?" LeMar asked Leo.

"Nah-hah," Leo replied.

"You know what he was talking about?" I asked Leo on the way home on the subway. Leo rolled his ambery eyes.

"Bridey, honey, here's the deal. Black street culture is the dominant culture of the country right now. Go to the Americana mall on Long Island and every rich poser in the place is talking like he's street. Therefore the expression 'to carry,' meaning 'You got a gun, white boy?' is understood from L.A. to NYC."

"In other words, you can speak street."

"Can. Won't. It's so lame. Look at me. I am what I am. It's insulting for me to talk to these people that way. Look at how Tequila won't even let her daughter speak that way in her home. She treats street slang like it's obscene. It's doubly obscene for some white kid like me to pretend it's my first language. It's like Americans in Europe, when they act as though if they speak English really, really loud, Czech people, or Spaniards, or Greeks will be able to understand them. There was this asshole—"

"Hey!"

"—okay, moron in my class at Biltmore who was a white rapper? He'd be wearing big pants, his Ralph Lauren boxers hanging out, a baseball cap on backward. He'd be going, 'The law of the gun, the law of the street/Life sucks the big one, when you ain't got enough to eat.' The guy had a screening room in his apartment!"

"And he's at?"

"Duke. Official home of the white homeboy with his own investment adviser."

"Yeah, but you had that friend, what was his name, Landon? He was a rapper. Alleged."

Leo began to thump in some complicated rhythm on the hard plastic subway seat, then chanted. "I'm curious, but you can call me inquisitive/If complacency's a function, I take the derivative."

"Wow. Algebra rap."

"Calculus, actually. It's not my thing, but he had a really good one about the First Amendment, too, and a great line about Tiananmen Square."

"Intelligentsia rap."

"Just poetry with some beats."

"You're smart."

The truth was that Leo had always had both smarts and sense, with sensitivity thrown in to boot. It was hard to say how this had come to pass. I think Meghan had been disconcerted by Leo's character. She liked a project. I know; I had been one of her favorites for many years. But I was pliant and tractable and, for a time, rather lost, whereas Leo was one of those children who seems a finished product almost from the beginning. It was all there at three: the honesty, the staunchness, a bit of a predilection for girl companions over boys, a contemplative streak that led him to wander away during parties and disappear into someone's den with *The New Yorker* to read the cartoons. There wasn't a whole lot of shaping required. He had most of his mother's steel and no need for all her striving. He had nothing to prove.

After the first week, all the women and children who stayed at the shelter and lived in the transitional housing loved him. He kept a basket of Tootsie Pops on the dashboard, and he gave one to each passenger, including the mothers, who were perpetually pissed off about the fact that, to the extent the bureaucracies cared about anything, they cared about their kids. They were treated as the unfortunate appendages; if "children are our future," as every dope running for office says every time he comes to a neighborhood in which the future is more of the same, then mothers are the past.

Leo didn't treat them that way. He slid open the side-panel door with a slight flourish, albeit the always annoying sound of worn and rusting tracks, and held out his arm as though he was inviting them to enter. "Good morning," he said. "I'm Leo Grater." One bad-tempered woman from the transitional building, who had been rude to so many landlords that we despaired of ever finding a place for her and her three timid children, sneered, "I know who you are. You get this job through, you know what. Connections."

"She's right, you know," Leo said to her kids, leaning down so his face was on a level with theirs. "Your mother is right. I got this job because my aunt works here. Do you want a Tootsie Pop?" Three heads bobbing like back-dash dolls. "That's bad for their teeth," the mother said. "Tomorrow I will bring carrot sticks," Leo said. Over two unseasonably warm days, the cup of carrot sticks on the dash curled and grew pale around the edges. "Throw that mess away," the mom said on day three as she took an orange pop.

Sometimes Leo had a lag at midday, when all the kids were at school and the mothers doing laundry or sneaking a smoke out in back of the shelter. Even the ones who had no money and had been burned out of their apartments couldn't seem to give up cigarettes.

"There's a police officer here to see you ladies," Leo came into our office and announced.

"Irving?"

"A real police officer, Bridey. In a uniform. Wearing a badge."

Tequila went out into the waiting room. There was the sound of mumbling, then the sound of Tequila's voice raised loud. "I never heard such foolishness!" she yelled.

Leo had always had good instincts, too. We were practically moving in tandem as we went to the door. Tequila had her finger right in the policeman's face. He was on the short side for a cop, had probably just squeaked by on the height requirement, which experience told me would make him irascible for life. Irving insisted that short cops were twice as likely to unholster their weapons, but I think he just made that up. He was over six feet tall, after all.

"I'm not here to argue, ma'am," the cop said. A young man in a cheap bomber jacket and a fraying tie stood behind him. He had "child services caseworker" written all over him. They lasted a year, maybe two, before the misery caught up with them and they decided that telemarketing was a more honorable profession.

"That's right, because that lady is a good lady and a good mother and she didn't hurt that child and I will tell you that right here right now and get no argument from anyone. From anyone!" Tequila has a tendency to come up on the balls of her feet when she's angry, perhaps the legacy of years of leaning over counters and desks and arguing with middle-level managers whose favorite sentence is "It's against our policy."

"I was just asked to check on the child. If you want me to come back with another officer, I can do that."

"Huh!" Tequila sounded as though she had just huffed and puffed and blown our house down.

"Can I help, Officer?" I asked. I had servility down to an art form. Meghan said that sometimes listening to me made her sick.

"He's saying Annette been beating on Delon, I say uh-uh, no way. And I bet I know which sorry bitch told them that because she's not getting all the attention anymore, now that she's back in Rikers where she belongs."

"I just need to take a look at the child, ma'am." I could tell the cop was not long out of the academy, that he still hadn't shaken the just-following-orders routine and learned to trust his instincts about the people he met and the stories they told him. Someone at the precinct had told him he had to take a good look at this kid at a homeless shelter, whose mom had no job, whose father was unknown, and he was bound and determined to do so.

"Officer, I appreciate that you've got a job to do, but this mother is really traumatized. She's been moving from place to place for months, and she's part of a group here who were displaced by that building collapse last month. She's going to be really distraught if she gets called in here with a uniformed officer. I don't know why the caseworker had to get all of you involved."

"The last time I came she threatened me," the caseworker said, pointing with his city-issued mechanical pencil at Tequila.

"You think that's threatening, you never been threatened," Tequila said. Tequila tends to be combative with caseworkers and cops. They are, after all, the people who had once taken her own kids to a foster home.

Leo had disappeared, and suddenly, incongruously, we heard him singing loudly, a nursery rhyme that began "Ride a cock horse to Banbury Cross," which our aunt Maureen had sung whenever anyone placed a baby in her outstretched arms and which both Meghan and I had sung, in our course, to Leo. When he was a toddler he would hug us around our knees as though we were tree trunks, strong and stalwart, and trill "Ride!" in a high, sweet voice until we lifted him on our shoulders, his hair a bright flag atop his round, freckled face. "Ride, Mama! Ride, Bridey!"

And now he himself was the tree, the horse, as he ducked through the doorway to the waiting room, Delon on his shoulders, his fat fingers entwined in Leo's overlong hair. Delon was wearing nothing but Spider-Man underpants, the action figures on them as wavy and indistinct as a mirage after many washings. His skin was smooth and brown, not a mark on it anywhere, and his mouth was open in an unabashed baby laugh, an intake of breath on the gallop, a hiccup on the dip, a smile so broad that you could see all his little pearl teeth.

"Hey, Delon," Leo said. "Can I put you down and catch my breath?" Leo lifted the child over his head and put his feet on the ground, where he stood sturdily, then took his small hands in his own big, bony ones and did a twisty dance and a hopping step, both of which Delon imitated carefully. "Up!" Delon demanded. "Pick me up!"

"You have lunch, Delon?" Leo asked.

"Baloney!" Delon yelled.

"You have breakfast?"

"Krispies! Rice Krispies!"

"You stand on your head?"

With a cry of triumph, Delon bent at the waist and put his palms on the floor. His butt faced us, displaying Spider-Man with his fists on his hips. It was the most complete demonstration of a child's physical well-being, and perhaps his mental one as well, that I had ever seen. "Ride!" he cried again and was carried off on Leo's shoulders.

After the police officer and the caseworker had retreated, Tequila sat down heavily at her desk. She took two Tylenol from her desk drawer, drank half a can of Coke without speaking, and tried to bring her breathing under control. Sometimes I thought working for us, where she had to relive the worst parts of her past, was too hard for her. Sometimes I thought it was an exorcism, other times a stroke of luck for the women we served. They had a virago on their side. Now it seemed they had an angel driving the van.

"I take back every bad thing I said about that boy getting the job," she said.

"You haven't said a thing."

"Not to you," she said, patting her neck with a tissue.

Fifteen minutes later, as I was finishing some paperwork in triplicate, Tequila rang through. "That nice man with the foolish name is wanting to speak to you," she said. I waited for the breathy voice of the overeducated executive assistant, but instead it was Edward Prevaricator himself on the phone.

"Ms. Fitzmaurice, I wonder if you've considered spending a week in Jamaica," he said in his courtly fashion.

"It's funny you should ask," I said. "I was thinking that very thing. But why are you thinking it?"

"I've found in business that timing is an important element of success. It seems to me the right time. Or at least that's what I gather from talking to your sister, and from the people who work for me down there. It's very beautiful there. Relaxing as well. I think you'd enjoy yourself."

"I'm sure I would. My only hesitation is that I got the impression my sister didn't want visitors."

"My experience is that want and need are often two different things," he replied. "Although my experience is also that strong-minded people often have an inability to discern the difference. May I offer the plane?"

"I like a man with a plane," said Tequila, who naturally had been listening in on the extension.

"I like a man who likes my sister. I just wonder how much he likes her."

"Too much is never enough," Tequila said. "That's a spy movie I saw on television."

"I think you're wrong about that," I said.

THE RITUALS SURROUNDING vacations among Manhattan's wealthiest and best-connected citizens are strange and specific. By vacations I don't mean country houses, which are part of the regular ebb and flow of life and which are frequently subjects for complaint—The kids never want to go! The caretaker missed the roof leak! The pipes froze!—as though having a six-thousand-square-foot, cedar-shingled cottage on five acres overlooking the ocean is nothing more or less than a constant test of character.

Just as most of the East Side of Manhattan gets away from town by taking up residence in places in Connecticut where they will repeatedly run into people from town, often the very same people with whom they attend parties and play the occasional game of tennis in town, the paths through foreign destinations are well-worn and familiar. In First Class airport lounges all over the world, you can see this played out as Investment Banker A steps to the bar for a vodka tonic and encounters Lawyer B, and both are overwhelmed by the sheer coincidence of being in Athens/Fiji/New Zealand/Beijing at the same moment in time, when only a week ago they, and both of their wives, now chatting in the deep leather chairs about their respective children, who may or may not be careening around the lounge tripping over and ripping out the cords of laptops belonging to business travelers, were in Manhattan.

"Quelle surprise!" as one of Evan's partners' wives once had said to Meghan in the First Class lounge in Nice, having landed in the copter from Monte Carlo. Meghan said she had replied, "Quelle throw-up!" but she hadn't really, she was just showing off.

But whereas once the parents and grandparents of some of these people (the ones with old money; the parents and grandparents of the others were working automobile assembly lines or driving city buses) encountered one another in Palm Beach or Paris, now the destinations are more remote. It has become axiomatic in New York City that the only place worth going to is one that is nearly impossible to reach. So no one with any real money goes to St. Thomas. Instead, you fly to St. Thomas, then take a small plane to a small island (unspoiled, everyone says), and then a water taxi to an even smaller one, an island that has virtually nothing on it except for several herds of goats and a four-star resort with a Pilates studio, a world-famous facialist, and a restaurant that can accommodate a wedding for a hundred in a pinch.

I am proud to say that my sister never saw the point of all this. Why go to a drafty castle at the ass-end of Scotland when you can go to a small hotel in Mayfair? Why take a train to some medieval village in northern Italy when there's the Hassler in Rome? And why take a chance on a puddle jumper to some off island in the Grenadines when Jamaica is a direct flight from New York?

"I just don't believe the ocean is that much better in Fiji than it is at Grosvenor's Cove," she'd once said.

"Same with Atlantic City," Irving had replied.

"Let's not get ridiculous," Meghan had said.

Of course, Meghan was interested neither in roughing it on vacation nor in going down-market. Grosvenor's Cove is a resort that had been founded by a British couple two marriages removed from the royal family sometime after the stock market crash of 1929, and it has that appealing air of colonialism that the old rich take for granted and the new find so bracing. It is still a kiss-kiss-what-are-YOU-doing-here place, but those who find themselves meeting friends at Grosvenor's Cove have a sense of confidence, are people who don't care when someone who has just come back from that little village an hour by camel from Morocco raises an eyebrow and says, "Jamaica?" In New York the climbers have outnumbered the confident, so there are now many guests at the Cove who are from Kansas City or New Orleans, but as Evan likes to say, it is good to have new blood, and if they try to take pictures of Meghan, she smiles and poses and then the manager asks them privately to stop. Like expensive resorts worldwide, it is utterly not of its place. In other words, if you turned down the reggae music and shut off the supply of ganja the staff discreetly provide to the more adventuresome or younger guests, it could be in Miami or Sardinia or Nice, any of those places that are warm and on the sea and are off-limits unless you have a staff badge or a platinum Amex.

But we were a world away from Grosvenor's Cove as the man Edward Prevaricator sent to meet me at the airport followed the steep S curves into and over the mountains that make up the undulating spine of the island. The cheesy American imports in Montego Bay, the Holiday Inns painted Caribbean pink, and the McDonald's with sunburned tourists shuffling through its air-conditioned interior gave way to some large, white villas at the ends of gated driveways and then to a ramshackle assemblage of lean-tos along the mountain road. Little girls in dresses held out mangoes and lobsters for sale as the car passed, and musky smoke rose from an old drum sawed in half that a man in a Georgetown T-shirt had turned into a barbecue for jerk chicken and beef. I admit, I had expected some variation on a black car, but the driver, a thin man named Derek with an impossibly long neck, was driving an electric blue GTO with the words "Big Boy" emblazoned in silver decal letters across the top of the windshield. On the twisting rutted roads we had passed "Slo Mon," "Love Mobile," and a red Hyundai with "Jesus Ride With Me" in gold script. Twice we stopped for livestock, once a befuddled goat, then a herd of bulky oxen with enormous horns.

We passed through one small town, and along the road single file were women and children in dress clothes: lavender skirts, enormous straw hats, flowered pillboxes, starched collars. They picked their way carefully among the stones on the shoulder, and occasionally one of the women would give a child a thump atop the head with a clutch purse.

"Is there some kind of festival?" I said to Derek, who had insisted I sit in the back.

"It is Sunday. They are going to church." He had a quiet voice that somehow sounded as though he didn't use it often, as though it was kept folded in a drawer and brought out for special occasions.

"And you don't go?" I said, trying to be friendly.

"I am a Seventh-Day Adventist. Our Sabbath is on the Saturday," he said in a stiff way that made me realize I had taken the wrong tack.

I remembered staying at Grosvenor's Cove with Evan, Meghan, and Leo for Meghan's forty-third birthday, and how we had remarked on how warm and friendly the staff had been, how one of the men taught Leo about windsurfing, how another took him to meet a boat delivering the lobsters to the disgruntled chef, a Paris expat. One of the hostesses in the restaurant sang lilting folk songs during the dinner sitting, and one of the waiters did little dance steps when he delivered our meals. There had undeniably been a falseness about the entire performance, particularly following the afternoon I got lost on my way back from the tennis court and came upon the staff quarters, a long barracks of cinder block outside of which those men and women we'd seen in white shirts and floral dresses sat on upturned crates in worn everyday clothes, their eyes unfriendly as I came around the corner of the dirt path.

"That way, missus," one woman said, pointing away from them.

Perhaps Derek's stiffness was that same resentment. But some of the children along the road smiled and waved at us, and one little boy ran alongside the car until his mother called sharply, "Lawrence!" and he slowed and disappeared. On either side of the road there were small low houses with metal grating protecting the porches, and alongside a few of them were raised burial plots, rough stone tombs sunk down a bit in the ground as though little by little they would bury themselves.

Tequila was from a town like this, she'd told me, and her mother buried alongside a house like one of these. Like the people who had boarded the flight with me, people who now lived in East New York, Brooklyn, and Jamaica, Queens, she had once gone home every summer with a duffel bag of clothes and an enormous assortment of consumer electronics. As the children had waited in the check-in aisle at Kennedy Airport, they had used appliance boxes as benches.

I had nothing for Meghan except detective novels. I didn't know what she needed or, more important, what she wanted.

"Do you know my sister?" I asked Derek. He nodded. For a long time he said nothing. Finally he cocked his head toward the backseat slightly and added, "She is a very good swimmer."

A minute later and we crested the mountain and saw far ahead of us the blue Caribbean. Below us the road twisted and turned as it made its way downhill, and far out on the horizon I could see a sailboat. The air was thick, and a long rodent crossed in front of the car as we stopped for a pothole.

"Mongoose," Derek said softly. "If he go to the sea, it is good luck. If he go to the mountain, bad luck."

"Which way was he going?"

Derek looked from one side of the road to the other. "Neither, I think."

Twice we passed small guesthouses, once with a young couple with hikers' backpacks out front consulting a map, but otherwise there was no sign of tourists and tourism. The road began to parallel the sea and at one point was almost upon it, and on the pebbly beach a man was soaping himself while standing waist deep in the water. Finally the car pulled up to a wooden gate painted a deep red. On either side were two enormous trees with red-brown trunks, a canopy of dim shade over the entrance. It was nothing like I had expected, no palatial villa, to be rented by the week. Down a path lined with old conch shells was a small one-story place, almost a pavilion, with a center room open to the ocean and the air. A small couch and two chairs were grouped around a low wooden table piled with books. A lizard ran across the floor, leapt at an insect, swallowed, and disappeared beneath an enormous philodendron whose speckled leaves covered most of the slope outside.

There was a patio and steps that led down to a narrow dock and a small stony beach. The sun had thrown a golden pathway from the horizon to the shore, and caught in its glare were a clutch of dugout canoes. I felt disoriented. That morning I had had coffee and a bagel in my apartment in New York as the May rain fell chill and hard against the window and the family across the yard, by the looks of it, slept in. Leo had spent the night at the house of a friend from Biltmore. "Tell her I said hi," he had said breezily of his mother.

"Do you want to send a note or something?"

"Saying what? Hi? What's up? Where are you? I'm still alive? I exist? No thanks. She knows."

"No wonder it used to take months for sailors to get here from England," I said aloud to no one. "It gave them time to get used to it."

A boy was standing on the end of the dock, his fists on his narrow hips, his thin legs apart. His head was in shadow, his hair rough and shaggy, and suddenly he raised his arm and waved back and forth at one of the dugouts, shouting something I couldn't hear. He was wearing khaki shorts to his knees and a shrunken T-shirt, and finally he let the shorts fall and dove into the water. He came up into the stripe of bright sun and began to swim, and in the light on the ruddy head and the sure length of the breaststroke I realized that what I had thought was a boy just short of manhood was my sister, wasted and shorn.

"Holy God," I said.

"You will have to wait a long time," said Derek. "She swims for many miles. My wife is cooking for her every night except for Saturday. She says someday she will swim to Cuba."

"And interview Fidel," I said.

On one side of the pavilion were two small bedrooms and a bath. Plantation beds with mosquito net canopies were in each. I could not tell which Meghan used because there was a framed photo of Leo in each with a small bouquet of some strange salmon-colored flower in a vase next to it. I changed into a bathing suit, some shorts, and rubber sandals, and followed the steps carefully to the dock. I looked out over the ocean. There was nothing, nothing, as far as you could see except for the dugouts. In one of them a man pointed at me, then spoke to his companion, and the two of them laughed. The coastline curved to a broad beach and the road running alongside it, and I could faintly hear the voices of the people bobbing up and down in a faint swell. I lay back on the dock. Above my head was a banana tree with green fruit. Somewhere in its branches a bird made a harsh braying sound. I fell asleep.

When I woke it was because of the sound of laughter again. Meghan was treading water near one of the dugouts. They handed her a net bag, and she looped it over one ankle, then struck out for the dock. As her arms curved overhead, her muscles were as clear as those in an anatomy book, and her freckles had almost merged into one expanse of mahogany brown. When she approached the pilings, her left hand rose from the water and wrapped itself around my ankle. Her right grabbed the splintering wood, and she arched out of the blue water like a red-gold fish. The men in the dugout watched. With one motion she pivoted, spraying water all over me.

"How is he?" she said fiercely. "That's all I want to know."

"I haven't seen him," I said. "I've talked to him a couple of times on the phone."

"What?" The insides of her frown lines were a paler color, as though she kept her face clenched when she was in the sun. "I thought he was living with you. Mercedes just sent me a fax saying he was living with you and working at the office in the Bronx. I was so relieved. I haven't been able to track him down anywhere."

"I thought you meant Evan."

"Evan? Who cares about Evan?"

"Leo's fine," I said. "He sends his love."

Meghan smiled and threw her arms around me tight, holding, releasing, holding, releasing, as though she was doing an exercise. The water was warm, but she felt cold. "You are one of the world's worst liars," she said. "I've always admired that. Learning not to lie is the hardest thing."

"Did you learn not to eat, too?"

She ran her fingers down her sides. Meghan has always been slender, and in times of trouble perhaps more than that. When she went on foreign assignments, she would sometimes look a little drawn on air, but I suspected she cultivated that: Look, America. Look how difficult is the work of bringing you the news! When we were children, I'd read the term *fighting weight* somewhere and thought that it applied to Meghan. In the months after our parents were killed, she had become so thin that she'd had to pin a fat handful of fabric at the side of her uniform skirt to hold it up. Every morning at breakfast, every afternoon when we arrived at our new home, she would make me food: cinnamon toast with cups of hot chocolate, cream donuts with glasses of milk. She even learned to make milk shakes in the blender, and she would sit at the table, hunched slightly forward, and watch me eat until I was done. By the time the school year was over, a roll of pink fat hung over the waistband of my underpants and the school nurse called my aunt and uncle in to say that Meghan must eat or she would have to leave school.

"I eat," Meghan said then. "I eat," she said now. It was probably true. You would have to eat a lot to underwrite the calories needed to swim to Cuba.

Derek's wife at first had cooked and served, but she and Meghan now had an arrangement in which she left the food in an ancient oven in the small kitchen. I couldn't understand how Meghan had lost any weight at all. That first night we had lobster stuffed with onion and bread crumbs, potatoes mashed with cheese, a local vegetable called callaloo, and some key lime pie. Meghan made me a rum punch while she drank beer. She wore an unfamiliar shift dress of cheap yellow cotton that hung straight to an inch or two above her knees. "I bought some stuff at an outdoor market a couple of weeks ago," she said.

After dinner we went out to the patio and lay on two old teak lounges placed side by side. The stars were so bright that they seemed to press down on us, and Meghan pointed suddenly to the sky. A shooting star moved in an arc away from us, then fizzled like a bum firework. Bats moved in careful figure eights overhead. For a long time we just lay there silently. Meghan went inside and got another beer and a joint from a little box on her bureau. I shook my head when she passed it over. Now that I was here, I didn't know how to begin. There was too much to say.

"What's the deal with this place anyhow?" I finally said.

"It's Edward's," she said. "Edward Prevaricator. He said you two know one another. He was at the Cove when I was there. One of the waiters took a picture of me with a cell phone and was peddling it to the tabloids. The waiter got fired, but the rest of the staff weren't so happy about that. And Sunday was coming, with a whole new group of tourists. Never mind the prices at that place. He took me out for a drive one day and we wound up here. He and his wife bought it twenty years ago from a friend. He said they used it maybe twice a year. She died about five years ago of breast cancer, and he's barely used it since. He just asked if I wanted to stay for a while. I went out running the first morning, and everybody was staring at me. Little kids, women carrying laundry baskets, the guy at the jerk stand up by the police station. I came back and said, You know, this isn't going to work, they all recognize me. He's such a nice man, he just gave me this little smile and said, I suspect few of them have ever seen a redhead before. That was it. Isn't that pathetic? These poor people, who get maybe two channels if they even have a television, and I'd convinced myself that I'm so important that they all recognize me. And it's all because I have red hair. Anyhow, I decided to stay."

"For how long?"

Meghan shrugged, took a long pull on her beer and a long pull on the joint. She was staring up at the sky. "You know who I've been thinking about?"

"Who?"

"Mother. Do you remember the bedside table? There were magazines and paperbacks and aspirin and a silver insulated pitcher of tea and a carafe of water and some prescription vials—I'm still not sure what those were—and the telephone and that little date book she had, it had a pink cover and the word *Secretary* on the front in gold script, and God, so much other stuff, sometimes there was a bakery box with cookies, sometimes there was a box of chocolates. And Life Savers. There was always a roll of peppermint Life Savers."

"I remember," I said, and for a moment I did. Not the pitcher or the date book, but the smell, of warm skin, Chanel No. 5, and peppermints. It hovered there on the edge of my memory, then skittered away the way the shooting star had done. The bedroom with its floral spread and slipper chair, the striped walls and the landscape above the bureau, the soft, rather puffy woman saying, "That's a sticky little face! Why is that little face so sticky?" For just an instant I had it. Somewhere it must live within me, but so deep that I would only ever glimpse the edges.

Meghan was talking, her voice slow and soft and changed somehow, the consonants not as sure of themselves as they'd once been. "She'd gotten her whole world down to one room and one trip," she said. "She almost never left that bed until she got up to get dressed and go out, and when she went out she never went anyplace except the club. Even at the club she never went anyplace but the dining room. I used to think she was just lazy. Stupid, too, for the longest time I thought she was stupid. Maybe she was. Hell, I'll never know now. But some nights I lie out here and think she had it all down. She knew where everything was in her room. She knew where everything was in her bathroom. She knew the menu at the club. She knew who would be there. Out the bedroom door, down the steps, into the car, up to the portico at the club, in the door, into the dining room. Then do the whole thing in reverse. There was no reason to do more. There was no reason to go anyplace else." She sighed, and I heard the clink of the bottle against the side of the chaise. The sound made another memory, and another, and I said, "She drank."

Meghan exploded with laughter and grabbed my arm. The smoke from her joint sent a slow coil into the air, and the bats moved off to the perimeter of the patio, down toward the big banana tree. "There's a news flash! She drank! He drank! Everyone drank! Manhattans, martinis, vodka gimlets, whiskey sours. Remember that sweet old man Daddy worked with, Roger Highwater, how plastered he used to get? How he would sing?" I shook my head. "Jesus, Bridget, you have a lousy memory."

"I just remember you. I just remember me and you."

I looked over at Meghan, and tears were bright on her cheeks. The moon was coming up and laying down a silver stripe on the ocean in what seemed like the same place as the gold one had been in the late afternoon. The repetitive trill we were hearing was either a bird, a cricket, or a frog.

"There's something so satisfying," Meghan said, "about living a life like this. You get up and you run a couple of miles. You come home and you eat. You read, you swim. There are three bathing suits, and you put one on. There are three pairs of shorts, and you change into one of them. There are ten books, and you choose one. You read, you swim, you eat, you drink. You sleep. No one needs you to do more. Maybe that was her deal."

"Except for one thing. She had children. Two daughters."

"Maybe she thought we didn't need her. Maybe she thought we had lives of our own and we didn't need her."

"Are you nuts? We were little kids. Of course we needed her."

"Did we? We were at school. Nelly made our meals. What did we need her to do?"

"You don't need a mother to do anything. A mother doesn't prove anything by being there. She proves something by not being there!"

"Ah, so now we finally get down to it." Meghan said the last four words slowly, with ellipses in her voice. Her face was dry now, and her mouth was drawn tight like a drawstring. I realized that she was drunk. Maybe it was only in that blurry netherworld that she'd finally made her peace with what she remembered of our childhood, or with herself.

"I didn't come to fight with you," I said. "I just miss you so much. And Leo does, too. He doesn't say anything, but how would you feel? He comes home from Spain, his mother is plastered all over the papers and his father is living in some hotel in Japan and the apartment where he grew up is empty and it's like he's supposed to roll with it. He can't talk to Evan about you because he thinks it's disloyal, and he can't talk to you because you're out here in the middle of nowhere."

"I've left him lots of messages. Once a week I go to Derek's and I use their phone and call Leo. I even bought a phone card so I could do it. I'm embarrassed at how many messages I've left. When I was at the Cove, I worked out exactly where he'd be and called and called and got nothing but a machine."

"At what number?"

"I don't know. It's Leo's number. His dorm room, I guess."

"He never uses the phone in his dorm room. None of them do. I don't even think they have phones hooked up to the jacks. They all use their cell phones."

"I called him at the apartment, too. I left so many messages at the apartment. Really long messages. Probably ridiculous messages."

"But he never goes there. Don't you have his cell phone number?"

"I do but it's in my own cell phone, and the battery ran out so there's no way for me to get it."

"E-mail? I know I packed your BlackBerry."

"Aah, the BlackBerry. You can't get a signal here. But one day Derek was taking me into town and I turned it on. We were coming over that big mountain and all of a sudden, boom! I'm connected. My God, it was the scariest moment since I've been here. It was like my whole life was sitting in my lap. Two hundred and eighteen messages, and not one from anyone I wanted to hear from. Reporters, co-workers, people who would tell you at a cocktail party they're my friends, only they're not. I felt like the thing had claws."

"So you just gave up on it."

"I tossed it off the end of a pier in town. It's at the bottom of the ocean. Where it belongs, in my opinion."

"That's mature," I said.

My sister set her mouth and looked south over the sea. Finally she said, "Leo could have gotten on the plane with you and be here talking to me right now."

"That's not his job, Meghan. He gets to be the kid. You get to be the mother. He doesn't take care of you. It's the other way around."

"Not always," she said lazily, finishing the joint.

"Come home," I said.

The trilling was loud and rhythmic, and while I waited for her to say something I found myself nearly lulled to sleep. But Meghan's eyes were still open, staring at the stars. She ran her hand through her hair, which curled at the crown like the ringlets she'd had in her baby pictures.

"Home is not a place," she said. "It's a series of arrangements. There is your job, and all the people you know through your job, and all the things that happen because of your job. There are your friends, and all the things you do with your friends, and all the people you meet because of your friends. There are your children. Or, in my case, your child. There is your marriage. It's the biggest arrangement of them all. You make me look smart and I make you look kind. You make me look rich and I make you look generous. You make me look interesting and I make you look credible. That's why after a while it's all one word. Kate-andsam. Motheranddaddy. It sounds like a corporation. It is not about whether people like each other or love each other or have sex with each other or want to be with each other. It is a deal. Does that sound harsh?"

"Yes."

"You are such a baby. Do you remember how you used to sit in your

walker and hold on to the back of my skirt and let me pull you around
the house?"

"No." If I had a memory, it was only one cobbled out of the hundreds
of retellings throughout my life.

"You had this wooden walker with big colored wooden beads on a
metal strip around the edge. I pulled you all over the house. You
couldn't move without me."

"I know."

"I married Evan. I loved him. He loved me. You wouldn't believe how
rare that is. I've met more people who didn't even like each other when
they got married than I can count. Whatever. But after a while you've
heard the same stories and the same jokes over and over. Plus there's all
the small shit. Kate and I got drunk one night and we agreed that if you
could get past listening to him chew you could get past anything. You
could even deal with infidelity if you could deal with the chewing
thing." Meghan made very loud chewing noises. She didn't sound like
Evan, whose habit of taking very tiny bites has always driven me insane.
She sounded exactly like Irving Lefkowitz. Maybe that was the point.

"Evan still insists that there's no one else."

Meghan waved her hand in the air. "Not the point. The point is after
a while you understand that you've made a deal. Meghanandevan. Totally separate from either of you individually. I had this shrink on the
show once who said the biggest single determinant of whether two people stay married is whether they're determined to stay married. I remember Josh called me in because I told the shrink that sounded like a
tautology, and Josh was worried that most of our viewers didn't know
what that meant. Probably because he didn't know what it meant. Jesus.
Josh." Meghan stubbed out the end of her joint on the stone of the patio.
"Now there's something that seems so far away. Josh." In the silence I
could hear what sounded like laughter from the beach. "Anyhow, what?
Oh, the shrink. That shrink was right. You made a deal, you keep to it.
It's like two trees. You can hang a hammock between two trees. You can't
hang a hammock with only one tree, or two trees that are too far apart."

"Did you just make that up?"

"No, Christ, I must be drunker than I thought. It's from some book I once had to interview the author of. God, it's amazing the crap your mind retains. Do I know anything I didn't learn through interviews with idiots?"

"Yeah, so the hammock was for Leo. What about Leo?"

"Leo was supposed to be in Boston this summer working at the public library as an intern, although apparently he changed his mind. Last summer he was down south. He called me twice when he was down there. Not that I'm complaining, but that's how it is. The summer before . . . Oh, damn, I'll remember. London! University College. Leo has a life that doesn't include me. Which is as it should be, I guess. Children stop needing their parents. Parents start needing their kids. Except for us orphans. No hammocks for us." Meghan giggled. "We are hammockless."

"Leo needs you. I need you. I miss you. Come home."

"To what? To a life in which I would be the woman who used to be Meghan Fitzmaurice? To a life as the extra woman at dinner parties where everyone else is married? Have you ever seen an interview with one of those Yankees players who is fat and fifty and standing there listening to someone talk about something great he did twenty-five years ago? That's what my life would be. I remember when Evan used to take me to those business dinners, before the men there were more interested in me than in him. There was this one really nice, smart woman who was always there. Julie. Julie something. And then she just disappeared. And finally I said to one of the other wives, I haven't seen Julie. Where's Julie been? And she said, Oh, her husband left her. Just like that. She'd been disappeared. It wasn't that her husband was gone. Her life was gone.

"Sometimes if I get stoned enough, I look out there and I feel like I can see New York on the horizon," she continued. "You know what it looks like? It looks like a mouthful of sharp silver teeth. It's the scariest thing you'd ever want to see. It's all right if you're nobody, and it's great if you're on the way up. But man, it is a place that is cruel to used-to-bes. Divorced wives, has-been writers, rich guys who aren't rich anymore. Actors who aren't famous anymore. Rise and shine, my Irish ass."

Meghan got up slowly from her chaise and stretched her arms over her head. "I'm going swimming," she said.

"You're crazy. You're drunk."

"You say that like it's a bad thing."

"And it's pitch black out there."

"I know. But if you open your eyes there are glowy things down at the bottom, like lightning bugs in the ocean. Come see."

When we were little, Meghan would put a jar of lightning bugs on the nightstand between our beds. I would go to sleep with the twinkle, first in front of my open eyes, then as an afterimage behind my closed ones. But in the morning the jar was always gone, the creatures freed, probably soon after I fell asleep. I never woke in the night, even when our parents came home late, stumbling up the steps.

This time I had to stay awake until Meghan returned from the endless expanse of black and silver water that lay before me. I was convinced if I didn't she would drown, and then I wondered if perhaps that was the point, that one night she would get wasted enough to stroke stroke stroke toward the horizon and then drift off to sleep above the glowy things. I lay on the chaise and listened to a faint slapping sound and couldn't tell whether it was her tireless arms or the ocean sliding toward and away from shore. There was another shooting star, and another. I closed my eyes for just a minute, and when I opened them again the sky was a clear violet-blue and there was a faint gold nimbus over the mountains as the sun struggled upward. I heard the slapping sound again, but this time it was Meghan's running shoes as they hit the macadam of the main village road outside the gates. "Get up," I think she said before she left, but maybe I just dreamed it.

F THE WORLD were different than it is, if Meghan were different than she is, I would have understood her decision completely. Not only would I have understood, I would have envied her. The air was so light and clear, and it smelled so good, like the water, the flowers, occasionally like the smell of smoke when the stalks of sugarcane were being burned off farther down the island. None of the things that normally concerned us were of any importance. I found it telling that sometimes I would mention something that was utterly of New York, about some acquaintance having a droopy eye because the doctor put the Botox in the wrong place, of another offering Amherst a new dormitory if only the college would accept a C student with a nasty Ecstasy habit. And neither of us could get any traction on the conversation. The thing about New York is that while you are in it, of it, it seems unequivocally the center of the universe. Your metabolism rises to meet it, so that your heart seems to beat faster, your mind to jump more quickly from one thing to another. The earth seems made of concrete all the way down to its core. But far enough away, it seems not only improbable but impossible. As we lay on the dock by the sea or hiked into the hills to see where the coffee grew, the lizards bragging of their prowess with the thrum of the bright flaps of skin at their throats, the hummingbirds hanging with a loud hum over some fuchsia flower, it was not only that the concerns of that other life seemed beside the point. It was that it was impossible to believe that another island, choked with steel uprights, underground trains, endless moving lines of people, existed in the same universe with this one.

I followed her routine. In the morning we had mango and papaya, then swam down to the beach and back. There was a double kayak, and we took it along the coast to a mangrove grove, looking for the crocodiles the fishermen had sworn took shelter there. There was lobster salad for lunch, and a couple of hours of reading in the shade when the sun was at its most brutal. In the late afternoon, Meghan again swam for an hour and I treaded water off the dock or on the narrow strip of sand at the beach while some of the children stripped out of their putty-colored school uniforms and washed themselves. At night, as we had that first night, we had dinner and lay on the chaises, talking. I talked a lot about my work, about the women in my parenting class, about Delon and Annette, about the building collapse and the refugees it had left behind for us to solace. "You should be really proud of what you do," Meghan said softly, and then she cleared her throat and said, "I am really proud of what you do." All these years later and it was just as it had been when I was a girl; my heart inflated with her approbation. The only difference was that when I was younger, when she said my essay was good or my dress was pretty, I thought she was saying so as a kindness. This time I realized she was speaking the truth.

"I should have done more of this kind of stuff in the city," she said the third night, our stomachs filled with goat curry. "Gone out to lunch with you, had a facial, maybe a bikini wax. Forty-seven years old and I've never had a bikini wax."

"You don't want a bikini wax," I said. "I had one once and it was like having your eyelashes ripped out."

"Yow. That's a vivid image. Okay, no waxing. How about a pedicure?"

"Meghan, you did all that stuff."

"No, not the way I'm talking about. Having lunch with the CEO of a publishing company, having a facial once a week to get rid of all the on-air crap in my skin and having it wedged in between a lunch speech and a dinner party—that's not what I'm talking about. I'm talking about living at non-warp speed. Like this."

"This is good. Do you want to snorkel tomorrow?"

"Yeah, let's snorkel. That's not what I meant, though." She reached across the small space between us as we lay on the lounges and took my hand. "I mean just lying around talking about stuff. When's the last time we did this?"

"We never did this."

"Ah, no, that's not true."

"Sure it is. Warp speed and all that."

"What about when we were kids?"

"You always went to bed later than I did. I was asleep by the time you came to bed. You studied a lot harder than I did. Look at what I'm reading." I held up the battered old hardcover I'd found on a bedroom shelf. "*A Tale of Two Cities*."

"Which we had to read in freshman English."

"Yeah, I didn't read it. I read the first chapter and the last chapter, and the paper you wrote on it."

"You get an A?"

"I didn't plagiarize it. I just got a sense of the thing from it. I got a B. I always got a B."

Meghan sighed. "Another obsession that seems incredibly inane at the moment."

"You know when we did this? We did it once. The morning you did the Gregor story."

"Jesus. The Gregor story."

The Gregor story is the linchpin of any profile of Meghan. She was working as a summer intern at the network affiliate in Boston and I was working as a waitress at a tourist trap by Faneuil Hall. She was twenty-one and I was seventeen. Evan was living with us, too, taking a summer class at Harvard in macroeconomics. There was a pullout couch in the living room where I slept. "Shhh, shhh, shhh," I would hear Meghan saying sometimes from the bedroom, when the two of them still had that kind of sex. It was the first time they'd had a double bed for the purpose instead of a college dorm twin.

"She called me once, a couple of years ago. Vanessa Gregor."

"I know. You told me. They're divorced, right?"

"Long time ago. I think they got divorced pretty soon after the fire."

Meghan was out having drinks, after work, late, with a young producer, who'd fallen in love with her, and two camera guys. They were at one of those small neighborhood places in an area where row houses were now called brownstones and the old plumbers and longshoremen were being supplanted by young publishing honchos and associates at law firms. They were all sitting at the front window when they saw flames leap from the third-floor window of a small house wreathed in scaffolding across the street. A man and woman were standing on the sidewalk screaming.

When Meghan had climbed under the covers of the sofa bed with me that morning, she'd still smelled like smoke. "At first I just wanted to help them," she said. "The woman had on this flimsy nightgown. You could see right through it. So I gave her the sweatshirt Al had in his trunk." Through the woman's screams and the sound of sirens growing louder, Meghan made out that the couple had six-month-old triplets. "The very first night! The first night!" the mother kept screaming. The first night in their own nursery on the top floor instead of their parents' room a floor below. Two boys and a girl. Three years of treatments. All the miscarriages. The firefighters tried and were pushed back by the flames. The husband had to be given oxygen in the ambulance, but the wife just kept talking. Her name was Vanessa.

Everything about life is so mysterious. If only the electricians had used a more experienced guy to wire the room instead of the apprentice. If only the smoke detectors had been in the right place instead of a corner of the stairwell where the air stayed deceptively clear. If only the weekend anchor who was dispatched to do the story had not had a flat tire and arrived after the eleven o'clock broadcast had already begun. If only the camera guy had not had an early assignment and so had his equipment in the car.

"I think it's a pretty big story," Meghan had whispered in my ear.

"This is what true tragedy looks like," she began. Her voice was quavering. Her forehead was shiny from the heat, and she wasn't wearing any makeup. There was a smudge of soot near the neck of her white T-shirt. Somehow it made the whole thing more compelling. Three children had died, three children whose parents had gone through years, tears, tens of thousands of dollars to have them. They put Meghan on the late news, but the story was also on the network morning show next day. Vanessa Gregor would not speak with anyone but Meghan. She stayed with the story and was hired the next year. She went network when she was twenty-four. That was her calling card: the story in which she looked like she was in it, instead of outside it.

She had known that morning, waiting for Evan to wake so she could tell him, too. She had been up all night, but she was more awake, more alive, than I had ever seen her. "I felt so bad for them," she said over and over, but then she would describe how she had written a kind of script for herself on a receipt she'd found in her pit of a purse, how she had decided not to put on lipstick, how the executive producer had decided they were cutting it close and had no choice but to let her do it, especially since the police lines had gone up. None of the other reporters could get close; because of the way Vanessa talked to Meghan, the way Meghan put her arm around Vanessa's shoulder, the police assumed she was a friend and left her alone. The camera guy shot her inside the police barricades. It made her seem so much closer to the story than anyone else.

"She's remarried," Meghan said. "They never had kids. I never asked, but I figure she just couldn't handle it. She sent me a crib quilt when Leo was born." Meghan was on the air up until she went into labor, and as she got bigger and bigger, the shots of her got tighter and tighter. She used to joke that in her ninth month she'd be just a mouth saying, "I'm Meghan Fitzmaurice."

"God, the Gregor story. I haven't thought about that in years," I said.

"Neither had I until I got here. But one night at dinner when I was still at the Cove, someone was talking about how she met her husband in the First Class lounge at LAX because her flight was delayed. It was one of those what-if stories, you know, if the flight had gone her life would have been completely different, his life would have been completely different, you know the deal. And all I could think of was all the things that came together on the Gregor story. Ed having his camera, Jill having the flat tire, the fire starting when it did, me eating at that place, I can't remember the name of it, it closed about a year later. And suddenly there I was." She tightened her hand around mine and squeezed. "And suddenly here I am." She smiled.

"Do you think you were so pissed at Greenstreet because of the Gregor story at some subliminal level—you know, because of the kids and the infertility and the surrogate? Or do you think it was all because of what had happened the day before with Evan?"

Meghan smiled again and shook her head. "Nah, I think it was only slightly about the Evan thing, and I don't think it had anything to do with the Gregor triplets. I wish it was that interesting. It was just the truth. I looked at Ben Greenstreet and I listened to him and I said to myself, This guy is a fucking asshole, something I've said to myself a million times before. The difference this time is that I said it out loud. I did the unthinkable. I told the truth on national television. That's what I'm getting killed for. Because if we told the truth, what the hell would happen? If we said, Nice to see you, Stan, but, jeez, this book is boring? If we said, I see you have a new movie and a new husband, isn't that interesting considering you can't act and you're a lesbian?"

"Now that's a show I would watch."

"Yeah, whatever."

"Someone wrote a column saying that, that guy from *The Washington Post*, the contrarian one? He said that you only said what any reasonable person wanted to say."

"Yeah, that and a MetroCard will get me on the subway."

"Maybe there are lots of people who think that."

"Doesn't matter. I'm cooked, Bridge. I told the truth, and I don't think I can stop. I think it's just going to keep tumbling out of my mouth, like the frogs did in that fairy tale." She looked over at me and smiled. "Tell the truth at a Manhattan book party? Tell the truth at a network press conference? Tell the truth sitting at dinner between two of the richest, most powerful, most boring men on earth? It's not that I can't do television. I can't do New York. I'm not even sure I can handle Montego Bay."

Yet in deference to me, two days later she arranged for Derek to take us to town, to Negril. I knew she hadn't been there, had gone only to the outdoor market at a little town about ten miles from the house. I knew it was a mistake as soon as we began to drive through the outskirts of town. It had once been a hippie haven, and it was still trying to hold up its end. The streets were lined with small shops and outdoor kiosks selling tie-dyed shirts, coconut shell bongs, and those knitted hats with Rasta dreads attached that American tourists find so amusing and love to wear for photographs. There were groups of sleepy young men at the street corners dressed like their counterparts in the Bronx—baggy shorts that fell below their knees, elaborate sneakers, the kinds of sleeveless T-shirts Leo and his friends casually called "wife beaters."

Derek was wearing dark dress slacks snugly belted, a pair of woven leather shoes, and a short-sleeved cotton shirt with a muted pattern ironed so professionally that it looked brand-new, although there was a hint of fraying around the back of the collar. That was all I could see of him through most of the ride, but you could read his back like a billboard as we drove on Negril's main street. Over the course of a few minutes, his neck grew longer and stiffer, his shoulders squarer, his chin higher. His disapproval filled the car, competing with my own chagrin. I did not know what Meghan was feeling. She was staring out the window.

We drifted down the street past a pink guesthouse with a ceiling fan whirring in its dim interior to an outdoor café with an enormous sign for Ting and a smaller one for the woman who was running for prime minister. A store sold hand-carved objects, fish and fishermen and women with baskets on their heads. To satisfy outsiders, Jamaica seemed to have conflated itself with all the other Caribbean islands and parts of Africa. There was steel-drum music on an old boom box and caftans of kente cloth. The woman who owned the place followed us around, picking up first one thing, then another: "Very pretty, this. That, too, everyone likes to bring that back home." I noticed that she seemed to be talking mainly to me. Did she recognize in Meghan's mahogany skin and ropy muscles the look of someone who had come to visit and then to stay? We drifted down to what looked like a bargain store catering to locals, and Meghan bought a package of boys' white T-shirts, size small, and some black rubber flip-flops.

On a side street we sat outside and had coffee and some scones. "At least they're not playing Bob Marley," Meghan said wearily, scraping back her damp hair with her fingers. "If I were a performer in this country, I'd hate that guy. It's all they play, everywhere. 'No Woman No Cry'—it's not even that good a song. It's the functional equivalent of Americans playing nothing but Elvis all the time."

"It's the functional equivalent of those cheesy stores in Times Square playing 'New York, New York' all the time. Which is exactly what they do. When Derek passed us on the road the other day, I think he was listening to country western music."

Two sunburned couples shambled by us, carrying beach bags and boogie boards, looking either pissed off or hungover or both, which is so often the case. A man sat down at the next table wearing khaki shorts and a Hawaiian shirt. All beach vacations are the same vacation. He ordered coffee and then opened a copy of *The New York Times*. It was shocking, like seeing a celebrity on the street. A phenomenon with which I was most familiar.

"What's happening in the world?" Meghan murmured.

The man looked at the front page. "The president's poll numbers are down. The Chinese are acquiring Wal-Mart. The Yankees are in a slump. There's no money left in the airline pension funds."

"Same old same old," Meghan said. "Except for the Wal-Mart thing. You made that one up."

"You're a sharp one," he said and went back to reading.

Derek had a friend named Percy, who owned a small boat and took tourists fishing and snorkeling. He lived on a back street that seemed to exist completely apart from the carnival midway quality of the main drag. It was a small cinder-block house painted a clear blue with an immense sailfish stenciled across its front. The fish had been painted around the grilles that covered window openings, so he had a strange curve to his back, as though somewhere in his family tree there was an eel. Derek's friend was dressed much like Derek except that his nicely pressed pants were shorts. His car was parked in the yard and had the words "Searching For Salvation" lettered across the top of the windshield. He offered to drive down to the grimy strip of beach where his powerboat was bobbing off a Styrofoam buoy, but we were just as happy to walk behind him after he'd changed into a pair of what looked like surfer's trunks and a thin T-shirt. He had a pronounced hitch in his step; Derek said he had had a nasty run-in with a propeller. "Very bad," he'd said quietly. In the bottom of his boat, Percy had a mesh bag with snorkel masks, fins, and a pair of water shoes he put on quickly, his back to us, as though it would be impolite to let us see his mangled foot.

After about a half hour of diesel fumes from his outboard, he made a wide U-turn and dropped anchor in perhaps twelve feet of water. The depth was hard to gauge because the bottom was as clear to me as his broad face, sand in remarkably even ridges with waving snake-grass here and there. Farther out we could see the suggestion of outcroppings beneath the surface, and he pointed in that direction as we stripped down to our suits and put our gear on.

Meghan has always liked to snorkel. She used to say it was the only time she really felt alone, although once over a reef in Anguilla someone had actually tapped her on the shoulder, startling her terribly, to ask if she was the morning show woman. ("I get that all the time," she said and went under again.) I like it for exactly the opposite reason, because there's so much company, but perhaps never as much as there was that day. There were snub-nosed fish so blindingly blue and yellow that they seemed to be lit from within, and puffer fish that would drift too close to my waving fingers and then inflate themselves in outrage at the intrusion. There were big schools of black-and-white angelfish, and some little bright yellow guys I didn't recognize. One of them came right up to my mask and stared at me as though he was trying to place the face. They were nibbling at the coral, shifting in the currents, swimming through an outcropping and appearing at the other end. Near the base of the coral, I glimpsed a lobster and an orange eel with an evil underbite.

Meghan stayed beside me for a while, then swam nearby and found a ray half buried in the sand. She dove deep and nudged it slightly with a finger, and it burst from its hiding place and began to propel itself rapidly, skimming the bottom with Meghan swimming strongly behind. I lost her in the fog of sand the ray kicked up, but I knew she would follow it until it had burrowed down again, then look for another. She loves to chase rays, something I've never understood. They frighten me, with their dark wings and their empty eyes.

I came up to look for the boat. It was drifting on its anchor, so it was farther away from us now. Percy had taken off his shirt and stood straight in the bow, then went into the water with almost no sound. He took a long time to surface, then went right down again. I saw Meghan's

snorkel tube up ahead and heard her garbled shout. I swam to her and
into a vast school of small silvery baitfish, thousands, maybe hundreds of
thousands of them, a bolt of rippling silver fabric unfurled in the water.
The sun hit them like sparks. Meghan took my hand, and together we
lay on the surface and watched them, so many of them that it seemed to
take forever for them to pass us by. Then she pulled, and we were following, swimming with and among them. "Paillettes!" I called through my
tube, but she couldn't hear me. We swam in front of them and then back
through them, separating the silver with our hands and our feet, little
wriggles all up and down us until we were both laughing.

It took us a moment to mark the change, the sharper, grittier feeling
on our ankles and a muffled noise to one side of our heads. I looked
down, and a school of large metallic fish were coming up from beneath
us, their mouths agape. And from above dozens of gulls were diving,
their sharp beaks indiscriminate as they tore through the water. Birds
and big fish, they were all around us, everywhere, tearing up, tearing
down, the water a whirlwind of sharp hard biting things, and for just a
moment, in a primitive gesture, we both thrashed in the water, our arms
outstretched, pushing back. I was stunned by the violence, by the power
of the natural world around us and how the birds and their prey were
blind to the two impotent humans who had blithely intruded. I inhaled
water through my snorkel tube, choked and coughed, surfaced to the
sight of the birds, spit swiftly. Then I grabbed Meghan's hand, took a
deep breath, and dove down, pulling her with me, hoping she had had
the wherewithal to hold her breath. The melee continued, and I prayed
we could get free from it, all the boiling roiling water and the casual in-
stinctive violence.

I got water in my tube again and started to cough, and when I came
up the boat was in front of us. I pulled on Meghan's hand. She felt like
dead weight as I towed her behind me, and I held on to her until Percy
pulled us one at a time into the boat, struggling to get me over the side.
We both lay on the floor, which was a little slimy. Meghan had a divot
ripped from the spot where her forehead met her scalp, and another on
one hand. Both were trickling blood.

"Oh my God," I said, and I started to shake.

Meghan lifted her hand to her brow. "I'm bleeding," she said. "I'm bleeding pretty badly."

"Me?" I said.

"I don't think so. Wow. Wow. That was scary."

"That is a very dangerous situation," Percy said. "I am very sorry. I did not see the birds until they were already diving. Should we find the doctor?"

"No, no. It was just very frightening. Have you ever been in there when that's happened?"

He shook his head. There were fine drops of water in his hair like crystal beads. "When we are diving and we see the baitfish, we move away. Soon there will be large fish, then large birds. One of my friends was once hit in the head by a pelican beak when he ventured too near. He lost an eye." He started the boat hastily and ripped toward shore.

Meghan leaned in and spoke into my ear over the noise from the outboard. "Have you ever noticed that everything said in an English accent sounds intelligent and everything said in a Jamaican accent sounds copacetic?" Her voice turned low and musical. "Ya, mon, he lost an eye. No problem. Jesus."

We were both quiet as the dock grew closer, both still breathing hard. On the shore, we pulled our clothes on over our wet suits. Derek's car was waiting next to the sailfish mural. He was giving lollipops to three small children in the yard. When he saw Meghan, he said something in patois to Percy in a dark voice. The children scattered like frightened fish. In his trunk he had a first-aid kit, and he put cream and a butterfly bandage on Meghan's forehead as she sat on the shallow front step of Percy's house.

"It's no big deal," she kept repeating. "I'm fine."

Back at the house, she walked directly from the car down the steps to the dock and stripped off her damp clothes. I followed slowly and sat watching her as she churned methodically, straight out into the setting sun and then back, out again and then back. After all those years of people counting off the seconds into her earpiece, I swear she has time wired into every bit of her body, so that it was almost exactly one hour when she climbed out. The butterfly bandage was somewhere floating in the Caribbean, and the triangular wound had stopped bleeding, but it looked deeper now. If she'd still had her old job, we would have been on a small plane to Miami and the office of a plastic surgeon, who would have dined out on saving Meghan Fitzmaurice's looks.

"Bridget, it's a cut. Stop looking at me as though I have forehead cancer."

"When was your last tetanus shot?"

"I had one two years ago when I did the show from that neighborhood where the plane crashed." She put her hands in her hair. "Jesus Christ, my whole life sounds surreal. I had a tetanus shot because I was talking into a microphone while standing in the wreckage of people's lives."

"It's your job," I said, picking up her clothes from the dock.

"That's what I'm saying. How strange is that? How sad is that? Hello, Mrs. Smith? I hear your husband is burned over half of his body. Oh, you want my autograph? Sure—but how about a wedding picture as a swap? It's a great visual! You want your picture taken with me? But what about your husband? Yep, still on the critical list."

"You're in a foul mood," I said, starting up the stairs.

Derek's wife had made some sort of fish in a pastry crust with rice and the callaloo again. For dessert there was banana ice cream. Meghan ate almost nothing. She drank nearly a full bottle of wine. She ate two spoonfuls of dessert, then wandered away from the table to stretch out on one of the chaises on the patio, one thin ankle over the other. And suddenly I did remember something about our mother, about the way twice a year she would make trips to New York for shopping and lunch, and how afterward she would be a flagrant dumb show of exhaustion, sighing, slumping, blue shadows beneath her eyes and at her temples, her soft white skin a faint gray. She would lie in bed wearing a pretty bed jacket for several days, shaking her head at the crowds, the crush, the end of the attentive salesperson and the well-made daiquiri. When I was little, I suddenly remembered, I had thought of going to New York as something like the time Meghan and I got lost in the woods behind the house and emerged on the wrong side of town, scratched, bitten, and bleeding. The saleswomen at Saks were mosquitoes, Fifth Avenue lined with brambles.

"That poor bastard," Meghan finally mumbled. "He probably took one look at the blood and thought he was well and truly screwed for all time. Derek talks him into taking these important Americans out in his boat, and one of them pulls a Tippi Hedren and gets pecked to death by birds. I wish I understood patois. I figure Derek said, Yo, man, you want to kill the white she-devils and get me fired?"

"Oh, please," I said. "They were both really worried."

"Yeah, right. I'd hate us if I were them. You know what one of the guys in town said one morning? I was running past the jerk stand, and I hear someone say, 'Get a job, missus.' I turned around, and there were three guys smiling at me. I still think it was the one with the gold tooth. You have to be pretty sharp, to get a gold tooth all the way out here."

"Everyone I've met has been really nice."

Meghan looked over at me with a half smile. "Ah, Bridget. The pure of heart. The friend to all humanity."

"Oh, shut up. I'm going inside if you don't stop. You're completely plastered and you're also being a complete bitch. All I want to do is be with you."

"No you don't. All you want is for things to be the way they were."

"Well, things were pretty good the way they were."

Meghan laughed, a deep throaty sound that was as unpleasant as a death rattle must be. "You have no idea, Bridget. I hated my life. I hated almost everything about it. I hated what I did at work, I hated how I always had to play a role, I hated that Evan and I had to pretend in front of people all the time that we were the happiest people on earth. I hated that I had no one to talk to about how much I hated everything. And I hated it even more because everyone else thought it was so great and that meant I couldn't even get out of it. Do you know what happened the week before it all blew up? I had a mammogram, and they came back in and said they had to shoot more pictures of one breast. And my first thought was Thank God, if I've got cancer I can stop. I thought that if I had cancer I could go home, get into bed, and watch old movies and cook soup from scratch. I could stay in my sweats all day and read trashy novels."

"Oh, give it a break. You wouldn't last a week."

She looked over at me, and in her eyes was a combination of shock and fury. "You wouldn't have taken a shot like that at me six months ago."

"I wasn't trying to take a shot. I was drawing an obvious conclusion."

"And a wrong one. All I was saying was that I kept thinking if I was sick, I could have a real life, a life like other people have."

"How could you not have told me you were feeling this way?"

"How could I even admit it? The whole world is telling you you have the perfect life. How can you say that you're trapped in a cage?"

"So get out of it. Do something else."

"Oh, Bridget," she said with a sour chuckle, picking up her rum punch. "What does someone like me do? Close your eyes and picture it, the way I have a million times lying out here. Meghan Fitzmaurice, covering the city council for the local network affiliate? Meghan Fitzmaurice, city editor of the local paper? Second-grade teacher? ER nurse? If you get too famous in America, you can't go down, you can only go out. I'm on the ledge and the window is closed. I lie out here every night and I'm glad I'm not getting up while it's still dark to read some crap off a teleprompter about some missing woman that no one's going to care about in six months. I'm glad I don't have to sit next to the governor at dinner and pretend he's interesting when he's the most boring man on earth. I hated that life. But it's ruined me. It's ruined my chances at anything else. I can't even reject it now because the whole world would think it was an excuse."

"Who cares what the world thinks?"

"Oh, honey, it's a little late for that attitude now."

"I feel as though you hid everything from me."

"Of course I did. You got all the best parts of my life, Bridge. And you loved it. How could I tell you how I really felt? I used to watch your eyes, at the dinner parties, at the screenings, when someone would talk to me on the street. You loved it. You loved the movie stars and the VIP entrance and the greenroom and the First Class lounge. You were hypnotized just like all the rest."

"Is that why you didn't tell me? Or did you want me to be just like everyone else, thinking you had the perfect husband and the perfect kid and the perfect life? You didn't have to be a martyr. I'm your sister. I'm not some groupie standing outside the studio with a hand-knitted afghan and a sign that says RISE AND SHINE."

"Oh, and you really wanted to know the truth, didn't you? Grow up. You're the one who gets to have illusions. I'm the one who has to deal with reality. That's *our* deal. Someone has to be the bitch so someone else gets to be the nice one. Someone has to be the one who pushes so someone else gets to be the one who takes it easy. Someone has to be the driven one so someone else can take their time and figure things out and follow their bliss." She was singsonging, mocking me, leaning forward with her eyes narrowed, the words tumbling from her slack mouth. The notch at her hairline glowed red. There was no doubt that she'd have a scar. "Someone has to be in charge so someone else can relax. Someone has to be willing to do everything so someone else can do nothing."

I felt sick to my stomach, and my voice was unsteady. "Jesus, Meghan. You sound like you hate me."

She fell back heavily onto the lounge and closed her eyes. There were no birds calling, no sounds from the beach or the boats. Finally there was just the sound of deep breathing, and I thought she had either fallen asleep or passed out from the sheer power of everything she'd said. I began to cry.

"I wasn't talking about you. I was talking about everybody. Everybody in the world. I don't hate you," she finally whispered. "I love you. You and Leo. You're the best things I ever did. But sometimes at night I'd sit in the kitchen of that apartment and I'd be so lonely and I'd think, What happened? It's not that it's a bad life; it's just so not real. The apartment, the cars, the speeches, the lunches, the show—none of it's real. Three real things: Evan. Leo. You. Evan's gone. Leo's going."

"Leo will always be around. Me, too."

"You know what the opposite of 'rise and shine' is, Bridge? 'Good night, and good luck.' But look what I have to show for it. A son who went to the annual mother-son school breakfast with his aunt, and a whole roomful of plaques and plates and crystal good-for-nothing things with my name on them. I don't hate you. I hate me." And then she was asleep, snoring faintly, her mouth open.

In the middle of the night, a bird cried loudly and woke me, and I looked over and she was gone. I looked into her room, but the bed was still made as Derek's wife had left it that morning, a white square floating in the black of the unlit interior. I was afraid that she had tried to go swimming again and I started down to the dock, but after only a few steps I was stopped by the shadows, the black spaces beneath the enormous canopy of rhododendron leaves, monochrome in the darkness, and the sharp profiles of bamboo and banana trees. The dock was partially in light, and I could see that there were two people on it, naked and entwined. I could not see their faces. I stepped back quickly and fell over an uneven step, then went inside but scarcely slept until morning, when I dozed off until I heard the sound of running shoes hitting the macadam out front.

At breakfast we had papaya with lime wedges and some kind of gingerbread. The coffee was strong, and the steam veiled our faces as we bent over it. "Whoa, honey, was I drunk last night!" Meghan said with a laugh as though nothing had happened. And somehow, with that one sentence, the sort of thing that is tossed off in every office in New York nearly every morning, to excuse everything from public urination to adultery, I knew that she would return. I didn't know when or how. But perhaps because our day trip had taken her a little too close to the world she'd left behind, or simply because she had finally revealed so much, she had recovered the muscle memory of how to lie, how to lie fluently, easily, as a matter of course. Who could blame her? Lying is always easier than telling the truth.

The next morning she stood on the drive with the sun behind her as I got into the car to go to the airport, and she put her hands on my shoulders and smiled a pure and simple smile. There were so many things I wanted to tell her and talk to her about, but during the course of the week there had not been the right time, the right place, the right opening. "You know what's so great about this place?" she said. "You can see everything so clearly here. You're on your own, kid. Take care of yourself." She started to walk into the house, then turned at the door. "Tell Leo to listen to those messages. Tell him I poured out my heart. Tell him he needs to come and see me. Tell him we'll talk."

GOT HOME on a Saturday night, which is the official moment of the city of New York. When I return after even a week away, I am always struck by it again, the bulk of it against the sky, the dwindling perspective drawings of the streets, the way everything is available here, everything possible: Ethiopian food, gay group sex, designer clothes for dogs, druggy dance clubs, six-foot-long hero sandwiches, all-night dry cleaners. New York runs on its own digitalis. One moment your heart is thump-thumping in a normal fashion. The next it's staccato, double time, leap-a-leap. "I love this girl!" someone screamed from the window of a taxi as I walked down Sixty-ninth Street in a light spring mist.

There was a note from Leo: "Went to Newport for the weekend. Love you a lot. Bought apples." He had, two dozen of them. Young men do not understand the basic law of produce: Things rot. Even apples. He had cleaned the apartment in his fashion. The sofa bed was folded into place, although a long tail of top sheet trailed from one corner of the cushion onto the floor. The dishwasher had been unloaded, although everything that had been in it was huddled together on the counter like a motley collection of glass and china friends. In the center of my bed a black-and-white kitten was sleeping. My grown cat, Kitty Foyle, was hunched like an orange meat loaf in the chair in the corner, keeping watch. She looked baleful. When she saw me, she moaned.

"Life is a constant surprise with kids," I remembered saying to Irving one evening after Leo had visited.

"Yeah, I got enough surprises in my life," Irving said. "Surprises are one of the few things I got in spades."

I was glad Leo was away, even though it meant the kitten would be a mystery for another day. The apartment felt quiet and peaceful. Nearly every drawer was open about an inch, and I went around the apartment closing them all. I await the research on why a person carrying a Y chromosome is unable to close a drawer entirely. "What?" Irving always said. "It is closed."

Inside the all-night Duane Reade drugstore, a Muslim girl in a head scarf was working the register alone. In the back, a thin man in a windbreaker was reading *Car and Driver*. An elderly man who lives on my block patrolled the aisle with his wheeled walker. It has a little basket screwed to the front, like a bicycle, and each day he comes into Duane Reade to buy just one thing. That way he will have errands to fill each day of the week. "Antacids," he was mumbling to himself. "Which aisle is antacids?" These are rhetorical questions. He doesn't like it if you answer him.

On the street, it was a party. Four couples came tumbling out of the Greek restaurant, the women loudly shouting something at one another of the "I was right, wasn't I?" variety. The men were unwrapping cigars and biting dramatically at the ends. Through the front window of one of the brownstones, trapped in a square of amber light, I could see a man and a woman in the foreground of some gathering, her head tipped toward him but turned down, his shoulder swiveled so it would touch her bare arm. He spoke and her chin floated north and she laughed, put out a hand to touch his arm, then drew back and lifted a glass to her lips. New York is full of pantomime. Once I watched an entire marriage proposal through the front window of a French restaurant from a coffee shop across the street. I could tell by the way the woman looked down at her ring that she found it a disappointment, and I wondered whether coincidence might be mischievous and allow me someday to see the night when she would throw it at him and break the engagement or, later still, demand a divorce.

On the stoop next to my building, a clutch of high school students were smoking cigarettes. One girl was wearing a frayed jacket that I'd seen in a magazine at the nail parlor; I remembered that it retailed at sixteen hundred dollars. "We do the same thing every weekend," she was saying. Probably it was true. The celebrity pizzeria, the walk through the Sheep Meadow in Central Park, the smoke on the West Side stoop, the drinking at the apartment where the parents were in Paris and the son said pugnaciously that if anyone touched the sculpture, they would die. Even New York kids who are not spoiled are spoiled just by waking up every morning with the UN blocking the view of the river from their bathroom window. Once I'd realized that my mother was wrong when she behaved as though the city was the most exhausting of enterprises, I had been on the train from Connecticut and in the city at every opportunity. There was a time when I thought the most exotic words in the world were "sushi on St. Mark's Place." When I'd gone into hiding on City Island, it was not to find peace and quiet but to place myself in the purgatory I believed I deserved.

Meghan had refused to go with me to the airport. She said it was because if Negril was depressing, Montego Bay would be unbearable, that she hated long car rides and her head ached slightly. But I thought Negril had suggested that there was a life beyond the bedroom with its plantation furniture, the patio with its chaises, the spliff and the swim and the dock. She was putting her hands over her ears to blot out its siren song. The morning of my flight a fax had flown across the kitchen floor. The network was formally cutting off her salary.

"Good thing I have thirty million bucks in investments," she said airily, waving it in front of her.

When she'd held my face in her hands the way she used to do sometimes when we were small, when she'd said, "You take care of yourself," it would have been the perfect time to blurt out my suspicions. Of course I should have done that that first night or the third or even in the car home from Negril, when I'd had to ask Derek to pull over so I could throw up by the side of a pasture filled with goats. But I'd told myself I wasn't certain, though the voice of running commentary in my brain—the voice that sometimes sounds suspiciously like Meghan's TV voice—was telling me that I was full of it. There's also a voice in my head that sounds remarkably like Tequila's; add the occasional bromide from my aunt Maureen, and it's impossible to imagine how I can hear myself think. As I'd stood at the counter of the drugstore and laid down a pint of rocky road ice cream, a Whitman's Sampler jumbo collection of creams, and a home pregnancy test, the Tequila voice muttered sarcastically,

"You got the candy, you got the ice cream, don't need to be bothering with the E.P.T. test because you know the answer."

The candy wasn't mine anyhow. Sunday morning I got up early into the milky white light and the city streets, which are deserted then, and always dirty with the sordid debris of weekend parties. I bought some bagels and cream cheese and packed them into a bag with the Whitman's Sampler, and took the train to Westchester. Our aunt Maureen lives in a faux Tudor building there, a place for older people, mainly women, that provides what are called support services, which means there's a free van for shopping and lunch outings and organized trips a couple of times a month to the Manhattan museums or theaters.

"There's my girl," she said as she opened her door, throwing her arms around me and taking the tote from my hand. "Coffee's on." Meghan says Maureen is the only person outside of commercials who actually says that: Coffee's on.

It's impossible to visit the apartment and not go immediately to the window, which frames a slice of one of the broadest parts of the Hudson River. There's a fringe of trees on the bank and, across the sweep of ruffled gray-green water, a steep embankment that looks as wild as it was when the Indians were the only people in New York, living a peaceful and uneventful life that would soon be marked by slaughter and betrayal. Maureen has a telescope on a stand, and an overstuffed chair that gives you mainly a view of treetops and sky. The light and the water are completely different, but in some ways it felt like the house where Meghan was living.

"You look wonderful," my aunt said, handing me a mug that said YOU ARE #1! on it. "Did you have a wonderful time?"

"*Wonderful* is not the word I'd use. It was weird, because for all the time the two of us spend together, we both realized we never really have that much time to talk. Really talk, I mean. But we really really talked. Let's just say that Meghan opened her mouth and everything came out."

"Like Pandora's box," Maureen said evenly. "Our Meg has had a lot to think about." Except for Evan, Maureen is the only one who is permitted to call Meghan by a diminutive. It is always preceded by the word *our*, and it occurred to me some time ago that it was to make the distinction between our Meg and their Meghan, the real woman and the public figure. Maybe there would no longer be the need for such a distinction.

"Did you have any idea of how unhappy she's been?"

"Oh, Bridget. Meghan has never been happy, not really. She has a little motor inside her, and it drives her. The problem is that when you have that kind of motor, there isn't really any destination. So then what do you do? You go as far as you can. But it's never quite far enough. This used to be a problem only for men, but now you girls have managed to make it your own along with everything else."

"Well, you know, this is all making me a little angry, because I thought things were pretty good. I mean, I knew her life was stressful. But I didn't think it was truly terrible. And now it turns out everyone knew but me. And I should have known before anyone."

Maureen went back into the kitchen to refill her own cup, and I went over to look at the photographs covering the wall of the dining nook. It ought to be the Meghan Fitzmaurice wall, of course. There is a photograph of Meghan with a small wizened man who, upon close examination, turns out to be the chief justice of the Supreme Court. There is Meghan at the Oscars, surrounded by movie actors and looking like just one of the crowd.

But there is me, too, at my graduation from Smith, standing on a beach in the Hamptons one summer, pretending to give Leo a good sock in the jaw while he holds his palms up and out, his eyes wide in play-horror. If you count the photographs on Aunt Maureen's wall, the number will always be equal. There will never be more space given to one niece than to the other. I know because I've counted. Maureen and our mother had been two sisters, too, and although she never said so, it was clear to me in hindsight that our aunt was bound and determined to see that in our case neither felt less favored.

"Do you know you don't have a picture up here of the two of us together?" I said.

My aunt Maureen nodded sharply. "I have one. It's that sweet one of the two of you with your arms around each other standing on the porch when you were young. It's on my bedside table. But here, no. Here the two of you are separate."

"Why? It seems so counterintuitive."

"Because you are separate, Bridget."

"Well, there's no denying we're different."

"Of course you are. I read a book or two when you first came to live with us, mainly to learn how to cope with Meghan. She was so angry, and it was difficult to think she wasn't angry at me."

"I know the feeling."

"She wasn't, you know. She was just angry at the way things turned out. And even then there was that motor. I think she was angry at how it drove her. In any event, one of the books I read said that the second child occupies the territory not already claimed by the first."

I laughed. "Ah. That's how I got penniless obscurity."

Maureen shook her head. "I would hope that one of the lessons of your trip was that that is not how things have turned out in the least."

"Do you think that accounts for my job? That being a social worker is being the anti-Meghan?"

"Now, it's funny that you should see it that way. I always assumed that your job was by way of imitating me. Maybe I was flattering myself."

"You could never flatter yourself as much as you deserve," I said, and I hugged her. "But here's something that worries me: If the second child gets the stuff the first doesn't want, what does that say about an only child? Where does that leave Leo?"

"I suspect an only child can either be everything or anything he pleases. Leo's taken the second tack. I wouldn't worry about that boy."

"I've never really been worried about Meghan before," I said, staring out into the tree branches.

"I don't believe that for a moment," Maureen said.

"She's really thin," I said.

"That's not new."

"Really thin. Thinner than she's been before."

Maureen got up from the table and went into the other room, came back with one of the supermarket tabloids. I looked at the front page. An aging movie star had found out her husband was gay. The lead singer of a band was sleeping with his ex-wife's sister. At the bottom was a small grainy photograph and a headline: "Meghan in Rehab?" The photo showed a redheaded woman in a hospital gown attached to an IV walking down a hospital corridor. The picture was shot from the back. At least the woman, whoever she was, had not had the humiliation of having her gown gape in back as hospital gowns are so wont to do.

"She's at some place in Colorado. The one they said that young actress went to last year."

"Or not. Because since we know Meghan isn't there, maybe that girl wasn't there, either. Maybe no one has ever been there. Maybe the place in Colorado doesn't even exist. Maybe Colorado doesn't exist. When did this come out?"

"I've been getting sympathetic looks at bridge for three or four days, so probably then. I was just worried that Leo might have seen it, or heard about it. I spoke to him Tuesday night. He seems to be enjoying his job. He said he had a surprise for you when you got back. I hope it's a good surprise. I've noticed that children's surprises sometimes tend to be a little miscalculated, if you get my drift."

I laughed; I was remembering a lifetime of unfortunate surprises. Aunt Maureen doesn't really care for surprises, perhaps because there were so many enormous ones: the fact that she never had children herself, that she was left almost overnight with her sister's instead of her own. That's why she likes the Whitman's Sampler instead of fancier chocolates. They still print a chart on the inside lid so you know exactly what you're getting.

"Like the box of baby ducks for Easter?" I asked.

"That comes to mind. And the time you cut your own hair. And when you painted the words to some poem on the walls of your room."

"Walt Whitman. *Leaves of Grass.*"

"I think Leo is past the writing-on-walls phase."

"Leo lives in a place where, if you want poetry on the walls, your mom hires a painter who does it in script and illuminates the letters appropriately."

"Don't be harsh. Besides, that nonsense doesn't have its claws into him. Look at that job you've gotten him. How many of those boys could do that job and win the trust of those people you work with? He's kept his footing. Our Meg, too."

"I think maybe she's lost her footing."

"She'll be fine."

"She says she can't come back."

Maureen poured us both more coffee. Her mug said NURSES DO IT WITH TENDER LOVING CARE.

"She just needs to use her imagination. She should use you as her model. You always found a way to reinvent yourself."

"Is that what we call it? I thought I was drifting aimlessly."

Maureen put her mug down with a heavy thunk. "No, you didn't. You thought Meghan thought you were drifting aimlessly. And she did, and it distressed her, not because it was a bad thing, but because it was something she had no knack for." Maureen picked up the blue bowl in the center of the table and took out the apples inside it, lining them up by her plate. She flipped the bowl over and pointed to my initials on the bottom. "You've done a lot that's concrete," she said. "Things that last. Don't underestimate that."

Perhaps it was the bowl, and the faint memory of how beautifully I'd shaped the clay, how the roundness had risen under my cupped hands as I'd sat at the wheel. But I suddenly found myself on the verge of tears. I opened my mouth, suspended in that state in which it seems that two ways are possible but one will grow fainter and then disappear as the words roll out on your tongue, as though just past your lips one possibility will vanish like the Cheshire Cat, leaving only a shimmering hint of its former self. It's that moment before you lean in to kiss a new man, the moment when you hold the unopened letter from a college in your hand, the moment when you know you are going to go one way or the other.

"I'm pregnant," I said.

"Well, that's a surprise."

"To me, too. I thought I was going through menopause."

"What are you going to do, Bridget?"

"I'm going to have a baby," I said, and a shiver shook me. It was the first time I had said the words aloud.

"I think that's a wonderful idea. Wonderful. The best idea in the world. How very lucky you are. Forty-three years old and pregnant." She took my hand in hers and smiled softly, my aunt who had been betrayed by her own barrenness, who had had to take secondhand motherhood.

"Irving doesn't want children."

"So what does he say about this one?"

"He doesn't know. I haven't told him. I didn't tell Meghan, either. I wasn't sure and I was afraid of what she'd say. You're the first person I've told."

Maureen sipped her coffee and smiled. "That makes sense. After all, I'm the grandma."

"And you're not upset?"

"Because you're not married? Oh, pooh. Two wonderful people with a baby they will both love. Think about what a great life she will have. Or he. But I have to admit, I'd love to have another girl. I bet a little girl would bring Irving around."

"He's pretty adamant about this. I'm not sure anything is going to bring him around. I might have to do this by myself."

Maureen stood to clear the plates. "Don't get up," she said. "Is that why you didn't drink your second cup of coffee? Do you need the name of a good OB? I still have an excellent medical network."

"I think I have a line on a woman that everyone seems to really like. But unless Meghan comes back soon, I might need a Lamaze partner." I had been Meghan's Lamaze partner. Evan faints during the company blood drive. They brought him in at the crucial moment to cut the cord and wound up having to give him oxygen and put him on a stool at one side of the birthing room.

Aunt Maureen put a glass of orange juice in front of my place. "If you need me, I will willingly be the oldest person on earth to go to Lamaze classes. But you shouldn't worry about Irving. The problem is that when most people think of having children, they think about having other people's children. They look at a bunch of four-year-olds screaming on the playground or some nasty teenager snarling at his parents and think, Not me. And then someone hands them their own child. And all of that other nonsense is forgotten. Irrelevant. They change in an instant."

She put the apples back in the bowl one by one. "It might not have happened to me with a baby in a hospital. But it happened to me, so I know exactly what I'm talking about."

MONDAY MORNINGS IN my part of the Bronx are quieter than you'd expect. Certainly quieter than Mondays on my Manhattan block, when the graphic artists, corporate lawyers, midlevel managers, and ad execs come trudging out of their lobbies and down their stoops, the *Times* tucked under their arms, the grim determination of the dedicated joyless worker in the set of their mouths and their shoulders.

But when I get off the train in the Bronx on Monday morning, the feeling of the place is different. Even the sandwich shop, with its siren smell of processed meat, is sleepier than usual. Ricky, who owns it, named it the Cubana Sandwich Shop even though he is Puerto Rican because he says everyone hates Puerto Ricans. His mother tends the plants on the sill, the world's largest and leggiest geraniums and an assortment of snake plants in terra-cotta pots, the kinds of plants that are purely an exercise in survival, not a display of beauty. Farther up the block there are a few shopkeepers sweeping Sunday's garbage into the gutter and some kids heading for school late with preternaturally furrowed brows. But in our neighborhood Monday morning is a bit of a sleeping-in day. Of course some people are long gone by the time I break into sharp daylight from the disorienting fluorescence of the subway station. The people who have to be at work at six, the people who clean the trains, who make the school breakfasts—their day is already half gone when mine begins. But many of the others are in bed, exhausted, from a weekend of work. Vacuuming corner offices, busing tables of twelve on Lexington Avenue, selling fruit and baked nuts from stands along Sixth Avenue to tourists who act as though they've never seen an almond. No Monday through Friday for the working poor: they take it where they can find it. Once I heard a young cop say that the streets were quiet on Monday morning because they were all on the government tit. Irving had been with me, picking up sandwiches at the Cubana for a bunch of guys working a big drug bust over at Hunts Point. He flicked the young guy. Flicking is the most demeaning thing an older officer can do to a young one, as though to suggest he's such an insect he's not worth a good slap. "Don't be ignorant," Irving said.

At my office I figured it wouldn't be slow at all. Mondays are almost always busy for us. Saturday dinners turn into Saturday parties turn into Saturday arguments. That's true everywhere, from Fifth Avenue to Staten Island, but in the precarious lives many of my women live, a Saturday argument can turn into Sunday morning on the street, a sister or an aunt whispering, "I'm sorry, baby, but he just don't want you here no more." There were more fires on the weekends, too, and more DV incidents, which is what we call it when a guy gets pissed that his wife is pissed that he has a pregnant girlfriend and turns her arm at that funny angle that makes it go snap so loud the kids, hiding in the next room, can hear it. Actually, sometimes we get the pregnant girlfriend instead, who's gotten kicked in the stomach because she wants to know when he's going to leave the wife. The answer being, When hell freezes over. Or, as Tequila said after one of her volcanic chesty "Huhs," "When Jesus climbs down from the cross, walks into Mickey D's, and orders an extra-value meal with a chocolate shake."

But my first day back at the office was quiet and the news was good. Two of our residents had gotten jobs. One lady who lunches sent up a flare for a housekeeper; another saw a sign for a job at a fancy take-out joint and called Alison to have one of our residents come down and try out. In New York it is, of course, who you know, even when you are homeless and are qualified only for a job that revolves around ammonia, rubber gloves, and a dust mop.

"Delon is going into a preschool program in the fall for toddlers." Mary, who oversees the kids at the transitional housing building, read from her notes at our staff meeting. "Annette is on a list for Section Eight housing. She may get a one-bedroom by July."

I nodded. Toddler programs are good. Housing is good. My mind was as untethered as a balloon with a snapped string. Perhaps it was the knowledge that by the time Annette got into Section 8 housing I would be in maternity clothes. How thrilled my parenting class women would be! Perhaps it was that Leo had not come home the evening before and that I was concerned about his welfare. "Where do you think he can be?" I'd asked Kate when I called to report on Meghan. "Probably wherever he is when he's at college and he's out all night," she said. "Calm Mom," Kate's coffee cup at Maureen's would have read.

Or perhaps it was being able to see Meghan now in my mind's eye, her arms moving so swiftly and surely through the lapis water, the muscles of her legs in high relief beneath the freckles and the dark skin, the drink and the joint in her hand. Soon I would have to send her a fax: BABY. Baby baby oh baby.

And of course there was Irving. I had been rehearsing a conversation with Irving for weeks now. They say that women intuitively know when they are pregnant—or, as one of my parenting students had once said, "I felt that bomb drop!"—and this had been true in my case. I had intuitively known it when I threw up at the faintest smell of clam sauce. I had intuitively known it when the idea of hot dogs made me nauseous. But I had ignored my intuition. There is something faintly ridiculous in pregnancy over forty-three.

It is more than faintly ridiculous to take a home pregnancy test, too, which I had found out Saturday night when I squatted over a stick in my windowless bathroom. And then it had occurred to me that that was the point. A dignified way of getting the news would not be the right preparation for what was to come: skirts with elasticized pouches, the signature flat-footed waddle, and the eventual intimate involvement in the bodily functions of another human being, one who would spit up on you as soon as look at you.

"Madonna and child," Meghan had said drily one morning as the nanny held the baby and she finished using an electric breast pump, which looked like a mysterious home appliance. She'd had one in her office, too, in the drawer beneath her Emmys. Maybe I could bring the actual baby and breast to the office instead. But that was among the logistics I hadn't figured out yet, including how I was going to afford

anything better than a resident delivering his first baby on our paltry
health insurance plan, how I was going to be able to buy diapers on my
good-works salary, and where I was going to put a baby in a one-bedroom
apartment. "They have kids, they wind up in the burbs," Irving had once
said with a shrug. Irving uses the term *burbs* the way epidemiologists use
the term *cholera epidemic*.

For a sixty-seven-year-old man raised by what sounds in anecdote like
the most fearful woman on earth and two older sisters whose motto was
apparently "I'm allergic," Irving is remarkably flexible, perhaps because
he's had to adapt to two wives and many girlfriends over his adult life.
There are few things on which he absolutely insists: white clam sauce,
not red; a suit and tie, not simply a jacket, in temple or church; no side-
burns under any circumstances; and no children. There was no negoti-
ating position in the news I had to deliver.

"We got to decide whether we're going to keep this chess club just for
our kids or for the whole neighborhood," Mary said, looking over her
notes.

"Since when do we have a chess club?" I said, shaking myself awake.

"Leo did it," Alison said. "We all let him go ahead because, honestly,
I don't think any of us thought the kids were going to go for chess. But
apparently he got them so invested in the knights and the king and some
story he told about all of them that there's a group who are playing every
day after school. He's got a couple of the middle school kids who
brought friends home, and the next thing we know we've got ten kids in
the living room playing or looking over each other's shoulders."

"You're a star!" I said after lunch at my desk, chicken soup and
saltines and Lord let it stay down, when Leo came banging into the
outer office.

"Wait, wait, hold that thought," he said, collapsing into the chair
across from my desk. Did they all do that, enter a room as though they
were ransacking it, fall into a chair as though they had been felled by a
blow or had fainted away? Suddenly I looked at Leo and saw him as a
succession of people—a baby, a toddler, a boy, a man. I looked down at
my lap and saw the future.

"First, can we keep the kitten? Second, how's my mom? Third, why am I a star? Fourth, have you seen Irving?"

"Yes, good, chess, no."

"Wow." He pitched forward, his elbows on my desk. "That was cool." He messed around with his hair, although it was hard to tell what effect he was after. If it was neatening, he'd missed it. "So, okay, we can keep the kitten, which is great. I found her in the yard and she was really freaking out, crying and everything, and I had to bring her home in my backpack, and man, that was an experience, let's just say I can't use that backpack anymore. And my mom's good, which is cool. And they told you about chess club, and you haven't seen Irving yet but you will tonight because he's taking me to the Yankees game, the commissioner's tickets, how cool is that?"

"How much coffee have you had today?"

"Sorry, I'm really hyper. We got up in Newport this morning and drove all the way back here. And I didn't get a lot of sleep while I was up there. But I had a whole lot of fun. You tell about the trip. I'll tell about the chess."

I must have talked for fifteen minutes, telling him about the little house, about the running and the swimming and the snorkeling, about the meals we had and some of the things we talked about. And yet as I spoke, all I could think of was how much we lie to one another with all the best intentions, how nearly every conversation has somewhere within it, often throughout it like veins in marble, obfuscation or avoidance or the kind of shading that shaves off the hard edges of the truth. Kindness and custom have turned us all into cowards.

"Come on, Bridey, how crazy is she?" Leo said, putting his big sneakers on my desk, laughing as I pushed them off.

"She's not crazy. She's a little hard. But her communication with you has been nothing but a comedy of errors. Apparently she left you endless messages on your dorm machine at school and the voice mail at the apartment."

"Neither of which I ever listen to. Yeah, I know. I'm going to have a Momathon tonight. I'm going to start with the first message at school and go straight through to the most recent one at the apartment. She says she thinks there are maybe fourteen messages in all. That's a lot of messages."

"You talked to her?"

"Not exactly. When I got here this morning, there was this long letter she sent on the fax machine. Handwritten and everything. I'm going to write her back, too. That'll be cool, you know. It gives you more time to think. And you can hang on to a letter afterwards."

"That's great. Speaking of something you can hang on to, she sent you something." From beneath my desk I lifted an enormous conch shell, speckled brown and cream, a gorgeous thing called Triton's trumpet. Percy had brought it the day after he took us snorkeling, as an apology, I imagine, and Meghan had asked me to bring it to Leo.

"Man," he said, turning it carefully in both hands, peering inside, holding it up to his ear. It seemed incomprehensible that a week ago this creature had been crawling in the grass in the warm blue water, and that what was left of him was in a cramped office in the Bronx, a gift from an absent mother to her boy-man.

"How did they get the guy out of there?" asked Leo. The one question he was certain to ask, the one best not answered. "They poured salt on him and he oozed out," I said.

He put the shell down on a pile of papers. "That's harsh," he said.

I nodded. "It's an empty house," I said.

When he'd left to go drive two of the women to job interviews, Tequila came in and picked the shell up. "That's a beauty, mon," she said in an amped-up accent. "How much you pay?"

"A gift."

She jerked her head toward the door. "You know how to play chess?"

I shook my head.

"It's hard, I tell you that. I was watching last week, the kids are like, this one only moves like that, that one only moves like this. Give me checkers instead. Nice and easy."

"So you think this is a waste of time."

She shook her head. She sat down in my chair, too, and put down the shell. "Princess Margaret's working with him on this. She got that job starting at the botanical garden, she gets off at three, I don't like her at home by herself. He's gonna pick her up when he has a drop-off over at the projects, then she goes home with me, keep her busy all day long."

"Give the girl a break, Tequila. During the school year all she does is study."

"My second one, Armand, got this friend named Marvin, always hanging around the house, coming by, picking Armand up to go out to KFC, whatever it is. But every time I see him he's looking at Princess Margaret."

"Beautiful girl," I said. Tequila nodded. That was just what she was thinking. A beautiful brilliant girl, one year away from changing her life as magically and as utterly as though a lamp had been rubbed, a jinn summoned, an improbable wish granted. I knew in her mind's eye Tequila could see it all, just slightly out of reach: the salary, the apartment, the professional man, the business card. But the pitfalls were considerable, and the greatest was a boy and a baby. Not so much a sleazebag who would beat and leave her, like Tequila's first husband; Princess Margaret was too smart for that. But an ordinary boy, someone who would go to work for the Transit Authority or Best Buy, wear a name tag, grow old without moving out or getting rich, the kind of man who would help lift her daughter a couple inches out of the projects when Tequila wanted her to fly, fly across the river to Manhattan, into a life where her own mother might sometimes be an embarrassment. That was the sacrifice she was willing to make. Children blow up your life, and then they leave.

I spent the afternoon amid the wreckage. One of the women in transitional housing was in danger of having her parental rights terminated because of some miscommunication between the courts, the child welfare workers, and her own attorney. She wanted her three-year-old daughter back, and foster parents out on Long Island wanted to adopt her. "You know what they're thinking," she said wearily. "Nice white couple with a house and a yard." When she left to go meet with a landlord who had a small apartment in a walk-up building, Annette was sitting in the chair outside my door. "Where's Delon?" I asked, and she started to cry. She ripped through a handful of tissues and explained that

Delon's father's girlfriend had just given birth to a second girl in as many years. Delon's father had decided that his best chance for a son was the one he already had, and he had stopped by Sunday to mention that he was figuring Delon should come and live with him. And his girlfriend.

"He's all, like, that boy growing up to be a sissy, all those women around. But he's all about bad business, Miz Fitz, and he is always using his hands. He say, 'spoil the rod and spoil the child.' " I wasn't going to correct her; I got the idea, and when the weather was warmer I'd get another look at the scars on her upper arms, which had been made with her own curling iron by Delon's father.

"Just keep the baby close, Annette. We'll tell everyone in the house he can't go with anyone but you. Where is he now?"

"He's watching the chest." It turned out that most of the residents thought we had a chest club now.

A letter about one of our kids who had a bad TB test, a letter about another who'd never been inoculated, a recommendation the charter school needed to enroll a boy whose mother was in transitional housing. When it's so cold in my back office that a decorative rime of crystalline frost appears around the edge of my window, I don't dare use a space heater. It's not just that the space heater is the official instrument of death and disaster in our neighborhood, that nearly every fire story includes the words "sparked by a space heater," with the lit oven in the unheated building and the candle flame for those without electricity running close behind. It's that we have so much paper in our offices, the vast written record of the nit-picking and inhuman social welfare bureaucracy. Our families do not have millstones, except in the metaphorical sense. They have great unyielding piles of paper that chronicle their broken hearts and broken promises.

At the bottom of the pile were papers that had come in the previous Monday asking for the whereabouts of a girl named Alezabeth Johnson. I remembered her vaguely, a chubby kid with dozens of little braids, a bow barrette at the end of each one, so that when she ran she made a clinking noise like dice being rattled in the hand. She, her mother, and her five brothers and sisters had stayed with us, sent from one of the city shelters. That had been maybe two years ago. The report I had was of her mother's suicide at Rikers Island. She'd cut her own throat with a Bic pen that had been sharpened into an ersatz blade. Three of the kids were in the foster care system. Two had been located living with her sister in Alabama. Poor people in New York City have sent their children south for decades, to get them away from the filth and the crime and the guns and the drugs, to get them back to wandering through fields, picking berries off bramble bushes, and going to church with a big Sunday supper after. None of them have realized yet that all the bad things from the city have migrated south, like birds, and that the biggest difference between Biloxi and the Bronx is that in one place their kids will wind up doing crack, and in the other it will be crystal meth.

But no one knew what had happened to Alezabeth, with her clicking head of hair, her poor mangled phonetic name. Sitting looking out my office window, I could let my imagination run wild. I was tired or perhaps I would have thought of the sunnier scenarios: sharing a room with a friend from school whose mother had decided to keep her on when her mother was busted, sent off to an aunt in Cleveland or Detroit or somewhere with an Indian name upstate that the system didn't know about. In fourth grade, in the choir. Instead all I thought was the worst. Killed by one of the men for whom her mother ran dope. Used as a sex toy for assorted pedophiles. Dead in the ER of one of the city hospitals of an asthma attack, undocumented, waiting in the morgue for the clock to run so some Rikers inmates on cemetery detail could toss her in one of the mass graves on Hart Island. I put my head down on the paper, on my desk, next to the shell with its infinite whorls, its secret spaces inside. I had figured having a baby was going to make me sick, and tired. I hadn't imagined how it would make me feel about the wreckage of little lives I saw every day in my work.

There's one thing I've never figured out about Irving Lefkowitz, and that is why he always shows up when you least want him. Have your hair highlighted and blown out by Mr. Victor of West Fifty-eighth Street, and Irving will be handling the local TV mokes for five days after a cop killing. Develop cold sores so bad that everyone suspects you have the syph, as Tequila once charmingly opined, and he'll be at the door with a bottle of good wine and a sex jones that very night.

So it was only natural that when I dozed off on my desk, then raised my head, the outline of a paper clip imprinted on my cheek, he would be standing in the doorway. In the interval between my waking and his sitting, I understood that he was angry. Cops tend, like old sinks, to have a hot tap and a cold one. It takes some doing for them to work it out to warm. He wasn't trying. If I'd been a criminal, I would have been terribly afraid.

But his voice was soft as he began. "Here's the thing we can never figure out. The bad guys don't even try most of the time. We get a line on someone who has capped a couple of people, and we find him asleep in his own bed, and in his sock drawer we find a loaded weapon. And it's the same weapon used to cap the victims. Or there's a couple thousand dollars' worth of stolen goods, and they're stacked neatly in the closet. It's like it's immaterial to them. Or maybe they're so delusional about apprehension that it never occurs to them."

I like the way Irving uses police jargon. I don't like it when his voice is low, slow. I think of it as his interrogation voice. He used a sweeping motion of his hand to indicate his clothes, the polo shirt, the neat slacks.

"So I'm at Midtown South and I have to get changed for the game, which I'm taking Leo to tonight. It's too long a distance to go to my apartment. But I recall that I have all the right clothes at your apartment from that trip to Coney Island. I change, I go to the bathroom. And what do I see in the bathroom?"

"What?"

"In the trash. Right there. Like it doesn't matter. Of course the real evidence has been hidden. But there's the box."

Irving said nothing as the silence dragged on. Again, a cop thing. Guilty people love to fill up a silence.

"A pregnancy test is not evidence of a crime," I finally said. "And I didn't hide anything. I put it away."

"That's not hiding?"

"You're talking about the little stick thing. I put it away." Then I was angry, too, angry and sick at heart. "I put it away to put in the baby book someday."

He slammed his hand down on the desk and leaned forward. "What have I said a hundred times? A hundred goddamn times? What have I said over and over again, Bridget?"

"I know. I'm sorry. I mean, I'm sorry, but I'm not sorry. I don't know how it happened, but it happened, and here we are. Can't you be happy at all?"

"Do I get any say in this?"

"Irving, I'm forty-three years old. I'm too old to have an abortion."

He stood up, rubbed his hand hard over the bottom of his face like he was trying to get his mouth, his chin, into some particular position. There was a Yankees hat sticking out of his back pants pocket.

"I'm too old to have a kid," he said.

"Just think about it. Don't make a snap decision."

"You think I haven't thought about this for years and years? I'm sixty-seven years old. You know how many times I've been asked if I have kids? I am not cut out for it. That's all there is to it."

"I'm sorry," I said again.

"I'm sorry, too," he said, shaking his head. "You have no idea how sorry I am." And then he left for the game. The Yankees lost, 4–3. Later Leo said Irving took it hard.

G OING OUT TO dinner with the Borowses would be funny if the maelstrom that develops around you did not feel so frantic, so desperate, so much like that news footage of people putting up plywood and throwing their dogs in the car to escape a hurricane. It's much worse even than going to a restaurant with Meghan, which usually results only in an assortment of unasked-for tastings and wines, and an obeisance so marked that it makes you feel a little dirty. But Kate, in her ever-present tribal jewelry, and Sam, with the trademark Hanes T-shirt and Levi's jeans beneath a thousand-dollar raw silk sport coat, are to a New York City restaurant what the pope is to a parish church. One slip and you're done. Or so all the restaurateurs believe. In fact the Borowses pay little attention when they are not working on their restaurant guide. They simply want decent food and good conversation. What they get is a waiter for every diner at the table and a recitation of specials that have appeared out of nowhere, in chef haiku:

> The arctic char
> Sautéed with baby capers—
> Served with mesclun salad.

When I first met the Borowses and began to dine out with them, the secret ingredient was always shiitake mushrooms, but that was a long time ago. In the course of our friendship, we have passed through pumpkin risotto, balsamic reduction, and peach salsa. "Please God, no lemongrass," Kate had muttered the last time we had dinner at a place that described itself as French-Thai.

So when they merely want to eat and relax, the Borowses always go to a venerable midpriced French restaurant on Fifty-eighth Street that they'd been going to since they were young. It has a middling rating in their guide because it has middling food, although like most French restaurants in New York it serves a good salad, good steak au poivre and tartare, and good liver. When we eat there, it is like eating normally instead of being Olympic judges at a skating rink. No figure eights. The elderly waiters pull their lips tight when we order something of which they disapprove, and then we change our orders. Unfortunately, now people go there because they have heard it is where the Borowses eat when they're not working.

"Oh, no," Kate muttered under her breath when she saw a woman approach our table with a bright white Chiclets smile and a cashmere shawl draped around her shoulders.

"Just the person I'm looking for," she said, bending for the air kiss. "Or people. I love you, too, Sam, as you know."

"And I appreciate it, Lisa," Sam replied. I didn't know the woman, but she must be truly awful for Sam to have taken that flat dry tone. He even manages to be nice to the mayor.

"I know you don't talk business at dinner, and neither do I, it's my new policy. Lunch, yes. Dinner, no. But I just wanted to give you my card because I have a young couple who are very interested in a certain apartment in a certain building that I keep hearing will go on the market soon. And I know you'd be the first to know when that happens, and I just thought I could make it easy for everyone. Cut out the second broker, all the look-sees. I know high-profile types hate having people traipse through their homes, and in certain situations, you don't know, instead of real prospects you might have reporters, although we try to screen and prequalify, as you would imagine—"

"I've got the card, Lisa. I'll call if the occasion arises." Kate's voice would have frozen a daiquiri. I suppose New York real estate agents are immune to that.

"Please don't think I'm trying to jump the gun. But this young couple have a toddler and another on the way, and the place would be perfect for them. He's a Wall Street guy, so they'd pay the full asking price. Honestly, I think she's a fan. You know how it goes, she'll tell her friends,

Guess whose apartment we're buying? It's absurd, but it can jack up the price. Two years ago I remember that singer's apartment was on the market, what was her name—"

"I have the card," Kate said, and now the tone of contempt and dismissal was unmistakable. Sam had his foot atop my instep.

"Did that woman just try to sell my sister's apartment?" I said as Lisa Real Estate crossed the room, adjusting the shawl.

"Jesus Christ, people are unbelievable," Kate muttered from between her teeth. She took the card and stuffed it in the bread basket, then took it out again. "I'm not going to take the chance that someone will find it and actually call her," she said.

"That's the third one this week," Sam said.

"The third what?"

"The third real estate agent. It's a big apartment with good views. On Central Park West."

"Someone lives there!" I said.

"I know, but Leo's in college, she's out of a job. And people have seen Evan out—"

"With a woman?"

"That's what I hear."

"God, I hate New York. Don't you hate it sometimes? Hate it and love it at the same time. That's what's so infuriating."

"Just like your relationship with Meghan."

"Oh, stop, Kate."

"Okay, I know. Bridget doesn't hate Meghan. Bridget loves Meghan. She loves Meghan, and Meghan makes her totally crazy. I feel exactly the same way. And if anyone else tries to talk to me about buying Meghan's apartment, I will personally kill and eat them. None of them seem to realize that it could be them, that all it would take is one misstep and suddenly your name is wiped off of every benefit committee list in New York."

"Is that happening?"

Kate shrugged. "A bit. Who cares?"

"That's weird. I'm supposed to go to a dinner next week at the home of one of our board members and I tried to weasel out because I hate those things. And she really really wanted me to come. And she knows Meghan is my sister."

"God, Bridget, you are an innocent. She's thrilled you're coming. She's telling everyone you're going to be there. They're going to read you like tea leaves. By the next day there will be women all over Manhattan having coffee and describing you as a good friend and saying that Meghan is fine or Meghan is terrible or whatever the hell they can divine from whether you eat dessert or take cream with your coffee. Or maybe not. Maybe you'll wind up at an entire ladies' lunch made up of decent people. Yeah, that'll happen. Speaking of which, guess who I ran into the other day on the street? That woman Ann Jensen."

"I remember her. She chaired that dinner for Manhattan Mothers. Oh, God, please don't tell me she wants to buy the apartment. That night she was acting like Meghan was the greatest thing since the facelift!"

"Honey, no offense to your sister's place, but Ann Jensen is strictly East Side. And I believe she has a triplex with a lap pool."

"Isn't she the one who was a call girl in L.A. and then married somebody really rich?" said Sam.

"I don't think so. I think she was somebody's assistant, then somebody's girlfriend. Then the wife of somebody."

"So she's not the one whose husband died in some weird accident and there were rumors that she or her trainer, I think, were involved?" I said.

"I know who you're talking about," Kate said. "That's somebody else."

"My God," said Sam, "this conversation is surreal."

"So what did she say?" I asked.

"Well, she has this annoying way of leaning in as though she's going to tell you the secret of life," Kate said. "And she told me about the Manhattan Mothers event, and how great Meghan was that night, and how it was only two days before what she called 'the incident.' And I was standing there thinking, What the hell will Sam say if it says in the tabs that I punched this woman's lights out on Fifty-seventh Street? So she leans in really close and asks if I'm in touch with Meghan, and before I can answer she says in this really tough voice, not at all like the way she usually talks, 'Tell her not to let the bastards break her.' And she got into a Bentley with a driver at the curb. Believe me, she meant it. It was as though her real self popped out right in front of Bergdorf's."

"Wow," I said. "You just never know."

"You don't, do you?"

"You don't?" said Sam.

"Oh, Sam," said Kate indulgently.

"You are ready to order?" said one of the grumpy waitstaff to me, since Sam and Kate always had the same thing, steak frites, every time. So do I, for that matter, but the waiters, like my sister's friends, have a hard time remembering my face. Liver and creamed spinach. My favorite meal is the kind of thing children are forced to eat as punishment. Sam tried to pour red wine into my glass, but I shook my head and took a deep breath.

"I'm pregnant," I said.

"Aaaaah!" Kate screamed so loudly that the real estate agent and her table stared over at us. The Borowses have three sons and two grandsons, and either will pull out baby pictures at the slightest provocation. This, too, sets them apart from most New Yorkers, especially the ones who insist their grandchildren call them something age-neutral, like Cherie or Belle. The first time a little boy with a full diaper called Kate "Nana," she became so unhinged with joy that her daughter-in-law had to put an ice bag on her eyes.

"Henri! Champagne over here! Cristal!"

"Sam, you idiot, she can't drink. You can't drink, right? None of them drink now."

"I don't believe I can drink. I haven't seen a doctor yet, but everything I've read suggests I shouldn't drink. Or eat swordfish, sushi, or processed meats."

Henri had a bottle of Cristal in one bucket and a bottle of Perrier in another. There's little he misses. "That's bull," Kate said. "I ate street dogs when I was pregnant. I loved street dogs."

"And salami," said Sam. He took her hand across the table. "And blue cheese. Saga blue with pear slices." They were, after all, food people.

"I'm beside myself. What does Irving say? Are you getting married?"

"Married? God, no."

"You should get married. Children need structure. Two parents. I know it's old-fashioned, but I am old-fashioned."

"What does Meghan say?" said Sam, clinking glasses with me.

"I haven't told Meghan yet."

I had, however, told everyone else. I told Ricky at the Cubana Sandwich Shop, my dry cleaner, and my dentist, who said some women have terrible trouble with their teeth during pregnancy. I told Alison and Tequila, both of whom screamed and danced around the office. "Girl, it's about time," Tequila shouted, shaking her butt in some ritualistic baby dance.

I told the women in my parenting group, who started screaming so loudly that the security guard from the front door, who manages to ignore blood in the lobby, came to the community room to make sure nothing catastrophic had happened. Once they quieted down, it was Maria who said thoughtfully, "Miz Fitz, you're too old for this."

"Get out, girl," said Charisse. "My mama had her last baby when she was thirty-seven years old. That's her best child, too, my sister Tanisse, who works the desk at the precinct typing and all that."

"I'm forty-three," I said.

"Oooooh," Charisse said thoughtfully. "You're not looking it." I was wearing a sacklike denim sundress I'd been wearing for five years. "When you due?"

"I think it's November."

"You need that prenatal stuff," one of the women said. "You know, the checkups, they give you vitamins, check you out."

"Don't go to that doctor up to Hillside Hospital," another said. "He's rough and he won't give you drugs for the pain."

"They don't give us drugs for the pain," Charisse said. "You on Medicaid, they go, Oh, none of that epidural stuff for you. You just lay there and yell." Charisse narrowed her eyes and picked at her cornrows. "Hold that dress tight against your belly." I had suddenly passed from teacher to student. They knew things, these women, that I had yet to learn. It was a mistake to focus on their deficits, as so many of the official types did. They knew things.

"Twins," Charisse said.

"Jesus God," I said. "Don't say that."

"Too big for just one. You what, three months? Look. She's big."

The entire parenting class tilted their heads to one side. Lips pursed, foreheads furrowed, fingers raised to lips. The rumination was broken by the security guard again, and all of us turned on him like a witches' coven interrupted by a feckless human. He proffered a big square box with a stack of paper plates atop it. "That young man drives the van, he thought you all might be needing this," he said.

"Can't argue with cake," Charisse said with a satisfied smile.

I'd told Leo the day after I'd told Irving. He was a wizard in our old van, adept at skirting the busiest intersections and maneuvering through the narrow side streets to get to the welfare offices or the Tubman projects. I had a late-afternoon meeting with a housing official so that we could see if a Tubman apartment that kept turning over would do for a family who had been in our transitional housing for more than a year.

It's difficult to believe that sentient humans designed most New York City housing projects, but Tubman is a particularly bad example of planning. One of its buildings backs up to the expressway. As a result, its residents are treated to car tires hitting pitted asphalt at fifty miles an hour at night and, during the day, the fumes from hundreds of idling engines working their way through stop-and-go traffic. Some years ago a researcher at one of the medical schools did a study showing that rates of upper respiratory infection, asthma, and attention deficit disorder were three times as high in that building as in the one farthest from the highway. It was the third story on the local news networks that night, after a pretty blond accountant who'd been found dead in her East Side apartment and the mayor's plan to offer free opera every week in Central Park.

Leo had found a parking spot at the side of that building, right across from a hydrant that is never used in the winter and is on all the time in the summer so the neighborhood kids can play in it and the guys can wash their cars. There were two cabdrivers there with buckets and rags, both black, both middle-aged, the kinds of black men who shame the young miscreants and criminals into leaving them alone by giving off an unmistakable but uncommon daddy vibe. The bravado boys avoid guys like this, ministers, store owners, cab and livery drivers, token clerks, as though they know that the men, as modest as their jobs may be, have achieved something they can never dream of. Most of them were still sleeping in their mothers' apartments even this late in the afternoon, or talking tough on the packed-down earth of the center courtyard that anchors the Tubman towers. An old woman in the building once told me that she had been among the original tenants, and that the city had sodded the four quadrants divided up by cement walkways and even planted a skinny shivering tree of some sort in the center of each. No one seemed to have made allowances for the facts not only that the children of Tubman would use the grass instead of the sidewalks but also that the four towers were so tall and boxy, so monolithic and forbidding, that except for about an hour in midsummer they blocked out the sun. The jagged stump of one of the trees still sticks out of the bare earth, and every couple of years a kid falls on it and pierces a cheek or a knee.

The good thing about the bulk of the buildings is that on warm days they provide plenty of shade, although after dark, shade becomes cover and crime blooms there in a way the trees never had. Both of the cabdrivers looked us over thoroughly as we sat in the car. Leo waved at one of them, who inclined his head slightly. Leo's freckles had darkened, and even wearing a Yankees hat and a T-shirt that said "Amsterdam Rocks!" he looked like Tom Sawyer's East Coast cousin.

There was such an improbability to the progression of him. My own life seemed a seamless skein unfurling beneath my feet, but Leo in my mind was a herky-jerky series of Leos, like a silent movie or a flip book. Meghan in a hammock in the first house they'd had in Connecticut, the one with the low ceilings and enormous Federal fireplace, reading some government report and drifting off to sleep as I watched random movements beneath her maternity shirt. Evan looking up from the toilet and missing Leo's first real boy pee, Leo's face as he looked at me the face of someone who has done something incredible. Meghan pointing my camera as Leo went to Biltmore for the first time in the navy uniform polo shirt and the khaki shorts. Leo diving in the lake, Leo debating the

question of the flat tax in the auditorium, Leo taking his friend Saman-
tha to the prom at the Waldorf. Leo driving me to Tubman, knowing his
way around.

"I'm going to have a baby," I told him, which is as different from "I'm
pregnant" as "I'm home" is from "I'm signing a lease."

"Shut up!" said Leo.

"Really."

"Shut up!" This is the current term of art for "you're kidding." I think
all those New York kids love it so much because they spent their childhoods with middle-aged nannies telling them the words were never allowed.

"Really."

"Bridey! A baby! I'm totally speechless. Wow. Wow. A baby." His
mouth was ajar. His hair was every which way. If I loved this baby as
much as I loved Leo, it would be so loved it would smile all the time. Or
maybe that's what all parents tell themselves, that if they love and love
and love, the smoke from that fire will warm its object until the end of
time. "It's a cousin!" Leo said. "It's a cousin, right?"

"Technically, yes. But if I had to guess, you'll be more like a big
brother. Maybe even an uncle."

"Wow. I can't believe my mom didn't say anything."

"You talked to your mom?"

"She sends me a letter every day now. Still by fax, though. She says
she's not sure how the mail service is there. She makes it sound as if she's
in the middle of nowhere."

"She is in the middle of nowhere."

"Wow, she must have been shocked by the news. The baby news."

"She doesn't know."

"Are you kidding? You didn't tell her?"

"I didn't know when I was there."

Leo looked at me and then threw his unruly head back and laughed.
"You're afraid," he crowed. "You're afraid of what she'll say. That's so
wack. You know what she'll do. She'll just spring into Meghan mode.
She'll have a list of what you should eat, what you should wear, what
doctor you should go to, what crib you should buy. Oh, man, you are so

lucky she's not doing the show anymore, or you'd have six months of sto-ries about older moms."

"Don't be mean." But he was right. Leo is never mean but always shrewd. He has perfect vision of the spiritual sort. He knew that his childhood had also been marked in five-minute segments or the occa-sional weeklong series: single-sex schools, self-esteem for boys, the role of team sports, how to choose the right college. Meghan eased into every life passage by turning it into a story designed to benefit all of America, and America liked it. Kate had said at dinner that she'd heard of a group of ditched wives on the East Side who called themselves the Meghan Fitzmaurice Society and who'd taken those two forbidden words she'd uttered at the end of the Greenstreet interview as their motto. "There's a substantial reservoir of support for her," Sam had said. "People think it's incredibly gutsy, just to walk away and leave the network holding the bag."

"On the other hand," Kate had said with her lower lip thrust out dra-matically, "we saw that putz Murphy at a party and he said she'll never work again."

Leo locked the van, and one of the drivers gave Leo the high sign, meaning he'd be on the lookout, although our van was so sad that it was hard to believe anyone would bother to steal it. Leo cut up the sidewalk along the backsides of the buildings and away from the busy center quad.

"You're going to C, right? Where Margaret lives? There's a back door that goes right into the corridor and to the director's office."

"Nobody's ever bothered to tell me that."

"Margaret uses it all the time. The other kids really hassle her a lot. All that Oreo stuff, thinks she's too good, you know. And a couple of the guys get really rowdy with her, say really bad stuff. The first time I was like, I am going to get so up in that guy's grille, and she was like, Hello, white boy, just step down and stay safe, and I was like, I'm not putting up with that crap. But then one of her brothers showed up. He's a good guy. The one who's going to be a cop. The other one is kind of sketchy. I mean, I think he's a good guy but he's got some sketchy friends."

"The one whose friend has a thing for Princess Margaret."

"She's ditching the Princess thing. She ditched it, like, two years ago at school. I mean, c'mon. It's just ridiculous. Oh, man, this door is locked up tight."

He was right; it wouldn't budge. We turned back and followed the path into the quadrangle, dark as a cellar and just as dank. The only way you could tell you were outside was by looking up at the small square of clouds that floated like a trompe l'oeil over the tops of the four buildings. Somebody'd burned up all the benches, and they'd had to remove the trash cans because during fights they always wound up being used as projectiles. Skull fracture, shattered pelvis, broken nose: you can do some real damage with a metal mesh can if you throw it hard enough. I watched as two teenage girls leaning on strollers unwrapped Little Debbie snack cakes and threw the wrappers on the ground. A toddler leaned out of one stroller and grabbed one of the wrappers. In another a baby slept, her bald head encircled by a beaded and beribboned headband in case anyone who missed her pink dress and Sleeping Beauty shoes made the mistake of thinking she was a boy.

"Miz Fitz! Miz Fitz!" One of the girls was waving her snack cake. I recognized her from a stay with her mother in the shelter three years before. I had given her a magic wand with a star atop it that for some reason had been in the goody bag at the Leukemia Society's black-tie dinner at the Pierre. She'd carried the wand around for weeks, until it turned from silver to gray.

"Hey, honey," I called back. Women at cocktail parties, girls at Tubman—it's remarkable how successfully that endearment covers up the fact that I can't remember names.

"I'm coming to your classes! The court say I got to go or they're gonna make my mother the guardian person for the baby, and I'm saying, Nuh-huh, if she's such a good guardian how come I got a baby when I'm fourteen? So I'm coming next week."

"I'll see you then. You take good care of her till I see you."

I looked sideways at Leo as we walked away. "Stop wincing. You got to learn early on not to wince. And not to assume. You know how old Tequila was when she had Baruch? She was fifteen. Some of them turn out all right."

"It's just that sometimes I feel like a fraud, being here. Like when I was in high school, we had this day called Community Service Day, and it was totally bogus, because we'd go to soup kitchens or whatever and all the girls from the girls' schools would use it as an opportunity to meet guys, and the next day we'd be talking about, wow, life is really hard for people in some places, and then we'd forget about the whole thing. It was like it was a museum exhibit: Now, boys and girls, here we are in the hood. Be careful and don't touch anything."

"Think how Princess Margaret must feel."

"It's a nightmare. She says Tequila is looking at this house over on Kelly Street to buy, get them all out of here."

As if to prove the point, the elevators opened and a group of young men sauntered out in gangsta uniform, long shorts, big shoes, hooded eyes as though they'd just rolled out of bed. I nodded. Leo nodded. They brushed past, way too close, to make the point that we were on their home ground, not the other way around. One of them was Tequila's son Armand. He'd flunked two of his courses spring term at community college. I figured one of the other guys was his friend Marvin. They were on the cusp, all of them. A lucky break, a decent job, and they'd go one way. A bad circle of friends, a pressing need for cash, and they'd go the other. The cusp was as good as it got in Tubman.

"Yo, Bus Boy!" one of them called as they strutted out the double glass doors. "Bus Boy! We talking to you! Bus Boy, that your girlfriend? She a little old for you."

"Shut up" I heard in a low voice. Armand, probably. He'd known me since he was thirteen.

"Bus Boy!" another cried. "You best not be going to Armand's place. His sister got other things to do."

Leo never looked up, but his shoulders were as stiff as if his T-shirt had been starched. The director's office was at the very back of the building, down another long corridor, but he was looking at his shoes the whole way.

"You having trouble here?"

"Nothing I can't deal with. I mean, I understand why they don't like me. I try to show my face as little as possible."

"Bus boy?"

"Because I drive the van."

I told him I needed him to wait in the director's office with me so he could drive me back, that I was tired and my feet hurt, both of which were true. But I also didn't want him walking out alone, and when we left we went through that back door. I almost asked for a key.

"Y OU'RE A WITCH," I said to Tequila once when we were watching a news bulletin on our grainy television in the transitional-housing living room. A political figure had announced that he was returning to private life to spend more time with his family several days before, and Tequila had turned down her mouth, raised her eyes, waved her hand, and said, "That man's trouble, mark my words. A lady friend, probably, or money. One or the other." It had turned out to be both, embezzlement for the purpose of keeping the lady friend, a former exotic dancer, in a love nest on Staten Island. "You're a witch," I said again.

"Let me tell you something. We know things."

"We who?"

"Black women, that's we who."

"Wait, we're supposed to pretend we're all the same, but it turns out you all got the intuition?"

"And you all got the money, the power, and the straight hair. Don't give me this all-the-same hoo-ha, sister girl."

"When you call me sister girl, I always know you're making fun of me."

"Damn straight." Tequila was the only person on earth with whom I'd ever had an honest conversation about race. Actually, we may be the two people in New York City to have had an honest conversation about race.

I remembered Tequila's insistence on race-based intuition the next time I went to teach parenting classes. Charisse looked at me and rolled her eyes around like she was going to have a fit. "So?" she said.

"Twins," I replied.

Pandemonium broke loose in the community room. The old woman across the hall was in the middle of making sweet potato pie, she told us, but she came across anyhow. "I thought somebody won the lottery," she said in her soft voice. You had to hand it to the women in my parenting class; their kids might wind up leaving school, going to jail, or if they prospered, leaving the neighborhood behind. But they still thought having two babies at once was almost as good as making a big win on the Lotto.

That's when I'd finally told Meghan, when I left the doctor's office after seeing those grainy moonscape images: a heart, a hand, an eye, a foot, a heart, a hand, an eye, a foot. The room filled with the thumping percussion of two heartbeats not quite in sync, so that they sounded like bad audio, stereo reverb, a three-second delay. My aunt Maureen took the train down to sit with me. We must have looked like inept mimes. An enormous grin followed by a quivering upper lip and then the tears. Unlike the heartbeats, we were almost exactly in sync.

"Yep, there are two," said the technician.

"Let's have an ice cream sundae," Maureen said. Hot fudge, too.

That afternoon I sat down and wrote, "Dear Meghan, I just found out that I am expecting twins. It was a shock for me and it will certainly be a shock for you. Please come home. Leo is fine and sends his love. XOXO Bridget."

Twenty minutes later I heard the laborious mechanical breathing of the old fax machine. Tequila came in with five sheets of paper. They were covered with lists: the names of neonatologists, of pediatricians, of prenatal yoga and exercise classes, of places to buy strollers, of the best strollers to buy.

"Score one for Leo Grater," I said aloud.

"Now you talking to yourself," Tequila called from her desk. The last page said: "I am wild with joy. XOXO M."

I faxed back the Polaroid from the sonogram, although by the time the fuzz of the image had become the fuzz of the Polaroid and then the fuzz of the fax it must have looked like a sleet storm at midnight. I sent a list of names, and she sent it back with big black lines through half of them; Fitzmaurice Lefkowitz, for one, did not make the cut. One day I sent along a couple of paragraphs about the yoga class, which was absurd on its face, a brace of women trying to find their centers when they were not only off center but off center in a slightly different fashion with each passing week. Another morning I sat down first thing and typed out a description of how Ricky at Cubana Sandwich Shop gave me two each time I ordered one and put hot sauce on everything for some complicated reason that apparently had to do with hair growth, although it was unclear whether the hair involved was mine or the babies'.

One afternoon as I was preparing to go home, Edward Prevaricator called. "Your sister wanted me to pass along this phone number," he said.

"She has a phone?"

"No, but Derek does. You remember Derek from your visit. He and his wife have a telephone, and if there is an emergency he can drive down to the house immediately."

I looked at the number on the paper. Leo's letters, my dispatches, a phone number: my sister was edging back into the world.

"I think your mother will come home soon," I said to Leo that afternoon as we sat on the front steps licking lemon ices.

"I don't think so. I told her to stay awhile longer."

"What? You did? Why?"

"I don't know. It seems like she's spending a lot of time thinking about stuff, and I just figure you guys don't get enough time thinking about stuff. When you're a kid, you spend all your time in your room listening to music, playing video games, but mainly thinking about stupid stuff. I mean, not all stupid—like when Jack Wallace's little brother had some weird cancer, he was thinking about important stuff. And when Nate's parents split. But like, the point is that we just have a lot of time to think. But you guys—there's just no time. Work, dinner, trips, whatever. It sounds like my mom has all this time to just think. And I figure she hasn't done that in a long time and maybe we should just leave her alone to do it."

"May I say something?"

"Oh, jeez, Bridey, whenever you say that it means you're going to say something really nice to me that's so over the top that I feel like a jerk."

"All I want to say is that if my kids grow up to be as great as you, I'll be the happiest woman on earth."

"I'll whip them into shape," Leo said, hiding his face in the paper cup of lemon ice.

If, as the old proverb goes, victory has a hundred fathers, these kids were going to have thousands of parents. In the muggy July evenings as I shuffled, splay-footed in flat sandals, from the subway station to my building, I was accosted by anonymous well-wishers, the familiar strangers I had known by sight but not by name. "You . . . are . . . glowing," gasped a woman who lived at the end of the block as she ran toward the park in shorts and a marathon T-shirt. "I'm so jealous," said a woman I'd seen with a toddler and a baby at the bodega on the corner, her hair always slightly untidy, spots on her clothes. Leo's friends Doug and Doug, who incredibly enough both dated girls named Caitlin, just bobbed their heads and said, "Cool. So, like, cool."

Sometimes at night Leo sprawled on the couch and sang softly to my stomach while we shared ice cream straight from the container. Mostly he sang a rock song he loved that began, "Today is the greatest day I've ever known."

Suddenly I understood what it feels like to be public property, to have people feel entitled to approach, to comment, to have an opinion. But because it was new to me, and because it would pass in the finite endless span of the pregnancy, I did not mind. I felt prosperous, as though I had so much, so much, as though I had been flat water and now I was carbonated. My apartment was too small and my body was so big and the future seemed so strange and yet so clear, too. At five I would walk them to the public school, the one with the gifted and talented program. At eight they would play soccer in the park, in one of the leagues; they would have brightly colored shirts and small muddy cleats. At sixteen they would stop speaking to me but never to each other, even if it was only to bicker and whine.

"Isn't it great that there's two, Bridey?" Leo said one night, and I looked at him in surprise, wondering why I had never really registered the faint nimbus of loneliness that had always encircled his sweet face.

There were two of us preparing, although it was in a most peculiar way. When I left the office now, there was almost always a squad car at the corner. Alison was delighted; the boyfriends, the common-law husbands, the exes were particularly bothersome in summer, and occasionally one would reel around the corner, determined to get his own back, and come face-to-face with two young officers in mirror shades. When I would come out at the end of the day, the patrol car would start up unabashedly and then follow me to the subway station. On the train a transit cop would sometimes saunter through the car where I sat, sweating in the summer heat, and I would wonder if he, too, had been sent.

It wasn't the first time I'd seen the fine hand of Irving Lefkowitz in my daily life. Several years back I'd stumbled down the corridor to the community room at Tubman, a corridor in which half the lights had burned out, and come upon a narrow young man in a do-rag who had a larger guy pressed back against the wall, a box cutter up and ready. "You don't want to be back here at this particular moment," he said. It was such an elegant locution that it stayed with me as I began to shake slightly and approached the security guard at the desk. "Uh-huh," he said and scribbled something on his log, which was a spiral notebook of the kind kids use. But he never moved from behind the faux wood desk he had shoved in one corner.

"Did anything bad happen at the Tubman projects yesterday?" I had asked Irving at dinner the next night.

"That is one of the more ridiculous questions you've ever asked me," he replied, putting down his fork and jamming a corner of a roll in his mouth, which he often does before he begins a long disquisition on the nature of crime in the city. "At one point they thought of setting up a satellite station house in the bottom floor of building A. The only reason they didn't is because they knew any officer assigned would apply for a transfer."

The next time I went to Tubman a patrol car trailed me there and back. "I can't have a black-and-white following me around the neighborhood," I told Irving. "It makes me stand out."

"See, I never thought of that. A tall woman with reddish hair, blue eyes, and skin so white you can practically see through it walking through an entirely black and Latino neighborhood wouldn't want anything that would interfere with her ability to melt right into her surroundings."

"Just can the shadow, Irving. I can't do my work with a police escort. Those people live there every day without a police escort. I can certainly manage." But that was then. This was now. This was us, not me. I didn't complain. I didn't demur. I ran my hand over the deepening shelf of my belly and let the police trail behind me.

Irving and I had enough to fight about anyway. Each time he saw me it was like he discovered my treachery anew, and his brow would tighten, his mouth thin. Sometimes we went to dinner together and didn't talk of it. Sometimes we talked of nothing else. The one thing we never did was to sleep together. Irving said he was inhibited by Leo sleeping on the sofa, and we couldn't go to his place. Irving kept a shabby apartment in Brooklyn with views from all rooms of a narrow air shaft. It looked like a safe house for material witnesses, which is what it was before Irving's second divorce, when he needed a temporary place to stay. He'd been there temporarily for twelve years.

In late July, during a week of heat and humidity so thick that the air felt like suede, he took me to a small and very elegant restaurant on West Fiftieth Street where we'd celebrated my birthday. I had a new dress, white with a tight bodice. My cleavage was a national monument. "Bridey!" crowed Leo, who was on his way out with the Caitlins to a club in Chelsea famous for its chocolate pudding shots. The headwaiter at Française did a faint minuet around me, as though he was afraid he might need to catch me and there was no telling in which direction I might fall. He brought a pillow for the small of my back. "She's fine, she's fine," said Irving.

The last time I had been there we had seen Fallujah Levine, who was rumored to have a lock on Meghan's job. "Give her all my love," she'd said earnestly, an actress playing the part of a newscaster playing the part of a sympathetic friend. But the restaurant was half empty on a summer evening. Everyone who mattered was eating in the Hamptons.

Without consulting the menu, Irving said he would have oysters and steak au poivre, medium rare. He was squirming like a man with a tack in his shoe.

"All right, so we'll get married," he said when the waiter left, looking at me sideways, holding a glass of red wine.

"I don't want to get married."

His glass hit the table with a sound like ice cracking. "What? What? You want to be a whatchamacallit?"

"A whatchamacallit?"

"You know what I'm talking about."

"No, I don't. I'm not a mind reader."

"A whatchamacallit. A single mother."

"No, I don't want to be a single mother. A single mother is someone who has to parent her children alone. I want to share parenting responsibilities with you."

He shook his head slowly. "Already we're getting into trouble here. You're using the word *parent* as a verb. *Parent* is a noun. You know better than that." He took a gulp of his wine and threw an oyster after it. I would have felt sorry for him if I'd been able to drink champagne or stomach oysters.

"I'm having a very difficult time with this and you don't seem to have a whole lot of sympathy for the position," he said. "I had a lousy father. My father had a lousy father. I'm not complaining, but there it is."

"So what? I had a lousy mother. Well, I think I did. But I did have Maureen, who was a great surrogate mother."

"Which is probably why your sister turned out to be a good mother."

"I'm surprised you'd say that."

"No, come on, you know I always give the devil his due. You can't spend time around that kid and not know that she did a good job." One of his cell phones started to hum in his pocket. He looked at the screen, pressed a button, and put it back.

"So you don't want to get married?"

"I don't think so. Look at what happened to Meghan. And you don't seem to do so well with it, either. I would like to live with you on a regular basis." I was not sure that that was true, but it seemed like the right thing to say. "If you want to buy me an expensive ring in honor of that, that would be fine. Although we might have to wait until the swelling goes down in my fingers."

"And you want me to do this whole thing where I go in with you, rub your feet, help you breathe?"

"Yeah. I would really like that. I think you'd really like it. I remember seeing Leo born. It was the most amazing moment of my life. There were two of us, and then there were three. Four, if you count Evan, who was sitting in the corner with his head between his knees. I don't see you as a fainter. And I think if you didn't see it you'd be sorry after."

"I've seen it. I delivered two babies when I was a patrolman. It happens all the time, you get to a car parked along the side of the Belt, there she is with her feet on the dash, screaming."

"Oh, great. That makes me feel a lot better."

Irving shook his head. "Sweetheart, you're going to be fine. I know you. A trouper. You given any thoughts to what you're going to call these kids?"

"I've eliminated some names already. Did you know Leo has three friends named Kate and two each named Sarah and Emily? I think the only thing they all have in common is that they're blond."

"Ask Tequila. She'll give you some doozies."

"Yeah, she explained hers to me once. Baruch after the college. Armand after some TV actor, Princess Margaret after Princess Margaret. And George."

"Washington? Foreman? Hamilton?"

"I think she just got tired. She's getting a second wind with me. The other day she suggested Meghan Jr."

"Over my dead body. Which is another thing. I'm too goddamn old. I'm going to look ridiculous. Not to mention the dying thing." That's what Irving always called it. The dying thing.

"Too late," I said, looking down at my evaporating lap. I looked up and saw the headwaiter leading Evan across the room. A woman was with him, and he had his hand at the small of her back, steering her to a table in a corner. It was a gesture as familiar to me as the up-and-over sweep of my sister's arm as she stroked her way across the sea. I covered my mouth with my hand.

"I have to go to the ladies' room," I said.

Anyone who has ever been single in New York knows how to use the restroom to take the measure of an old lover's new love. There are the mirrors over the bar, the big plate-glass window facing the street that reflects nearly as well as the mirrors do, the arbitrary room dividers with flower arrangements atop that make it possible to stand behind the delphiniums and hide in plain sight. One of these last served. Evan's companion was small, wiry, with enormous blue eyes and a funny fish mouth. He talked, she laughed. In only a few months he apparently had become hilarious. In the ladies' room, I watched the door as I washed my hands. I could hear Tequila's voice in my head, telling me to say "Rise and shine, bitch!" if she walked in. But I would have slunk out, although my ability to slink was severely compromised by my size. Brave in my imagination, not in fact.

Back at the table there was a chocolate mousse at my place. It was the first time I can ever remember that I was not joyful at the sight. From across the room, I imagined I could hear the faint sound of feminine laughter.

"So no deal on the marriage proposal?" Irving said casually.

"That wasn't a proposal," I muttered. "That was a capitulation."

"I can't figure out how to get this right."

"Whatever. Let's get a check." We rode home in a taxi in silence. I looked out the window, which reflected Irving looking at me. A metaphor for all relationships. If I had turned to him, chances were better than even that he would have turned away. And so on, and so forth, the emotional concomitant of the White Rock girl.

"I'm not going to come up," he said when we got to my door.

So the next afternoon when he appeared suddenly in the doorway of my office, I thought for a moment he had come to make peace, to abnegate himself through Lamaze classes, to vow to give up cigars and so live long enough to watch his children grow. He looked like a door himself, so big and boxy, almost Frankensteinian, his shoulders raised, his head bowed. He looked down at me, and I saw that for the first time in all the years I had known him he looked as though he'd been crying. Unthinkingly I put my hand down to my belly.

"Meghan," I whispered.

"Leo," he said.

HAVE BEEN at this hospital so many times before, but this was the first time the staff thought I was the patient. Usually I am with a woman who is bleeding, a child who is gasping for breath, a teenager who is screaming as her baby threatens to be born. Now the staff, taken in by the size of my belly, assumed it was my turn. A woman with a clipboard approached. "My nephew has been shot," I groaned loudly, and she lost interest. A pregnant woman about to give birth is a person of interest; a relative awaiting news of a gunshot victim is a bystander. "Take a seat," she said. Outside Irving yelled into one of his phones.

There is usually something oddly soothing about the emergency room of a large New York City hospital. There is nothing that can come through the double doors that the doctors and nurses there have not seen, and for that matter saved. A man with his leg in a plastic bag filled with ice in the ambulance next to him. A woman whose hair has been caught in a meat grinder, effectively scalping her. A child catatonic after being placed in scalding water. We social workers can hear the indictment before the mother actually opens her mouth: she wouldn't stop crying.

In New York you can measure how badly a person is hurt by how quickly they take him into a treatment room. If you've hammered a nail through your palm or broken your leg in a fall, you will have to wait. People with AIDS are bleeding from head wounds suffered in lovers' quarrels, yet behind the scrim of their surgical masks the staff appear unruffled, even unmoved. There is an abbreviation for gunshot wounds: GSW. It is all over the charts on the receptionist nurse's battered metal desk. Those are the only people not required to immediately provide insurance information, the ones on bloodied gurneys that sweep through the doors and move forward like planes poised to land, to disgorge mangled cargo.

Leo had apparently gone right in, surrounded by an honor guard of emergency medical technicians and police officers. He'd been shot in the back as he locked the van outside the Tubman projects. When Irving came inside, he flashed his badge and demanded we be taken into the treatment area. But all we could see was the curtain of the cubicle where they were treating him. I heard doctors barking orders and could see on the greenish linoleum floor a pair of shorts and a T-shirt scissored into sections. It was the black T-shirt that said "I'll Sleep When I'm Dead."

"No," I said without meaning to say it.

"I'm sitting you down," Irving said, and he pulled a chair from another cubicle where an elderly man was crying softly. I dropped down and leaned back against the tiled wall. I listened for the sound of Leo crying, screaming, talking, but all I could hear were the medical people. Their jargon sounded as though it was part of a television show. One of the nurses came out and looked through narrowed eyes from my face to my belly.

"You with us, Mom? You okay?"

"My nephew. Leo. Leo Grater. Is he alive?"

She knelt in front of me. She was wearing a smock with lollipops printed on it. Our aunt Maureen had had one like it before she retired. "We're stabilizing him. They'll talk to you soon. We don't know exactly what's going on yet. They're going to run some tests. How old is he?"

"Nineteen. Do you need his social or date of birth?"

She patted my hand. "There's plenty of time for that."

Irving made a tight circle, into the waiting area, back to the treatment area, outside to answer the phone, back to the waiting area. He was juggling a crisis: a personal heartbreak, a police matter, a public relations nightmare, all in the same package. I knew there was some part of him that was happy he could get through the first two before the third hit because Leo's last name was not Fitzmaurice.

The gurney flew by, a wild tuft of auburn hair waving from a junk pile of tubes, bags, even paperwork stacked atop his chest on a clipboard.

"CT scan," the nice nurse said, riding shotgun with her hand on one of the rails. Irving pulled one of the doctors aside. "Commish," a detective in an old seersucker suit called. Irving began the circuit again, talking in a low voice to the police, carrying his cell phone out onto the pavement, laying his hand on my shoulder. Each time he returned he had something from the vending machine. There was a stack in my lap: Milky Way, Gatorade, Cheez Doodles, M&M's peanuts. Slumber party food. I felt a dead weight in my midsection and wondered if I'd harmed the babies with adrenaline. Then one stirred, a soft fishy U-turn of a movement. I would call him Leo Jr. I would call her Meghan Jr. I would reconstruct the entire fractured landscape of my life out of spare parts. I would not cry because that would mean things were every bit as bad as I knew they were.

When Evan came in, he looked like a completely different person from the one I had seen just the night before in the restaurant. He was gray and drawn, and I wondered if I looked the same way.

"How is he?" he asked Irving.

"They don't really know anything yet. They're not holding out on us, the doctors don't really know. He got shot in the back pretty far down. I think they're trying to figure out where the bullet is and whether they can get to it." He put his hand on his chest where his own scar was. "A bullet wound is not as bad as it sounds." He had his TV voice on.

"Who did it?"

Irving shook his head. "We don't know that, either. We got cops all over the project. Apparently there were a group of thug wannabes who had been giving him a hard time."

"I know," I said. "I know those guys. They called him Bus Boy. Tequila knows who they are."

"He never said anything to me about guys giving him a hard time. He made it sound like he spent all his time driving women to doctors' appointments and teaching kids to play chess."

The nice nurse was back. "Is this Dad?" she said, leading Evan away. We use titles to establish the pecking order, those of us in the so-called helping professions. In the title department, Evan outranked me. He disappeared through yet another set of doors, rooting through an inside jacket pocket for his wallet, looking for his insurance card. I had handed him the M&M's. I drank the Gatorade.

"One of the guys is Tequila's son," I said softly to Irving.

"I'm on it," he said. It looked as if he had gag toys in his pocket: all of his cell phones were vibrating, ruffling the fabric of his gray slacks. The reporters probably already knew that a white kid, a freshman at Amherst, a Central Park West resident, had been shot at a Bronx housing complex. That was a good story for them. Soon one of them would figure out whose son he was. That would turn it into the lead of the local news. It would probably be a while before the officers at Tubman knew who had done the shooting. A man could be shot in the middle of the complex on a summer day with kids playing in the dirt, mothers talking by the lobby doors, old people leaning on the windowsills looking out. When the cops arrived, it was always the same: no one had seen anything. If you saw bad things, you made the people who did the bad things angry. And when they were angry, they would do bad things to you. Or, as Charisse told me once, her hand on my shoulder, explaining how come no one had given up a guy who stabbed his wife two days after he got out of prison upstate, "Karma is a boomerang." I wasn't sure whether she was referring to the need to keep quiet or the inevitability of retribution, which had led the husband to take a header off the roof of a building the following month. Everyone knew the dead woman's brother had pushed him off, but no one knew a thing.

I didn't know what time of day it was. The hospital lighting made a constant sickly overcast daytime. After a while everyone seemed to have forgotten about me. Irving was outside somewhere. Evan had not returned. A nurse's aide bundled up the gauze and wrappings and other trash from the cubicle. A police officer came in and put what was left of Leo's shorts and T-shirt in an evidence envelope. I wondered what had happened to his big guy sneakers, his size elevens. Sometimes when I looked at his bony feet and hairy legs propped on my coffee table, I thought of the small bowed pink parentheses that had confounded me when I first tried to change him as a baby. My throat seized and I opened my mouth, looking for air, and a thin high wail came out. No one seemed to notice as they wheeled another gurney into the cubicle Leo had occupied, this one with a large elderly woman in the throes of what sounded like an asthma attack, her face obscured by the oxygen mask.

"You're going to need to get out of the way," one of the EMTs said.

I wandered back out into the general waiting area, past two little kids playing with action figures on the floor and an old man answering the questions of the woman with a clipboard. The clock told me I had been in the hospital for nearly six hours. I sat down in the waiting area and paged through a tattered women's magazine without seeing a thing. The place was nearly full. It looked like every other waiting area for poor people, a little grubby, a little stuffy, no pictures on the walls except for placards identifying the first signs of heart disease, the routine for breast self-examination, and the Heimlich maneuver. The girl next to me was using a stubby pencil to draw her way out of a maze in a copy of *Highlights for Children*. They'd had the same magazine in the dentist's office when Meghan and I were kids. It didn't look like it had changed at all.

Through the doors I could see the silver shimmy of headlights on the asphalt and a slate-colored night sky. There were two police cars at the far curb, and Irving was sitting in one of them talking on a cell phone. I watched him for a long time. Once he threw one of the phones across the asphalt, and a young cop got out of the squad car and picked it up. Irving made some notes on a narrow notebook he always kept in his breast pocket, then took the phone back from the uniformed cop without even looking up. Once he came inside to check on me. "I'm just waiting," I said. "Do what you have to do." Irving handed me a box of animal crackers from the vending machine and went back outside.

"Do you want these?" I said to the girl next to me.

"I'm not supposed to," she said.

"I know I'm a stranger, but I'm not a bad stranger. You can take them."

"I have sugar diabetes. My grandmama says I got to watch what I eat."

She finished the maze and started some sort of word puzzle. I left the animal crackers on a chair and a little boy carried them off. When his mother looked up, I nodded at her, and she nodded at him. I looked back out and suddenly saw Irving swivel in the seat of the patrol car, the door open, and then he vanished because a limousine had pulled up and blocked my view.

She stepped to the front desk and said, in a way that was undeniable and could not possibly be ignored, "I am Meghan Fitzmaurice." It had been months since I had seen the look the nurse got on her face as she stared up at that wiry figure, brown and freckled, untidy and painfully upright. My God, the look said. You really are.

"Can we not turn this into a photo op?" I heard Irving say, and then I noticed the silver stars pulsating through the glass doors and realized they were flashbulbs, like sharp little bullets of bright light. My sister has an uncanny ability to turn herself into the person the public thinks that she is, as well as what's perhaps an even uncannier ability to turn it off. That's why we can often do an entire six-mile loop in Central Park without anyone looking at her twice. The phrase she uses is apt: she puts out the light. The spotlight is something that shines from within at least as much as the glare from without.

She had never looked less like the woman that nurse thought she knew so well than she did at that moment. Her hair was still a rough reddish nimbus of choppy curls, and her freckles were so dark that she looked like a member of some unknown race. The brown of her skin meant that the scar on her forehead shone as though fluorescent. Her arms jutted, muscular, from the sleeves of a cotton dress she'd gotten in an outdoor market, laundered so the pattern was almost indecipherable. I had always joked that Meghan was the knife and I was the spoon. It had never been more true.

But my sister had turned the light on through sheer force of her blinding will, and the nurse was on her feet, and everything was about to change, as everything always had.

Meghan saw me across a row of plastic chairs, and put out her hand. In just a few minutes we were down a long corridor and into a room that looked like someone's office, with a conference table to one side and a couch. "Lie down, Bridget," she said. "You look exhausted."

"How did you get here so fast?"

"Private jet," she said.

A doctor I hadn't seen before came into the office through a side door, and when I squinted at his name tag I knew why. He was the president of the hospital, and as he shook hands all around I realized we were in his office. On a credenza was a big photograph of a boy in a blue and white soccer uniform, one cleated foot up on the ball. I hated the doctor and his kid with a feeling not unlike heartburn. Perhaps it really was heartburn; my stomach was empty, and the babies were restless. After having given up coffee and wine, after having eaten yogurt and fish—but only fish low in mercury—I was probably delivering a chemical cocktail made up of equal parts fear, guilt, and rage.

"We have our neurosurgery team working on him right now," the doctor was saying, playing nervously with a stethoscope. I wondered if he normally kept one in his pocket or if this was a special occasion. I thought of the day Leo was taking some of the families to Orchard Beach and helping one of the boys change into his trunks. The kid had a thick ropy scar in the shape of a cross that stretched from one end of his belly to the other, from his sternum to his pubis. It looked as though it had been done with a blunt scalpel by a blind man.

"Jerome, what'd you do, man?" Leo had asked, trying to keep his voice soft.

"When I was little I had a thing called a hernia and the doctors had to fix it up," Jerome replied.

"No, dude, I had hernia surgery, it doesn't look like this. You must have had something else."

"Leo!" I'd called from the office. I remembered Leo's surgery. He'd been two years old and his anesthetic was delivered by a woman wearing a Power Rangers mask after he'd had a strawberry sedative lollipop. Meghan sat through the surgery in one corner of the operating room. His scars looked like the faintest of pencil marks, each barely an inch long, each tucked into the fold of his groin, as though the surgeon was worried that someday he'd want to pose nude for a Calvin Klein commercial.

"Dude," I'd said quietly in my office. "That's what a hernia scar looks like if you have surgery in a public hospital after the thing has strangulated and they let a resident learn the ropes on you."

"Doctor, let's cut to the chase," Meghan said, pacing in front of the doctor's desk. "First of all, are you the same person I was talking to on the car phone?"

"I believe that was our chief of staff, Dr. Patel."

Megan looked down at her palm. She'd taken notes on her hand, something she does from time to time. "That's right. He was polite but not terribly informative. He told me that my son was likely to live, that he was unconscious, and that he had suffered what appeared to be a spinal injury. I asked if he was going to be a quadriplegic."

"It's too soon to tell, but that seems unlikely," the doctor said. "The injury to the spinal cord is lower. Quadriplegia results only from an injury high up."

Meghan stopped and leaned forward on his desk. She knows obfuscation when she sees it; she's slashed and burned it enough on national television. "Paraplegia?" she said.

"We're not certain yet."

"But it's possible."

"It's possible."

I covered my face with my hands. Irving put his hand atop my head.

Evan came in then, and he took Meghan in his arms and put his chin atop her head as I'd seen him do so many times before. How soothing he must once have found it, that she was so much smaller than he was. Was it when he realized that that was an optical illusion that he had begun to look elsewhere?

"Oh, Jesus Christ, Ev," she murmured.

"I know, Meg, I know. It's going to be all right. They're still trying to figure out what's going on."

"Have you seen him?"

"Sort of. You can't really see that much of him, between the doctors and the nurses and the equipment. And he's not conscious. I mean, he doesn't know whether we're there or not."

"I need to be where he is."

Evan looked over her head at the doctor. "They're going to be working on him for a while," the doctor said. "It might be easier for you to make yourself comfortable here. I'll send for something to eat."

Meghan shook her head. It made Evan's chin move as though he was a ventriloquist's dummy.

"As close as we can possibly get," she said into his shirtfront.

They left the office hand in hand. That was the deal she'd talked about as we looked at the stars, the one you hear about in songs growing up, the one in the books and in the movies. If you're hurt, your mother and father will be there together, holding on to each other, holding you, holding everything together. And they were.

"You're welcome to stay here," the doctor said.

"I have to make some calls," Irving said. "But the lady definitely needs a more comfortable place to hang out than the waiting room." Irving eased me back on the office couch and took off my shoes. He covered me with his jacket, but a moment later a nurse appeared with a blanket and a pillow, and Irving put his jacket back on. We were interrupted again, this time by an aide with a hospital meal on a tray. Irving lifted the metal dome. "Mystery meat," he said. "They never let you down in these places."

"You know, don't you?" I said. "You know how bad."

"It's what the doctor said. Maybe paralysis. It seems like he's concussed, too. They're not clear on why he won't come to. Although if he can't move his legs I'd just as soon he stayed out for a while longer."

"You've got to get these guys," I said.

"We're on it. Believe me, we're on it. In a couple of hours the mayor, the governor, maybe the president will be on it, too. It's going to be really bad. I got to get way out in front of all that. And I gotta get downtown because somebody's going to want to have a press conference soon. Your sister walked into the hospital and the stealth phase was over."

"Go. I'm fine. I'm just going to lie here. Just do one thing for me?"

"You want a Three Musketeers?"

"The soccer picture over there? Turn it around so I don't have to look at it."

Irving put it in a drawer of the credenza. "I love this kid as much as you do," he said.

"I know, but don't say anything else like that. I just can't start crying. I can't. If I do I won't stop. Do you know where my sister is?"

"She'll find you," Irving said. "Don't worry."

EGHAN SAT BY his bed all day and all night. Evan brought her a stack of books and some magazines, culling the ones that had items about where she was, what her future held, and how Fallujah Levine was doing hosting the show. She never touched any of them. She sat straight in a chair pulled close to the side of the bed. It was a recliner chair in reddish leather, handsome, really, and in the middle of the night she could have leaned back and slept. She never did when I was there. Her eyes went from the heart monitor to Leo's face and back again.

For perhaps forty-five minutes of every hour, she talked. Her voice was soft and faintly sibilant, as though she was letting diction take a holiday, as though it would penetrate Leo's muddied unconscious only if it sounded like Mommy, not Meghan Fitzmaurice. The doctors had decided to keep him in a drug-induced coma while they waited to see if the swelling to his spinal cord would go down, but Meghan was convinced he could hear, and so she spoke to him. "I remember that time when you were three and you fell out of the canoe at the house in Connecticut," she would begin, and even I would be lulled into a state somewhere between meditation and sleep as she went on: the fright, the fish, the warm bath, the hot chocolate. She talked of his first day at Biltmore, of the game at which he got hit in the eye with a lacrosse ball, of the paper he wrote on Greek mythology in which he likened the sirens to the Beatles, of the girl he had dated in eighth grade whose lip had been cut up by Leo's braces and whose parents had called in high dudgeon. "And I said to Gaby's mother on the phone, you should consider it a privilege that your daughter was kissed by my son!" That was how that one ended.

Word by word, phrase by phrase, she built a detailed panorama of an idyllic childhood. My sister had wanted to be a writer, not a celebrity, and she was never so eloquent as during those days. When she would finish, stop, take a drink of water, I would feel as though there was one unspoken sentence hanging always in the air: And they lived happily ever after.

"Do you remember the story of the Three Billy Goats Gruff?" she said one afternoon as she stopped to drink some tea just outside the doorway. "Mother used to read it to us in her bed. There was a troll, I think."

I shook my head, and she looked at me. Her eyes were so clear and her skin translucent, the color of amber. She looked years younger than when she'd gone away. It was as though she was searching for something in my own eyes, and finally she said, almost pleading, "You don't, do you? I'm not sure I do, either."

"Memory's a swamp," I said. "It's hard to tell the snakes from the shadows."

She put a hand out to my arm and brushed my belly instead. "That's a smart thing to say, Bridget Anne," she said in a half-mocking tone.

"I think it's a line from a country western song. And don't sound so surprised. I've always been smart."

"So you got smarter," Meghan said. "Me, I got tan. And thin. The dream of every New York woman, right? And meanwhile my son almost got killed."

Once a day Mercedes came with Leo's favorite foods wrapped in a heat blanket so that when she opened the container the aroma surrounded the bed. Macaroni and cheese, beef stew, sauce Bolognese, peach pie. I don't know what happened to the food afterward. Meghan and I never ate any of it. A black car took Mercedes back to the apartment. Meghan went there every afternoon to take a shower and change her clothes. She was usually back in an hour.

"Anything?" she would say, and I would shake my head.

Leo had lasted two days in that Bronx hospital. The director was astonished, then truculent when my sister announced that an ambulance would be moving him. A team of neuroscientists from the Manhattan hospital habitually rated best in the nation for everything from heart transplants to mental health supervised the move. Leo was taken directly to what is known in New York as the Four Seasons floor. Not only does it appear to have been decorated by those who decorate the luxury hotels but it states in its brochures that it was. The fabrics are all toile, the furniture mahogany, the bathrooms marble. It was the floor of the hospital to which millionaire hedge fund managers came to have angioplasty or young movie stars to give birth, where socialites whose liposuction had gone terribly wrong lay in comas with a manicurist on call once a week. If not for the respirator, the IV lines, and the monitors, it might have been possible to think that Leo and Meghan had gone on one of those little trips they used to take occasionally, when she had to give a speech and she felt it was time he saw Madrid, or Bangkok, or Prague, usually with an embassy escort.

Sometimes, especially at night, I felt as though I was underwater, or underground. When you are from New York and you meet people from other parts of the country—or even the suburbs of New Jersey—they will express surprise that you manage to live where you do. None of them seems to understand how rude this is. How surprised they would be if you said, Gosh, it's hard to understand how you manage to survive in the stifling upper-class confines of Sterling Silver, Connecticut, or Gee, don't you get kind of tired of the sheer boredom of life in Little Town, Iowa? But those same people feel not the slightest hesitation in saying, I don't know how you manage to live here, while standing in front of the Metropolitan Museum of Art or in the middle of Central Park. Sometimes they try to turn the insult on its head by congratulating you on mastering the pace, or the press of people. But mainly they mention the noise.

What they don't understand is that there's no noise to New York if you're rich enough. There is a hermetically sealed office, the backseat of a car with darkened windows, an apartment with triple-glazed windows. The New York apartment of a certain size is so utterly soundproofed that I remember once leaving a dinner table to go to the bathroom—a ploy that I perfected to get through polite conversation with some of the big-money blowhards with whom I had been partnered—and standing at the window astonished as a fierce thunderstorm barreled across Manhattan. Grabby fingers of lightning arced from charcoal gray clouds into the blowing branches of trees in Central Park. Rain fell so hard that it was almost impossible to see the traffic on the street eleven stories below other than as a series of ruddy smears of brake lights. Faintly I could feel a vibration that I suspected was the kettledrum of thunder. But I couldn't hear a thing.

I remember that the man on my right had been talking about a massive lawsuit some years before that had involved the very cooperative building in which we were now eating swordfish and orzo. "Don't worry, Stephen, it was before you bought the place," he brayed when our host had looked wary. It turned out that the residents had been able to hear a faint whir in their back pantries when the elevator passed their floor. "Did any of the residents actually go into their back pantries?" I asked. "Aha!" said the man, using his fork for emphasis. "That's why it took so long for them to get on it. One of the housekeepers finally made a fuss."

The elevator had been rendered utterly soundless. And when we left the dinner party, the storm had blown through as though it had never happened at all, with nothing left but wet sidewalks and a string of black-car drivers who had placed striped golf umbrellas in the front seats, close at hand.

The Four Seasons floor of the hospital was soundless in precisely that way, or at least to the extent that a hospital can ever be soundless. Below it was a busy Manhattan avenue, on which the trucks blew horns, the cars came to a grinding halt, the pedestrians shouted at cabs, and the bicyclists shouted at the pedestrians. It was all a dumb show out the windows of the Four Seasons floor, a mime city. I lived completely and utterly in two bodies, in my own, which seemed to have taken on a life of its own—or two lives, I suppose, since my own participation often seemed negligible—and in Leo's. A machine breathed for him, with a sound a bit like an obscene phone caller with asthma. I often found myself unconsciously breathing in tandem with him, and occasionally I became dizzy because of it.

Edward Prevaricator was on the hospital board. He had also sent the private plane, and provided the car that hovered at a side entrance all day and all night, for Mercedes, for Meghan, for me. He was an unobtrusive presence, coming in once a day for a few minutes just to ask Meghan how she was and to offer her the use of the plane to bring in that specialist from Miami, this one from Geneva. "He's stinking rich," Meghan said wearily one day after he left. "Machine parts or something. Plants all over the Midwest. It's kind of refreshing actually, to meet someone who made his money by actually making something as opposed to just making more money."

Evan was there every day, too, but the more time passed the less he put his arm around Meghan's shoulder or took her hand. It was hard to blame him. Meghan was as thin and hard as a bamboo pole, her eyes glowing with a slightly maniacal shine. I waited and waited for her to weep. Perhaps, like me, she did it in the car or in the shower.

Alison and Tequila would arrive most days after work, and we would come out to the common room to meet them. The common room on the Four Seasons floor was a three-story skylit atrium with Oriental rugs, living room furniture groupings, and a grand piano. The pianist came at four and left at seven every day, so we sat and talked to the plaintive strains of "Für Elise" or, if he was in a jauntier mood, "Send in the Clowns."

"The cops are all over the projects," Tequila said somberly when Meghan had drifted back to the room to check on Leo. "They saying it was those boys that Armand was hanging with. Armand's over to his aunt in Queens. I told the officers, I said they can talk to him whenever but I want him out of the house while this happening."

"You need to get a lawyer," I said.

"We don't need no lawyer. It wasn't him. I know that boy. He's got his troubles, but he didn't do this. He wasn't with them. He was over to the college signing up for his summer courses, and he had to wait and wait for the adviser to sign, and I told him, That professor, he saved your butt, boy. He says they didn't say nothing to him about doing this. They knew, those boys, that he wouldn't go along, or maybe it just happened, you know, just sudden and careless. He told the officers all he knows. They can't find the other boys. That tells you something, right there. All four gone missing, all at once. Huh."

"Is Margaret all right?"

"She wants to come here, I say no. I don't want her seeing him like that. She thinks she started all the trouble, says those boys were hassling her about her white boyfriend. She says, Mommy, he wasn't my boyfriend, he was just my friend. I don't want her coming here."

"Tequila, would you like some roses?" Meghan said, emerging from the nurses' station with a vase of white long-stemmed flowers. The arrangements had come in an unceasing cavalcade once the story had gotten out that the young man shot in the projects in what was assumed to be a drug deal gone wrong was Meghan Fitzmaurice's son, a volunteer at a charity for homeless women.

The president of the network, Meghan's agent, the managing partner in Evan's firm, the head of the Biltmore School, dozens of people who had sat at their dinner table and gossiped about them after: they all sent enormous bouquets. Delphiniums, peonies, orchids, of course. They were all summarily sent down to the oncology floor after Mercedes collected the cards to make a list for thank-you notes. The Borowses sent chocolate chip cookies, the ones Kate makes herself. They were the only thing I ever saw Meghan eat during those days.

At the end of the week, Alison and Tequila came with a folder of drawings the kids had made. "Dude, Get Well Soon, Darren," said one with a stick figure of a man standing over what appeared to be a chessboard. "I am so sad that you are sik," said another from one little girl, construction paper cut into the shape of a lopsided heart. In all there were eleven cards and letters, including one from Annette, Delon's mother, a Hallmark card that said on the front "May God Bless You and Hold You in His Hand."

Irving would appear at odd times, two in the morning, two in the afternoon, his suit spotted, his tie loosened at the throat. The ICU had a family-only policy, but his deputy commissioner's badge trumped that. He sometimes appeared to be the only person Meghan was interested in talking to, and she would walk around and around the atrium with him, her flip-flops slapping the marble at the margins of the rug. Her face would be set and her eyes down, but her mouth would work whether she was speaking or he was. Occasionally he would stop and bend his head to speak to her with the fierce and dark intensity that I had seen only from time to time, and only on television.

"I'm thanking God your sister doesn't have a carry permit," he said when he made me sit down in the small parlor where afternoon tea was served to the visitors to the Four Seasons floor. There was chamomile, mint, and Earl Grey tea, and cucumber and smoked salmon tea sandwiches. Watching Irving eat tea sandwiches is like watching a bear eat berries.

"She'll be better when you catch the guy," I said.

"Yeah, people always think that. It's bull. I mean, we'll get this guy, but he'll just turn out to be some mook showing off for his homeboys. There won't be anything biblical about it, which is what people always want. They want it to be big, epic, to mean something. None of it means something. Eat a sandwich. You have to keep up your strength."

"I probably shouldn't ask this, but do you guys think Tequila's son is involved?"

Irving's mouth was full. He shook his head and swallowed. "Nah, he's clear. All these guys we're hearing about are his friends, though. The thing is, most of them aren't real players. A couple of them don't even have juvie problems, they're pretty clean. I think one of them had a thing for the daughter. Maybe it was just something that got out of hand. We don't know yet but it won't be long. We'll pop somebody for something else, drugs or an assault, and they'll say, Yo, you guys want to trade some jail time for information? And there we'll be. We'll get the guy. And we'll nail him."

"Did you tell Meghan all this?"

"Sure. Like I said, it's not going to make her feel any better. And you know that kid, it's not going to make him feel any better. He's a champ, that kid. It's gonna be tough, but he's a champ and he'll get by. Oh, hell, don't cry."

"I just want him to wake up," I said, wrapping some of the salmon sandwiches in a napkin. "Oh, madam, I'll take care of that," said the young woman who served the tea. She brought out a fancy white box full of the sandwiches and an assortment of scones, and I took them back to the room, back to Meghan. The next morning I threw them away, untouched.

That was the morning the doctor told Meghan and Evan that he and his colleagues suspected Leo's spinal cord might be irreparably damaged. When Meghan left for the apartment that afternoon, her back looked bowed, as though her own spine had been damaged, as though it was too slender a thing to hold her up any longer.

I went into the bathroom and turned on the taps full blast and sobbed, sitting on the toilet seat, my belly heavy on my thighs. Perhaps she was right; perhaps he could hear. I wouldn't want him to hear the horrible retching sounds that were coming from inside me. Finally I splashed water on my flaming face and sat down in the chair that was still slightly warm from Meghan's weight.

"Do you remember that day I went on the field trip to the Bronx Zoo with your class?" I whispered. "You got into that big argument with Andrew, I think that was his name, Andrew Backus, about whether an opossum was a marsupial. I think he was Australian, or he'd just been to Australia, and he was so full of himself, one of those fat kids with a loud voice, and he kept saying, No, no, only Australia had marsupials. Your voice was so high then, and you were very polite, you waited until he was done with all his spitting and screaming, and then you said in this very dignified way, 'The opossum is the only American marsupial.' And one of the zoo guys heard you and said, 'That's right. Most people don't know that.' Man, the wind just went out of his sails. I remember afterwards I said to your dad, I think that kid lost ten pounds of bullshit. You went to school and repeated that and got in trouble. I got you in trouble."

His heartbeat on the machine continued to count out a monotonous even pattern. Kerthunk, kerthunk. "Wake up, kidlet," I said after each anecdote. Kerthunk, kerthunk. It was oddly soothing, the minutiae of memory, the details dragged up from the undifferentiated tedium of the past. Who cared what was true and what was a trick of the mind, which was the snake and which the shadow? I went on to the story about the doorman coming up to complain that Leo and his friends were mooning double-decker tourist buses from the library windows, and the time we went to the San Gennaro festival and Leo threw up calzone on Irving's shoes after chugging a Coke.

"Wake up," I was murmuring, and then I pushed the recliner back and fell asleep. Hormones, I thought dismissively to myself. Once I blinked and a nurse was there, changing an IV bag, humming under her breath. Later I shifted positions and saw Evan in the straight chair on the other side of the bed. "Shhh, it's okay, Bridge," he said quietly, and I slid down the slope of sleep again.

T HE DAYS WENT by slowly and almost soundlessly, neither day nor night. I slept often, listening to Meghan tell stories, watching the lines around Evan's mouth deepen, hearing the doctors murmur in the halls. There was a nightmarish shape to each day: the updates from Irving, the conferences with the doctors, the constant dozes from which I always woke momentarily unsure of where I was and, for just a blessed instant, ignorant of all that had happened. Maybe that was why Meghan never napped, because if she did she would smell the sweet equatorial air, hear the white pebbles rolling up and down the beach, and imagine herself swimming to shore, chasing the rays from their hiding spaces in the sand. And then she would wake to this.

"I'm having those contractions," I said to Evan one day as we sat on either side of the bed, during one of those rare times when Meghan had left the hospital.

"You are? Are you sure? Should I call the nurse?"

"Not the real contractions, the fake kind." A nurse came in to adjust the IV and smiled reflexively at us both. "They're some sort of practice contractions. They have a strange name. Like Ezra Pound. Ezra Pound contractions."

"Ezra Pound?"

"Braxton Hicks," murmured the nurse.

"That's it. I'm having Braxton Hicks contractions."

"Absolutely normal at this stage," said the nurse. "And that's from someone who spent eleven years in labor and delivery." She patted my shoulder on her way out.

"Ezra Pound," Evan said. "Bridge, I miss the wackiness you brought into my life."

"Yeah? I miss stuff, too, Ev."

"Like what? Or should I even ask?"

"I don't know. I miss my illusions, mainly. It turns out I had a lot of them. Which is strange when you think about it. I mean, of all of us I probably have the most real-world job. Well, maybe not as much as Irving, but close. You'd think I'd be more realistic than the rest of you put together."

"That's false logic. If you were really realistic, you'd be a partner at some law firm with two kids in private school and hot-and-cold running nannies."

"You say that like it's a bad thing." And we both laughed a little. I hoped Leo could hear us; it was the kind of interchange that he loved, the kind of remark he so often made. Maybe I was trying to speak for him as well as to him. I noticed the light playing on the sheen of coppery stubble on his head. I remembered how terrified I had been of the soft spot on his skull when he was an infant. "Can't he wear a helmet?" I'd asked once.

"You seeing somebody, Ev?" I said in a quiet companionable sort of voice.

He stared down at his hands, then nodded without looking at me. "I don't know what it is. I don't know where it will wind up. I don't know." His eyes slewed sideways to Leo, and for a moment his mouth twisted.

"I saw you," I said. "I saw you at dinner. At Française."

"I know. I saw you, too. There was a mirror on the wall and I could see you and Irving." Both of us smiled.

"Like an O. Henry story," I said. "I saw you and you saw me and neither of us said anything to one another."

"I thought about it, but you and Irving looked like you were fighting."

"He asked me to marry him."

"Oh, that explains it."

I laughed again. "I miss you, too, Ev. Maybe someday . . ." I shrugged as my voice trailed off. I was having another contraction. Braxton Hicks.

"Maybe."

I slept, and then I dreamed. Leo and I were skydiving. He was young, perhaps seven or eight. We were both nervous and happy, unconcerned with the fact that Meghan had been kept in the dark about our plans. We leapt, and our chutes didn't open, and the spires of the city rose to meet us, and I woke to the sound of a sharp click as Evan turned the television on.

Ever since the start of the pregnancy, I had found it difficult to move from sleep to consciousness. Sometimes I thought a part of my mind was deep inside with the pair of them, lulled by the motion, listening to the heartbeats, dreaming the dreams of those poised between two worlds. So it took me a minute or two to realize that I was looking at a shot on the TV screen of the front door of a building in the Tubman projects, police officers in flak jackets on either side. The camera pulled back and showed the broad quadrangle of dirt at its center; it was empty of everything except police and police cars.

"What?" I said.

Evan turned up the sound. A local reporter was stumbling over her words, caught in midsentence ". . . will be exiting the building in just a few minutes, we're told. It's unclear whether this was a hostage situation or a surrender. What we do know is that for at least an hour a resident of the projects has been inside one of the apartments there with a young woman and another person who has been identified by police as Meghan Fitzmaurice." The local reporter seemed flustered, working live without a script, but she was smart enough to know that she didn't have to identify Meghan further.

One of the nurses stood in the doorway, too, as Evan switched from channel to channel, finally settling on the network for which Meghan had so famously been the public face. They interviewed a woman with a toddler in her arms, who said the police refused to let her back into her apartment. "This baby is getting hungry, too," she said peevishly, and as if on cue her little girl keened, "I wanna sandwich." They interviewed a young man, who said it wasn't fair that a clutch of cops showed up for "some TV lady" and paid scant attention when items were taken from people's apartments, which had apparently happened to his girlfriend recently.

They interviewed Charisse as a group of kids jumped up and down behind her, until she turned and waved them off with her fierce bottom lip thrust out over her chin. "Meghan's boy, he got shot here and she's upstairs talking to the person who did it, and she's going to bring him out before there's any more trouble," she said. "He showed up here, he's sorry, he came to apologize to a girl here who is a friend of Meghan's boy, and things got a little out of hand and the girl's mother called Meghan and told her to come over. You can't get the cops to come right over here and have things stay calm, you know what I mean? You don't know what would happen with that boy in there if the cops come, breaking down the door. So she called Meghan and she came in and she's talking to him now. She'll take care of business with this boy. You know she will."

"Jesus Christ," I said.

"What the hell is she talking about?" Evan said.

"She's taking a terrible chance," said the nurse.

"Oh, come on. That's a preposterous story," Evan said.

"No, it's not," I said.

Evan didn't have the advantage of knowing Tequila, of knowing how strategy forms in a mind sharpened by years of mistreatment at the hands of mindless authority. If she found a criminal in her home with Princess Margaret, even a remorseful criminal, she would ask herself how best to turn him over to the authorities without getting her children hurt, or her daughter's name sullied, or the child welfare bureaucracy interested in her family again. How lucky she was, to have on her desk pad the number of a person so well-known that instead she herself would become the center of attention, a person so powerful that she would surely be able to make things right.

We sat and watched for what seemed like a long time, although when I looked at the grandfather clock out in the hallway I saw that only fifteen minutes had passed. The local stations were all afraid to cut away, and even CNN had gone live to a shot of the doors of the Tubman projects. The traffic helicopters hovered overhead, and I wondered what it sounded like in Tequila's apartment, where the windows would have been open. The soundless New York exists only for the wealthy. For the poor there is always sound: the cars whooshing past on the highway on their way to someplace else, the subway clanking along the elevated line, the screaming fights in the courtyard, the sound of gunshots at night. Their lives are so noisy that maybe the guy who had shot Leo didn't even notice the sound of rotors. Maybe he slept in every morning, stayed out every night drinking a forty-ounce and blowing a bone with the boys, so that he thought the freckled woman sitting on Tequila's velour couch was just some white lady Princess Margaret had gotten to know at that fancy school she went to.

Meghan Meghan Meghan, all the reporters said, as though she had never gone away. There's never much happening in a hostage story until the very end, so most channels took the opportunity to reprise the Ben Greenstreet episode, and one of the cable shows, the right-wing one, even reran the footage with the obligatory dead air over the offending words. But Meghan's own network did not. I thought that it was self-protection, but afterward I wondered whether even then the big guys could see what was coming and were hedging their bets.

Then suddenly the local reporter interrupted the monologue she was doing to fill airtime, about the size of the projects and the crime rate there, which was even worse than I'd always suspected. She got a vacant look on her face, the look my sister had once told me meant you were listening to something in your earphone and therefore were never going to be good enough for network, and then she said, "Excuse me, Dan, but we've just been told that the suspect is going to be exiting the building in just a moment and that Meghan Fitzmaurice will be with him." The camera took in the front door of the building, and sure enough, there was movement at the end of the long hallway, a blur of blue and white that materialized as though a Polaroid was developing behind the smeared glass, resolving itself into a clear picture as the doors swung open, the police still holding back.

Ah, how lucky she has always been in even the small things, our Meghan. That morning she had put on a plain white linen dress, so that she shone in the weak sunlight falling between the brick towers. She looked like a saint in a stained glass window, whittled away from body to simply soul, all eyes. Next to her was Armand's friend Marvin, his head down. He was wearing a baseball cap, which made him look as though he was hiding his face. His hands hung limply at his sides, and I was certain he had been told that if they went into his pockets the guns would be raised and maybe even used. Meghan put one hand on his shoulder, and he appeared to flinch. She raised her chin slightly and looked out into the quadrangle as though she was there to talk to the residents grouped in small knots on the packed earth, not the phalanx of old electronic friends, the television cameras set up in a half circle.

"This man came here today to turn himself in to police. He is wanted in connection with the shooting here two weeks ago of my son, Leo Grater. Before he gave himself up, he wanted to speak to me and turn over the weapon used in that shooting. He is a person of faith who felt that God wanted him to do this before he spoke to the police. I knew that the New York City Police Department was looking for him, and it was important to me that no harm come to him before he could give himself up."

"No harm come to him," Evan said. "No harm. Let them shoot the scumbag right now."

"Shhhhhh."

"The police department was extremely cooperative in accommodating my desire to speak to him. I thank them." She took her hand from Marvin's shoulder, and he looked up, plainly terrified, as though Meghan's touch was all that stood between him and a couple of good body shots from an automatic weapon. "I am not the only mother who has had a child shot in these projects," she said. "They all deserve justice." Then she nodded at the police officer nearest her as though by prearranged signal, and he and several others stepped forward and cuffed the kid. Even at a distance the news cameras picked up the sound of Meghan saying, "Don't hurt him." The police put Marvin in the back of one car, and Meghan got in the back of another, and suddenly Irving was standing in her place, in front of the door of the Tubman building where Tequila lived.

"At approximately twelve forty-five P.M. a suspect surrendered himself in the shooting of Leo Grater at the Tubman projects," he said. "The suspect expressed the wish to surrender peacefully to Mr. Grater's mother at the apartment of a mutual friend. Mr. Grater's mother came from his hospital bed, where he is being treated for his injuries, to the Tubman projects and met with the suspect, who is identified as Marvin White, nineteen, a lifelong resident of the projects. Mr. White had with him the firearm he used in the shooting, which he turned over to Mr. Grater's mother. He expressed to her his remorse about his actions and his hope that her son would recover fully from his injuries. He is now on his way to central booking. That's all for now."

"Commissioner," one of the reporters cried, "does the suspect know who the victim's mother is?"

Irving sighed. You could hear and see it: shoulders up, chin down. "I have no idea," he said.

"Jesus Christ," Evan said. I couldn't speak. Another nurse came to the door of the room. "Someone from the police department called to say that Mrs. Grater will be back in about an hour," she said.

"Mrs. Grater," Evan said with contempt. "Mrs. Grater. Jesus."

I was exhausted. "She's right, you know," I said wearily. "That could have been a bloodbath, with that guy holed up in Tequila's apartment. Meghan probably kept the whole thing from blowing up."

"Oh, was that the point of that exercise? The police could have gone in there and gotten him. That's their job."

"They could have shot up the apartment."

"You believe that was what she was thinking? You're amazing, Bridget. Do you stay up nights inventing excuses for her?"

"It is what it is, Ev," I said with a shrug.

"Oh, can everyone stop saying that. Nothing is what it is. What is this—a hospital room or a fancy hotel? What is she, a martyr or a mother? What are you, a sister or an assistant? Do you live in this city? Nothing is what it is. No one looks their age. No one screws their spouse. No one likes their job. It is what it is? Where? What? When?" He stood up and walked out, then turned on his heel and shot back into the room, his fists clenched. "Let me tell you how a guy feels when someone shoots his son. He feels powerless. He wants to find the guy who did it and rip him apart with his bare hands. And instead he has to sit here and do nothing except wonder whether his son will be able to speak, and read, and feed himself, and walk again."

He pointed up at the television. "And then she goes out and takes over. And she doesn't even tell me. She doesn't think, Well, maybe his father would want to be part of this. Maybe he could help me. Maybe he would at least want to know who the animal is who did this to his boy. Because it's always been about her. You couldn't figure out why I left, Bridge? I was never really there. I was an incidental character in the Meghan Fitzmaurice show. And, honest to God, you know as well as I do that you are, too." Evan shook his head, his mouth working. "I want to see my son when she's not here. Tell her that. We'll have to divide up the time. I won't be in the room with her."

The set stayed on, telling me everything I already knew about my sister. Over and over again they replayed the clip of Meghan with her hand on Marvin's shoulder. "Don't hurt him," she said. "Don't hurt him. Don't hurt him." Then they returned to regularly scheduled programming, which was a soap opera, which seemed just right.

It was at least three hours before she came back into the room. The set was still on but with the sound muted. I was eating a tuna sandwich and reclining again, my swollen ankles elevated. Meghan's dress was creased at the hips as though she had been sitting for a long time. She still shone as though she'd soaked up the light from the sun and the cameras and stored it deep inside.

"Anything?" she said, standing over Leo and looking down at his pale freckled face.

"Anything?" I said, the ubiquitous echo. "That's all you're going to say? Anything? Anything up with you? Want to give me a report on your day, on what the hell you were doing and what that was all about?"

She looked up at the set. A beautiful blonde was emoting soundlessly to a silver-haired man. I often wondered how Meghan felt when she looked at a TV set. Was it the way a cicada felt looking at its shed skin, its transparent shadow?

"Did they interrupt scheduled programming?" she said.

"Oh, come off it. Of course they did. Look, Meghan's back. Oh, look, Bob, Meghan Fitzmaurice is back, and now she's the star of her own personal drama. Well, actually, it's her son's drama, but let's not quibble. She's the hostage! Rise and shine!"

"Shut up, Bridget. You don't know what the hell you're talking about."

"I don't think there was a whole lot of mystery to that performance, Meghan."

"You don't know what you're talking about," she repeated. "Your friend Tequila called me. Her daughter called her and said this guy was in the apartment with a gun, crying, yelling, waving it around. It wasn't a hostage situation. He spent an hour emoting, gave up the gun, talked about finding Jesus, blah blah blah. Tequila figured I could get him out of there and away from her daughter. And that's what I did. I went over there and I pretended to listen to the guy and then I called Irving and I took care of business. I don't know who called the TV people, but it wasn't me. I just did what Tequila asked me to do."

"Oh, come off it. 'They all deserve justice.' 'Don't hurt him.' Compassionate Meghan, forgiving Meghan."

"I don't know why you're so angry. You know how things work up there. You know what a mess that could have turned into. You know I'm right."

And that, of course, was exactly why I was so angry. "You try to run everything!" I cried.

"Somebody has to," my sister replied.

"Oh, now we've moved on to take-charge Meghan, who gets to have her career back and feel so good about herself at the same time. Not to mention that she gets to do it all for the benefit of the folks watching at home."

"Don't be stupid. You know what the cameras were good for? For insurance. It's all too public now. No judge will give this guy a slap on the wrist. They will all know the whole world is watching. And they won't be able to deal it down, lowball him or give him a pass. That son of a bitch will pay. He will pay for what he did to my boy. He will pay and pay and pay and pay."

"I don't believe you."

Meghan sat down in the chair Evan had left. Her face was flat; the light was gone. "You're right. You want to know what I was really doing? I was cleaning up your goddamn mess. Leo wouldn't have even known these people if it wasn't for you. He wouldn't have even been in that shithole if it wasn't for you. What you saw there? That was me cleaning up Bridget's mess. Of course, because that's what I do, don't I? That's what I've always done. My whole life."

"You know, Meghan, there might have been a time when I would have swallowed that. But no more. Here's what I believe: I believe you just bought your own rehabilitation on Leo's back. I believe I'm going to spend the next ten years watching spots about urban violence and spinal cord injuries and the rights of the disabled so that you can be a star again. And if I figure out that's true, I will never speak to you again as long as I live. Never."

Out in the hospital atrium, I sat down heavily at one of the small tables. Without a word, the young aide brought me what I'd been having the last few days, a pot of chamomile tea and a pumpkin scone. The twins were perambulating wildly beneath my rib cage as though they, too, were undone and enraged. I took off my shoes, and when I tried to get up to leave, to go somewhere, anywhere, I found that I couldn't get them back on my swollen feet, and I began to cry. Wordlessly the aide returned with a box of tissues and a stack of magazines. Perhaps she did not realize that one of them, one of the older ones, had my sister's picture on the cover. "Meghan!" it said. "Fit and nearing 50!" The pianist was playing what seemed to be an endless medley of New York songs. Taking the A train, in a New York state of mind. After about a half hour, he wound up with a rendition of "New York, New York." If you can make it here, you can make it anywhere.

"I hate this song," Irving said, falling into the chair opposite me. "Sweetheart?" he called to the hospital aide. "Sweetheart, is there any way you could get a tired guy a beer? I don't do the tea thing, and I'm really running on empty here."

"I'm sorry, sir, but we don't serve alcohol in the hospital."

"Yeah, I guess I figured that. I just thought maybe an exception could be made." He looked at me looking hard at him and added, "I think my pal here could use a drink, too."

"I could use an explanation."

"Not from me. I got dragged into this thing at the last minute. I still have to get a fill from the number one participant, who is around here somewhere. I'm just the guy who called the cops and kept things cool. But that was not my show."

"Yeah, I know exactly whose show it was. *Show* is exactly the right word for it."

Irving pulled a cigar from his breast pocket and rolled it between his thumb and finger. "I think you're being hasty about this. I'm the last guy who wants your average civilian involved in something like that, and I'm going to rip Tequila the next time I see her about what she did. But you know as well as I do that your sister might have actually helped keep things under control there. Not great for the department, because one of the city columnists will be pounding the drum about how one little white woman could keep things cool when the cops usually can't. But bottom line, she went in, she came out with the guy, we got the guy, she walked away, no one hurt. Finito."

"Oh please. Finito? On what planet? She'll be all over the news for the next two weeks."

"If anyone can deal with that, she can."

"That's not what I mean. I mean she used this. She used this to get herself back on the map. And you helped her. You helped her."

Irving looked at me, the cigar pivoting in his hand. The aide brought him a flowered teapot and a matching cup. He waved her away, but she put it down and winked. Irving looked inside the pot and smiled. I could smell the beer from where I sat. He poured from the teapot into the cup and sipped, then gulped.

"Thanks, sweetheart," he called across the room.

"You're not going to say anything to me?"

"I'm trying to modulate my temper before I do. So let me start at the beginning. You have a sister. She's two people. She's that person that everyone thinks they know. They make up stuff about her, in their own heads and in the papers, and some of it is right on the money and most of it is crap. Then she's the person she really is, whatever that means. And she probably figures there's nobody who knows who that is except your aunt, maybe, and you. It turns out that even her husband can't tell the difference. And right now it seems like you can't, either. You're making the kind of judgment about what happened that reporters will make, and gossip columnists, and all those morons your sister invites over for dinner, the ones that eat her little bitty lamb chops and then trash her behind her back. And I gotta say, from where I'm sitting, the idea that you're in that camp is pretty heinous."

"You don't know her."

"Yeah, I do. You're the one who doesn't. You can't see straight when she's around. What's your problem, that if she winds up right back where she started from then so will you? That's a joke. Everything's changed. She crashed and burned, and you stood up. You can't go back, even if you wanted to, and Jesus, it would be sad if you wanted to. You can't go back because you're a different person and so is she. Look at her. It's gone, whatever you call it, that idea she had that she was untouchable. That way of looking like she had the world by the tail. And look at yourself. Poor little Bridget? Give me a break. She was as phony as big bad Meghan was. Stop playing cartoons in your head. Stop believing what you see on TV. Your sister is weak and broken and sad. And she needs somebody to see her that way, to let her be that way in one little corner of the world. And there's nobody available except you. You hear me? You think you owe her? Well, payback time is here."

"You're taking her side?"

Irving shook his head hard, like he was trying to shake something loose. He leaned back in the chair and sighed. "I just don't get it. I just don't get it. You're so damn smart about everybody else. And then you get inside your own head and you wander around like you're in the woods without a compass."

"You're taking her side. You are. I can't believe it."

"There are no sides. You love somebody and you help them, and you give them a break. And they do things you don't like but you love them so you go along."

"Like a deal."

Irving shook his head. "If it's like a deal, you're screwed," he said. "A deal means you're expecting something back. What I'm talking about is just taking it as it comes."

"I'm not sure I can forgive her."

"For what?"

"For that dog-and-pony show she just put on. I just don't see it the way you do. I still think she was trying to rehabilitate her reputation out there."

"Bridget, let me tell you something. And I want you to listen to this, because I'm saying it out of respect. You would have done the same god-damn thing."

"I wouldn't have had the cameras there."

Irving sighed again. "Forget the cameras. Who cares? It's not whether people are watching when you do it. It's what you do. People will see what they want. It's only the ones inside who know the truth. I've told you a million times: Don't ever make the mistake of confusing a good story and the truth."

"I'm still trying to figure out which this was."

"Ah," said Irving, finishing the last inch of beer from the flowered pot. "This was one of those rare cases that was both at the same time."

SEE CLEARLY now in retrospect that Irving was right. He can be irritating that way, although he is also good about admitting his own errors of judgment. A month after the twins were born he was walking one of them across the bedroom floor just before dawn when I heard him say, "Okay, I admit it. I was totally wrong about this. Totally." On the other hand, I think he said it because he thought I was asleep.

Of course, I was right about my sister, too. Rehabilitation was exactly what happened, although the shape of it was clear only as the years went by. To her credit, Meghan handled the aftermath of the afternoon at the Tubman houses flawlessly, which I suppose should have come as no surprise. She didn't do interviews; the requests from reporters piled up beside the phone, although Mercedes told them that Miss Fitzmaurice would not be calling back. The only messages she returned, when she came home from the hospital to sleep for an hour or two, were those from old friends. She didn't start going out to lunch with network executives until Leo had left the hospital and gone to the rehabilitation facility, where the staff began the work of teaching him to negotiate the world from a wheelchair.

The rehab hospital was an hour north of the city, its turreted stone buildings set along wide paths in the middle of the woods. Even the local cabdrivers who took me from the train station had a hard time finding it. But dozens of people came to see Leo during the months that he was there. His friends from Biltmore drove from the north and the south, from Vassar and Princeton and Colgate and Yale. A few of them were discomfited by the sight of Leo Grater, lacrosse player, track-and-field hurdler, long-legged soccer ace, sitting in the motorized chair, his calves merely filler within the legs of his pants. But most of them gave him one afternoon to vent and then went on as before. There were a couple of weeks after Meghan showed him the tape of Marvin's surrender when Leo was sullen and silent, even with me. The guy took a plea and still got the maximum, not for assault but for attempted murder. He writes Leo once a month every month, on the anniversary of the day he shot him.

One afternoon we were sitting in the sunroom overlooking a small pond, and I asked Leo whether he had dreamed during that time in the hospital, those weeks when the doctors kept him chemically unconscious to give him time to heal. He nodded. His hair had grown in darker, less wavy, and of course he looked older now. "I dreamed I was running," he said. That was the only time I cried in front of him. "Let it go, Bridey," he muttered.

His friends came down from Amherst, too, and some of the kids from the Bronx took the train up with their mothers, who sat uncomfortably in the waiting room, hoping no one blamed them for what had happened. Leo played chess with the kids in the sunroom, and he flexed his biceps to show them how strong he'd gotten. Delon came, too. "I'm sorry someone shot you with a gun," he said solemnly, and Leo said, "I'm sorry, too." Then he put Delon on his lap and took him for a ride down one of the outdoor pathways, the little boy clinging to the handrails of the chair with that same terrified look of joy he'd had when Leo put him on his shoulders and exhibited him for the cop and the caseworker that afternoon so long ago.

Princess Margaret visited almost every Saturday. Often she hitched a ride with one of Leo's friends. She went to Amherst, too. They gave her the biggest grant they had to offer, a free ride for college and an additional three-year scholarship endowed by an alumna for postgraduate work. Tequila had decided that she would be a lawyer.

Leo transferred to Columbia after he finished rehab. He called it the crip-friendly Ivy, but I suspect he wanted to be close to the therapist he had found. She was a fifty-year-old Irish-American woman, slender and self-contained, a marathon runner with the most muscled calves I had ever seen. I'd laughed when I went in to talk to her for the first time.

"And he chose you out of all the shrinks in town," I'd said.

"Occasionally the human psyche is mysterious," she'd replied in a light voice. "But not often."

She'd come to Leo's graduation as his guest, and so had Margaret and Tequila, and Irving, of course, and Aunt Maureen, who had moved into an assisted living facility, and Evan and his wife, Juliet, and their daughter, who was six months old and slept through the ceremony in her stroller, and Edward Prevaricator, who had married my sister the year before. Each graduate was supposed to have only four tickets to Class Day, but Edward had become a trustee of the university, and we had as many tickets as we liked. We were already sitting in a special section near the stage when he and Meghan arrived, and like a cornfield in an August breeze, the crowd began to make that faint repetitive whispering noise I know so well, that resolved itself into spoken words only if you listened closely, or knew in advance what they would be saying: There she is. There she is. Meghan Fitzmaurice. That day I remembered what she had said to me one afternoon down by the blue water in Jamaica about how she felt in exile: "The past seems improbable, the present infinite."

"What about the future?" I'd asked.

"What future?" she had replied.

"Leo almost missed the procession," she whispered to me as she took her seat between Irving and Edward. "He and his friends were carrying on upstairs. I think most of them are already drunk. And God knows what they're wearing under their robes. I think one of them is naked."

"Really naked?" my son said, his eyes enormous.

His sister was at the end of the row on Margaret's lap, her thumb stuck firmly in her mouth, her free hand playing with a curl that hung down on her forehead. Perhaps that was why Leo had wanted to go to school in New York City, too, because of Max and Isabelle. Max and Isabelle Fitzmaurice Lefkowitz. "Aw, jeez," Irving had said. "They sound like a law firm."

"Your uncle Leo is not a good boy, Max," Meghan whispered.

"He's not a boy," Max said, pursing his lips. "He's a man."

And it was so. As his name was called, he steered himself effortlessly up the ramp to the platform, and from the other students there was a great deep shout. He waved, and his classmates began to chant "Le-o, Le-o," and Max and Isabelle picked it up, too. Evan's daughter rose from the stroller and let out a cry at the noise, then as quickly slumped down and fell back to sleep, and Evan reached over and put his hand on Meghan's. Her eyes were full of tears. There was a flash, and I knew someone, perhaps just another parent, perhaps a press photographer at the edges of the crowd, had taken her picture. Three helicopters circled overhead, above the shaded amphitheater the limestone buildings of the university created as they leaned toward the center lawn. Watching, watching, although this time watching not us but the pageantry below. New York is a city in which everyone is always watching, in which I suppose everyone feels recognized. When Irving and I had moved into the bigger apartment on Ninety-seventh Street the month after the twins were born, a woman stopped me on the stoop as I carried the last of the lamps out of the old place. "Congratulations!" she said, a palpable thrill in her voice, and I looked at her, confused, and suddenly saw that she was the woman who lived across the backyard, with the son, now gone to college, and the daughter, who looked a year or two from leaving. I had watched her life from across a hundred feet of atmosphere, and it turned out she had watched mine, too. We embraced.

"Didn't it creep you out that she'd been watching you?" Meghan said when we were having lunch with our aunt, and then was vaguely indignant as the two of us hooted with raucous laughter.

My sister is for all intents and purposes herself again, which is to say that everyone knows who she is and thinks well of her. Slowly but surely over the last four years, it became clear that Meghan Fitzmaurice, the hard-as-flint morning news cookie who'd filthy-mouthed a guest, had been transmuted into Meghan Fitzmaurice, the devoted mother who walked her son's assailant into the arms of the police and sat by her son's bedside and her son's wheelchair as he recovered. In each successive story the Greenstreet interview was pushed lower as the standoff at the projects grew larger. The audience didn't realize until the opportunity presented itself that what Meghan Fitzmaurice needed to make her perfect was a whiff of tragedy and a measure of comeuppance.

She has a different job and a different audience now, too. She does a show called *Day's End* that runs for a half hour each night at 11:30. She and a guest in conversation, usually about something significant: the secretary of state on the Middle East, the president of Harvard on the future of higher education. No interviews with actresses unless the actresses are smart and serious and willing to be crossed. Meghan had not lost that, that ability to say, "Oh, come on. Didn't you really take on this role for the money, pure and simple?" People say they find it refreshing.

One night Irving and I were watching, and he said thoughtfully, "Nobody maintains the fiction better." At first I thought it was a criticism and I was a little surprised, since Meghan has been so devoted to the twins and Irving has come to like her more for it. But then I realized that he had gotten to the heart of the thing, not only for her, but for all of us. Meghan once managed to convince people that what they were seeing was a conversation on a couch between two people, two people who happened to be America's best-known TV personality and a popular actress, or an esteemed writer, or a distinguished doctor, or sometimes just an average citizen, jittery and glassy-eyed, caught in an extraordinary situation and rewarded by four minutes on morning television. There was a coffee table and a wall of books and a window with a view, although the view was a photograph wallpapered onto a backdrop and the books had never been read and the living room was in the middle of a vast hangar of a place filled with technical people and assistants and producers.

Now Meghan convinces people that she is merely sitting at a table deconstructing the great issues of the day, although most of them have been deconstructed in advance by the production staff and the questions committed to memory before the red light goes on. But still the fiction is maintained, of spontaneity, of genuine engagement, of a conversation at a table empty of everything but water glasses, paper, and pencils.

Isn't that what we all do, really? Irving works to maintain the fiction that the New York City Police Department has matters always in hand, although no one knows better than he that that is illusory. I once worked to maintain the fiction that the women I helped would find homes, find work, find the future palatable if not ideal, when I knew that that was often not remotely true. And now that I am the deputy commissioner for homeless services—Edward is a college friend of the mayor's, and Irving has served him well—I maintain the fiction that we will get people off the streets and into shelters, if not apartments. Occasionally we even manage to do so.

Last winter, after New York had had three nights when the temperature had fallen below ten degrees, Meghan decided to do a half hour on the homeless. "Do you want to come on?" she said and then answered herself, "Too weird, huh?" The lines are brighter now. She has not done a program about paralysis, or the rights of the disabled, or gun violence. Marvin writes to her from prison, too, but she does not read the letters. Leo does not read the ones he receives, but he keeps them, unopened, in a drawer in the small apartment with the widened doorways he has uptown. He is going to Columbia's journalism school in the fall, and if I had to guess, I would guess he knows that a good story lies between the lines of those letters. "I am my mother's son," he said to me one day when we were discussing his future. And he is. He is harder, harsher, tougher. He is a person with something to prove now. I sometimes wonder where my sweet soft Leo went, and then Max and Isabelle run into the room and swing off his powerfully muscled arms, and for just a little while he is there.

Meghan still leaves dinner parties early, not because she has to go to bed but because she has to go to work. But the other guests leave, too, to watch who Meghan talks to and what they say. We get a different kind of comment on the street than we once did. A man in a dark topcoat will bark, "Good job with the chairman of the Fed!," the sort of man who, five years ago, would have told her that his wife was a big fan.

Meghan says that Edward is her biggest fan, and this is undoubtedly true. In the beginning he was little more to me than a series of conspicuously kind and thoughtful gestures. Theater tickets, private museum tours, box lunches from Française at the rehab facility, a prototype wheelchair afterward. Meghan held him at arm's length for the first year, and he neither complained nor retreated. He is almost twenty years older than she is, and because of that I was casually dismissive of the relationship, ironic since Edward and Irving are almost exactly the same age.

Then one night when Max and Isabelle were a year old I called, crying, because they had the croup. Their coughing was so abrupt and harsh that they sounded like angry seals, and their faces had gone scarlet with the strain. The pediatrician said to turn on the shower until steam filled the room and sit with them there, although she did not say how to keep two babies who had just learned to walk from putting their hands beneath the scalding spray. I sat in the bathroom and wept in a miasma of steam and self-pity, my sister broadcasting live from a college campus in Chicago, my children's father in Las Vegas at a law enforcement convention.

I spent most of that night with Edward, I on the floor with Max, he on the toilet with Isabelle. I had seen him as one of those silver-haired aristos whom Meghan had always pointed out as resembling our father, except that his eyes beneath the hood of age were uncommonly kind. But condensation humanized him, and by the time we emerged I knew of his youthful disinclination to go into the family business, the heart attack his father suffered that forced his hand, his wife's long struggle with breast cancer, and his deep affection for the more old-fashioned writers: Trollope, Dickens, and Henry James. His silver hair was plastered to his forehead, and he made rice cereal for the children and an omelet for me, although I knew he'd had a private chef since he'd bought a duplex apartment overlooking the East River ten years before. He was a widower with two grown sons, and he said that one, the one who was the English professor, not the one who'd taken over the daily running of the business, had had croup a dozen times when he was small, and that he'd felt a flush of nostalgia sitting there with a baby on his knee in the steamy bathroom. "I like the little guys," he said, smelling Isabelle's hair.

He and Meghan were married last year in the living room of his apartment, in front of a wall of windows that framed the East River and a great big piece of Queens. At the start of the twilight ceremony, a fireboat sent an enormous spray of water into the air. His sons and hers surrounded the couple, and as they turned toward each other, I saw the faint surprise in her eyes and I knew she was feeling, perhaps not that she loved him, but that she was enormously content. He made everything so easy.

Which made it doubly difficult for her when, after the graduation ceremony, the two of us found ourselves stranded in upper Manhattan, or at least stranded by Meghan's measure. Leo had gone off to a lunch and a picnic and a party and a party, and Edward to a board meeting downtown. There had been a cavalcade of black cars, and we had seen everybody off triumphantly: Evan, Irving, Tequila back to the office, Maureen to the home of an old friend on Long Island. It was only when we stood at the curb with the twins, our programs rolled damply in our perspiring hands, that we realized we had come up one car short, and not a cab to be found in the press of gowned graduates and departing family. The silver scar on Meghan's forehead glowed in the way it does when she is angry or upset or simply rattled. It bisects a constellation of freckles like a shooting star.

"This is not how I pictured this," Meghan said grimly as we pushed through the subway turnstile.

"We're holding the pole. We're not letting go," said Isabelle, repeating the instructions given to her on a hundred rides on the Broadway local.

"I guess it could be worse," Meghan said, keeping her head low. "We could live in L.A."

"Bite your tongue."

It was a party on the train, half the passengers in Columbia blue gowns, some of them already feeling the effects of too much champagne. An old man surprised us all by launching into a shaky a cappella version of "Pomp and Circumstance" at 110th Street. By 96th Street, when we left the train, he had already begun to bore the other passengers. The attention span of the average New Yorker is roughly the amount of time it takes to travel from one local stop to another.

"I can't believe you take the subway," a young woman carrying a mortarboard in one hand and a leather diploma folder in the other said to Meghan as she pushed by us on the way up the steep subway stairs. So many things Meghan does that people can't believe: flies commercial, calls for takeout, buys the paper at the newsstand. Of course, most of them are things she doesn't do anymore. There is the plane for trips, and Derek and his wife for meals and errands. They had come to live in Brooklyn when Edward sold the Jamaica house after he and Meghan married. Mercedes works for us now, caring for our children.

Our personal favorite was the woman who had said one night, at the Waldorf, "I can't believe you go to the ladies' room."

"Famous people are like Barbie," Meghan said afterward. "They can't even be bothered to urinate."

At the corner of Ninety-sixth Street and Broadway, we blinked in the May sunshine. A few torn clouds moved across the sky, then disappeared behind a new forty-two-story apartment tower that had been built where a six-story brick walk-up once stood. Two double strollers angled for room on the sidewalk. In my neighborhood, the double stroller has become the official icon of the city, the late-in-life babies side by side. If you're put on hold at my pharmacy, and of course you always are, the recorded message tells you that the place is the largest single supplier of fertility drugs in the nation. Ah, New York, where we are all so busy that sometimes we even forget to reproduce, and then find ourselves paying richly for the privilege. Everyone assumed our children were the result of a clinic, a series of painful tests, and a petri dish, and I had stopped suggesting otherwise.

"Ah, here are some cabs," Meghan said.

"Come home with us for a while," I said. "I'll make grilled cheese."

"Do you have sweet pickles?"

"My feet are hurting," roared Isabelle. "My feet are hurting very very much."

"That settles it," said Meghan, holding Isabelle on her hip. Max immediately put his arms up, and I lifted him, too. Standing there, we balanced each other perfectly, but not in the way we once had. My sister had been transmuted by what had happened to her and what had happened to her son. Sometimes now, Leo complained, she looked at him with a question in her eyes. He couldn't figure out what she wanted. But all she wanted was to know that everything would be fine, that the past does not matter. And of course it does. In every city she visits, she meets with doctors who are experts on spinal cord injuries. If walking were ever to be for sale, Meghan would buy it for Leo with Edward's money.

No one else would see or know, but something had broken inside her, and I could see where the spirit had been forcibly mended. Maybe it had cracked before, when the housekeeper shrieked as the police told her about our parents, when Evan began to make comments about the shallow and transitory nature of morning television. Or maybe it had hap-

pened in Jamaica, or in the hospital room, or even in the Tubman projects. For years I had not seen. Now I could not unsee. Does someone
have to break so someone else can be whole?

I shifted Max to the other side. He tried a tentative pull at my earring,
and I shook him off. "No way, José," I said, and he replied, as always,
"I'm not José!"

We started down the block, and it was then we realized a young
woman was standing beside us, waiting for us to see her, to acknowledge
her. She pushed her sunglasses up into a head of tight black curls as she
looked at Meghan. I watched my sister arrange her face into the sort of
pleasant attentiveness, signifying nothing, that she had long ago developed for these occasions. The girl was nervous, worrying the strap of her
shoulder bag, and she began with that thing a fifty-one-year-old woman
least likes to hear.

"I've been watching you since I was a little girl," she said. "And I just
wanted to say, to say that, I'm a journalism student at Columbia, I'm interested in making documentaries, I'm just a huge admirer, huge, the
interview you did last week with that geneticist was amazing, it was the
first time I understood any of that. Oh, God, I'm babbling, I'm sorry, I'm
invading your privacy, I just had to say you're an incredible role model to
us. All of us. All of us women."

Isabelle squinted suspiciously. "What's your name?" Meghan asked.

"My name?"

"Yes."

"Eve."

"Do you have a pen, Eve?"

The girl was carrying one of those big shoulder bags that all journalists carry. Meghan had had one, when she was young.

"I do," the young woman said. "I always have a pen in my purse. And
a notebook. I always have a pen and a notebook."

"Good." Meghan dictated her office number, not the one I had, that
went straight to her, but the public number. "Call and tell my assistant
that I told you to call. Her name is Tequila. Like the liquor. You can
come someday and have coffee."

"Oh my God, really? Thank you. Thank you so much."

"You're a nice person," I said when we were out of earshot.

"I'm hungry," Isabelle whined.

"You don't have to carry her the whole way home."

"Sure I do," Meghan said.

I smiled at my sister and said in a falsetto voice, "I've been watching you since I was a little girl."

"Goddamn straight."

Isabelle lifted her head. "Don't swear, Aunt Meghan," she said. "It's not nice."

"I know, sweetheart. I just forgot." Isabelle put her head back down, and my sister looked at me over it. "I've been watching you, too," she said.

"I know," I said.

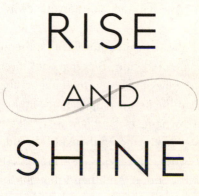

RISE AND SHINE

ANNA QUINDLEN

A READER'S GUIDE

A CONVERSATION
WITH ANNA QUINDLEN

Reader's Circle: We love the premise of *Rise and Shine*—two sisters living in New York City, with two very different career trajectories. In dreaming up this novel, what came to you first: the sisters, the setting, or Megan's on-air slip? And how did your storyline evolve from there?

Anna Quindlen: I always begin a novel with a theme. *Black and Blue* began with the theme of identity, *Blessings* with the theme of redemption. *Rise and Shine* grew out of constant thoughts about the disconnect in modern American life between appearance and reality. The more I thought about that disconnect, about how we've all come to believe that what looks good is good, the more I thought I should write about someone famous. That's where the dissonance is greatest, it seems to me, and the public interest is weirdest. And then I thought that the story would be best told by someone on the outside looking in. (Yes, I have read *Gatsby*. Many, many times.) That's where the idea of the sisters eventually came into play: one the doer, the other the watcher. And over time I realized that in doing that I had given the story, which is essentially a comedy of manners, greater resonance than it might have had otherwise. I find that I almost always make the right decisions for purely accidental reasons.

RC: Bridget and Meghan's relationship seems to ring true for readers—the sisters are each other's number one fan and critic. Do you have a sister of your own, or any siblings? Did your experiences with them help shape Bridget and Meghan's relationship? How?

AQ: I have a sister, and three brothers who fall between us on the birth-order ladder. My sister and I agree that our relationship bears little resemblance to that of Bridget and Meghan. I am not that controlling, and she is not that compliant. Perhaps the one aspect of their relationship that is taken from our lives has to do with our jobs. My sister is a public school teacher. She makes far, far less money than I do, and gets almost no public attention for her work. Yet I believe what she does is infinitely more important and more difficult than what I do. And certainly that mirrors Meghan's feelings about Bridget's job as a social worker.

RC: Do you believe in the birth-order convention, that the elder child is a natural leader, who strives to please others and can be controlling, while the younger child is charming but irresponsible, and looks to others for guidance and discipline? Did the study of birth order influence you in writing about the Fitzmaurice sisters? Does birth order ring true in your own experience, or do you think it's a bogus label?

AQ: Well, I recently got an email from a very irate reader complaining that I was perpetuating birth order stereotypes in a way I would never dare do about gender, sexual orientation, and the like. So I'm more equivocal about answering these questions now! But my experience, as both the eldest in a large family and the mother of three, is that certain birth order conventions frequently apply. But maybe it's more useful and illuminating to put it the way Aunt Maureen puts it in the novel: Successive children fill the spaces not already occupied. So if extrovert, or leader, or wild child, or whatever, is already taken by one of your siblings, you may feel compelled—or free—to shape your identity otherwise. That's certainly what happened with the Fitzmaurice sisters.

RC: Do you share any qualities and/or characteristics with Meghan? Bridget?

AQ: I am like both Meghan and Bridget. For years I had the sort of laser focus that Meghan had, and I have some of her rather cynical attitudes about the affluent around her. But, like Bridget, I have always been interested in trying to do something about the situation of the poor and disenfranchised in New York and in the rest of America, in my case through the columns I've written.

RC: There are several interesting male characters in the book: Irving, the gritty cop; Edward, the smooth operator; Evan, the seemingly reliable yet duplicitous husband; and Leo, the upbeat, loveable young man. Who is your favorite among them, if you can pick one? And what qualities do you find most (or least) attractive in men in general?

AQ: Most female readers of a certain age seem to fall hard for Irving Lefkowitz. I can totally understand that; we've had it up to here with the sensitive man, and Irving is pure retro. He also really, really likes women, and he really likes Bridget. I assume the reader shares that sentiment; I certainly do. But if I had to pick just one male character in the book as my personal favorite, it would be Leo. Some critics have suggested that he's too good to be true, but I've met a fair number of teenage boys like him: smart, self-deprecating, truly inclined to do the right thing. Obviously one of the reasons I love him so is that he's based, in part, on both of my sons.

RC: Your portrait of New York is loving, yet you see the city—and its residents—for what they are. What do you love about the city? What do you hate? Can you ever imagine leaving New York, or is it home to you?

AQ: I made New York City a major character in this book because I thought it would make my task as a novelist easier. I've covered New York for more than thirty-five years as a reporter and columnist, and I know from long experience that it's a storyteller's dream. It's so polyglot, so vivid, so sharply drawn, that writing about it is as easy as finding a cab outside the Carlyle (or finding crack on certain corners in certain parts of the Bronx). But like any great character, part of its greatness, part of its power, is in its manifest flaws. New York is a city where it's particularly hard to be poor, not only because everything costs twice as much here as it does elsewhere but because over-the-top affluence is part of its identity. Yet it's a city, as the novel makes clear, where affluence and want exist almost side by side. I hate the ways in which the rich are too often blind to their own conspicuous consumption. With what some East Side women spend on Botox and fillers a year, they could put a kid through parochial school, which could change a life completely. What I love is the flip side of that: that there is such enormous generosity. And I love other things too, of course. I love that you can always get a decent Ethiopian meal. I like the places in Central Park in which you can feel as if you're on top of a mountain, not in the middle of town. I like the way the subway can take you to the beach in a half hour, then back to the roar and glare of Times Square. New York is just more alive than any other place else I've ever been. People never really leave. I can't tell you how often in promoting this book, in Atlanta or Orlando or Minneapolis, someone has said to me, "I'm a New Yorker." They may have lived elsewhere for most of their life, but they're still New Yorkers.

RC: Meghan goes off the radar in Jamaica. What do you do to "go dark" and have time for yourself to get away and regroup?

AQ: We have a house that's in the middle of nowhere in Pennsylvania. I spend the entire summer there. It's a good place to write because there's really nothing else to do. After the third time rowing across the pond in the canoe, I think, well, hell, and I go inside and work. Occasionally there will be a bear or eagle sighting to break up my day. But it's pretty easy for me to be off the grid in Manhattan, too. I'm not as visually identifiable as Meghan is, so I don't get much attention in the city. New Yorkers are so accustomed to seeing the truly famous that they are very cool about it. Usually they just smile. It's interesting for me to go to cities that have a small clutch of well-known writers. In those places they are a BIG DEAL. Here no one cares.

RC: Have you ever had a career-defining moment, either positive (like Meghan's first big scoop), or negative, like Meghan's on-air gaff? How did you grow from it?

AQ: I had one fairly substantial setback as a reporter when I was much younger. There was the perception that I had blown a major, major story, although the truth was much more complicated than that. But, like Meghan, I came to understand rather quickly that the truth was less important than the spin. It was thought that I had certain glaring deficits as a reporter, the chief one being that I could write a pretty feature but was a washout with hard news. Over the space of several days I tried to scope out assignments that could exorcise that perception if I filled them in a satisfactory fashion. In this way I became a member of *The New York Times* City Hall bureau for two years. It wasn't my dream job, but after two years of council hearings, budget reports, and the like, many of which ended up on page one, there was no longer the sense that I couldn't do hard news.

RC: CNN anchor Kyra Phillips left her microphone on as she chatted in the ladies' room. What did you think of this story, which broke the same week *Rise and Shine* went on sale? Did you imagine such a thing could happen as you wrote the book?

AQ: I always say that if you can imagine it, it can happen. While several interviewers were skeptical about Meghan blurting out an obscenity into a "hot mike," I was certain such a thing was possible. Of course, after the CNN blooper, interviewers kept asking me whether I'd had it in mind when I wrote the book, illustrating the simple fact that even well-connected reporters don't understand the nine-month lag time between finishing a novel and publishing one.

QUESTIONS AND TOPICS
FOR DISCUSSION

1. *Rise and Shine* centers on the unique bond of sisterhood—potentially one of the most supportive, competitive, and difficult relationships in life. Describe Bridget and Meghan's relationship and how each woman views her sister and herself. What roles does each play? Does this portrait of sisterhood reflect your own relationship with a sibling, or perhaps with a close friend? Do you identify with one of the Fitzmaurice sisters more than with the other?

2. Meghan's audacious on-air slip, and its repercussions, incites the novel's forward action. How would you judge the seasoned anchorwoman's mistake? Was she wrong to let her personal opinion and emotions show? Do you believe that the network's reaction was justified? Finally, what do you think was the public's response to Meghan's fall from grace?

3. Describe Anna Quindlen's portrait of New York City. Is the Big Apple "unequivocally the center of the universe," as some New Yorkers believe? Compare Bridget and Tequila's experiences at the shelter with Meghan's worldview from the Upper East Side. How does Quindlen attempt to capture all sides of the city?

4. Describe Meghan and Bridget's conflicting perceptions and memories of their mother. How does the loss of their mother shape the Fitzgerald sisters's lives and ways of relating to each other? What role does Aunt Maureen play?

5. Is Evan justified in leaving Meghan, or do you agree with Bridget, that there must have been another woman in the picture right from the start? What factors led to the failure of their relationship? How does Bridget deal with the breakup? Meghan?

6. Meghan retreats to Jamaica to escape the turmoil in her life, and in doing so detaches from her old persona and responsibilities. What did

you think of this episode? Was Meghan being selfish by isolating herself? Was this period in Meghan's life necessary and inevitable? How does it affect Leo? Bridget? Discuss the outcome of the trip. Does Meghan sustain her growth of character when she reenters the real world? How about Bridget?

7. What attracts Bridget to Irving Lefkowitz? Describe Irving's attitude toward children and his reaction to Bridget's unexpected news. Will this relationship work for Bridget? Why or why not?

8. Bridget's daily experiences in New York City is marked by relationships with "familiar strangers." What does she mean by this? Are there "familiar strangers" in your own life?

9. Discuss Meghan's role in apprehending the shooter in the Tubman projects. Was her involvement self-serving, or was she defending her son and the safety of others? What were her true motivations, and how were her actions perceived? Do you agree with Meghan's decision to take matters into her own hands?

10. Quindlen writes in the first person, from Bridget's perspective. What effect does this narrative viewpoint have on the story? How would the book be different if it were told from Meghan's point of view?

11. In the last few pages of the novel, Quindlen writes, "Does someone have to break so someone else can be whole?" (p. 268). Who in *Rise and Shine* breaks, and who has been made whole? Is there more than one way to think about this question?

12. The cover for *Rise and Shine* shows a beautiful butterfly, a symbol of metamorphosis. How does the concept of change apply to the characters in the novel? Consider especially Meghan and Bridget, Evan, Leo, Irving, Tequila, and Princess Margaret. Have you undergone changes similar to theirs in your own life? Finally, how did your opinion of the Fitzmaurice sisters, and your assessment of their relative strengths and weaknesses, evolve over the course of the novel?

13. What do you think defines a "successful" life? According to your de-

finition, who is the most successful character in *Rise and Shine*? Does success equal happiness? How does that concept play out in the novel, and what do Bridget and Meghan come to understand by the end?

14. Does *Rise and Shine* have a happy ending? What new directions and challenges face the Fitzmaurice sisters, Leo, Irving, and the others?